Rosie Clarke was born in Swindon. Her family moved to Cambridgeshire when she was nine, but she left at the age of fifteen to work as a hairdresser in her father's business. She was married at eighteen and ran her own hairdressing business for some years.

Rosie loves to write and has penned over one hundred novels under different pseudonyms. She writes about the beauty of nature and sometimes puts a little into her books, though they are mostly about love and romance.

Also by Rosie Clarke:

The Downstairs Maid

Rosie Clarke

Emma

EBURY
PRESS

1 3 5 7 9 10 8 6 4 2

First published as *The Ties That Bind* in 1999 by Severn House Publishers Ltd.

This edition published in 2015 by Ebury Press, an imprint of Ebury Publishing
A Random House Group Company

The Random House Group Limited Reg. No. 954009

Addresses for companies within the Random House Group can be found at:
www.randomhouse.co.uk

A CIP catalogue record for this book is available from the British Library

The Random House Group Limited supports The Forest Stewardship Council®
(FSC®), the leading international forest-certification organisation. Our books
carrying the FSC label are printed on FSC®-certified paper. FSC is the only
forest-certification scheme supported by the leading environmental organisations,
including Greenpeace. Our paper procurement policy can be found at:
www.randomhouse.co.uk/environment

Printed and bound by CPI Group (UK) Ltd, Croydon, CR0 4YY

ISBN 9780091956103

To buy books by your favourite authors and register for offers visit:
www.randomhouse.co.uk

Chapter One

'Tell my fortune, Gran,' I begged, offering my hand palm-up across the scrubbed pine kitchen table. 'Oh, please – just this once.'

She puffed on her clay pipe, silently regarding me from those wise old eyes, and considered. Known affectionately to March townsfolk as Old Mother Jacobs, my grandmother disliked telling fortunes for her family because she was afraid of what she might see. She had read her husband's death in the tea leaves and it had frightened her so much that she had tried to ignore her gift ever since, which was a shame because there was no doubting she had the 'sight'.

'Please, Gran . . .'

'Maybe just this once then . . . seeing as you've brought me baccy.'

'I didn't do it for that, Gran.'

'No, that you didn't, you're a good girl.'

Gran took my hand in hers. Her skin felt rough and callused from years of hard work; her fingers were misshapen claws spotted with age and twisted with the rheumatics. I waited eagerly as she puffed on her pipe, looked thoughtful, then began to trace the lifeline on my hand with a yellowed fingernail.

'You've a long life ahead of you, girl,' she said at last. 'A long, hard road to travel by the looks of it. You'll not have easy times.'

My life had never been easy. I wanted Gran to tell me about the future. 'I don't mind work,' I said, dismissing her warning. 'Will I marry? Will I have children?'

Sometimes I was afraid that my life would never change. I had been working in Father's shop ever since I'd left school at fifteen. I hadn't wanted to leave. My teacher had been sure I was bright enough to win a place at college, that I could go on to become a teacher myself, but my father had refused to listen.

'If you're bright enough for that, you can keep the books for me,' he had told me when I'd begged him to let me stay on at school. 'You'll not need to go out and earn a living. The business will be yours one day, so you may as well learn how to look after things. I don't want to employ anyone else, Emma. May as well keep the money in the family.'

My father was very careful with his money; some people said he was mean, though not within his hearing.

'You will have a child,' Gran said, nodding her head. 'Perhaps more than one. There's a break in the line here. It means . . .' She shook her head and let go of my hand. 'Nothing. It's all nonsense. Why I let you persuade me I don't know. You'll marry if you want, Emma. You ain't a beauty but there's something grand about you – goodness knows where it comes from. Not from me or your father, that's for sure – but mayhap your father's folk. There was always a mystery about Harold Robinson. Nobody knew where he came from twenty-odd years ago when he set up shop and they're none the wiser now. A close man, your father – in more ways than one.'

No, I wasn't pretty; Gran was right about that. I had thick, dark hair, which I brushed back off my face and secured into a coil at the nape of the neck, and my eyes were brown, but there was nothing remarkable about me that I could see.

'Pretty isn't everything,' Gran said, taking another puff of her pipe. 'You've got something men like. Your destiny is in your own hands, girl. Don't you worry, things will come right one of these days. You won't always be tied to your father's shop.'

'You are a pet!' I flew round the table and hugged her. She smelled of baking and carbolic, familiar and much loved. 'Shall I wash the tea things before I go?'

'Am I the invalid now, that I can't wash a couple of plates?' She scowled at me, but the fierce look hid a warm heart. 'Be off with you, Emma. It's a lovely day. Take a bit of a walk and get some air into you. Your father keeps you indoors too much.'

'At least he lets me visit you once a week.'

'I'd have something to say if he didn't.' She gave me a long, speculative look. 'You're a good lass, Emma. I look forward to your visits – but if ever you want to do a bit of courtin' on a Wednesday afternoon, you don't need to worry over me. I shan't grumble if you don't come.'

'You're a wicked woman,' I said, laughing. 'At the moment there's no lad I'd rather spend my time with – if there was I would tell you.'

'I know that.' Gran's eyes had a naughty glint, reminding me that she had by all accounts been a bit of a lass in her youth. 'But there's a few lads have noticed you, lass. Your father won't be able to hang on to you for ever, no matter how hard he tries.'

'Bless you,' I said and kissed her cheek. 'I don't know what I'd do without you, Gran.'

She was looking at me, an odd sadness in her eyes that made me wonder what she was thinking.

'You're not ill, Gran?' I asked, a cold chill at the base of my spine.

'No, I'm not ill. Get off with you, before the day's wasted!'

I smiled as I left my grandmother's cottage. It was built close to the railway line and Gran spent most of her time these days sitting at her back door, puffing her pipe and waving to folk in the trains which rattled past. She was known to almost everyone in March, a small, busy, Cambridgeshire town which had one of the largest marshalling yards in Europe and had become prosperous because of it, and to many travellers who passed through on their daily journeys to and from work.

Her husband, Jack Jacobs, had worked all his life as a railwayman, ending his days as a crossing keeper. After his death, Gran had rented her tiny cottage from the railway, living on her meagre savings and gifts of fruit or vegetables from the gardens of people who knew and liked her.

Remembering a conversation with my father earlier that morning, I frowned. I had asked him for something to take Gran as a gift, but he had refused me.

'I've no money to be wasting on Mother Jacobs,' he'd muttered. 'She'll get by without charity from me; she always has.'

'I wasn't asking for money, Father. Just some tobacco or a bar of Fry's dark chocolate. She likes that.'

'You've got your wages. Buy her something yourself if you're so set on it.'

I had intended to do that anyway. But it wouldn't have hurt Father to give me something for Gran. He made more than enough money, and I ought to know. I kept the books for him, though I had no idea what he did with all the profits. Neither my mother nor I saw much of them. He certainly didn't pay me much of a wage.

I mulled over my grandmother's words. It was true that Father didn't give me much time away from the shop, which sold newspapers, sweets, tobacco and various odds and ends, like stationery, lighters and boot-laces. He had once considered selling food, too, but there was a large greengrocer's next door and a general grocer's at the end of the road, so in the end he had decided to stick to the trade he knew best.

I was thankful he had decided against branching out. I already worked long hours for the eight shillings a week he paid me. I could have earned more in the new corset factory, which had recently set up in town, but Father had refused to hear a word about it.

'No daughter of Harold Robinson is going to work there,' he had told me when I'd mentioned it. 'Common as muck, that's what those women are. You should think more of yourself, Emma, and thank your lucky stars for the home you've got. You don't need more money. You've a bed to sleep in, food in your stomach, and your mother will make you a new dress when you need one.'

My mother was good with her needle. She always looked smart herself, a slim, trim, attractive woman who had once been a looker, but had a permanent droop to her mouth these days. I had never minded wearing the dresses and blouses she made me for everyday, but I did want a smart, tailor-made costume for best. I'd seen one in a shop in the main street, and every Wednesday on my way back from visiting Gran, I popped in to look at it. Just to make sure it was still there.

That afternoon, I panicked when I glanced through the costume rail. It had gone! Disappointment swept over me. I had been saving, but I'd left it too long.

'Don't look like that.' Mrs Henty came through from the back. 'I've put it by for you, Emma. Someone else was looking at it on Saturday, and I didn't want it to go.'

'But it will be ages before I can save enough to pay you.'

'How much have you saved so far?' Mrs Henty gave me an encouraging smile.

'Ten shillings – and I should be able to put another two by this week.'

'Well, let's see – how about this? You pay me a deposit, then bring in what you can until you've paid the rest off.'

I thought about the costume. It had a long, slim skirt that flared out slightly into a frill of box pleats just above my ankles; the jacket was three-quarter length and in the new swagger or jigger style, which hung like a kind of triangle over the tight skirt and looked very stylish; and the shade was a soft green, which suited my colouring.

'It was really kind of you to put it by for me,' I said, making the big decision. 'I would like to pay so much a week, if you're sure you don't mind?'

My father would be angry if he knew what I was doing; he didn't believe in owing anything to anyone, but if I didn't decide now someone else would buy my costume.

'I'd rather you had it than anyone else,' Mrs Henty said. 'That woman on Saturday wanted it for a wedding, but it would be wasted on her. No, it's your costume, Emma. That lovely green looks just right on you, dear.'

'I might be able to pay you more soon, if my father gives me another two shillings a week. He said he would if I got up earlier to sort out the papers for the boys to deliver, and I have all this week.'

'You make him pay you the extra,' Mrs Henty advised. 'He can afford it. He must know what a treasure he's got in you, dear. Goodness knows I'd love to have you working for me.'

'Father would never let me,' I said with a sigh of regret. 'I only wish I could work for you, Mrs Henty. You have such lovely clothes.'

She smiled and nodded as I went out. It was an impossible dream, of course. Father would find some reason why he didn't want his daughter to work in a dress shop.

Mother had the table spread when I got in. She knew I always had a cup of tea and a piece of cake with Gran, but it was nearly six and Father would be up for his supper at half past. It was our chance for a quiet gossip before I went down to take Father's place in the shop.

'How was your grandmother?' she asked as I took off my coat and hat, hanging them on the pegs in the hall. 'Pleased with the baccy, I expect?'

'She always is.' I followed my mother into the sitting room, which was a good size and furnished with a modern sideboard, painted bookcases and a comfortable three-piece suite. There were several pieces of brightly coloured pottery standing about and prints of famous paintings on the walls. Father might be cautious about giving either my mother or me money, but he was fond of saying he liked a nice home, and spent his money on things that appealed to him. 'She can't afford much for herself these days – though she never seems to go hungry. Someone brought eggs and tomatoes for her while I was there.'

'Aye, your Gran is well liked,' Mother said with a nod of satisfaction. 'My father was popular, too. Most of the lads from the railway pop in to see Mother Jacobs now and then – for his sake, I reckon. They've not forgotten how he warned their fathers and uncles when the signals were down that time – saved a few lives he did, and ran himself ragged to do it.'

There was a gleam of pride in my mother's eyes as she spoke of her father, a gleam that was not often there these days. I remembered a time when I was a small child and she had seemed happier. She and my father had not quarrelled so often in those days, at least not in my hearing – but that was a long time ago.

My mother was justifiably proud of Grandfather Jack. Having been told the story many times, I knew it well. It had happened several years ago, when I was still a toddler. Some twenty-odd men had been working on repairs to the rails when a non-stop through train had been accidentally shunted on to the wrong line. Only Jack's quick thinking and a desperate dash across the back land had averted what could have been a terrible accident.

'Yes, I know,' I said. 'Gran was well. She sent you her love.'

My mother gave me a disbelieving look. Mother Jacobs had never had much patience with her own daughter. She had been against Greta's marriage to Harold Robinson in the first place, and thought she should stand up to her husband more – but then, she wasn't married to him. Besides, he respected her, grudgingly. She didn't know what a tyrant he could be if thwarted. Only Mum and I knew that.

Gran's own marriage had been happy, producing three strapping great sons besides my mother, all of whom worked for the railways but were scattered far and wide over the country. My mother was the only one of Gran's children who still lived near enough to visit her, so it was a pity they didn't get on as well as they might.

'What else did you do this afternoon?' Mother asked. 'Did you go for a walk?'

'After I left Gran's.' I sighed as I recalled my time of freedom, which was over all too soon. 'It was lovely by the river, Mum. Oh, and I met Richard Gillows on the way to Gran's. He walked with me for a few minutes. Asked about you and Father, same as usual.' I pulled a wry face: Richard was not my favourite person. 'He always seems to have his break at the same time on my afternoon off.'

'I expect it's the finish of his shift. He's on local runs at the moment, isn't he? Just as far as Ely or Littleport. It will be different if they put him back on the Cambridge and London run.'

Richard was a train driver. In his late twenties, he was a tall, burly man, good-looking I supposed, in a rather coarse way, with black hair and narrow-set eyes. He had a decent job and was respected, though there were whispers that he liked his drink. Not that there was anything wrong with that. Most men enjoyed a few beers in the pub now and then. As long as it wasn't any more serious, it wouldn't be frowned on in our community.

'You don't fancy him, do you?' My mother looked at me curiously as we sat down to the dining table. 'He's quite a looker. Most girls would go weak at the knees if he changed shifts just so as he could walk with them for a few minutes.'

'Not me.' I sighed as my mother pushed a plate of buttered muffins in front of me. 'Do you think I'll ever meet anyone, Mum? A man I could really love and respect?'

'There aren't many about would be good enough for you, Emma – and you don't want to marry for the sake of comfort the way I did. Look where that got me!'

'Oh, Mum,' I said, feeling unhappy as I saw the disappointed drag to her mouth. 'It's obvious you and Father don't get on – but do you honestly wish you had never married him?'

'If it wasn't for you, I would.' She reached out and squeezed my hand affectionately. Her eyes held a sad, reminiscent expression. 'I liked him well enough to begin with, and I thought we could make each other happy. He was kind to me, and I respected him, even looked up to him – but it wasn't real love. There was someone else I cared for and he asked me first, but I was young and silly. We quarrelled and I sent him away. Then Harold came after me. I turned him down for a start, but I suppose my head was turned by the thought of having my own shop and house . . . pretty clothes and holidays at Margate or Bournemouth, that's what I expected.' Her whole body drooped with defeat. 'All I got was a life of penny-pinching and scrimping. Your father says it's all he can do to keep the shop going these days.'

'That's not true, Mum. We make a reasonable profit

but . . .' I frowned. 'He takes the money out every night, says he has to pay bills, but I see the bills. He can't spend it all, because he only goes for a drink twice a week and then he comes home sober. So what does he do with the rest of it?'

'I wish I knew,' Mother said, sighing. She broke off, looking guilty and a bit frightened as she heard the tread of heavy boots on the stairs. 'You'd best get off, Emma. You know what he's like.'

I wiped the butter from my mouth with a spotless, starched white napkin, then pushed back my chair. My mother was a good housekeeper, but then my father was a particular man and would have complained if everything wasn't to his liking.

I met my father at the top of the stairs. He was a large, heavy man with dark hair greying at the sides and a sour expression. He always dressed in black, with a striped waistcoat and a white shirt, come summer or winter. He was usually fair enough in his dealings with me, but that evening he was clearly out of temper, because he glared at me, his eyes an unforgiving grey.

'Gossiping with your mother I suppose? Get down there before someone comes in, Emma. Who knows what that idiot I employ will do if he's left alone for five minutes.'

'Yes, Father.'

I ran down the stairs, relieved to escape. Father's

assistant – a spotty-faced, ginger-haired youth of sixteen, who received no more wages than I did – was selling Woodbines to a boy I knew wasn't old enough to smoke.

'Ben!' I stopped him as he was about to hand over the cigarettes. 'Have you asked how old he is?'

'I'm seventeen, miss,' the boy squeaked. 'Honest I am.'

'No, you're not,' I contradicted. 'I know you, Tim Green. You're not yet fourteen. Give him his money back, Ben.'

'You ain't got no right. I've paid me money, I want me fags.'

'I'll tell your mother – and she'll give you a strapping.'

'Ah, go on, miss. Let me 'ave just the one. I can pay. I ain't after stealing it like some.'

'Buy some humbugs or liquorice pipes instead. You can have some of those sweet cigarettes if you like. Besides, smoking stunts your growth, haven't you heard that?'

As he was nearly my own height, that hardly seemed much of a threat, but it was all I could come up with on the spur of the moment. It was glamorous to smoke; all the film stars did it, and most men I knew – and quite a few of the women, too, though the more refined of them did it in private, because some people still felt it wasn't quite nice for ladies to smoke in public. And this was 1938!

'And it stops your *thing* growing,' Ben supplied helpfully. 'You'd best have a barley twist instead.'

'Oh, go on then,' the lad said reluctantly. 'But I don't believe you about the *thing*. Our Mark's is as long as that—' he measured an impossible twelve inches on the counter, '—and he's bin smokin' since he were nine.'

'Get away with you!' I said, hard put not to laugh, and gave him the biggest barley twist in the jar, which should have cost more than the smaller ones. 'And don't try that here again until you're older.'

Tim Green laughed and ran out, clutching his sticky sweet triumphantly, well aware he'd done well for his halfpenny.

'I'm sorry, Emma,' Ben said. 'I never thought to ask how old he was . . . and he only wanted the one. All the kids do it. It don't do them no harm. Me Dad says it's good for your lungs – clears him out when he has a good cough in the mornings.'

'I know, but we're not supposed to sell them to children. Besides, my father doesn't encourage them in here. He says they steal more than they buy – and it gives the shop a bad name.'

Ben was about to continue his protest when the bell went and two customers entered. Ben served one of our regulars with an evening paper and some pear drops, while I waited for the second customer to speak. He was a stranger. Dressed in a smart grey pin-striped suit, Homburg hat, starched white collar, plain waistcoat and spotted tie, he was obviously a gentlemen. We didn't get many in dressed like that, and when he spoke I knew he was from what my father would call the upper class – one of the gentry, but not an aristocrat.

My father was very class conscious. He thought of himself as middle-class, because he owned his own business, and looked down on anyone who ranked beneath him in the accepted hierarchy.

'I should like a box of those cigars, please,' the stranger said, seeming to notice me at last. 'A box of Cadburys' milk chocolates, the evening paper – and twenty Players.'

'Yes, sir.' I reached down the items he had indicated from the shelf behind me. 'These are the best Havanas. That will be ten shillings and threepence altogether, sir.'

'Cheap at the price, I expect?' His eyes were deep blue and very bright, as though he was laughing at me. I noticed his hair looked dark and thick where it was visible beneath his hat. 'You weren't here when I popped in for a newspaper earlier, were you?'

'No . . .' I felt myself growing warm beneath his quizzical gaze. I had never met anyone quite like this; Father would have served him himself if he'd been here. 'It was my afternoon off. I went to see my grandmother.'

'And now you have to work again. What a shame.'

'I don't mind, not really. Father will come down when he's had his supper. It's only for an hour or so.'

'Fortunate for me I didn't leave it until later, then.'

'I beg your pardon, sir?'

'Paul Greenslade.' He tipped his hat and I saw his hair was thick and wavy. He was rather handsome, a bit like the film stars I'd seen in magazines. 'I suppose you would think it an awful cheek if I asked you to come to the pictures with me this evening? I'm on my own, you see, and feeling lonely.'

I could feel my cheeks turning a bright red. This wasn't the first time a customer had asked me out, of course, but it was usually just one of the local lads being cheeky, and I always said no. And I'd only been to the pictures a couple of times, with Mum and Gran as a birthday treat. I hadn't ever been asked out by a stranger before – nor had any man looked at me in quite this way. It made me feel a bit wobbly inside.

'No, I don't think it's a cheek,' I said, my voice sort of breathy and excited. 'It's very kind of you – but I can't come.'

'Why? You don't have to work after your father comes down, do you? We could just about catch the last showing.'

'I'm finished for the day then.' I dropped my gaze as he gave me an amused, questioning look. 'Father wouldn't let me go out with you. He's very strict.'

'Now that is a shame.' He took a pound note from his wallet and handed it to me. 'Do you think your father might relent if I asked him?'

'No, please don't,' I said. 'It would make him angry.'

17

He looked disappointed. 'Another time then.' He tipped his hat again, going out as three working men came in together. 'Goodbye – Miss Robinson, is it? It was nice meeting you.'

I was too busy serving the men to reply. For several minutes both Ben and I had a succession of customers; after a while it tailed off and finally the shop was empty.

Ben gave me an odd look when we had time to breathe again. 'You should have gone out with the toff, Emma. Missed your chance for a good time there.'

'I didn't know him,' I replied, thinking how much fun it would have been if I'd dared to accept his offer. 'Father would never have let me go out with a man I'd never met before. Only common girls let strangers pick them up just like that.'

Girls like me didn't do that sort of thing, but I thought perhaps the ones who did had a lot more excitement in their lives.

'You're not common,' Ben said, giving me an admiring glance. He daren't say it, of course, but I suspected he had a bit of a crush on me in his way. 'I never meant that, you know I didn't. I just thought you would've liked it, Emma. Most girls would jump at the chance to go out with a man like him.'

I shook my head and turned away to tidy the shelf behind me. I agreed with him in my heart, but I knew what people thought of girls who went off with a man at the drop of a hat. Especially in a town like ours, where everyone knew each other, and a stranger walking down the street caused heads to turn. I wasn't fast and I wasn't cheap – but I had liked the stranger's smile. If we had met properly, been introduced by someone Father knew . . . but there was no point in dreaming. Mr Greenslade had probably been passing through and I would never see him again.

The shop began to fill up once more. Three girls came in. I knew them all by sight, though they were older than me. They all worked at the railway canteen. Two had scarves wound round their heads like turbans; they were both wearing bright red lipstick and one of them had a cigarette dangling from the corner of her mouth – exactly what Father meant when he spoke of the factory women as common. The third girl, however, looked different. She was pretty, with soft fair hair that she wore in a pageboy bob. Her perfume wafted towards me across the counter, flowery and rather nice.

'Hello, Emma,' she said in her usual friendly manner. 'Could I have a small bar of Fry's milk chocolate please – and a quarter of Tom Thumb drops for our Terry? He's had the measles and I promised him a treat.'

'Poor lad,' I said, feeling sorry for her brother. 'I had measles when I was eleven; it was horrible.'

'Well, Ma says I've had it, and she put Freddie in with me so that he took it, too, but our Terry wasn't born then. Still, he's had most things now. It was the mumps before Christmas, proper poorly he was with that, and the chicken pox last summer.'

'Bless him,' I said and added an extra half-ounce of sweets for the same price. 'You look nice, Sheila. Off out somewhere?'

'My boyfriend is taking me to the dance at the Women's Institute,' she said, looking happy. 'They have them most weeks. You should come, Emma. It's fun.'

I felt a pang of envy as I looked at the pretty dress she was wearing. It had a narrow skirt that flared out in a frill at the hem and the jacket was belted, with wide, padded shoulders. She looked a treat and I thought it would be wonderful to be going somewhere nice dressed up like that.

'I wish I could!' I sighed enviously. 'You're so lucky, Sheila.'

'Eric would fix you up with one of his mates,' Sheila offered, warming to the idea. 'We could go next week as a foursome if you like?'

'Emma! Your mother needs you upstairs.'

I jumped as my father spoke. I had not been aware of him standing just behind me, and, glancing round, I saw he was annoyed. He didn't approve of my gossiping with the canteen girls, but I'd always liked Sheila, who was only a year older than me, but seemed very sophisticated.

'Thanks, Sheila,' I said, ignoring my father's frown of disapproval. 'I'll ask Mum if I can come.'

I gave Sheila her change, slipped past my father and up the stairs before the shop emptied, giving Father no chance to lecture me. With any luck, he would have forgotten all about it by the time he closed up for the night.

'I'd let you go,' my mother said later that evening when I asked about the dance. 'You know I would, Emma – but your father would raise the roof. We'd never hear the last of it.'

'No, I suppose not.' I sighed as my hopes were dashed. 'I didn't really expect you to say yes.'

'Don't look so disappointed, love.' Mother patted my hand to console me. 'Those dances aren't up to much, anyway. One day you'll find a nice young man, and he'll take you somewhere decent.'

'Shall I?' I gazed at her, feeling close to desperation. 'Will it happen, Mum? Shall I ever be able to go out like other girls?'

'It will have to be someone your father likes and approves of, you know that – but the time will come, Emma. I promise you.'

I smothered my doubts and kissed her goodnight. I was usually in bed by a quarter to nine, because I had to be up to check the papers by soon after five, and I liked to read in bed. Reading was one of the few pleasures I was allowed, and even that brought a frown of censure from Father if he saw me with what he termed 'trashy' library novels.

I sat at my dressing table, brushing my hair and pulling faces in the mirror. If only I were as pretty as Sheila! Then perhaps someone would come along and sweep me off my feet. He would be tall and handsome, and very rich, and naturally he would fall instantly in love with me. We would run away together, to somewhere exciting like America or Paris, and my life would never be lonely or boring again.

Suddenly, I laughed at myself. That was what came of reading too many romance stories. I never met any exciting men – or I hadn't until this evening.

I got into bed, my book unopened, as I thought about Paul Greenslade. He was just like Clark Gable or Spencer Tracy: handsome, dashing, a gentleman.

My father might not allow me to go to the cinema very much, but I was as star-struck as the rest of my generation. I read all the magazines about the Hollywood film stars and lingered outside the cinema whenever I had the chance, feasting my eyes on the magical posters of the latest films.

I smiled as I recalled the look of disappointment in Paul Greenslade's eyes when I'd turned him down. It was almost like something out of the movies. Only in a film he wouldn't give up; he would keep following me until I agreed to go out with him.

The only man I knew who did that was Richard Gillows and I wished he wouldn't. He was all right in his own way, I supposed, but I didn't like him much. There was something about the way he looked at me that made me feel uncomfortable.

I opened my book. I was foolish to dream of having a more exciting life. No matter what Gran or my mother said to comfort me, I was certain that nothing was ever going to change.

I went to church that Sunday with Mother as usual. Afterwards, we stood talking to friends for a few minutes before starting to walk home. It was as we stopped to look in a shop window that Richard Gillows crossed the road to speak to us.

'Evening, Mrs Robinson – Emma,' he said, raising his trilby hat. 'Been to church then?'

Dressed in a single-breasted, dark navy pin-striped suit with wide shoulders and a matching waistcoat, he looked much smarter than he usually did when I met him on his way home from work. Almost a gentleman, I thought, even if his suit had come from the thirty-shilling tailor's.

'Yes, we usually go on Sunday morning,' Mother replied. 'How are you, Richard?'

'Very well, thank you.'

'Going somewhere special?'

'Just out to dinner with a friend.' Richard hesitated, his dark eyes intent on me. 'I've been asked to a church social at the church hall a week on Wednesday. I wondered if Emma might like to come?'

'Would you, Emma?' My mother glanced at me, but I kept quiet and she looked at him again. 'We should have to ask Mr Robinson. Perhaps Emma could let you know?'

'It starts at six. I'd have her home by nine.'

'Well, we'll see.' She smiled at him. 'Come along, Emma. Your father will be waiting for his dinner.'

After walking in silence for a few minutes, Mother turned to me. 'Would you like to go with him? I'm sure your father would agree if I persuaded him a little. He gets on well with Richard – and a church social isn't like a public dance.'

As Richard well knew! He'd chosen his target well.

'I'm not sure.' I wrinkled my nose. 'It would be nice to go out, but he might take it as a sign I liked him – that I wanted him to court me.'

'He isn't all that bad,' Mother said. 'Especially when he's dressed up. You could do worse, Emma. If you were courting him, your father would have to let you go to the pictures and things.'

'I don't know.' Richard had looked different and I

supposed I might get to like him if I let myself. 'I'd like to think about it for a day or two.'

'Well, don't think about it too long,' she said. 'I doubt he'll hang around for ever. If you don't want him, there's plenty of girls who will.'

Chapter Two

It had just started to rain that afternoon, and foolishly I had come out in only a thin dress and cardigan. I peered anxiously up at the sky, which was overcast but not black. Was it going to be simply a shower or should I go back for my coat and umbrella?

'Get in before it really starts. I'll give you a lift wherever you're going.'

The man's voice startled me, making me swing round sharply. I'd been vaguely aware of the car pulling into the kerb behind me, but hadn't taken much notice. I didn't know anyone who owned a car, though several of Father's business friends had vans for delivering goods.

No one around here had a car like this one! It was too luxurious, too expensive. Staring at the driver fixedly for a moment, I was surprised to discover I recognized him.

'Mr Greenslade . . .'

'You remembered. I'm flattered.' He leaned across to

open the passenger-side door. 'Come on, Miss Robinson. I'm not dangerous. I won't ravish you against your will. Tell me where you want to go and I'll deliver you safely – scout's honour!'

His teasing made me laugh. I'd never met anyone like this before. I glanced over my shoulder, wondering if anyone was watching, noting the fact that Emma Robinson was talking to a stranger, then felt a surge of rebellion. Who cared? I had a perfect excuse for getting into the car, because the rain was getting worse. Besides, he wasn't a complete stranger. I had sort of met him before. He had been into the shop to buy cigarettes at least three times now, and on two of those occasions my father had served him personally. He hadn't asked me out or even seemed to notice me particularly after the first time, which was probably just as well.

'Thank you,' I said, making up my mind and sliding into the car beside him. The seats were covered in leather and smelled nice. 'This is a Bentley, isn't it? I've never seen one close to before.'

'It belongs to my father,' he said, glancing my way as he pulled away from the kerb. 'I couldn't afford this on my salary. I shall have to wait until the old boy snuffs it and leaves me this one.'

I was a little shocked by his casual reference to his father's death, but didn't let it show. The rich were different. I'd heard my father say it often enough, and was sure he was right. They had different moral values, different standards to ordinary folk.

'It's lovely,' I said, to cover a slight awkwardness. 'If you meant it about giving me a lift, I'm going to my grandmother's. She lives in a cottage by the line. Mother Jacobs they call her – but you wouldn't know that, not being local.'

'As a matter of fact I have heard of her. I'm working for the railway myself at the moment. I'm an architect. I design things – bridges, tunnels, boring things like that.'

'That's why you're here several times a week, then?' I looked at him curiously. 'At least, you've been into the shop a few times this past week.'

'You noticed? Yes, I've been having preliminary meetings, discussions with civil engineers. They're talking about a new bridge on the Peterborough line, but at the rate we're going it will never get built.'

A roll of thunder sounded overhead and the sky opened, sending down the rain in torrents.

'It was just as well I happened along,' he said. 'You would have been soaked to the skin in this.'

'Yes, I'm very grateful. But you're right about that bridge,' I said, feeling confident because this was something I knew about. 'Gran says it has always been like that – arguments, disagreements. When they were first building the railway they couldn't agree on who should build and own various bits of the line. It was almost abandoned at one stage. Gran says it was a wonder they ever sorted it out.'

He shot an amused look at me, then indicated to turn right. 'You're fond of your grandmother, aren't you?'

'Yes. She's special. I visit her every Wednesday and most Sundays. I like talking to Gran. She knows everything.'

'Does she indeed?'

The look in his eyes made me blush. I suspected he was laughing at me. Of course, he must think I was very unsophisticated, just a common shop-girl, not educated or glamorous like the girls he was used to meeting in his world.

'Well, not everything. No one could, of course – but she knows a great deal about the railways. Her husband worked for them all his life. And she knows a lot of other things – about plants and herbs.'

'She's a wise woman.' Paul Greenslade nodded. 'She sounds interesting. I should like to meet her.'

'Would you really?' I stared at him a little suspiciously. 'You're not saying it just to please me?'

'No, I mean it. I've been told she's quite a character.'

I frowned, not sure I liked the way he'd said that – as if Gran were an oddity. I didn't mind him laughing at me, but I wouldn't let anyone make fun of Gran.

'I'll have to ask her,' I said. 'She won't have you in her house unless she likes the look of you.'

*

The rain had eased slightly by the time we reached the isolated cottage. I hesitated, then turned to look at Paul, my hand on the car door handle.

'Do you want to come in if she says yes?'

He glanced at his wristwatch, which was gold-cased and obviously expensive. 'Perhaps not now. I have an appointment. What time will you be leaving here?'

'About four – why?'

'Why don't I pick you up? It looks as if it may rain all afternoon. I could take you home.'

'Wouldn't that be a lot of trouble?' I was doubtful, unsure whether to take up the offer or not. Why should he go to so much bother for my sake? 'It would be out of your way.'

'I'll be here at four,' he said, giving me a smile that made my stomach lurch. 'Have a nice visit, Emma.'

'Thank you.'

I stood watching as he drove away, then turned and walked up the garden path to Gran's front door. The brass knocker was polished so bright you could almost see your face in it and the step had been scrubbed fresh that morning.

Gran must have been watching from her window, because she opened the door as I approached, eyes lively with curiosity.

'Who was that, then?' she asked. 'Not local. I don't

suppose he'd be that architect from Cambridge? They tell me he drives a fancy car sometimes.'

'Oh, Gran,' I cried and hugged her. That afternoon she smelled of lavender and herbs, as if she had been making up some of her cures and poultices. 'You do know everything! Who told you about Paul Greenslade?'

'Paul, is it?' Her eyes were bright and curious, studying me from beneath her sparse lashes. 'That sounds as if you know him. How did you meet him – and what are you doing accepting a ride in his car?'

'It was raining and he offered me a lift,' I explained and Gran nodded, looking thoughtful. 'He wants to meet you. He's coming to fetch me later.'

'Bring him in,' she said. 'I'd best have a look at him. If he's interested in my girl, I want to see what sort of a man he is.'

'Oh, Gran,' I cried, laughing. 'I'm sure he isn't. He was just being kind because it was raining.'

'And why did he ask you out then? Was that just kindness?'

'Oh, that . . .' I felt my cheeks getting warm as her eyes seemed to probe my mind. 'I expect it was an impulse. He was new here and didn't know anyone. I suppose he thought I looked harmless.'

'Thought you were available more like,' Gran said with a snort. 'His sort and yours don't often mix, Emma. I'm not saying it never happens, so don't pull a face. If this Mr Greenslade is a decent man, there's no harm in your seeing him, but you shouldn't expect too much.'

'I'm not seeing him, Gran!'

'But you might if he gets his way. I know men, lass. None of them go out of their way for a girl unless they're interested – and when the man is from Mr Greenslade's class it usually means trouble for a girl like you.'

I didn't argue; I knew my grandmother was right. Gentlemen just didn't marry shop-girls, not in real life. They might flirt with them, or seduce them, but they didn't marry them. I supposed I ought not to have let him give me a lift in the first place.

'You won't say anything to Father? About Paul giving me a lift this afternoon?'

She screwed up her face, the soft skin wrinkled and mottled with age. 'What do you take me for? I may be old, but I'm not daft, girl – and I'm not against your having a little fun. I just don't want you hurt.'

'I shan't be. Really, Gran. I know he wouldn't be interested in marrying a girl like me. Besides, Father would never let me go out with him, so there's not much chance of my getting into trouble, is there?'

'Harold might be brought to see sense,' Gran said, the light of battle in her eyes. 'But only if this man is the right sort, Emma. Otherwise, you'd best stay clear of him.'

*

'Well, did I pass inspection?' Paul asked as he was driving me home later that afternoon. 'I'd heard Mother Jacobs was a strong-minded woman, but I wasn't prepared for the Inquisition.'

'Not that bad, surely?'

I laughed, feeling happy. Gran had liked him. He'd answered all her questions – some of which were almost impertinent – with a good will and a smile. In fact, he had charmed her into inviting him to call for a cup of tea whenever he was in the district.

'She really liked you. I don't think she expected or wanted to, but she did. I was surprised.'

Paul glanced my way, his brows arched. 'Why? Don't you like me?'

'Yes, of course I do.' I blushed, feeling silly. He must think me a complete idiot. 'Well . . . I mean, I think I would if I knew you, which I don't, of course.'

'Come to the pictures with me this evening? We could have a drink first and get to know each other better.'

'I can't,' I said, a catch in my voice. 'I wish I could, Paul – but I can't.'

He had told both Gran and me to call him Paul and I'd done so without realizing it. I twisted a piece of skirt between my fingers, feeling nervous and excited all at once. I badly wanted to say yes to him but knew I mustn't; it would only lead to arguments.

'Because of your father?'

'Yes. You don't know what he's like. Gran only asked questions because she cares about me – Father cares what people think and say. He would think you were after only one thing.'

My cheeks flamed scarlet as he shot me an amused look. How naive I must sound! He wouldn't want to go out with me now.

'I like you,' he said. 'It's a shame you can't come out with me. I think we might have got on really well.'

'I wish I could.' I could hear the wistful note in my voice, but couldn't help myself. He was offering me the world I had often longed to enter, and I knew it would probably be my only chance. 'I'd give anything to come out with you, Paul, really I would – but my father would half kill me if I did so without his permission.'

'And he wouldn't give it?'

'He would just shout at me – and my mother.'

'We can't have that, can we?' Paul pulled the car into the kerb at the end of the main street, keeping the engine running. 'Perhaps you had better get out here?'

'Yes, that might be best.' Tears of disappointment were misting my eyes. 'Thank you for keeping me dry, Paul.'

'My pleasure.' He leaned towards me, giving me a brief kiss on the mouth. 'Maybe I'll see you again like this, Emma? If your father doesn't know he can't be angry, can he?'

'Next Wednesday?' I couldn't bear to look at him.

'But you wouldn't want . . . I mean . . .' I floundered to an embarrassed halt.

'We'll see,' he murmured. 'Take care of yourself – and remember that dreams do sometimes come true.'

I fumbled for the door handle, pressed it and got out of the car, walking away without looking back. He must think I was a timid mouse! Most girls of nineteen and a half went out with anyone they fancied these days. I supposed I could too – if I were willing to risk a row with my father. Sometimes I thought about defying him. I imagined myself packing my clothes, walking out of the house, finding myself a job where they paid decent wages . . . but he would only take it out on my mother.

I couldn't desert her. She hadn't been really well for several years now – not since her last miscarriage. I suspected that Father hit her sometimes. It didn't happen often, but she'd had terrible bruises on her face on two occasions. She had pretended she'd walked into a door, but the shame in her eyes had made me think otherwise.

It must be so awful to be married to a man you didn't love! My father wasn't too bad with me, providing I did as he told me and didn't argue. Perhaps because he knew I could walk out if I really wanted to – or I would be able to in another eighteen months, when I was twenty-one. Until then, he could compel me to live under his roof, though I'd often thought that if I caused enough fuss he would probably just wash his hands of me.

If it wasn't for my mother . . . I squashed the rebellious thoughts. Mother wasn't well enough to go out to work and earn her own living. My father wouldn't give her a penny if she left him, and he'd made sure she never had enough money to save anything for herself. So she didn't have much choice. And I couldn't desert her; I couldn't leave her there alone with him.

There was no point in wishing for the moon! I made an effort to shut out my feelings of disappointment and ran into the shop as the rain started to fall faster again. Father gave me a long hard look.

'You should have taken a coat,' he muttered. 'I don't want you going down with a chill. It's been raining for the past half-hour – why aren't you wet?'

Feeling apprehensive, I avoided the suspicious look in his eyes.

'I got a lift in Mr Baker's van,' I lied. 'Mary had been out delivering meat near Gran's and she gave me a ride home.'

Mary Baker was two years older than me and drove her father's van to the outlying houses and cottages in the area for the old folk who found it difficult to buy their supplies of fresh meat. Mary and I had known each other at school and were in much the same situation, neither of us having a great deal of time to spare. Mary's father, however, allowed her more freedom when her work was done.

I crossed my fingers behind my back, but I knew Mary would back me up if I asked. We didn't often see one another, but were good friends. Mary was the only one of my school-friends that Father actually liked. He sometimes invited both her and her father to dinner with us on a Saturday night.

'Get up to your mother, then,' Father said with a grunt. A customer had come in and his attention was instantly diverted. 'I'll be up for my tea as usual.'

'Yes, Father.'

Running upstairs, I felt guilt for having lied to him. But it was his own fault. If he were more reasonable, more like Mary's father, I should not have had to lie. I'd done nothing wrong, except . . . A little smile tugged at the corners of my mouth as I remembered that brief kiss and its effect on my heart. It had beat so frantically that I felt breathless. I'd wished Paul would take me in his arms and kiss me properly – the way it happened in the romantic books I liked to read.

How wicked of me! I ought to have slapped him or acted as if I were insulted – but I'd liked it. I had enjoyed the sensation it gave me, the warm feeling I'd experienced inside. At first, I'd wanted to cry because it had seemed as though he were saying goodbye, and I was afraid he wouldn't want to see me any more – but then he'd smiled and hinted that we might be seeing each other again.

If only we could! If only we could meet often, go

dancing and . . . My mind careered on wildly, making up a life so wonderful it could only be imagined.

I jumped guiltily. Mother was standing in the kitchen doorway, a milk jug in her hand. I'd been dreaming and hadn't noticed her there.

'Father doesn't know,' I said, glancing over my shoulder. 'He thinks Mary Baker gave me a lift home – but it was someone else.' I felt a warm glow of pleasure spread through me. 'He's a gentleman, Mum. Gran likes him. He's an architect from Cambridge working with the railway and his name is Paul Greenslade. He's asked me twice now to go to the pictures, but of course I said I couldn't. Father would never agree.'

'No, he wouldn't!' She looked really alarmed. 'Where did you meet this man, Emma? Your father will kill you if he knows you've been meeting someone secretly.'

'I haven't been with him,' I said. 'Not like that, anyway. I haven't done anything wrong. He came into the shop one evening and I served him – and this afternoon he gave me a lift to Gran's because it was raining so hard. He wanted to meet her and came back at four to bring me home. She liked him. Honest, Mum. Gran thinks he's all right.'

'Well, that's something I suppose.'

She sighed, her shoulders drooping under the burden of her unhappy life. 'It was bound to happen one day, of course. I've tried talking to Harold about you growing up, needing more freedom, but of course he never listens. Just be careful, Emma, that's all. I know it's hard on you, your father being the way he is, so strict, but . . .'

'I've told Paul I can't go out with him. I don't suppose I'll see him again. He's bound to know lots of girls – girls who aren't treated as if they're children, who are allowed to say yes when someone asks them out. Why should he bother with me?'

Oh, Emma . . .' She gazed at me sadly. 'Don't look like that, darling. I wish I could help. I could try talking to Harold again, but I don't think it would make much difference. You know how irritable your father can be.'

'No, you mustn't,' I said quickly as I saw how tired and worn she seemed. I didn't want Father to take his anger out on her. 'It doesn't matter, Mum. I liked Paul, but he's only here for a little while. I doubt if I shall see him again.'

I went out into the hall as Father was coming up the stairs for his meal. I waited for him to reach the top, but was surprised when he lingered, giving me a thoughtful glance.

'Richard Gillows was here a few minutes ago. He was asking after you, Emma.'

'Was he?'

'He's fond of you, that lad, asked me if I would allow

you to go to the church social – you and your mother, that is.'

'Oh . . .' I waited warily. Father was looking pleased with himself, and that warned me that I wasn't going to like this. 'He asked Mum the other day when we came out of church.'

'You didn't tell me. She didn't mention it.'

'I asked her not to, because I didn't want to go.'

'Not go? Why?' His brows furrowed in surprise. 'Well, I said you would. It will do you and your mother good to get out of the house for once. She has been looking a bit peaky lately.'

'I wish you hadn't said I would go.'

'Nonsense! Don't be so selfish, Emma. Richard is a decent young man. You and your mother will be safe enough with him.'

It was always useless to argue with Father in this mood. I didn't say anything as I passed him, going on down the stairs. How could he have arranged the outing without consulting me? It was worse than if he'd refused permission.

I was tempted to feign illness on the night but realized that would only be cutting off my nose to spite my face. If I was truthful, I would enjoy the church social, and, if my mother was there, it wouldn't be like going on a proper date with Richard Gillows.

It was so unfair! Why couldn't it have been Paul

Greenslade who'd spoken to Father about taking me out?

Paul came into the shop the next morning. I was weighing out some pear drops for a regular customer. I glanced at Paul once, giving him a nervous smile. He hardly seemed to notice me, but spent several minutes talking to Father.

'He's an interesting chap,' my father remarked after Paul had left. 'Educated. Knowledgeable. Been to university I expect. You can always tell that sort. He was telling me about a new bridge he's been discussing with the Railway Board.'

'Did you like him?' I held my breath.

'Like him?' Father frowned. 'Don't know the man. Seems interesting, that's all. You don't have to like someone to appreciate their quality. Not our sort really.'

'Oh . . .' My heart sank. I might have known. I turned my back on my father and started to tidy the rack of newspapers and magazines.

'Thought any more about the church social?'

'I expect it will be enjoyable, Father. It usually is.'

'I don't approve of time wasting,' he grumbled. 'But you're a sensible girl, Emma. You do your work well and there's no harm in something like that now and then.'

'Do you need me?' I asked, still not looking at him. 'Only I ought to enter some bills into the accounts.'

'You get on,' he said. 'I'll call you if I need help.'

'All right.'

'Emma?'

I stopped at the door leading to the back stairs. 'Yes, Father?'

'There will be an extra half a crown in your wages this week.'

'Thank you.'

I went upstairs. At least I could pay Mrs Henty some more on my costume. It would have been nice to wear it for the social, but I had a pretty dress Mother had made me: that would do.

I was halfway to Gran's the next Wednesday afternoon when the blast of a car horn made me jump half out of my skin. Glancing over my shoulder I saw it was Paul and my heart began to beat wildly. I hadn't truly expected him to come.

'You made me jump,' I said, half accusing.

'Sorry.' He leaned across and opened the passenger-side door. 'Jump in. I'll give you a lift to your grandmother's.'

'Thank you.' I obeyed eagerly, without hesitation. At that moment I didn't care who saw me or what my father would say if he heard about it. I was overjoyed that Paul had sought me out once more.

'I shan't be able to fetch you today,' he said, 'but I've bought a few things for Mrs Jacobs – a tin of biscuits, some tea and sugar. Tell her I'll call one day this week. I'd like to have a little chat with her.'

'What about?' I looked at him curiously. 'It was kind of you to buy her these things, Paul.'

'I'm trying to soften her up,' he said and grinned disarmingly. 'Maybe she can tell me how I can get through that briar hedge your father has built around you.'

Did he really mean that? I looked at him shyly. 'Is that why you spent some time talking to him the other day?'

'What do you think?'

'I think he respects you. He said you were interesting.'

'That's something.' Paul stopped the car. We were a few yards from my grandmother's cottage, which was isolated out here by the line. I would have hated to live in such a place, but she liked it. There was no one around to see us. 'I've got to find a way of seeing you properly.' Paul looked at me intently. 'I can't get you out of my head, Emma. I'm not a complete rogue. Surely there's something I can do to make your father see that?'

'Gran is the one to ask,' I replied, cheeks flushed. 'She is the only person Father ever listens to, and that's only because she is so stubborn. She makes such a fuss that in the end he gives in to make her keep quiet.'

Paul laughed, then leaned towards me. He ran his fingers down my cheek, then gave me a long, lingering kiss on the lips.

'I'll find time to see Mrs Jacobs tomorrow,' he promised. 'Tell her I'll come about noon.'

His words caused my heart to take a little skip of joy.

There was no mistaking the expression in his eyes. He really did like me. He must do to go to all this trouble for my sake.

'I'll tell her to expect you,' I said. 'Goodbye, Paul – and thank you.'

'My pleasure,' he said and smiled.

I couldn't help showing my excitement as I got out of the car, waved to Paul and then watched as he drove away. If he was really serious about seeing me, it might just be possible to persuade Father. After all, he'd agreed to my going to the church social with Richard Gillows.

My spirits lifted as I ran the last few yards to Gran's house. Perhaps things were about to change for the better.

I was on thorns wondering if Paul would come to the shop after he'd talked to my grandmother the next day. Every time the shop bell went my head jerked up expectantly, my heart beginning to race in anticipation, but he didn't come. Nor the next day either.

By Saturday I had almost given up hope of seeing him, but then, at five to six that evening, he came into the shop and bought several expensive items from Father. He spent a few minutes asking his advice about various brands of cigars, explaining that he wanted the best as a gift for his own father.

'Decent chap that,' Father remarked after he'd gone. 'Seems to think a lot of his father. Wanted only the best for him. Too many young people have too little respect for their parents these days.'

I was glowing as I listened to Father's praise of Paul. He had given me one meaningful look before he left, which I was sure meant this was all part of the plan for gaining Father's confidence. And it did seem to be working!

I went to bed happily that night, clutching an Ethel M. Dell novel I had not previously read and a small bar of milk chocolate.

Perhaps, just now and then, dreams did come true.

Chapter Three

When I attended church with my mother the next morning, I was wearing a full-skirted light blue summer dress, a hip-length white jacket with a belt and a pretty straw hat I'd trimmed with ribbons myself. Paul was sitting in the pew we usually occupied. My heart jerked giddily as I saw him, and I was glad I'd taken so much trouble with my appearance.

My mother took her place next to him. He smiled a friendly greeting and offered her a hymn book.

I was trembling with excitement, though trying not to let it show. Throughout the service I was acutely conscious of Paul sitting there. The sermon seemed to go on and on endlessly, causing me to fidget. Would it never end?

At last it was over, but my nervousness increased as Paul followed us out into the brilliant sunshine. The vicar was waiting in the porch to speak with his parishioners and – wonder of wonders! – he seemed to know Paul. I held my breath. He was actually going to introduce him to my mother.

'Have you met Mr Greenslade?' he asked, smiling in his gentle manner. 'This is Mrs Robinson and her daughter, Emma. Both of them regularly attend my services, I'm pleased to say. Mr Robinson owns the newsagent and tobacconist in the High Street.'

'I've met Mr Robinson several times,' Paul said, looking with interest at my mother. 'And I believe I've seen Emma before . . .'

My heart was racing wildly as Mother looked at him, eyes narrowing. I held my breath lest she disapprove of him, but I need not have worried. She was no more proof against his charm than Gran and I had been. She was soon smiling, accepting a lift for us both in his car – me sitting in the back behind them – and issuing an invitation for tea that afternoon.

'We're just simple people, Mr Greenslade, but you would be welcome,' she said. 'There's not much to do here at weekends, unless you have friends.'

'You are so kind, Mrs Robinson,' he said. His manner was so easy, so pleasant. I was not surprised my mother had succumbed. 'I hardly know anyone in town, but was obliged to stay over for business reasons. I accept your hospitality gladly.'

'Then we shall expect you at half past three, Mr Greenslade.'

'Please do call me Paul. All my friends do. It was a pleasure meeting you, Mrs Robinson – and Emma, of course.'

I was barely able to suppress the laughter bubbling up inside me. I'd hardly spoken a word the whole time, but it didn't matter. Paul obviously knew exactly what he was about, and I was afraid of spoiling the effect by saying something out of place.

How clever he was to get himself introduced by the vicar! Surely Father could not object to my knowing him now.

'Well,' Mother said later, when we were back in the house. 'So that's your Paul Greenslade, Emma. I must admit I did like him. An educated man. Respectable.'

'What will Father say when he knows you've invited him to tea?'

'We'll worry about that afterwards. He won't make a fuss while we've got company, and I can put up with his grumbles afterwards. If I were you, I should pop round to Mary Baker's and ask if she and her father can come to tea. It won't look so obvious if we have other guests.'

'Oh, Mum!' We smiled naughtily at each other. 'How clever you are. I'll go straight away.'

Slipping out of the back door so that Father wouldn't see me, I managed to get away without being questioned. When I knocked at Mary's house my friend invited me in at once. Mary was a quiet, dark-haired girl, but that morning she was looking excited and animated.

'I'm glad you've come, Emma,' she said. 'I wanted you to be the first to know. Joe Edwards has asked me to marry him, and I've said yes. He's going to live here and help Dad out the back – which means I shan't have to do so much and my father won't be left on his own when I marry.'

'I'm so pleased for you.' I gave her a quick hug. 'I was going to ask you and your father for tea, but I expect you have plans of your own?'

'We should like to come – if I can bring Joe? He's from Chatteris and it will be nice for him to meet our friends.'

'Of course you can.' The more the better, I thought. 'That would be lovely. I'll tell Mum to expect all of you then?'

I felt a surge of happiness as I walked home. Mary's engagement could not have come at a better time. My father liked Mr Baker, and when he heard the news he might start thinking about my future. It might make him realize I was no longer a child.

'Hello, Emma.' The man's deep voice broke into my thoughts. I sighed and stopped walking, turning to look at Richard Gillows as he came up to me. 'I missed you this Wednesday. Didn't you go to your grandmother's?'

'I went earlier,' I lied, feeling guilty as he looked at me hard. 'How are you, Richard?'

'Same as usual. You haven't forgotten you're going to the church social with me next week?'

'No, I haven't forgotten.' My heart sank as I saw the expression on his face. He looked so pleased with himself! 'Me and my mother,' I reminded him.

A chill had begun to form at the nape of my neck. I didn't know why but there was something in the way Richard looked at me that made me feel very nervous.

'That's right. You and your Mum. I'll pick you up at a quarter past six. Your father will have had his dinner by then. Be ready.'

I didn't answer. It was obvious from the confident way he looked at me that he considered the outing a sign that I was willing to be courted. I wished Father hadn't accepted the invitation for me. If only I dare change my mind! But it would cause too much fuss in the house.

Why let it bother me? It didn't matter. I dismissed the uneasiness I always felt when Richard made a point of walking with me. Paul was coming to tea. Surely he would find a way of persuading Father to let him take me out!

Father accepted his unexpected guests with surprising graciousness that afternoon. Mother had set the table with the best linen, a bone china tea service which usually lived in the sideboard, and some silver spoons she'd been given as a wedding present but seldom used because they were too precious.

Paul spent most of the time discussing cricket and politics with my father. I was spoken to only a couple of times by either of them, and talked mainly to Mary and her fiancé.

It was only towards the end of the visit that Paul mentioned a film he was interested in seeing the next week.

'I don't suppose you would care to come as my guests?' he asked. 'You and Mrs Robinson – and Emma, of course.' He smiled in Mother's direction.

'I've no time for going to the cinema,' Father replied, 'but I dare say Mrs Robinson and Emma might enjoy it.'

'That's settled, then,' Paul said before he could change his mind. 'Shall we say tomorrow? I'll be here at six-thirty – if that's convenient, sir?'

Afterwards, I thought it must have been the way he called my father *sir* that made him agree. I could hardly believe he had and found it difficult not to let my excitement show.

'I ought to be going,' Paul said, glancing at his watch. 'This has been such a pleasure. Mrs Robinson, thank you so much for the excellent tea. I shall look forward to seeing you tomorrow.'

'See Mr Greenslade out, Emma,' my mother said. 'There's a good girl.'

I got to my feet at once, only too eager to obey. A few minutes alone with Paul was more than I had dared to hope for.

Downstairs in the shop, Paul reached out for me, giving me a swift kiss on the mouth. He looked triumphant as he let me go.

'There – that wasn't so difficult, was it?'

'I don't know how you managed it.' I was dazzled by his cleverness. I could never have believed it would be so easy, but then, I had never met anyone like Paul before.

'Mrs Jacobs gave me a few hints.' He smiled to himself. 'She's a wise old bird, that grandmother of yours. Next time, I'll get your father to let us go out on our own.'

'I don't mind Mum coming.'

'I do . . .' The expression in his eyes made me tingle all over. I almost had to pinch myself to make sure this was really happening. 'I want you to myself, Emma – but this is better than not seeing you at all.'

'Yes. Much better.' I felt suddenly alive, full of expectation as I gazed up at him. 'Oh, Paul! You've no idea how much this means to me.'

'Haven't I?' His mouth quirked at the corners. 'You show your feelings, Emma – but I feel just the same. I would like . . .'

I was eager to hear what else he had to say, but, hearing the clatter of feet on the stairs, I knew that Mary and her fiancé were coming down. I moved away from him quickly.

'I'll see you tomorrow, Paul.'

'You'll see me in my dreams before that,' he whispered and went out just as Mary came into the shop.

'Dad has stopped for a chat with your father,' she said and came to kiss me goodbye. 'It was lovely having tea with you.' The happiness seemed to shine out of her as she looked at Joe. 'We're going to the social on Wednesday. We'll probably see you there. Mrs Robinson said you were going with Richard Gillows.'

'Mum and me,' I agreed with a giggle. 'That's twice we're going out in one week. Wonders will never cease!'

'It's different with Richard, though, isn't it?' Mary said, arching her brows. 'He's been sweet on you for a long time.' She glanced at the pretty amethyst ring on her left hand. 'You'll be wearing one of these soon.'

I shook my head as my friend went out, but Mary only smiled mysteriously, as if she knew something I didn't.

She couldn't think I wanted to marry Richard? I shuddered inwardly. I couldn't think of anything I wanted less.

The visit to the cinema the following evening was even better than I had expected. Paul bought chocolates for me and my mother from the shop, then came upstairs to wait while we finished getting ready.

'Don't worry, sir,' Paul said to my father as he escorted us from the shop. 'I'll have them both safely home by ten at the latest.'

'I'll have locked up by then.' Father frowned at my mother. 'You've got your back door key, Greta?'

'Yes, Harold. Don't forget to take your medicine at nine.'

He grunted assent, declining to answer and staring moodily after us as we went out.

'Is Father ill?' I asked my mother as Paul opened the car doors for us to get in. 'He hasn't mentioned anything to me.'

'It's just his usual trouble,' she replied. 'I suggested he visit the doctor, but he insists a good dose of syrup of figs will see him right.'

It was cheaper than visiting the doctor, of course. I was thoughtful. I recalled Father rubbing his chest a couple of times that afternoon but hadn't taken much notice. He suffered with indigestion and stomach trouble periodically, though he usually made little of it.

'Isn't this exciting?' I said to my mother, pushing Father and his health problems from my mind. 'I'm looking forward to it, aren't you?'

The film showing that night was *Morning Glory* and starred Katherine Hepburn. She had been voted the best actress of 1932 for her part in it and I'd wanted to see it the first time it had come to town. I hadn't been allowed to go and hadn't really expected to see it this time either.

'Paul, I want you to take me to my mother's,' Mother

said, surprising me as he started the car. 'You can fetch me afterwards if you will.'

'Mum?' I stared at her. 'Do you mean it?'

'I've no interest in playing gooseberry. Besides, it's ages since I spent time with your grandmother. You can tell me about the film on the way home. Harold will be bound to ask.'

'This is awfully good of you, Mrs Robinson,' Paul said, glancing at her. 'Are you sure you don't mind?'

'All I ask is that you look after Emma. I'm trusting you to take care of her.'

'And I shall. Believe me.'

It took only a few minutes to deliver Mother to the little cottage by the line, and a few more to reach the cinema. Paul bought three tickets and gave the stubs to me.

'Keep them in case your father wants proof.'

He seemed to think of everything. I slipped them into my coat pocket. It was very wrong of us to deceive Father like this, but I couldn't feel guilty. If he had been more reasonable, this wouldn't have been necessary.

I was thrilled as we slipped into the very back row of the cinema. The programme had just begun with the Pathe News and the lights were down. No one even looked at us.

After a few minutes, Paul put his arm about my

shoulders. I turned to him at once and he kissed me. It was a long, lingering kiss this time and my head swam. I felt slightly dizzy and breathless. I was falling in love with him. I must be!

We sat close together throughout the film, drawing apart only when the lights went up in the interval. I hardly knew what was happening on the screen. It was heaven just sitting there in the dark with Paul. He smelled so good. I wasn't sure whether it was the expensive hair oil he had used, but something had an intoxicating effect on me.

I wanted to stay there forever, sitting with him in the dark, but all too soon it was over and we had to leave. Paul kissed me again in the car, just before we fetched my mother. He held me so close that I felt as if I were a part of him – I wanted to be. My skin went hot all over as I realized what I was thinking.

'I had a wonderful time this evening,' he whispered. 'Did you enjoy yourself, darling?'

He had called me darling! My throat contracted with emotion. He did care for me. He must! Oh, he must love me, because I couldn't bear it now if he didn't.

'It was lovely,' I said. 'I don't know how to thank you.'

'There's no need.' He touched my mouth with his forefinger, sending little shivers of pleasure all over me. 'Just think of me before you go to sleep.'

'I always do,' I confessed impulsively, then blushed because it sounded so forward.

'You're so sweet, Emma. 'Do you know how lovely you are?'

'I'm not pretty,' I denied, hanging my head. 'I know I'm not.'

'Sometimes you are beautiful,' he said and sighed heavily. 'We had better collect your mother or we shall be late. And if we sit here any longer I might forget to be a gentleman.'

I laughed, certain he was only teasing me. I was still laughing as I went into the cottage to fetch my mother. She and Gran gave each other a knowing look.

'It seems you've enjoyed yourself,' Gran said.

'Oh, I have!'

'We'd best get back,' Mother said. 'Harold will be looking at the clock and wondering.'

'You can tell me all about it on Wednesday,' my grandmother said, giving me a wicked look.

'Of course I will.' I kissed her. 'Thanks, Gran. It wouldn't have happened without you. I'm so happy.'

In the car Paul described the film to my mother word for word.

'I've seen it before,' he confessed as I questioned with my eyes. I could only remember bits. 'It was well worth seeing again – wasn't it?' He winked at me.

'Oh yes,' I agreed, smothering a laugh.

'I'm going to be in Cambridge for the rest of the week,' Paul said as he dropped us outside our door. 'But I'll see you after church on Sunday.'

'You must come to dinner this time,' said Mother. 'We call it dinner but I expect you say lunch?'

'I call it a perfect opportunity,' he replied with a teasing look in his eyes. 'You are a terrific woman, Mrs Robinson. Emma is lucky to have such an understanding mother.'

'You don't have to flatter me, Paul,' she murmured, amused but still liking him. 'I'm entirely on your side – and Emma's, of course.'

'For which I shall be eternally grateful.'

He got out of the car and opened the door for her and then me.

'Good night, Mrs Robinson. Until Sunday, Emma.'

'Good night, Paul – and thank you.'

Later, when I was brushing my hair in front of the dressing table mirror, Mother entered, putting a finger to her lips.

'Was it as exciting as you expected?' she asked softly. 'Keep your voice down, love. Your father is still up.'

I nodded, barely controlling my desire to blurt it all out.

'It was wonderful. I'm so happy, Mum.'

'Don't get your hopes too high, love. I'll try to

persuade your father to let you see him on your own, but I can't promise.'

'It doesn't matter. As long as he doesn't find out what you did tonight. I don't want you to be in trouble, Mum.'

'Don't worry about me.' There was an odd, faraway expression in her eyes. 'I've put up with Harold's moods for years. I dare say I can manage for a bit longer.'

Overcome with sympathy and affection for her, I stood up and kissed her cheek.

'I'm glad Mary is going to the social on Wednesday. I don't want to be on our own with Richard Gillows all the time.'

'Don't let your father know you don't like Richard just yet,' she advised. 'If things work out for you and Paul . . . but we mustn't go too fast. You said yourself he wouldn't be here long. If he's serious, I'll bring Harold round somehow – but it's too soon to think about that. You mustn't set your heart on him, love. He's charming and I like him but . . . well, men don't always mean everything they say.'

'I know.' I met her serious gaze steadily. 'I like him a lot, Mum – but I know he must meet lots of girls prettier than me.'

'You're pretty enough,' she said. 'Who know what makes people fall in love? It isn't just looks.'

'No, I don't suppose it is. Not always.'

Paul was so good-looking! He was everything I had

ever dreamed of in the man I hoped to marry one day.

'Well, we'll see,' she said. 'Go to bed now. You've got to be up early tomorrow. Don't oversleep or there will be no more trips to the cinema for either of us!'

I was up at my usual time. I had started to sort the newspapers the next morning when Sheila Tomms came into the shop.

'Hello, Emma. Can I have a quarter of toffee pieces please?'

'Yes, of course. Shall I break them up small for you?'

Sheila nodded. 'I saw you last night.' She pulled a mischievous face at me. 'Who was that man? He's really dishy – just like Clark Gable without the moustache.'

'His name is Paul,' I said, then put a finger to my lips. 'Don't say anything. My father might hear.'

'Mum's the word.' She grinned at me. 'Are you going to the social tomorrow?'

I nodded.

'Might see you there then.'

'Yes. We can have a proper chat there.'

'Righto. I'm off. I'll be late for work else.'

She went out. I watched her mount her bike and pedal off. Several men were passing on their cycles. Most of the railway workers went to the depot on bikes; it was a fair distance to the marshalling yards, which were vast and sometimes eerie and desolate, especially on a misty morning. I had been there with my grandfather a couple of times when I was small, and though I never ventured further than Gran's these days, from the top of the bank just past her cottage it was possible to see part of the yards and the engines standing idle or being shunted around.

'Who was that just now?' Father asked as he came through from the back. 'You were talking to someone.'

'A girl I knew at school. Sheila Tomms.'

'Oh, that one.' He glared at me, clearly in one of his moods. 'Common as muck and no better than she ought to be from what I hear.'

'Sheila is all right.' I was defensive. 'Better than most.'

'I don't like you mixing with girls like that. She'll get herself in trouble before she's finished, the lads she hangs about with all the time. I wonder her father allows it. I'd soon put a stop to her little games.'

'Her father is dead. And she's going steady.'

'He's after what he can get. Or else he's a fool. No man wants second-hand goods. You mind my words, girl. I might seem an old fool to you, but one day you'll thank me. When a decent chap asks you a certain question, you will realize a girl's reputation is worth something.'

I bent my head over the piles of papers, marking them with the numbers of the various houses and putting them into hessian rucksacks ready for the delivery boys, who would start arriving at any moment. My father had never spoken to me so openly before and it made me feel awkward.

Why was he suddenly beginning to talk to me as an adult? I suspected he had something particular on his mind. Was it possible that Mary Baker's engagement had set him thinking? I'd believed he would resist all requests for me to go courting, but he seemed to be changing his mind.

He had mentioned a decent man. I knew he was very class conscious – was he flattered at the idea of me being asked out by a gentleman? Paul had gone out of his way to gain his good opinion. Perhaps my father liked the thought of his daughter marrying into a class above his own.

The idea made me smile inwardly. If only . . . if only my dreams would come true.

Wednesday was very warm for June. It was more like July or August, sticky, muggy heat with a hint of thunder in the air.

I wore a blue-and-white summer frock with a squared neckline and tight sleeves to the elbow. I had added a wide white leather belt and white shoes. My mother lent me a soft shawl to drape over my shoulders.

'You look very nice,' Richard said when he came to fetch us. He presented us both with a small bunch of flowers from his garden. 'Are you ready then?'

Richard was dressed in his best suit with a white shirt and spotted tie. He looked smart, his hair slicked down with water and parted in the middle. I noticed some of the girls glancing enviously my way as we walked into the church hall.

I knew most of the people at the social. I had gone to school with several of the girls, and seen the men either in Father's shop or the street. There were a few fresh faces but not many.

Mary and Joe came up to us almost at once, and after an exchange of greetings the two men went off to fetch some drinks: orangeade for the ladies and shandies for themselves.

The evening started with a Tombola and some party games, and then someone put a record on the gramophone and the dancing started.

I danced a two-step with Richard, then swopped partners with Mary for the fox-trot. When I looked for my mother, I was surprised to see her dancing with a rather nice-looking man who was probably a year or so younger than my father. He had thick brown hair, dark eyes and a cheerful manner.

'This is Bert Fitch,' Mother introduced us afterwards. 'We used to know each other years ago.'

'I went away to work,' he explained. 'I've just returned to March and taken a job as a crossing keeper – same as your grandfather, Emma. It's not that I need to work; I've a nice bit put by for a rainy day, but I like something to do as a hobby. Not being married, you need to keep busy.'

Something passed between him and my mother at that moment. A look that made her blush and drop her gaze. I was curious, but Richard was asking me to dance again.

'It's the barn dance,' he said. 'We don't want to miss that.'

I gave him my hand. The barn dance was fun. I'd always enjoyed this part of the evening, not that I'd been to many socials. My father had brought me and my mother a few times when I was younger, and last year, when Mother was unwell, he had allowed me to go with Mary and her father to the Christmas party.

The barn dance meant I got to dance with most of the men in the room. I smiled at them all, thoroughly enjoying myself, and was sorry when it ended.

I went to the cloakroom afterwards to tidy myself, and saw Sheila was there, putting on some fresh lipstick.

'That's a pretty colour.'

'It's a *Tangee*,' she replied, showing me. 'I bought it in Woolworth's. It cost me a shilling – but it was worth it. I could have got a cheaper one, but this has a pretty case.'

'It's lovely,' I agreed. 'I wish I dare buy one, but my father won't let me wear it.'

'He needn't know if you rub it off before you go in.' She offered me the stick. 'Go on, try it.'

'I'd better not. We're going home soon.'

'Had a good time?' She looked slightly envious. 'You're doing all right. Clark Gable at the pictures and now Richard Gillows. You're a sly one, Emma.'

'It was just coincidence.' I blushed as she pulled a disbelieving face. 'I didn't want to come with Richard this evening, but my father arranged it.'

'I'm not surprised.' Sheila looked thoughtful. 'They drink together sometimes down the pub – did you know that?'

'No. I knew he liked Richard, that's all.'

'You want to watch it,' she advised. 'Richard always had an eye to the main chance. He'll get his feet under the table at your house if he can.'

'What do you mean?'

'Everyone knows Harold Robinson must have a packet stashed away. Stands to reason: that shop is open all hours and he doesn't spend much. The money must be sitting in the bank somewhere.'

'You think Richard is interested in me because of the money?'

'Not just because of that.' She patted her hair in front of the misty mirror. 'But it helps. He used to play around, but these days he's not interested. I reckon he's got marriage on his mind, Emma.'

'Well, I haven't! Not to him anyway.'

Sheila went into a fit of the giggles.

'And there was me thinking you never had any fun.'

She winked at me. 'You watch out, love. I wouldn't marry Richard, even if he is a good-looking devil. You be careful of him. He likes his drink too much and can be mean when he's had a few.'

I watched as she walked away, hips swaying. Sheila sounded as if she knew Richard well. Had she been out with him in the past? She had been with a lot of different men. My father hadn't been making that up. In a small town that kind of behaviour soon led to gossip. Sheila probably wasn't as innocent as she might be, but I liked her. I believed the warning about Richard Gillows had been given in good faith and without malice.

Later that evening, I lay in bed and thought about what Sheila had told me. It made me all the more certain that I was right to feel the way I did about Richard. His manner had become progressively more possessive throughout the evening. He was obviously beginning to think of me as his girl – but was he planning to ask me to marry him?

The thought sent a shudder down my spine. I didn't even want to consider it. I couldn't bear the idea of Richard kissing me the way Paul had. There was always a lingering smell of the railways about Richard, even when he was dressed up: grease or oil or burning. I wasn't exactly sure what it was but I didn't much like it.

Paul smelled like a wood after rain. I closed my eyes as I lay back against the pillows, remembering the way he had held me . . . the way I had wanted to melt into his arms, to surrender my whole self to him.

If I couldn't have Paul I wouldn't have anyone, I decided. I certainly wasn't going to marry Richard. No one could force me to do that, not even my father. I would run away from home first!

But perhaps it was all imagination. Richard hadn't said anything. He had paid me more attention these past few weeks, but that didn't mean he wanted to marry me – did it?

Paul was in church that Sunday morning. He took my mother and me home afterwards and stayed for lunch, which was roast beef and lovely, light crispy Yorkshire pudding with lashings of gravy and vegetables.

Mother usually did the cooking and cleaning herself, but since her last illness, she'd had help in the house three mornings a week. On Sunday she left her helper to prepare everything for lunch, apart from the Yorkshire batter, which she made herself and left to stand in a cool place while we attended church.

'That was delicious,' Paul complimented her after-wards. 'I've never had Yorkshire pudding like that before. The way my mother's cook makes it, it's always soggy and heavy.'

'Greta is a good cook, I'll say that for her.' Father patted his stomach. 'The trouble is, it tempts me to eat too much and I suffer for it later.' He glared at my mother as if to blame her for his indigestion.

'Harold is a martyr to his stomach,' she said. 'It's a shame because he enjoys a good meal.'

'My father is much the same,' Paul said. 'He swears by Carter's pills. Have you tried them, sir?'

After the table had been cleared, I helped my mother to wash up in the kitchen. I could still hear the men's voices but it was impossible to make out what they were saying. However, when I returned to the parlour they were drinking a glass of the brandy Paul had brought, and my father seemed to be in a mellow mood.

'Paul has invited you to a concert in Cambridge next Saturday afternoon,' he announced. 'What do you say to that, Emma?'

'A concert?' I stared in surprise. 'It sounds nice.'

'It will do you good,' Father said. 'Improve your mind. Your mother is too busy to come with you, but you may go if you promise to behave yourself.'

'Of course I shall, Father.'

My heart was racing. Was he really going to let me go alone? And on a Saturday afternoon, which was often our busiest day in the shop?

'That's settled, then,' Paul said. 'I shall call for you at one. My mother will be pleased to meet you, Emma. And to return the hospitality your parents have so kindly shown me.'

I was puzzled as I took him downstairs shortly afterwards.

'Are we going to the concert with your mother?'

'You'll see.' He gave me a mysterious look and kissed me briefly on the lips. 'Just trust me, Emma. Trust me . . .'

Chapter Four

'I'm going out with a special friend on Saturday,' I explained to Mrs Henty that Wednesday afternoon. 'I know I still owe you thirty-five shillings – but could I possibly wear the costume this weekend? I'll bring it back afterwards and keep paying until I've settled in full.'

Mrs Henty hesitated. I knew she wouldn't normally consider giving credit. She didn't mind her customers paying weekly, but she always put the goods by until they were paid for. I was about to apologize for asking when she nodded and smiled at me.

'Seeing as it's you, Emma, of course you can take it. And you needn't bring it back. I'll trust you for the money.'

'I'll pay five shillings on Saturday,' I promised. 'This is very good of you, Mrs Henty. Perhaps one day I'll be able to do something for you.'

'You could always come and work for me. I would be willing to pay you fifteen shillings a week – more when you'd learned the trade.'

'I wish I could.' I must have sounded wistful, because she looked at me with sympathy. 'Father wouldn't let me, of course.'

'You're too useful to him,' she said and smiled. 'Wait a few minutes. I'll pack the costume for you.'

Mother was surprised when I showed her the costume later.

'I thought you still owed nearly two pounds on that?'

'Thirty-five shillings. I've promised to pay five shillings a week from now on.'

'Will you be able to manage?' She looked doubtful. 'I'll help you if you can't – but don't tell your father you still owe Mrs Henty. He wouldn't approve.'

'I couldn't wear my old costume to meet Paul's mother, could I?'

'No, of course not, love – and this one does suit you.' She reached out to pat my cheek. 'You can borrow my best cream silk blouse and my pearl earrings. You'll want to look smart.'

'I'm so nervous,' I said. I had thought of nothing else all week. 'Paul must like me quite a lot, mustn't he – if he's taking me to meet his mother?'

'It does sound promising,' she admitted, though still

looking a little doubtful. 'I was surprised when he said it. After all, you only met him a few weeks ago.'

I knew she was right. I sometimes felt as if I had known Paul all my life, but it was only a few weeks since he'd come into the shop for the first time, and rather soon for him to be taking me home . . . unless he was serious about me.

The thought made me tingle all over with excitement. I had tried very hard not to get too excited, not to hope for too much, but I couldn't stop myself dreaming. I was in love with Paul and it really did seem as though he felt the same.

I couldn't wait for the weekend to come!

'How is your friend?' Sheila Tomms asked when she popped into the shop on Friday morning. 'The one that looks a bit like Clark Gable – have you seen him recently?'

'Paul has been busy this week but I'm seeing him this weekend.' I was glad my father wasn't in the shop to hear me. He had gone out on business, leaving Ben and I to hold the fort. 'He came to dinner last Sunday and he's taking me to meet his mother tomorrow.'

Sheila arched her brows. 'Sounds promising. Lucky you. I wish I could meet someone like that.'

'I thought you were going steady with Eric Brown?'

'I was . . .' She pulled a face. 'We broke up last night.'

'I'm sorry. What happened – or shouldn't I ask?'

'Eric was all right.' She sighed. 'We quarrelled over – well, it doesn't matter. It's finished and that's that. I suppose I'll find someone else.' She laughed, shaking her hair back from her face with a gesture of defiance. 'Maybe Richard Gillows. Since you don't want him – you don't, do you?'

'No!' I made a wry face at her. 'You can have him and welcome.'

'Maybe I shall, then.'

Sheila was still laughing as she went out of the shop. I wasn't sure whether she was serious or joking about Richard.

'She's a right caution that one,' Ben said as the door closed behind her. 'I'm not surprised she fell out with her bloke. They're saying as she's up the spout and it ain't Eric's neither.'

'Ben!' I gave him a sharp look. 'I don't want any of that talk here, thank you. If my father heard you he would sack you immediately.'

'Lucky he ain't here then, eh?'

Ben's cheeky grin made me smile despite myself. I wondered if the story was true. People loved to talk, but the old saying 'no smoke without fire' often proved accurate. I felt sorry for Sheila if she was having a baby. There was bound to be gossip in a small town like this, and a lot of people would turn their noses up at her.

I began to tidy the shelves. I did them every morning,

but the young lads turned everything over, reading as many of the comics for free as they could and sorting through the box of marbles in the hope of finding one they hadn't already got in their collections. Some of them weren't above stealing something if I didn't keep a sharp eye on them.

'You sweet on the toff then?' asked Ben. 'You want to be careful of his sort, Emma. He'll have your knickers off soon as look at you.'

'Ben! I shan't warn you again about that sort of talk. I'm going to the stockroom. You can call me if you get busy.'

I was frowning as I went into the crowded stockroom. It was packed from floor to ceiling with boxes against the walls, some containing fresh stock but others crammed with forgotten oddments, old papers and paid bills. Father really ought to throw most of this stuff out, I thought, as I looked round at the dust that had accumulated over the years. There was no sense in harbouring rubbish. I'd suggested having a clear out to my father several times, but he always made some excuse.

Opening the top drawer of an old chest, I frowned as I saw the collection of small bottles and pill boxes. What on earth were they? There were so many of them, some of the labels faded and indistinct. I picked one or two out, glancing at the printing on the packaging; they were all remedies for indigestion or stomach trouble. Some of them looked as if they had been there for years. Reading the list of ingredients for one medicine, I was startled to see it contained arsenic.

Surely that was poison? Did Father know what he was taking? He could end up by making himself really ill if he wasn't careful. It would be so much better if he went to the doctor instead of treating himself in this haphazard way.

'What are you doing, Emma?'

I jumped as I heard Father's voice behind me.

'I was thinking of tidying the stockroom,' I said. 'I just happened to look in this drawer and found these. You've had some of these pills for ages, Father. Don't you think you should throw them away and ask the doctor for something to settle your stomach?'

'Who asked you to pry into my affairs?' He glared at me. 'When I want your advice I'll ask for it – until then keep out of here and leave things alone. If I wanted this place sorted I would do it myself.'

'Yes, Father.'

I turned away, cheeks flaming. Why did he always have to be so harsh? I had only been trying to help. I was upset and annoyed with him for being the way he was, and yet couldn't help feeling concern. He was my father, even if he didn't show me any real affection. Sometimes I felt like leaving home, but I didn't wish him any harm, and I certainly didn't want him to poison himself with those pills.

I spoke to my mother about the pills when I went up to have my meal later.

'I'm sure he ought not to be taking half of them,' I said. 'One of the bottles has a label that says the preparation contains arsenic. I thought that was poison?'

'It is.' She gave me an odd look. 'Are you sure you read the label right?'

'Yes.' I frowned. 'I read something once in a book about people taking small doses of arsenic as a medicine, but I can't remember what it was supposed to cure.'

'Folk used all sorts years ago,' Mother said. 'No one goes to the doctor if they can help it. Harold is always looking for something different to cure his own troubles. I suppose he knows what he's doing. I've never been able to tell him anything. If I had my way he would go to the doctor, but you know what he is.'

'It just seems so silly, Mum.' I looked at her and sighed. 'Ben said he thought Sheila Tomms might be having a baby. Have you heard anything?'

'No, I haven't – but it wouldn't surprise me. She's a silly girl, Emma. If she carries on the way she is no one will marry her. I've seen what happens to her sort before and I'd have thought she'd have more sense.'

'I feel sorry for her if it's true.'

'So do I,' Mother admitted. 'Her mother won't be able to help her much. She will probably have to go away where no one knows her. Her life will be a misery if she stays round here. You've heard the way they gossip. She'll lose her job for starters.'

'I wonder who the father is? If it's true, that is.'

'Goodness knows. Let's just hope he decides to do the decent thing and marry her!'

I found it difficult to sleep that night. It was partly excitement, but other things kept running through my mind – like those pills in Father's drawer. Why did he leave them there and not in his bedroom? And why buy a medicine that contained a dangerous substance?

I couldn't answer either question so tried thinking about something else.

Was Sheila pregnant – and if so, who was the father?

Why did she keep mentioning Richard? Making out she didn't like him much one minute, then saying she was going to go out with him the next?

It didn't matter. I turned over and closed my eyes, making a conscious effort to get to sleep. If I lay here thinking all night, I would have shadows under my eyes in the morning, and I wanted to look my best for Paul.

Paul brought flowers for my mother when he collected me the next day – a beautiful bouquet of scented roses and lilies, which must have come from a high-class florist and which were obviously expensive.

'To say thank you.' He smiled as he presented them,

then turned to me. 'You look lovely, Emma. That colour suits you – you should wear it more often.'

I thanked him, feeling both nervous and excited as I went out to the car with him. Would his parents like me? Would they think me suitable for their son?

'Where is the concert being held?' I asked as he drew away from the kerb. 'I've never been to one before. I'm afraid I don't know much about music – not classical music anyway.'

'I'll teach you,' he said, sending me a smile that set my heart on a dizzy spin. 'Trust me, Emma. I promise you it's going to be fun.'

I glanced out of the window. It was an overcast day, much cooler than it had been for a while. I was glad I'd asked Mrs Henty for the costume. It wouldn't have been warm enough for a summer dress.

For some time the roads were almost deserted except for the occasional farm cart, a delivery van or one of the buses that ran between the various small towns and villages. The fields on either side were low-lying, the earth often black fen soil, rich and fertile. It was only when we turned off the country roads and headed towards Cambridge that we started to meet more cars and lorries.

'We'll soon be there.' Paul smiled at me. 'It's a surprise, Emma. I didn't think you would really want to go to a concert. We can find something better to do than that, can't we?'

He was turning off the main road as he spoke, though we were still some distance from the town itself, in a quiet road with several rather nice-looking houses in large gardens. Paul manoeuvred the car into a gateway flanked by red brick pillars and drove down a long, tree-lined drive.

'Are we going to your house?'

'Yes. We can listen to as much music as you like there. My parents have a large collection of classical, opera and dance records. We'll put the gramophone on. You can tell your father you've been listening to Mozart and Bach. You won't have to tell any lies.'

My heart started to beat very fast. I'd thought we would go to the concert before having tea with his parents. Now it seemed we would be with them all afternoon.

I looked out of the window. We passed a tennis court and what looked as if it might once have been a stable block, though it was not tumbling into disrepair. Beyond the stables I could see the roof of what seemed to be an extremely large building. As the car swept round the corner of the stable block I saw wide lawns, a grey stone terrace with roses growing over the low walls – and the house itself.

'Oh, Paul!' I gasped. 'It's huge.'

'Not really, there are much larger houses than this, believe me. Don't be overly impressed. We only use one wing. The rest of the place is falling down. One of these days we shall have to pull the whole thing down in the interests of safety.'

I was shocked. I had never seen a house like it, except in magazines or books. It appeared to be built in three sections, with a central block and two wings, and I thought it must be very old. I hadn't expected anything this grand, though as I got out of the car I could see what Paul meant. Parts of the roof had gaping holes and the walls looked as if they might be crumbling away in one wing. Even so, with all the land around it, it must be a valuable property.

'Your family must be wealthy, Paul!'

My stomach was tying itself in knots. What was I doing here? This was going to be worse than I'd imagined.

'If only,' he said, pulling a wry face. 'We were rich at the beginning of the last century but the money was frittered away by Grandfather Greenslade. These days we live on the bank and past glory. Things are what you might call tight where money is concerned.'

Paul might not consider his family wealthy, but I knew instinctively that what he thought of as being 'tight' would probably seem like riches to my family.

I ought not to have come here – this wasn't my world. I felt so nervous that I wanted to run away. My feet seemed glued to the ground and I hung back as Paul took my arm.

'What's the matter?'

'You shouldn't have brought me here, Paul. Your parents won't like me. I'm not the sort of girl they expect you to bring home. I can't meet them. I'm sorry. I just can't.'

He frowned. 'Silly Emma. You won't have to meet them; they're not here. They went away for the weekend. We shall have the house all to ourselves.'

'Really?' My relief was so overwhelming that I laughed. 'Oh, Paul! You might have told me sooner. I've been so nervous all the way here.'

'I wouldn't put you through that ordeal yet,' Paul said, giving me a brief kiss on the lips. 'When we're married we'll just turn up and give them the news.'

'When we're . . .' I was so bemused by what he'd just said that I made no further resistance as he led me towards some French windows, unlocked them and drew me inside to a small parlour. He gazed down into my face for a moment, then took me into his arms, kissing me so thoroughly that I was trembling when he let me go.

'Poor darling,' he said, running the tip of one finger down my cheek. 'You were scared to death, weren't you? I'd better give you a drop of brandy. You look pale.'

He left me standing as he went over to a rather grand looking eight-legged sideboard, where there was a silver tray with glasses and decanters.

'Here you are,' he said, handing me a large glass which contained a tiny measure of brandy. 'Drink this – and then take your coat off. I'll put some music on and then see what I can find for us to eat. Mother's cook prepared a few bits and pieces before she went off for the weekend; there's bound to be something decent in the larder. She knew I might pop home and tends to spoil me.'

I sipped the drink experimentally. It was very strong and made me gasp, but it gave me a nice warm feeling when I swallowed it.

'That's right.' Paul nodded approvingly. 'Sip it slowly. I haven't given you enough to make you drunk, but it will settle your nerves. It's medicinal, darling.'

I set the glass down on a little round table. It was highly polished and had a reddish-brown colour, rather like the magnificent sideboard. I thought it might be mahogany and antique. All the furniture looked as if it could be very old. It was elegant but too formal for my own tastes. I wondered how people sat comfortably in the hard, button-backed chairs. The only thing that looked comfortable was a sofa with high sides that seemed to be tied at each end with a tasselled rope.

Having taken off my jacket, I picked up my drink and went to sit on the settee. The cushions were soft so I slipped off my shoes, curling my legs up beside me on the seat and sipping more of the brandy. Paul had been right. It was relaxing me. I felt much better now. I closed my eyes, listening to the music. It had a soft, dreamy quality.

'You're not falling asleep, I hope?'

I opened my eyes as Paul came back into the room. He was carrying a wooden tray, which he set down on a side table in an alcove next to the fireplace.

'Mrs Moxon has come up trumps,' he said. 'She has made us some delicious canapes and I've opened a bottle of wine. I thought you might prefer medium to dry. It's chilling in the ice bucket . . . but we've plenty of time, haven't we?'

'Oh yes,' I responded eagerly. 'Hours yet.'

'And you do think this was a good idea of mine – better than some boring old concert?'

'Much better.'

I turned to him as he came to sit beside me on the settee. I could smell the woody scent that always clung about him. It was intoxicating. I felt a little odd, as if I were floating on air. Perhaps it was the brandy, but I'd only had a few sips. No, it was just the way Paul was looking at me. It made me feel funny inside.

I loved him so! No one had ever looked at me in that way before. His expression was so intent, so compelling!

'You are lovely. Do you know that, Emma?'

I shook my head. 'I'm not pretty.'

'No – you're beautiful.'

He leaned towards me, his mouth touching mine gently at first, then in a more demanding way that made me feel strange.

'Do you know what you mean to me, Emma? Do you know how I've longed to be alone with you like this? To hold you in my arms and make love to you . . .'

'Paul, I love you.'

'My sweet girl.'

He reached for me. I went into his arms willingly. It was all happening just as it had in my dreams. I surrendered my lips to his kisses. He had never kissed me quite this way before, his tongue probing inside my mouth, teasing and provoking sensations that set my senses spinning. It was wonderful. I was melting inside, head spinning.

Paul was easing me back on the settee, his mouth working against my throat as he whispered things . . . exciting, frightening, wonderful things that made me tremble. Now he was lying on top of me. I was thrilled and yet nervous. What was going to happen? His hand was caressing my breasts over the top of my silk blouse. His touch made me tingle all over. I was breathless. My stomach spiralled with a strange new sensation that made me gasp. Paul was sliding his hand up my leg . . . right to the top of my inner thigh.

I made a little murmur of protest. This shouldn't be happening. It was wrong. I ought to stop him.

'Paul . . . we mustn't.'

He was gazing down at me, eyes mesmerising me, sapping my will. There was such an odd look on his face; his mouth was soft and loose. I knew he wanted to make love to me. This was real, this was passion. Not something out of a book. It was happening now – to me.

'Trust me, darling,' he whispered huskily. 'I'll look after you. We're going to be married. There's nothing to be frightened of – unless you don't love me?'

'You know I love you, Paul.'

'Then just relax, darling. Trust me. It's all going to be wonderful for us.'

He was kissing me again, tongue flicking inside my mouth. I was melting, losing the will to resist. How could this be wrong when it felt so lovely? His hand stroked the inside of my thigh, gently, so that I felt my whole self responding to this wonderful new sensation. I moaned, my back arching towards him instinctively. His fingers slipped inside my French knickers, seeking out the sensitive essence of my womanhood. I jerked with pleasure as he touched me *there,* stroking gently yet insistently with the tip of his finger.

'You're so wet,' he murmured throatily against my ear. 'You want me as much as I want you, don't you? Say it, darling. Say it.'

'I want you,' I whispered. 'I love you, Paul.'

I was being carried away on a tide of emotion, swept ever forward with the relentless surge of a passion I had not known existed.

I felt him lifting himself. What was he doing? Something hot and soft was pressing against me there, where his finger had been. Now it was nudging at me, pushing into me. It felt huge and hard as he suddenly thrust up inside me. I realized what he was doing and was frightened.

'No, Paul . . . we mustn't . . . not that.'

He wasn't listening. His breath rasped against my ear as he thrust himself right into me. I gave a cry of pain, which he smothered with a kiss. He was crushing me, hurting me. I struggled, trying to push him off, trying to stop him. This was wrong! The warm feeling I'd felt earlier had vanished. I didn't want this to happen, not like this.

He was too strong for me. I felt tears come to my eyes as I realized he wasn't going to stop. He didn't care that he was upsetting me. He wasn't going to stop. He wasn't going to stop . . .

All of a sudden it was over. I felt him jerk and he groaned loudly, then slumped down on me, his breathing rasping in my ear. For a few minutes he lay on top of me, then rolled away and sat up.

I was crying as I sat up. I felt ashamed and somehow used. I couldn't look at him.

'You should have said no earlier,' Paul muttered, looking annoyed. 'I thought you wanted it. You said you wanted me – what did you expect?'

'I did – I do.' I took the handkerchief he offered and wiped my cheeks. 'I love you. I just didn't want it to happen yet, not like that. It was wrong.'

'Not for me.' He sounded sulky. 'You know I love you.

Don't make so much fuss, Emma. It always hurts a bit the first time. You will enjoy it more the next time we do it.'

'Can I use the bathroom please?'

'Yes, of course. Down the hall – the last door to your right.'

I left quickly. I was hurt and humiliated. Paul had done what he wanted without bothering how I felt. How could he love me and do that?

I found the bathroom and locked myself in. It was a huge, old-fashioned room, and in the middle of the floor was a large Victorian bath with legs.

I needed a bath; I felt dirty. Turning on the taps, I discovered the water was barely warm. The boiler must have been shut off for the weekend. Paul's parents had expected the house to be empty, of course. There had never been any intention of introducing me.

I ran sufficient for my needs, took my clothes off and got in. It felt cold and made me shiver but I had to wash down there. I jumped out as soon as I had cleaned myself, wrapping myself in a towel to get warm again.

I saw blood on my knickers and rinsed them under the cold tap, wetting only as much as I had to and rubbing them with the towel to dry the damp patches.

It must have been at least half an hour before I felt sufficiently in control of my emotions to face Paul.

I believed our future relationship depended on what I

did now. He had expected me to be more sophisticated. I *had* made a fuss but it had shocked me, the whole business. Somehow I'd always thought it would be more romantic, nicer – but perhaps Paul was right. Perhaps it got better the more you did it.

I finished dressing and used a comb from the painted wall cabinet to tidy my hair, then walked back down the hall. Approaching the room I'd left earlier, I heard voices – Paul's and another man's. I hesitated, feeling nervous, reluctant to go in. It was difficult enough to face Paul, let alone a stranger.

'For goodness sake!' Paul raised his voice irritably. 'Couldn't you just do as I asked, Jon? I asked you to deliver the money. I didn't appoint you guardian of my morals.'

'She was nervous of going through with it. She asked for my advice and I felt obliged to give it. I thought it was wrong and told her so. And besides . . .'

The man stopped speaking as I walked in. He stared at me, his greenish eyes opening wide in surprise. He was as tall as Paul, but thin and wiry with sandy-coloured hair and gentle, rather ordinary features. As he stared at me, a look of disgust came over his face. 'Damn you, Paul!' he said and took a fat envelope from his pocket, tossing it on to the settee. 'Do your own dirty work in future. You deserve whatever is coming to you!'

He walked past me into the hall. A moment or two

later I heard a door slam and then the sound of a car starting. Paul hadn't spoken. His face was white and he looked worried.

'I'm sorry,' I said. 'I wasn't sure whether to come in or not.'

'It was only my cousin Jonathan,' he muttered, still angry. 'Take no notice of him. He's a sanctimonious fool. Are you feeling better now?'

'Yes, thank you. I'm sorry if I was silly just now. It – it was my first time and I was frightened.'

His frown eased. 'Yes, I know. I'm sorry, Emma. I shouldn't have rushed you. It's just that I wanted you so very much. I really do care about you, darling.'

'I love you, Paul. Don't be cross with me.'

He moved towards me, smiling now. 'I'm not angry with you, darling. I'm the one at fault. I've been clumsy and I've hurt you. Forgive me, please?'

'It was silly . . .'

He reached out, drawing me to him, his lips moving against my hair as he made soothing noises. His kiss was gentle this time, understanding.

'Feeling more the thing? I've behaved like a brute, darling.'

'It – it doesn't matter.'

I was lying. It did matter, but I was scared of losing him. He would think me an ignorant country girl, which of course I was.

'Have a glass of wine and a canape. It will make you feel better.' He offered me a plate. Some of the food had been eaten and I thought he might have waited for me. 'These little salmon things are very good.'

I took one and bit into it. The pastry melted on my tongue and the soft filling tasted delicious, but my throat was so tight I could hardly swallow. I took a sip of wine to help it down.

Paul nodded his approval. 'That's right. Sit down, darling. Listen to the music. This is Mozart . . . you can tell your father you listened to the Requiem Mass, that should impress him.'

I sat down. The envelope was still lying on the settee where his cousin had thrown it. I saw it had split open and there was money inside – a lot of money. Perhaps two hundred pounds.

Paul saw I had noticed. 'I asked Jon to settle a debt for me. He made a mess of things. I shall have to take care of it myself.'

'Is that why you were so angry just now?'

'Partly.' He was frowning again. 'It's just a nuisance. Nothing important. Forget it, Emma. Come here and let me hold you. We won't do anything else, I promise. Not until you're ready. I'll be more gentle with you next time. Just remember I love you and want to marry you.'

'Do you really, Paul?'

'Of course I do, Emma. Silly girl! I've never been

to so much trouble to get a girl to come out with me before, believe me. Just trust me. I promise everything will be perfect.'

I lay thinking after I got to bed that night. Paul had promised we wouldn't do anything else if I let him hold me – but he hadn't kept his word. I hadn't struggled the second time, and it hadn't hurt quite as much, but I'd still felt empty and disappointed afterwards.

Tears trickled down my cheeks as I remembered the lies I'd told my parents when I'd got home. I felt so guilty! Particularly about lying to my mother, who had trusted me.

What had I done? Why had I let it happen?

I wasn't sure. The brandy had made me feel relaxed, but I hadn't drunk enough to become intoxicated. I had known what was happening. I'd wanted Paul to kiss and touch me, but I hadn't expected him to go all the way. Was that naive of me? I supposed it was. Men were like that – and yet I had believed Paul would take more care of me. He knew how strict my father was – how difficult things would be for me if . . . but I dare not even think about that!

'Don't worry,' Paul had said as he dropped me outside the shop at a quarter to nine that evening. 'We've done nothing wrong, darling. We love each other and we're going to be married. I'll speak to your father soon,

I promise. And I'll bring you an engagement ring next weekend.'

'Paul . . . do you think I—?'

'No, I don't.' He kissed the tip of my nose, giving me a teasing look. 'It doesn't happen the first time. Don't give it another thought, Emma. You're not pregnant. Besides, we'll be married within a couple of months. I promise.'

Supposing my father refused his permission? Supposing I was pregnant despite Paul's reassurances to the contrary?

A shudder of fear ran through me. I couldn't face my father if that happened. I would rather run away!

Chapter Five

'Do you enjoy yourself at the concert?'

I carefully avoided Gran's eyes as I replied, 'It was all right. I think I like the ballads and dance music we get on the wireless better.'

'And what about Paul's mother? Was she nice?'

'Yes.' I could feel my cheeks burning as I lied. 'A bit posh.'

Gran drew on her clay pipe, studying me in silence. I felt uneasy beneath her knowing gaze. But she couldn't know what had really happened, could she?

'You are friendly with Sheila Tomms, aren't you?'

A tingle went down my spine. Gran wasn't saying, but somehow she had guessed my secret.

'Yes, I know her. Why?'

'There was talk of her being in trouble,' Gran said. 'She's a nice lass, always polite to me, thoughtful.'

'Is the talk true?'

Emma

'Aye, I reckon so. I reckon that's why she's gone off so sudden.' Gran shook her head. 'She should have come to me when she first missed her flow. I would have given her something to bring it on.'

'Can you do that?'

'Aye.' Another puff of the pipe. 'But only for a few weeks. Safely, that is. If the baby is more than six weeks or so the dose needed would be too strong. It could kill the mother then, as well as the child. It has to be straight after the first missed flow.'

'Isn't it wrong to do that?'

'Some might say so. It depends on the mother's circumstances. I wouldn't do it for everyone.'

'Is it dangerous?'

'There are other, more dangerous ways of doing it. In London there's places where they'll do it up to three months or more. I've heard of women bleeding to death after visiting houses like that. My way is safer, more natural. It's just a herbal drink.'

'Does it always work?'

'Mostly. If you know what you're doing.'

I got up and started to clear the table. What would Gran say if I told her I might need her medicines?

'You said Sheila had gone off?' I bent over the sink, rinsing the crockery. 'Who told you that?'

'Her mother told me – said she went out on Friday night and hasn't been back since.'

'She was in the shop on Friday, buying some sweets. She was laughing . . . cheerful.' I frowned. 'It seems odd. Why didn't she say if she was thinking of going away?'

'Maybe she wanted to keep it a secret – or she might have made up her mind quick.'

'I suppose so.' I felt a cold trickle down my spine, though I wasn't sure what was bothering me. 'She didn't sound as though she was thinking of leaving town.'

'What did she say to you?'

'Oh . . . just silly things.' I dried my hands on the towel next to the sink. 'I'd best get home now.'

'Not getting a lift today then?'

'No.' I avoided looking at her. 'Paul expects to be busy until the weekend.'

'Oh well, the walk won't hurt you, lass.' Gran caught my hand as I moved past her chair. 'If you're ever worried about anything, you can always talk to me.'

'Yes.' My eyes pricked with tears. 'I love you, Gran.'

'I'm always here if you need me, love. There's no one else I care for as I do you. I'll always be on your side, no matter what.'

She did know! I bent to kiss her cheek, then left quickly before the tears could start.

I walked slowly, eyes cast down, as I left Gran's cottage. She *had* guessed the truth somehow. I felt awful as the shame washed over me. She had said nothing to censure me – but others would! Why on earth had I let it happen?

I had looked for Paul on my way to Gran's that afternoon, but he hadn't appeared. I tried not to feel frightened or let down, though I knew he had been annoyed by my lack of sophistication. Just because he hadn't come didn't mean he had deserted me. He was a busy man with a responsible job. I couldn't expect him to be here every Wednesday.

'Hello, Emma. Penny for them?'

I jumped at the sound of Richard's voice. I hadn't realized he was following me. My heart thumped as I swung round to face him.

'You frightened me. Sneaking up like that!'

'I wasn't.' His eyes narrowed as he studied me. 'You were dreaming.'

'Yes, I suppose I was,' I admitted.

'Sorry if I scared you. You know I wouldn't hurt you, Emma.' He sounded sincere, and I was sorry that I had snapped at him.

'It was just the shock. I haven't seen you since the church social.'

'I was on a different shift last week.'

'Oh.' I felt vaguely guilty, though I had no idea why I should. 'Have you seen Sheila recently?'

Something flickered in his eyes. 'What do you mean? Sheila who?'

Was he angry or nervous? I couldn't be sure.

'Sheila Tomms. She was talking about you the other—'
I gasped as he grabbed my arm. 'You're hurting me!'

'Sorry.' He let go instantly. 'I don't know what she told
you – but if it concerned me it was a lie. I don't go out
with girls like that.'

I rubbed at my arm. It was tender where he had dug
his fingers too hard into my flesh. 'She didn't say that –
only that she liked you.'

'I wonder why she said that? We've hardly spoken.'

'She thinks you're good-looking.'

'It's what you think that matters to me, Emma.' He
took my arm again, more gently this time. 'You must
know you're the only girl I care about.'

'No . . .' I moved away from him, not wanting him to
like me too much. 'Please don't. I don't want you to say
things like that to me.'

'Is there someone else?' His gaze narrowed in
suspicion. 'Is it that toff I saw you with once? He's an
architect or something . . . comes from Cambridge.'

'What's it to you if it is?'

'I didn't think you were fool enough to fall for his
sort.' Richard glared at me. 'He'll sweet-talk you, Emma,
but he won't marry you. Don't fall for him or he'll break
your heart.'

'If he does it's my business,' I snapped. 'I'm not your
girl, Richard Gillows; you don't own me and I'll do as
I please.'

I walked off, head in the air, leaving him to stare after me in dismay.

I could hardly bear to be out of the shop that week in case Paul came in. My heart raced every time the bell went, but it was never him. He had promised to be in church without fail on Sunday, but when we got there that morning his usual place was empty.

'Don't be too disappointed, love,' Mother said, squeezing my arm gently. 'I expect he's too busy to come.'

The look on her face told me she didn't believe her own words. She probably thought Paul's mother had disapproved of the relationship. If only it was that simple.

I was almost sure my period was a couple of days late. I didn't keep the exact dates of my monthly flow, because I'd never had reason before this, but I would normally have expected it to come by now.

No, I was being silly, letting my imagination play tricks on me. Paul had told me it didn't happen just like that. I couldn't have fallen for a baby; we had only made love twice.

'It takes some women years to conceive,' he'd said with a teasing kiss. 'So why should you happen to fall just because we made love a couple of times?'

Why wasn't Paul here to reassure me with his smile?

I felt wretched throughout the service. He had

promised to bring me an engagement ring, so where was he?

My eyes were gritty with tiredness and I felt as if I wanted to weep. When Mother stopped to talk to friends after the service it was all I could do to stop myself walking off.

'Have you heard about the murder?'

Mrs Henty came bustling up to us full of the news. She looked shocked, her complexion an odd yellowish-white.

'Murder – who has been murdered?' Mother asked in hushed tones. 'When did it happen?'

'Over a week ago, so they're saying. The body has been in the river for several days. Some eel fishermen found it caught in a bed of reeds. It had been swept down river for some distance – but the police discovered a bus ticket in her pocket and they're making inquiries in March. And I've heard Sheila Tomms has been missing for just over a week . . .'

'Sheila . . . they think it may be her?' I felt the colour drain from my face as I stared at her, horrified. 'Oh no! Why would anyone want to murder her?'

'Who knows?' Mrs Henty frowned. 'I thought it was odd when I heard she'd gone off without a word. She was in the shop on Friday morning, putting a deposit on a new dress she fancied.'

I felt the sickness rise in my throat. I had thought it strange when Gran said Sheila had gone off somewhere.

It hadn't made sense. Not after the way Sheila had been talking that morning in the shop.

'How was she murdered?'

'I don't know the details,' Mrs Henty said. 'I've only just heard about the body being found.'

'So it could have been suicide,' my mother said. 'If she was in trouble she might have taken her own life.'

'From what I've heard the police think it was murder,' said Mrs Henty with a shake of her head. 'It's a terrible thing, whatever happened. Poor girl. She might not have been all she ought, but she didn't deserve this.'

'No, indeed she didn't,' Mother said. 'There's a good many girls have done as much or worse, I dare say.'

Mother and I walked home in silence. Just before we got to the shop, I turned to look at her.

'Do you think it was murder, Mum – or suicide?'

'I've no idea. I expect it will come out at the inquest. Poor girl. I liked Sheila, despite her flighty ways. I don't like to think of her ending her life in the river, however it happened.'

'No,' I said. 'Nor do I.'

Suddenly, my own problems seemed much less than I'd thought. After all, it was only a week since I'd seen Paul. He would probably be in touch soon. He loved me. He had said it so many times. He must mean it – mustn't he?

*

The local paper was full of the story the next week. The dead girl had been identified as having lived in Peterborough; she had been visiting friends in the area and a man had been taken in for questioning and then released. So far the police had no further clues about the attack on her.

'It's a terrible thing – but thank goodness it wasn't Sheila,' my mother said when I took the newspaper up to show her that morning. 'It makes you wonder where she has gone, though, doesn't it?'

'Yes. I'm relieved – but I keep wondering why she went off so suddenly. Eric came into the shop this morning. He asked me if I'd any idea of where she might have gone. He seemed really upset. I suppose he had been worried in case it was her.' I was thoughtful. 'He said she used to talk about me a lot. I think he really cares about her, Mum. Perhaps he's wishing they hadn't broken up now.'

'You said they'd had a row?'

'She was a bit upset over it – but not miserable enough to do anything silly. At least, she didn't seem that way to me.'

'Maybe she decided she'd had enough of this town. If she was having a baby—' Mother frowned, '—she might have gone away to have it. To avoid the gossip.'

'Yes, she might.'

I turned away, biting my lower lip. I was definitely late with my period. What was I going to do if I had fallen for a baby? My mother would be disappointed and hurt – and my father would kill me!

'Is something wrong?' Mother asked, looking at me anxiously. 'You've been a bit quiet recently. Is it because Paul hasn't been in touch?'

'I expected him before this,' I admitted, only just managing to keep my voice steady. 'I know he's busy, but . . .'

'He'll come.'

'Will he?' Looking directly at her, I saw the love and concern she could not hide. 'You warned me not to expect too much, didn't you?'

'I was only being cautious.' She gave me a comforting smile. 'Paul cares about you, darling. It shows when he looks at you. Besides, he wouldn't have taken you to meet his mother if he didn't. He's probably just too busy.'

I longed to blurt out the truth but was afraid of the consequences. And besides, it was only a week and a half since I'd seen Paul, though it seemed much longer. He was sure to come soon.

'I'd better get back to the shop,' I said. 'I only popped up to tell you the news.'

'I'm glad you did,' she said. 'I shouldn't want to think of Sheila ending up in the river – though it's a shame about that other poor girl. The police don't seem to know what happened – or why.'

'I'm sorry for her, of course I am, but I can't help

thinking about Sheila. It's a bit of a mystery where she has gone, isn't it?'

I was thoughtful as I went back downstairs. I wished Sheila would walk into the shop the way she used to. I would have liked to talk to her, perhaps confide in her.

'There you are!' Father was putting an envelope into his pocket as I went into the shop. He glared at me, seeming angry for some reason. 'I'm going out, Emma. I've a bit of business to take care of. Look after things here while I'm gone.'

'Yes, Father.'

Ben pulled a face at me behind his back.

'He's in a rare old mood this morning,' he said as Father went out, closing the door with a snap. 'Must have got out of bed the wrong side – or maybe it was that letter. It seemed to annoy him, whatever it was.'

I could only agree about Father's mood. His temper hadn't improved of late. I had noticed him rubbing at his chest several times and thought he might be feeling unwell. He ought to visit the doctor, of course, but it was no use telling him that, because he wouldn't listen.

'I think we'll do some stock checking, Ben,' I said. 'We're getting short of stationery and need to re-order. Go on then!' I gave him a little push in the right direction and turned as a customer came in. 'Oh!'

For a moment as I waited to serve the customer my heart missed a beat. It was Paul's cousin. I was certain of it, even though I had only seen him for a few seconds at the Greenslades' house that afternoon. My mouth was dry and I felt breathless. Was something wrong with Paul? Had his cousin come to bring me a message?

'Hello.' There was a puzzled look in his eyes, as if he had recognized me but couldn't quite place me. 'I know this is an awful cheek, but I haven't come in to buy anything. I'm looking for the offices of Barker, Barker and Dobson. They're a small firm of solicitors.'

'Yes, I know them.' Should I mention Paul, or would it look forward? 'Keep on down the High Street and turn left at the end. You can't miss it: there's a big sign.'

'I work with a firm of solicitors in London,' he said, seeming inclined to linger. 'Barker's have asked us to take a case for them. As I was coming this way I said I would look in on them personally. It's better than phone calls or letters, don't you think?'

I nodded. My heart was beating very fast. I wanted to ask him about Paul but somehow couldn't. He'd seemed angry when he'd seen me at the Greenslades' house. He might think it impertinent of me if I asked questions.

'I think I will have a packet of fruit drops,' he said, hesitating for a moment. I thought he was on the verge of saying something else, but he just handed me the money over the counter. 'Thank you – and for the directions. Miss Robinson, is it?' I nodded. 'Good morning.'

I stared after him as he went out. What an idiot I was

to just let him go. Why couldn't I have been natural, asked after Paul in a casual way? Yet to do so would have seemed as if I were running after Paul and I wasn't reduced to that yet. Not quite.

I was almost certain I was having Paul's baby now. I was three weeks late. I stared at my pale face in the dressing mirror. Did it show? I'd heard people say you could tell when a woman was pregnant by something in their eyes, but didn't know if it was true or just an old wives' tale.

What was I going to do?

I was so frightened! I hadn't slept well for over a week. Every time someone came into the shop I jumped, thinking it might be Paul. Where was he? Why hadn't he come as he'd promised?

I had thought about writing to him, but when I tried it all looked so awful on paper. How could I say, 'I'm pregnant, please come and marry me before my father finds out'? It was impossible. I needed to talk to him, to see his smile . . . to hear him say he loved me.

Tears stung my eyes. I had really believed him when he said it . . . when he'd told me we would be married very soon.

I would never have let it happen if I hadn't trusted him. Why had I? I'd known it was wrong. How dangerous it could be, particularly for me.

My father would kill me when he found out.

I closed my eyes. I couldn't bear to look at myself in the mirror, couldn't bear the thought of what everyone would say . . . of all the gossip and sniggers behind my back.

Gran would help me! I could ask for one of her special cures. But supposing Paul came back after I'd done it? How could I tell him I had killed his child?

I didn't want to kill my baby. I wanted to marry Paul and have the child as his wife.

If he knew I was pregnant he would marry me. Of course he would. He loved me. Hadn't he told me so? I was sure he would marry me if he knew.

'Where are you, Paul?' I whispered into the darkness as I turned out my light and crawled into bed. 'Why don't you come? Please come. I need you.'

Why hadn't he tried to contact me? If he was too busy he could surely have written. Was he ill?

I wished now that I'd found the courage to ask his cousin if he was ill. He had looked quite nice. Not handsome like Paul, of course, but nice. I had been silly to let the opportunity slip.

I had to do something. I couldn't just let things drift. I had to see Paul, talk to him. He was sure to do what was right when he knew . . . and if he didn't? A shudder went through me. I couldn't bear to think about that, not yet.

Paul loved me. He would marry me. Of course he would!

I came to a decision. If he wasn't waiting for me in church the next morning, I would catch a train and go to his house the following Wednesday afternoon.

The next few days were the longest of my life. I had been sure Paul would be in church that Sunday, but he wasn't. He didn't come to the shop that week either.

Had he deliberately deserted me? Perhaps he'd had an accident. I convinced myself it was the latter. Paul wouldn't break his promise without a good reason – would he? He had gone to so much trouble to get me to go out with him. Surely he must have cared for me a little!

Did he think I was cheap because I'd let him make love to me? My father spoke of girls who were easy with contempt, dismissing them as trash. Did Paul think I was easy?

All I felt like doing was weeping, but I couldn't, not during the day. I was terrified that my father would suspect something, but he seemed preoccupied with his own concerns. I'd noticed him grimacing a few times, as though in pain.

Mother had guessed there was something wrong, though. I had seen the worried expression in her eyes. Sometimes I thought telling her would be even worse than telling Father. He would be angry, but Mother would be upset.

Oh, why had I been such a fool?

On Wednesday morning I was up early. I had all my jobs done before I went upstairs to change into my green costume.

'Wearing your best costume to visit Gran?' Mother gave me a long, hard look as I came out of the bedroom.

'Yes. She asked to see it.' My cheeks felt warm as I avoided her eyes. 'I might go for a walk afterwards. Don't worry if I'm a little late back.'

'Emma – is there something I should know? You would tell me, wouldn't you?'

'I'm going to see Paul. I'm going to find out if it's over.'

'Emma . . .' She looked at me sadly. 'Don't run after him, love. Don't lower yourself that way.'

'I have to.' My voice almost broke. 'I have to, Mum. I love him.'

I ran down the stairs and went out the back way. Mother called for me to come back but I ignored the request. I had to see Paul again, even if it was for the last time.

I just had to!

I took a taxi from Cambridge station out to Paul's house. It was extravagant and cost most of the money in my purse, but I was too restless to wait for a bus and I thought it might be a long way to walk.

It would have taken ages. I hadn't realized it was

as far out of town as this – at least five or six miles. Looking ruefully at the few pennies left in my hand, I knew I would have to walk back to the station. I hadn't enough money left for a bus, let alone a taxi. But perhaps Paul would take me – or at least provide the money for my fare.

What would he say when I turned up uninvited at his house? Perhaps I ought to have written first, just to say I was coming. I had attempted it once or twice but didn't know how to express my feelings on paper. I couldn't just demand that he marry me, even though he had given me his promise.

Why had he changed his mind?

It was quite warm now, the air rather heavy as though there might be a storm later. I felt a little sick as I walked past the tennis courts. Supposing Paul wasn't here? I hadn't considered that – but now I thought it might be better, less embarrassing. I could leave a message asking him to contact me.

I was almost at the house. Ought I to go round to the main door – or the French windows Paul had used when he brought me here?

I stopped walking as I saw the windows were open. Two women were standing just inside the house, and, as I hesitated uncertainly, they came out. I knew at once that they had seen me. It was too late to retreat. I had to go on.

As I got nearer I saw that one of them was obviously the lady of the house and the other a servant – probably the housekeeper.

Paul's mother was staring at me fixedly. It had to be her! I could see a certain likeness in their features. Besides, her manner made it clear that this was her territory.

My mouth went dry. I felt faint, my head swimming. How unfortunate that Mrs Greenslade should witness my arrival! I'd hoped the door would be answered either by Paul himself or a maid.

Mrs Greenslade looked extremely angry. I sensed her hostility even before she spoke.

'Who are you? Why have you come here?'

I was taken aback by the ferocity of her opening words. I couldn't answer immediately. She was formidable: a tall, thin woman with greying hair and sharp features. She was wearing a dark green gored skirt, a white linen blouse and a black fitted jacket. Her shoes were the kind of heavy lace-ups my mother wouldn't have been seen dead in.

'I . . .' I took a deep breath and licked my lips nervously. 'I've come to see Paul. Please – would you tell him I'm here?'

'You little slut!' Mrs Greenslade's mouth thinned. 'How dare you come here? I suppose you thought I believed your filthy lies about my son? Well, let me tell you, I've dealt with your sort before and you'll get nothing here. I threw your letter into the fire as it deserved.'

'What lies? What letter?'

I took an involuntary step backwards as she moved threateningly towards me. What was she talking about? I hadn't written to her or Paul.

'My son isn't here,' she went on. 'He's away, but that makes no difference. If you try to blacken his name I'll have you in court before you know where you are. And as for my son promising you a thousand pounds—' Mrs Greenslade seemed to swell up like an angry toad. 'I've never heard anything so ridiculous in my life. Just take yourself off and don't try blackmailing me or my family again.'

'I haven't. I wouldn't—' I stared at her in dismay. 'I don't know what you're talking about. I haven't written any letter. I just want to see Paul. He loves me. We are going to be married . . .'

The words died on my lips as I saw the scorn and hatred in her face. There was no point in trying to tell this woman anything. She had obviously mistaken me for someone else, but even if she had let me speak the result would have been the same. Paul's mother despised me for being what I was – a girl from a class lower than her own, someone who didn't belong in a house like this. And she was right. Of course she was right. I'd known it instinctively when Paul brought me here. I could never be a part of this family and had been fooling myself to believe for one moment I could.

I raised my head, looking at Mrs Greenslade with a quiet dignity. 'Please tell Paul that Emma Robinson was here,' I said. 'I have no wish to blackmail him or anyone else – but I do wish to speak to him. It is quite important.'

For a moment she looked uncertain, as if she realized she had made a mistake.

'What did you say your name was?'

'Emma Robinson.' I smiled slightly. 'Paul will know – if you tell him.'

I turned and walked away, head high, knowing that she was disconcerted. She *had* mistaken me for someone else but it made no difference. I could not think my reception would have been any warmer if Mrs Greenslade had known the truth.

Chapter Six

Pride kept me going until I was out of sight of the house, then the awfulness of it hit me and I gasped, feeling as if someone had punched me in the stomach. Paul wasn't going to marry me. He had never had any intention of doing so . . . all his sweet talk and promises had simply been for one thing.

I could hear Father's voice in my head, ranting on about the kind of girl who dropped her knickers for the price of a few drinks or a cheap present.

'Girls like that deserve all they get.' He had said it over and over again in my hearing. 'Cheap little whores, that's what they are. Fools! No man respects a girl who lets him do what he wants just like that.'

Tears stung my eyes, flowing over and running down my cheeks. I was powerless to stop them. I felt sick and dizzy – cheap! Paul must have thought I was easy. I had never tried to hide the fact that I wanted to go out with him, wanted him to kiss me. I had returned his kisses with all the natural warmth and loving in my heart, believing that he loved me.

'Oh, Paul,' I wept bitterly, stopping to lean against the trunk of a tree as a storm of emotion swept over me. 'Paul . . . Oh, Paul . . . how could you? How could you do this to me?'

My heart felt as if it were being torn apart. I wanted to lay down where I stood and die. What was the point in living when Paul didn't love me, had used me, deserted me? Even my fear of discovery had faded into insignificance besides my grief. I loved Paul . . . loved him so much. How was I going to bear this?

I leaned my head against the tree trunk, covering my face with both hands. I was consumed with grief, uncaring of what happened to me now, wanting only to die of the pain.

'Hey . . . something the matter?'

The man's voice made me glance up. I knew him at once. It was Paul's cousin. He had a couple of golden retrievers running at his heels and had obviously returned from walking them across the fields.

'No. I have to go!'

I turned away and started walking very fast. I had to get away. It was all too much. I couldn't bear any more! My eyes were blinded by tears and I didn't realize I had turned the wrong way, was walking in the opposite direction I needed to take for the town and railway station.

'Hang on . . . No, Rufus! Go back.' I could hear footsteps as the man ran after me. 'Miss . . . Miss Robinson! Please wait. Please!'

I kept on walking. The last thing I wanted was another confrontation with a member of Paul's family. I blinked hard, feeling for my handkerchief and discovering I hadn't got one.

'Here – take mine.' He had caught up with me and thrust his large, white handkerchief under my nose. 'Stop a minute. You're upset. You can't leave like this. What happened to make you cry like that? Did you come to see Paul?'

At the mention of Paul's name I stopped and swung round to face him. He stared at me for a moment, concern in his eyes, then reached out to wipe the tears from my cheeks with his handkerchief. I swallowed hard and took it from him, finishing the job and blowing my nose.

'Keep it,' he said as I hesitated over returning it. 'Please let me help you. How did you come here?'

'By train and taxi. I have to get back—'

'You're going the wrong way.' He smiled in a gentle, helpful way. 'Look, there's a small hotel just up the road where they serve teas in the afternoon. Why don't you let me buy you some tea? You need to sit down for a while – and if you tell me what's wrong I might be able to help.'

My first instinct was to refuse. At that moment I just wanted to run away and hide, but the practical side of my nature warned against it. Perhaps he could help me, if only to lend me the taxi fare to the station.

I blew my nose hard. 'Do I look awful?'

'No – just a little bit red about the eyes. Don't worry. I know the people at the hotel. They won't take any notice. I'll tell them you're feeling a little bit under the weather if you like? You look peaky so they will believe me.'

'You . . . you're very kind,' I said in a small voice. 'I was hoping Paul might take me to the station in his car. You see . . . I spent all my money on the taxi coming here.'

'Paul isn't here.' He frowned. 'He has gone abroad – to America. A brilliant opportunity came up, but he had to leave at once. Did they tell you that, up at the house?'

'Mrs Greenslade said he was away.' I swallowed hard. Paul had gone to America! There really was no chance of him coming back to rescue me. 'She seemed to think I was someone else . . . that I'd sent her a letter. I'm not sure what she meant, but she accused me of demanding a thousand pounds for something.'

'Oh, Lord!' He looked shocked. 'Did she mention that exact sum?'

'Yes. Do you know what it is all about?'

He had taken my arm now and was gently but firmly

leading me towards the small hotel I could see on the opposite side of the road.

'Yes, I do actually, but I would rather not say. It is all rather unpleasant.'

I chewed my lip nervously. What didn't he want to tell me? I almost asked, then decided it didn't matter. Nothing mattered now.

He took me inside the hotel and turned to the left. The tearoom was empty of customers, rather dark and old-fashioned; there was a smell of something I couldn't place but which reminded me of dusty old books. It was mixed with the overpowering scent from a vase of stocks on the windowsill. My companion directed me to a small table by the window, then went to order our tea from a woman behind the reception desk. I looked at myself in my compact mirror, wishing I had some face powder to cover my red nose.

Paul's cousin came back and I closed my bag, giving him a tentative look. He sat down in the chair next to me and smiled.

'I forgot to say – I'm Paul's cousin. Jonathan Reece. Please call me Jon, I prefer it.'

'I'm Emma. Emma Robinson. Paul said you were his cousin Jonathan, but I didn't know your surname. Do you remember seeing me at the Greenslades' house that afternoon?'

He nodded. 'I was almost certain it was you when

I came into your father's shop, but I didn't like to say anything in case I was mistaken. You told me where to find Barker, Barker and Dobson's.'

'Yes.' I breathed deeply as my nerves began to settle. 'Do you have Paul's address? It's very important that I get a message to him.'

He was silent for a moment, studying me intently. 'Yes, I can see that. Are you in trouble? A certain kind of trouble?'

'How did you know?' My eyes met his apprehensively. 'Does it show?'

'No. I just guessed. I knew it had to be urgent or you wouldn't have spent all your money to get here.'

A little nerve was flicking in his cheek. I thought he looked angry and my head jerked up. Paul's family might not think I was good enough for him, but I wasn't going to be treated as though I were trash.

'Paul asked me to marry him. I would never have . . . not if I hadn't thought he meant it.'

'He asked you to marry him?' There was a look of such surprise in his eyes that I was suddenly angry.

'Why shouldn't he have? I know I'm not of his class but I'm respectable. My father owns his shop. I'm not cheap. I've never been out with a man before. I know I was foolish to let Paul . . . but I was in love with him.' My eyes filled with tears as I stared at him, but I held my head high.

'I'm sorry I upset you,' Jonathan Reece said. 'I didn't mean to imply that you weren't good enough for Paul. In fact I think you're a damned sight too good for him!'

Now there was no doubt that he was angry, but now I thought it was Paul not me who had caused that anger.

'Why are you looking at me like that?'

He was about to answer when the waitress brought our tea, and by the time she had gone I could see by his expression that he had changed his mind about what he was going to say.

'Have you thought what you will do?' he asked when we were alone and I had poured the tea. 'I mean – what will your father say?'

I blinked hard. 'My mother will be upset – and my father will half kill me. He has always been very strict.'

'This must be very difficult for you.' He looked at me thoughtfully. 'Do you want the child? There are things that can be done if—'

'I know. My grandmother told me.'

'She knows about this?'

I shook my head. 'I haven't told her but she may have guessed. She was talking about someone else – but it was meant to let me know she would help if I asked.'

'Are you going to ask?'

'I don't know. I don't want to kill my baby.' I crossed my arms over myself in a protective manner. 'I'm not sure what I ought to do, but I know this much. It's Paul's baby. If I told him he would marry me.' I saw the disbelief in Jonathan Reece's eyes. 'You don't believe me, do you?'

'I don't know. I believe he promised to marry you.'

'But he was lying, wasn't he?' I nodded to myself as he kept silent. 'I know I was foolish to be taken in. I realized that after I met his mother. He couldn't marry a girl like me – his family would never permit it.'

'My aunt might not like the idea,' Jonathan agreed. 'But if Paul's father knew, I think he would demand that Paul do the decent thing.' He gave me a long, thoughtful look. 'Do you want me to do that? Shall I tell him? Shall I make Paul come back to England and marry you?'

'No!' My head shot up. I looked at him proudly. 'I wouldn't want that. If he doesn't love me—' I choked back my emotion and gave him a watery smile. 'As Gran would say, I've made my bed and I must lie on it.'

'Your Gran sounds interesting.'

'Yes, she is.' I sipped my tea, but found it almost impossible to swallow the tasteless liquid. I was in a state of shock and he was sympathetic. I found myself telling him what was on my mind. 'I don't know what to do. My father will be so angry.'

'Will he turn you out?'

'I don't know. He might.'

'You could go away. Have the baby somewhere you aren't known, buy yourself a wedding ring . . . pretend to be a widow.'

'I don't have any money.' I glanced up. The suggestion appealed to me, presenting a way of escape, but it was not possible. 'How would I manage?'

'Paul should give you money,' Jonathan said. 'It is the least he can do in the circumstances.'

I felt a flicker of hope. 'If I could go before my father found out, it might be all right. I should have to tell my mother, of course.'

'Supposing I give you this for now.' He took out his wallet and extracted five pound notes. 'It will see you home safely and—'

'But that's your money. Why should you give me anything?' I shook my head as he held out the notes. 'No, I can't take it – not all that. I should be grateful if you would lend me a few shillings for the taxi to the station, but five pounds is too much.' I glanced up at the elaborately cased clock on the wall. 'I shall have to go soon or I'll miss my train.''

'I'm going to take you home in my uncle's car. I'll fetch it in a minute. You needn't come back to the house. Stay here while I bring it over.'

'No . . . please.' I blushed. 'I would rather go by train. Honestly. I want to be alone. You've been very kind, but I'm all right now.'

'Are you?' His eyes narrowed as he studied my face. He was clearly anxious for me. 'You won't do anything silly, will you?'

'No. I promise I shan't.' I forced a smile. 'All right, I'll take your money for now – in case of emergencies – but you must let me pay it back out of whatever Paul gives you for me.'

'I can't promise a lump sum,' he said. 'But a regular payment – a few pounds a month until the baby is born and you can find work – I can promise that Paul will provide that much.'

'It would make all the difference,' I said. 'I have some experience in book work. I do my father's accounts for the shop. I think I could find a job – but it would have to be somewhere away from March. Somewhere my father couldn't find me and fetch me back.'

'This is my card.' Jonathan took a small, neat business card from his waistcoat pocket. 'If you are ever in any difficulty you can get in touch with me at this address. The telephone number is my office so it's only in dire emergency.'

'Oh, I wouldn't phone you at work!' I blushed furiously. 'I don't want to be a nuisance to you.'

'You wouldn't – and you can use that number if you have to.' He gave me the card. 'I'll call and see you at the weekend. If you're not there, will you get in touch with me?'

'I'll write to you,' I said. 'I might go to London. I've always thought I might like to live there.'

'Be sure and let me know where you are. Don't try to manage alone, will you? Keep in touch.'

'Yes, I shall. Thank you.' I looked at him shyly. 'I don't know what I would have done if you hadn't come when you did.'

'It was lucky I was staying with my aunt and uncle for the week.'

'Yes, it was.'

'I'll ask the receptionist to ring for a taxi, shall I?'

'Yes, please.'

I watched as he went off to arrange it, tucking the five notes safely inside my bag. It was more money than I'd ever had at one time in my life. I felt awkward about taking it, but it represented a way of escape if I needed it – and I would pay it back one day. I wasn't sure Paul would be willing to support me and my child, but it didn't matter. I would manage somehow.

My chin went up and I felt a new determination. I had often thought of finding myself a job somewhere else. Well, now I had no choice. I had to leave home before my father discovered I was pregnant and made life unbearable for my mother and I.

'The taxi will be here in five minutes,' Jonathan Reece said, joining me once more. 'Shall I come to the station with you?'

'No. It's kind of you to offer, but I shall be best on my own.' I stood up and offered him my hand. 'I shall never forget what you've done for me, Mr Reece – but I can manage now.'

'Please do call me Jon,' he said and held my hand for a moment. 'I should like to be your friend. I'll be in touch soon. I won't let you down, I promise.'

'No,' I replied softly. 'I don't believe you will.'

Sitting on the train home, I thought about my plans for the future. With the money in my purse I could go to London and rent a room somewhere. It would be months before the baby began to show. I could find work for the time being and save – and if Jonathan Reece actually persuaded Paul to give me a regular income, I would manage.

But I wouldn't rely on that; I was going to stand on my own two feet from now on. I glanced at myself. It was a pity I'd bought this costume. I ought to pay Mrs Henty the money I owed before I left, but that wouldn't leave sufficient for me to keep myself going while I looked for work. No, I would have to send the money when I found a job.

I refused to dwell on the difficulties of my situation or on the hard knot of grief in my breast. If I let myself think about Paul and the way he had let me down I would go mad, so I wouldn't think about it, not now. I had to make plans for myself and my child. For the first time I began to think of the baby growing inside me as a person.

I was going to have a baby! Despite all the trouble it was going to cause me, I felt a warm glow. It was what I had always wanted – children and a place of my own.

But until now I'd thought there would be a husband to love and care for me. Once again the tightness in my throat almost choked me. How could I go on? What did anything matter now that Paul had deserted me? A wave of self-pity washed over me but I fought it down. I wasn't going to give in. No matter how much it hurt!

My head went up once more. I began to make plans. I would tell my mother first and then leave. My eyes pricked with tears of shame. She was going to be so disappointed in me.

'I'm sorry, Mum,' I whispered. 'I'm so sorry.'

A new worry started to creep into my mind. I could escape – but what about my mother? Would Father take it out on her when he discovered I had gone?

Perhaps it would be all right if he thought I had simply run off to find a new job. He would be angry but not as much as if he knew the truth. I didn't want Mum to suffer in my stead.

I frowned, twisting the handle of my bag nervously. Jonathan Reece had put the idea into my head but he didn't know what Father was like. He had such a temper.

He might take it out on my mother if I ran off – but what else could I do?

I mustn't waver! I would wait until the weekend, then slip away when Father thought I was in church and catch the train to London that afternoon.

'Emma,' Mother called to me as I came upstairs. 'Thank goodness you're home! Your father has been up for his supper – and he was very cross when I had to tell him you weren't back.'

'I'm sorry, Mum. The train was late – there was a delay of some kind on the line. Signals down or something.'

I went into my bedroom to take off my costume and hang it in the wardrobe, slipping into one of my working skirts and blouses. She followed me to the door, standing there to watch as I ran a comb through my hair.

'You've been crying. Your eyes are red.'

'Yes.' I turned to look at her. 'I told you I was going to see Paul. He wasn't there but his mother was. She told me he has gone away.'

'Without letting you know? That wasn't very nice of him. I thought he had better manners. I'm disappointed in him. What did Mrs Greenslade say to you?'

'She thought I was someone else. She wasn't very nice.'

'I thought you had met her before, when he took you to that concert?'

I shook my head, cheeks firing.

'No. She wasn't at the house – and we didn't go to the concert. Paul played records of classical music so I could say I had been listening to it.' I raised my head, tears hovering on my lashes. 'I'm sorry, Mum. I hated lying to you. I believed we were going to the concert and then tea with his mother. Honestly. I didn't deliberately deceive you.'

'So Paul took you to his house and his parents weren't there?'

'No one was there – except his cousin. He dropped by for a few minutes to talk to Paul.' I lowered my gaze, not wanting to look at her. 'I met his cousin again today. He was very kind. He lent me some money for my fare back to the station and told me Paul had a new job in America. He isn't like Mrs Greenslade. His name is Jonathan Reece and—'

'Emma!' The unusual sharpness in my mother's voice made me falter. 'Stop rattling on about nothing. What happened that afternoon?'

I shot a quick look at her and then away as I saw the expression in her eyes. She was hurt, anxious and disappointed – and that made me feel worse than anything else. Even the knowledge that Paul had deserted me hadn't been as hard to accept as this.

'I'm sorry, Mum,' I whispered. 'I know I shouldn't have. It was wrong and silly but—' Tears trickled down my cheeks as I raised my eyes to meet hers. 'He wanted to and I loved him. I loved him so much I let him do what he . . .'

'Oh, Emma.'

'Please don't hate me,' I begged. 'I love you, Mum. I know I've let you down and I'm sorry. I'm so very sorry.'

'You've let yourself down, Emma.'

'Yes, I know.' A sob escaped me. 'I wish I hadn't.'

'If your father suspected—' She gasped as she suddenly guessed why I had gone to see Paul that afternoon. 'No! Oh, my God! What are we going to do? Harold will be furious.'

'I know. I'm sorry. Paul said he would marry me. I believed him.'

'There's no chance of that, I suppose?'

'No. I should have known, Mum. His family would never have allowed it even if . . .' I blinked rapidly but warded off another bout of weeping. 'His cousin is going to make him pay me something for the child's keep.'

Mother frowned. 'What are you saying? Harold will make your life a misery but he won't throw you out. He wouldn't want to pay anyone else to do your work.'

'He doesn't have to know, Mum. I could go away and find myself a job somewhere else. If Paul helps me to keep the child, I need not stay here.'

'Supposing he won't? Do you realize how hard things could get? Bringing up a child alone isn't easy.'

'Yes.' I looked her in the eyes. 'I know it won't

be easy, but it's better than staying here and having Father take it out on us both. It might not be so bad if he thinks I've gone off because I'm not satisfied with my wages.'

'He would raise the roof . . .' She was thoughtful for a moment. 'I could give you a pound or two. Nothing much, but enough to pay your fare and rent for a week or two.'

'I've got five pounds. Mr Reece lent it to me. I shall pay him back when Paul gives me the money.'

'Oh, Emma.' My mother started to cry softly. 'I never thought this would happen to you . . . not you.'

'I'm sorry, Mum. Please forgive me. Please!'

She held her arms open and I moved into them. We embraced, both weeping.

'I shall miss you,' she said, 'but I think perhaps it's best that you go. If you are set on going it should be quickly, before your father finds out—'

'Finds out what?' The harsh, angry voice made us both freeze. Mother released me as we both swung round, staring into Father's cold, hard eyes. 'Running away, Emma? Don't I pay you enough?' His gaze narrowed as I remained silent. 'Or is there another reason for this sudden flight? Perhaps I can guess.'

He took a step towards me, raising his fist as if to hit me. I retreated two steps, but continued to face him defiantly. Something in my eyes must have made him hesitate, because he merely shook his fist at me, his expression one of disgust. 'You deserve a thrashing, you little slut! I've a good mind to take my belt to you.'

'No, Harold!' my mother cried. 'Don't you dare hit her. I'll leave you and take her with me if you do.'

'Leave? You?' He turned disbelieving eyes on her. 'You haven't the courage to walk out on me. You never did have.'

'I mean it, Harold.'

He moved towards her, his lips curled in a sneer. I thought he was going to hit her and I rushed towards him, but he pushed me away and turned his blazing eyes on her.

'You bitch!' he snarled. 'Do you think I don't know why you married me? It wasn't the money, was it? It was the bastard you were carrying in your belly. You were frightened of the gossips. You married me rather than let everyone know your shame.'

'No! That isn't true,' she cried, her face proud despite the fear in her eyes. 'I've sworn it enough times, Harold. Emma *is* your daughter. I tripped and fell – that's why she was born early. I give you my word she *is* yours. Fetch the Bible and I'll swear on it again if you wish.'

'You're a lying whore – just like your daughter.'

He gave her a rough push towards the door, making her stumble and almost fall.

'Get out of here. I want to talk to Emma alone.'

She struggled but he was too strong for her. She was forcibly ejected and the door locked behind her. She beat against it with her fists, screaming at him defiantly.

'If you hurt her I shall leave you – and I'll tell everyone what kind of a man you really are. I'll blacken your name in this town, Harold Robinson. I mean it! See if your customers will buy from you then. People will spit at you in the street!'

'Be quiet, woman. I'll deal with you later.'

'Don't hurt her,' I said as he turned to me. 'Please, Father. This isn't her fault. It's mine. I know I've done wrong. If you want to take it out on someone – make it me. Thrash me with your belt. I deserve it.'

His eyes narrowed. 'It's what I ought to do. I ought to break your neck before I let you bring shame on my name.'

'Do it. I deserve it.' I met his glaring look without flinching. 'If you don't, I shall leave this house in the morning.'

'You won't leave, nor will your mother. I'll make certain of that. You will stay in this room until I decide what to do about this.'

'Why don't you let us leave? Since you hate us both so much.'

'And have the whole town laughing at me?' He shook his head. 'The only reason I didn't throw your mother out years ago was because I had my pride. She cheated me of my rights, Emma. I could have thrown her out, shown her up for what she was – but I'm not one for washing my dirty linen in public.'

'She made a mistake.' I looked at him, searching for any hint of softness in his face, any kindness. 'Couldn't you have found the strength to forgive her?'

'I might have – if she'd shown any sign of caring.' His eyes narrowed. 'You'll not get round me, Emma. I'll not have you flaunting your shame to the world.'

'You can't keep me locked up forever.'

'Who's to stop me? Be sensible, girl!' He glared at me, torn between frustration and his determination to have his way. 'Let's sort this business out as best we can. You're not much use to me here are you? I want you back in the shop where you belong.'

'I don't want to work for you.'

'Then you'll stay here until you come to your senses!'

He took a step towards me and I thought he was going to hit me. Then he shook his head.

'No. I'm not going to make it that easy for you, Emma. It's her I'll punish. Remember that. Every time you defy me she suffers.'

'That isn't fair. She isn't strong. You know that.'

'Think on it. I'll give you until the morning to come to your senses. Work for me, and I'll treat her fair, same as I always have. She would have had worse treatment from some, believe me. A lady of leisure she's always been, with a woman to come in and do the heavy work.

There's not many of her friends can claim that, for all her grumbling.'

I looked at him and wondered if he had loved her at the beginning. Perhaps all the faults had not been on his side. How was I to know? I had never asked him why he was so harsh with her. I had thought him hard and uncaring, but it must have hurt him to know she had never really loved him.

'I know that, Father. It's just . . .' I shook my head, refusing to plead with him. However hurt he might have been in the past, he had no need to threaten her because of what I'd done. I looked at him resentfully. 'You don't have the right to force me to work for you.'

'Don't I?' His mouth hardened and I knew he was angry again. 'Think of it from my side for once. I've looked after the both of you, and many a man would have treated you worse. You've got until morning, Emma. After that I'll start punishing *her* for your sins.'

He went to the door, unlocked it and showed me the key. 'This stays in my pocket until you give me your word you'll do whatever I decide is best.'

'You can't do that!'

'Just watch me.'

Mother opened the door, her face pale, eyes desperate. 'Emma,' she cried. 'Don't give into his blackmail—'

He grabbed her by the arm, pushing her back out of the door again.

'Don't hurt her! Please,' I begged, tears starting to my eyes. I was desperate to stop all this anger and bitterness, and I knew I had deserved my father's anger. 'I will work for you, if that's what you want. I shan't leave. I promise. I promise, Father.'

He gave my mother a shove backwards: she lost her balance, fell to the floor in the hallway and lay there gasping for breath. Father stared at her for a moment, and I thought there was a hint of pain in his eyes as he reached out and pulled her roughly back to her feet, but the pain – if it was ever there – was replaced by anger as he looked at me again.

'I'm locking you in for the night,' he said quietly. 'Think about this, Emma. Think about what happens if you break your word. If you run off behind my back I'll find you, I promise. I'll find you one day. And you'll both regret it.'

I closed my eyes as he locked the door behind him. He was determined to keep me here, and it seemed I had no choice.

I sank to my knees on the floor, all the defiance crushed out of me. I had always known my father had a violent temper. But until this evening, I had not suspected the awful truth behind his harsh treatment of both me and my mother.

Harold Robinson did not believe I was his child.

Chapter Seven

At last my tears had dried. I had hardly slept all night and now felt drained of emotion, frightened and unwell. What was I going to do – what could I do? I knew Father would eventually have to let me out of my bedroom, because I was of very little use to him locked in here, but that wouldn't change my situation much.

We could go to the police, of course, but I doubted we would get much help. Angry husbands often made threats against their wives and children, especially when the daughter had brought shame on their name. The police would probably advise me to go home and tell my father I was sorry. Harold Robinson might not be liked but he *was* respected in the town. And he hadn't beaten me: he was far too clever for that. He knew there were ways of making us suffer without the kind of brutality that would give us cause to seek protection from the police.

I started up as the door was unlocked and he came

in. My mother followed, bringing a tray of tea and some toast.

'Are you all right, Emma?' she asked, looking at me anxiously.

'Yes, Mum. Don't worry.'

She put the tray down and departed, giving me a look that spoke volumes over her shoulder. Any courage she might have had the previous evening had gone and she was obviously nervous.

'Well,' Father said, entering the room. 'Have you thought it over?'

'Yes.' I raised my head as his eyes seemed to bore into me. 'You are my father whatever you say. Mum wouldn't lie.'

'I've accepted it for the look of things,' he muttered. 'I'll not start to deny you publicly now – unless you defy me.'

'You've made it impossible for me to do that, haven't you?'

'So you're going to be sensible.' He nodded, eyes glittering with satisfaction. 'I thought you might. Behave properly and nothing need change, Emma. We'll go on as before.'

'What about the child? I shan't be able to keep it a secret for long. Aren't you afraid of what people will say?'

'I've been thinking about that.' He gave me a hard look. 'I'll arrange things.'

'You can't cover this up. Why don't you let me go away? No one need know the truth.'

'I've told you. I'll not be made a fool of in this town. Do you think the gossips wouldn't get hold of the tale?'

'But—'

'Eat your breakfast and come down to the shop. You'll do as you're told, or you know what will happen. Every defiant look, every sullen word, believe me . . . your mother will pay for it.'

'You don't have to tell me again.'

He nodded, a gleam of satisfaction in his eyes. 'As long as we understand each other.'

He turned and went out of the room. As soon as he had gone, my mother rushed back in. I looked at the dark bruises on her arm and felt sick with fear.

'Mum!' I cried. 'He hurt you.'

She touched her arm. 'He has done it before, but not where it shows, and not often. He was too angry to think last night. We should leave now, while he's in the shop, Emma. Go to the police.'

'You know that wouldn't stop him,' I said. 'We can't go. He would come after us.'

'He has hated me ever since he discovered I wasn't a virgin on our wedding night.' She blinked away her tears. 'There was someone else before him and he has never forgiven me for it.'

'Am I his daughter, Mum? Please tell me the truth.'

'Yes, Emma. God forgive me, I wish you weren't!'

'Oh, Mum.' I moved towards her and we hugged. 'I'm so sorry. So sorry for bringing all this on you.'

'It's not your fault. If that unnatural man had given you more freedom you might have known a bit more – been aware of what men are. I blame myself. I encouraged Paul here.'

'No, Mum. I knew it was wrong. I just didn't think . . . until it was too late. It was nice kissing and . . . but it went too far.'

'You're not the first to get caught like that.' She sighed and gave me a little push away from her. 'Don't think I don't understand, because I do. None better. Something similar happened to me, except that in my case it was my own fault. I sent him off because I thought he would never amount to anything. I wanted more than a railwayman's cottage. I was a fool and I've regretted it – but there was nothing I could do once I realized what a mistake I'd made.'

'Oh, Mum! I'm so sorry.'

'It's too long ago to cry over. You had better get ready and go down to the shop, love. Until we can sort something out.'

'Yes, I know. It's all right, don't worry. I'm not afraid of him anymore.'

She nodded. I knew she had accepted the situation,

at least for the time being. Neither of us wanted to stay here, but what else could we do?

Perhaps Jonathan Reece could help? He worked for a firm of lawyers, didn't he? I wasn't sure if anyone could help me, but I might ask Paul's cousin when he came at the weekend – if I got the chance.

That Saturday, I waited with some misgivings for Jonathan to come into the shop. It was going to be difficult if Father was there when he arrived. I should probably be sent upstairs and forbidden to speak to him – and he would take it out on my mother later if I disobeyed. I felt slightly relieved when evening came and Jonathan hadn't been in.

He had promised he wouldn't let me down, but perhaps he hadn't been able to get in touch with Paul. Somehow I was still sure that Jonathan would come when he could – besides, it didn't matter. I didn't really need money now, though I had decided to take what was offered. Why shouldn't I? My child might need it one day, even if I didn't.

I was having supper when Father came upstairs after closing the shop. It was earlier than usual and I was surprised when he announced his intention of going out.

'I'm off now,' he said, giving us a hard stare. 'I may be late back – so don't bother waiting up for me.'

'Where are you going?' Mother asked.

'Mind your own business. I'll tell you both what you need to know when I'm ready.'

'I hate you, Harold Robinson.'

'Aye, I know it. The feeling is mutual.'

He turned round and walked out, leaving silence behind him.

'What is he up to?' my mother asked. 'He's up to something, I know he is – something neither of us is going to like.'

'It doesn't matter, Mum,' I said. 'If we had enough money we could go where he wouldn't be able to find us – maybe to America or somewhere far away.'

'I wish I knew what he does with his money!'

'It's in a bank somewhere, I expect.'

'Harold Robinson put his money in a bank?' She snorted with disbelief. 'He doesn't trust them. No, it will be in property or the like. If I could just get my hands on some of it, I'd show him.'

'How much would it cost for a passage to Australia for us both?'

'Far more than either of us are ever likely to have – we would need money to live on as well, remember. Forget it, Emma. As long as he doesn't hit you I can put up with him – for the time being.'

I nodded reluctantly. She seemed to have accepted the situation. It was all we could do for the moment – but perhaps one day it might be different. If I could somehow get enough money together . . .

I went to church with my mother the next morning. Father had insisted that we go, because people might think it strange if we didn't. He had seemed in a good mood at breakfast, smiling and nodding to himself as if he knew something that pleased him.

'He's definitely got something up his sleeve,' Mother said as we walked to church. 'Did you see the way he was grinning to himself? What has he done, that's what I'd like to know.'

'Was he very late in last night?'

'It was past eleven when I heard him come in. He didn't come upstairs for an hour or more. I pretended to be asleep but I could smell the whisky on his breath.'

'I didn't think he drank whisky!' I stared at her. 'Was he drunk?'

'Not so as you'd notice. He'd had a few, but he never drinks too much. He might lose control – and Harold likes to be in control.'

'I wonder why he closed the shop early? It couldn't have been because he wanted to go to the pub. There would have been plenty of time for that later.'

'I've got a nasty feeling about that,' she said and frowned. 'It was something that amused him, I know that.'

I nodded but we had reached the church. We went in

and took our usual places. I had half-hoped Paul would be there, but of course that was impossible: he was far away and even if he had wanted he couldn't have returned so quickly.

Kneeling down, I closed my eyes and whispered a prayer, though without much hope of it being answered. Then, sensing someone beside me, I glanced to my left and saw it was Richard Gillows. He smiled as I sat back on the pew and picked up my prayer book.

'Surprised?' he whispered. 'I came to see you, Emma.'

I put a finger to my lips as the vicar began to speak. He nodded but there was a look of expectancy in his eyes, which made me uneasy. I had never known Richard to come to church before.

Throughout the service I was very conscious of him sitting next to me. He had a good strong voice and sang the hymns with confidence. Every now and then he shot me a knowing look, which made me more and more uncomfortable.

When we left the church he kept close by my side. I tried to walk on ahead, but he caught my arm, holding me back.

'I'd like a word, please,' he said, and then, as my mother looked at him, 'I've spoken to Mr Robinson. He says it's all right if I take Emma for a walk.'

'Emma . . .' Mother looked at me, then nodded. 'You'd best go with him, love.'

I let Richard take my arm as we turned away. My chest felt tight and I found it difficult to breathe. So this was what Father had looked so pleased about that morning! He had obviously been talking to Richard about me . . . arranging things. I knew what Richard was going to say to me even before he started, which he did when we reached the river bank.

'You know I'm mighty fond of you, Emma. Always have been.'

'Please don't say it, Richard.' My eyes filled with tears. 'I don't love you. I'm sorry but I don't.'

'I reckon I know that.' His forehead creased. 'It was that smarmy toff as turned your head. Before he came, I reckon you liked me well enough.'

I turned my face aside, holding back my tears.

'Please, Richard . . . don't.'

He caught my hand as I would have walked away. 'I love you, Emma. I'm not much of a man with words and I know you don't love me – but I'd be good to you. I'd work for you and try to make a good life for us both.'

'Oh, Richard.' I felt terrible. I had never wanted his attentions but was now humbled by his words. 'You don't understand. You don't know what I've done.'

'Why don't you tell me?'

His voice was so gentle, so understanding. Suddenly the tears were flowing as I blurted out the truth.

'Father shouldn't have encouraged you,' I said. 'You won't want to marry me now.'

'Why not?'

'Because I'm having another man's child.'

He was silent for a moment. I broke away from him.

'Don't go, Emma. I love you. I still want to marry you.'

'You can't. You can't want to.' I started walking back the way we had come but he ran after me, catching my arm, swinging me round to face him. 'Please – leave me alone.'

'Emma! Don't run away from me. Listen to me.' I stopped and looked at him, struck by the urgency in his voice. 'I do want to marry you. I won't say I don't mind about the child – but it's something I can live with. I want you to be my wife.'

'No, Richard – no. It wouldn't work.'

'Why not? It makes sense.' He gave me an impatient shake. 'Do you want everyone talking about you, laughing behind your back?' I shook my head, not looking him in the face. 'Well, then! They'll think it's mine – maybe a bit early but that's better than being unwed, isn't it?' I nodded reluctantly. 'Marry me, Emma.'

'I don't know . . .'

I felt my will to resist weakening. It would be one way out of the mess I was in – one way of saving Father's pride and making things easier on my mother.

'Think about it, Emma. I'll walk you home and then come back this evening for my answer.

'It will still be no. It wouldn't be fair to you.'

'You let me worry about that.'

I remained silent, not speaking once as we walked home. At the door I turned to him.

'I'll think about it.'

'I shall be here at six. Don't be stubborn, Emma. I'll be good to you. You know I love you.'

I inclined my head, accepting it without comment. He stood staring after me as I left him and went into the house.

Father was waiting at the top of the stairs. He looked at me expectantly.

'Richard asked me to marry him,' I said, 'but you know that, don't you?'

'I gave him my permission to ask you.' His eyes narrowed. 'I hope you were sensible?'

'I've told him I'll think about it.'

'It's him or no one,' Father said. 'Turn him down and I'll make you sorry.'

'Yes,' I said. 'I suppose you will.'

I went into my bedroom and closed the door. When it was opened almost at once I flinched, waiting for his next onslaught, but it was my mother.

'You should think carefully,' she said. 'I don't want to push you into anything, love – but it is a way out for you. If you defy Harold over this he'll make your life a misery.'

'And yours.'

'It doesn't matter about me. I am thinking of you. There are worse men about than Richard Gillows.'

'Yes, I expect so.' I sank down on the edge of the bed with a sigh. 'I don't love him, Mum.'

'Does he make you shudder when he touches you?'

'No.' I stared at her, understanding what she meant. 'He's not that bad. I don't actually dislike him but I don't love him either.'

'He isn't Paul?' She nodded as I didn't answer. 'No one will be, Emma. You're not likely to meet anyone like that again. He was out of our league. You know that, don't you?'

'Yes, but—' I felt the lump in my throat, choking me. 'But I still love him, Mum. I know he didn't love me. I know he won't marry me – but I still love him.'

'We could still go away – take a chance.'

'It's too much of a risk.'

'Don't marry Richard if you really can't bear the thought of it. I've wished a thousand times I had thought more about what I was doing before I married. Have the child and brazen it out. It doesn't matter what people think.'

'I've told Richard I'll give him an answer this evening.'

'Oh, Emma.' She looked at me sadly. 'It's all such a mess . . . all such a mess.'

*

I saw the letters waiting on the mat when I went downstairs the following Monday morning. I slipped the one addressed to me into my pocket and took the others through to the stockroom for Father. He was looking at something in his rolltop desk, but shut it hurriedly when I entered. I caught a glimpse of something shiny but wasn't sure what it was. He obviously didn't want me to see.

'Two letters,' I said, handing them to him. 'Do you want me to help in the shop this morning – or shall I get on with the accounts?'

He opened the envelopes I had given him, frowned as he saw they were bills and tossed them onto the desk.

'You can get on upstairs,' he muttered. 'I'll call you if we're busy.' I turned away but waited as he began to speak again. 'I'm glad you were sensible. Richard is a decent man. He'll make you a good husband.'

'Will he?' My tone was flat, emotionless. I had been feeling numb since giving Richard my answer.

'You'll see. I know you are angry with me for forcing you into it but everything will turn out for the best. Richard will live here with us. He can help out with some of the heavier jobs when he's not on a shift. It will make things easier all round.'

'Yes, Father. If you say so.' He gave me an odd look, as if he didn't quite believe my submissive manner; then put his hand in his pocket and brought out ten pounds. 'You'll have things to buy for the wedding. I'll be paying for the reception, so don't expect anything more. You're lucky to get this after the way you've behaved.'

'Thank you. I'm sure the money will be useful.'

I turned away and went out. At the moment there was no defiance left in me. The realisation that I would probably never see Paul again, that he had never loved me, was just beginning to sink in. I had been too shocked and upset at first to do anything but cry. Now I was thinking and it hurt. I felt stupid and used. I had been such a naive fool, and I wasn't unintelligent. I ought to have had more sense.

My moods seemed to fluctuate between anger and shame. It really stung to know that I had been so easy. Paul must have thought it a great joke. How he must have laughed!

How could he? How could he have done this to me? Why had he bothered? It must have seemed like a game to him, a challenge that had lost its interest once I'd been silly enough to give him what he wanted. I remembered his annoyance because I had cried. He had decided that I was just a stupid country girl and had broken it off quickly, before he got caught out.

I wished I could hate him. He deserved that I should, but my foolish heart still ached for him.

Going into my bedroom, I opened my letter. It was

from Jonathan Reece. I had expected it would be, though a part of me had hoped for a minute that it might have been Paul. Foolish, foolish thought! Paul wasn't going to write to me. He had left me without a backward glance.

Dear Emma, Jonathan had written. *I hope you don't mind me calling you that? I just wanted to apologise for not coming last weekend. My uncle died suddenly and . . .*

Paul's father had died! My heart took a flying leap. Surely that meant Paul would come home? If Jonathan had told him I was . . . The hope died in me almost as soon as it was born. Paul didn't want to marry me. He wouldn't have gone off the way he had if he had cared for me.

I finished reading Jonathan's letter, then sat looking at the ten pounds he had sent me. He promised there would be more next month and every following month. What ought I to do about it? I still had most of the money he'd lent me the afternoon we had met at Paul's home. Should I give it back now that I was to be married? I didn't really need it – but was it mine by right?

Folding the letter carefully, I hid it at the very back of my dressing table drawer. I would keep the money for the time being but write to Jonathan Reece and tell him I was to be married.

As I closed the drawer, I caught sight of my pale face in the mirror. Was that me? It didn't look like me – but then, I wasn't the same girl anymore. The old Emma would never have agreed to marry a man she didn't love.

For a moment I felt a surge of despair. How could I marry Richard? It was wrong and unnatural. I would do better to run away than agree to this marriage. Yet I knew that was impossible. Mother could never work in a shop or a factory, and I wasn't sure I could earn enough to keep both of us and a child. Even if Paul continued to send money it would be hard – and there would always be the threat of discovery hanging over our heads.

Was I a coward to take the easy way out? I would have liked to consult Gran, but Father had banned me from visiting her.

'When you're married you can go,' he had told me. 'Until then you will stay in this house – unless Richard takes you somewhere.'

'He won't have time. He's working extra hours for the next couple of weeks so that he can take me for a holiday.'

I hadn't been able to bring myself to use the word honeymoon. Sometimes, when I allowed myself to think what it would be like being married to Richard, I felt sick. How could I lie in his arms and let him do what Paul had done?

Yet perhaps it didn't matter. Nothing seemed to matter anymore. My senses were dulled. I felt as if my life were over. None of my dreams were ever going to come true, so I might as well let Richard and my father have their way.

I might even die when the child came. Women often did. Why not me?

'Your mother told me what was going on here.' Gran came puffing up the stairs that Sunday afternoon. 'You haven't been to see me, so I decided I'd best come to you.'

'I am sorry, Gran.' I hugged her. 'Father wouldn't let me. I think he's afraid I might run away.'

'Is that what you want?'

'No, not now. I thought about it, but it wouldn't be sensible.'

'What has being sensible got to do with it?'

'Did Mum tell you about the baby? Richard knows but still wants to marry me.'

'And what do you want?'

'Nothing I can have.'

'Still mooning over that rogue?' She frowned at me. 'Tell Richard you've changed your mind. It's not too late to get rid of the child. It would have been better if you'd come to me sooner but if we're careful—'

'No! I don't want to kill my baby, Gran.'

'I was afraid of that.' She shook her head over it. 'You're too soft-hearted, lass.'

'You won't change her mind,' Mother said, bustling in with a tray of tea. 'Harold went wild at first, but he'll not make things too hard for her as long as he needs her in that shop. And who knows, it may turn out for the best.'

'You always did talk nonsense!' Gran gave her a sharp look. 'What's going on in your head, Greta? I know you and your schemes.'

'Nothing important.' Mother smiled at me. 'I want what's best for Emma, that's all. She is entitled to more than she's had so far, but things won't always be this way.'

'Neither of you will get much while Harold's around.'

'Oh, I don't know.' Her smile was serene, mysterious. 'None of us wanted this to happen but it has. We've just got to make the best of a bad job,' she said, an odd glint in her eyes. 'I've put up with his temper and meanness for years, but I shan't anymore.'

'What do you mean?

I looked at my mother in surprise. She wasn't exactly smiling but she did seem . . . satisfied. Yes, that was the right word.

'I just shan't, that's all.'

A look passed between her and Gran that puzzled me, but then it was gone and I thought I had imagined it.

I was relieved my mother had stopped wearing that haunted, frightened expression, but I couldn't help wondering why.

Chapter Eight

I stood at the window, looking out at the back yard, with its washing lines and tubs of summer flowers. Beyond it was Mother's garden, where roses bloomed in profusion. Today was my wedding day and the sun was already high in the sky, not a cloud to be seen. It was going to be really beautiful by the time we left for church.

I turned to glance at the dress hanging on the front of the wardrobe. It was so pretty! All shiny and white. I touched it with reverent fingers. I'd never worn anything like this, and knew it looked just right on me, though I felt a little guilty about wearing it: white was meant for virgins, wasn't it?

'How do you feel?' Mother's voice from the doorway startled me, making me swing round hurriedly. She smiled at me. 'Don't worry, love. I was nervous on my wedding morning but I soon got over it. Richard is a better man than your father ever was, believe me.'

'Is he?' I felt a panicky sensation in my stomach. I looked at her in silent appeal, hoping against hope that she would say something to make me feel better, yet knowing there was nothing she could say. 'He has been really nice to me since I said I'd marry him.'

'He's fond of you,' my mother said. 'If not, I'd tell you to run off to London, Emma. Harold might create hell, but I doubt if he would follow you.'

I turned the pretty little cluster ring on my finger. It was set with pearls and tiny rose diamonds. Richard had given it to me when we'd sat in church together, to hear the banns read out for the first time.

'We don't want people thinking I'm too mean to give you a ring, do we?' he'd said. 'I hope it fits, but you can wind a bit of cotton round it if it slips, can't you?'

It had fitted perfectly. I liked the ring and the simulated pearl beads Richard had sent me as a wedding present. He had been generous with his gifts, and was also taking me to Yarmouth for a week in a hotel for our honeymoon.

'And why shouldn't he be nice to you?' Mother smiled and kissed my cheek. 'He loves you, Emma. You've been honest with him from the start and he's accepted you made a mistake. If he still wants to marry you he must think the world of you. Why else would he marry you?'

'He keeps telling me he loves me,' I said, looking at her doubtfully. Some of the tension drained out of me. There really was no reason for him to marry me if he didn't, was there? 'You do like him, don't you, Mum? I know Gran thinks I shouldn't marry him.'

'Take no notice of your Gran, love. She means well but she doesn't understand how difficult your father would have made things for you if you'd refused to take Richard. I think it's the best thing you can do in the circumstances.'

I nodded. Mother seemed almost serene these days. There was an air of contentment about her. Why? What had changed? Certainly not Father's temper. He seemed to get more irritable every day. I suspected he was having trouble with his stomach again.

'I'll leave you to get dressed,' Mother said. 'Your father will be up for his breakfast in a few minutes. He's fretting over leaving Ben alone in the shop this afternoon, but he wouldn't listen when I told him to shut the place for once, so he'll have to bear the consequences.'

'I think he doesn't always feel well,' I said. 'But he insists it's nothing but wind and gets cross if I mention it.'

'Feeling sorry for him?'

'No.' I met her eyes. 'I used to think he ought to see a doctor but now I don't care. If he won't spare the time for the treatment he needs it's his own fault.'

'It's only indigestion. If he ate more slowly – or a bit less – he wouldn't suffer so much. It is his own fault. He's brought it on himself. He should go to the doctor.'

'Yes, he should.'

As my mother went out, I sat down at the dressing

table and began to take out the grips I'd used to pin my hair up the previous night. I was lucky in having a natural wave in the front, but wanted it to fluff out a little for the wedding photographs.

I thought about Father. It couldn't be very pleasant being in pain a lot of the time, and he certainly was. I'd noticed him grimacing on several occasions recently.

But he deserved to suffer for the way he'd treated my mother! My heart hardened against him as I began to brush my hair into soft waves and curls. If he hadn't been such a tyrant I wouldn't have been marrying Richard Gillows. At least not yet. I could have thought about it more, decided what I wanted to do.

If I was unhappy it would be his fault!

My breath caught as Richard slipped the wide gold band on my finger. He smiled at me and I felt a flutter of nerves in my stomach. Until this moment it had all seemed like one of the stories I read before I went to sleep at night; I'd half expected to wake up and find it was all a bad dream.

Oh, Paul. Paul, I love you!

I smothered the cry from my heart as I walked out of church with my hand on my husband's arm. The sun was shining brightly and it was very warm. I could smell the scent of roses and lilies from my bouquet, hear the loud pealing of the bells. The bells were ringing so loudly that I couldn't hear what Richard was saying to me. I leaned my head towards him, trying to catch the words.

'I said you look beautiful, Emma. I can't wait to be alone with you.'

I nodded, trying not to think of what would happen once the reception was over and we left to begin our honeymoon. We were staying at a hotel in Ely overnight and catching a train to the coast early in the morning.

'I love you, Emma.'

I smiled up at him. It was time to forget my dreams. Paul had never loved me. I had to start fresh. Mother was right. I must try to make a go of my marriage. I looked up into his eyes.

'Can you forgive me – for what I did?'

'It's over,' he promised. 'Just be good to me, love, that's all I ask.'

'I will,' I said. 'I will. I promise.'

The photographer called everyone to order.

'Smile please. Look this way, Mrs Gillows. We want nice, happy pictures, don't we?'

Everyone had gathered in the churchyard. I looked round for my mother. She was standing just to the left of Father. He was rubbing at his stomach. He said something to Mother; she took a small box out of her bag and gave it to him.

'Now the bride's parents,' the photographer said, waving at them enthusiastically. 'A nice big group – and you, Mrs Jacobs. Come on, everyone – smile, please!'

Father stood next to me for the picture. I heard his stifled groan and glanced at him anxiously. He really was in a lot of pain.

'Are you all right?'

'A touch of wind,' he muttered. 'It'll pass.'

I nodded, smiled for the camera again, then felt Richard take my arm and push me towards the cars waiting to take us to the reception in a small local hotel.

'I think my father is ill,' I said as we dodged the deluge of confetti and got into the back of the first car. 'He was in pain just now.'

'He'll be all right,' Richard said and reached out for me as the car drew away from the kerb. 'Give me a kiss. I've been waiting for this for a long time.'

When his arms closed round me I felt trapped. I wanted to push him away and jump out of the car, but of course I couldn't. His mouth was eager, demanding. He seemed to take without giving – but what else could I expect? I let him kiss me, staying perfectly still until he let me go and sat back.

'Stop worrying,' he said and frowned at me. 'Harold will be fine. It's just his stomach trouble again. He's had it for years.'

'Yes, I know.'

'Relax. Everything will be all right.'

'Yes, of course.'

I could see he was put out because I hadn't responded

to his kiss. I would have to try harder next time, because I wanted him to be kind to me. I might just be able to bear being married to him if he was kind.

I noticed my father didn't eat much at the reception. I saw him grimace a couple of times, but he got up and made a speech about being proud to hand his daughter over to a decent man.

'To the bride and groom!'

Father took only a sip of his drink, then sat down quickly. He looked pale but sat through the rest of the toasts, only disappearing rather hurriedly into the cloak-rooms when Richard and I started moving about the room, talking to our guests, thanking them for all the lovely presents we had been given.

'You look beautiful,' Mary Baker said and kissed me. 'You sly thing! I knew you and Richard were going steady, of course – your father told mine the night we came to tea – but I didn't think you would be married before me.'

'Nor did I,' I replied truthfully. 'I'm as surprised as you are.'

'Well, just be happy.' Mary squeezed my hand. 'It all went well, didn't it? Your mum looks pretty in that pink dress.'

'You look pretty, too.'

'Did you know Sheila Tomms is back?' Mary asked suddenly.

'No – is she? Have you seen her?' I stared at her in surprise. Even though I no longer thought Sheila might have been murdered, I had wondered about her a lot. 'Do you know where she went?'

'I know what they're saying.' Mary pulled a face. 'You don't want to hear about—' She broke off as there was a murmur of consternation from the other side of the room. 'What's happened? That's your father, Emma. I think he just fell over.'

I turned and saw several people gathered about a man lying on the floor. I started to walk towards him, but before I got more than halfway he was sitting up. Mary's father and another guest pulled him to his feet and someone gave him a chair.

Mother came to meet me.

'It's all right, Emma. Nothing to worry about.'

'What's wrong, Mum?'

'He was sick in the toilets,' she said. 'It left him feeling a bit dizzy. He's all right. Just his usual trouble. Nothing to worry about.'

'Are you sure? Should we call a doctor?' I looked at her anxiously.

'He says he doesn't want one. You know your father.'

'But he hasn't been like this before.'

'He would hate it if I made a fuss in front of everyone. If he's no better after we get home this evening, I'll send for the doctor then.' She glanced at her watch. 'You ought to go home and change, love. Otherwise you'll miss your train. Your Gran will go with you. I'd better stay here with Harold.'

'You look a treat in that dress.' Gran embraced me. 'I was against this, Emma, you know that – but now that you've married the man, be good to him. There's no point in looking backwards.'

'I know that. I'll try my best to be a good wife to him.'

'Aye, well, remember that tonight. For most men being a good wife starts in the honeymoon bed. Be warm and willing if you can't be more. You don't want to start out on the wrong foot, do you?'

'No, I don't.' I smiled at her. She was so good to me and I loved her so much. 'Like I always say, Gran, you're a wise old bird.'

'My advice is to get a little tiddly. It helps get over the strangeness of having a great lump of a man in your bed. They're unnatural, awkward creatures at the best of times – but a good one is no bad thing to have around.'

After all the nervous tension of the past few hours and Father's collapse, Gran's no nonsense words had lifted the gloom. I went into a peal of delighted laughter and clutched at her arm.

'Oh, Gran,' I giggled. 'What a thing to say!'

'Lust wears off after the first two or three children come, but mutual respect and affection lasts forever. It's worth putting your man first to have peace in the house, lass. And a little caring brings its own rewards.'

'I'll remember,' I promised and hugged her again.

I was smiling as we went back to the reception. Richard was waiting for me. Remembering Gran's advice, I gave him a look of welcome and his response was instantaneous.

'You look beautiful,' he said huskily and reached out for me.

This time I went easily into his arms. He gave me a long, passionate kiss, which brought some cheers from his friends and a lot of laughter.

'We'd best get off or we'll miss our train.'

'I'll just say goodbye to Mum.'

I hugged my mother.

'Be happy, Emma – that's all I want.'

'I shall. Don't worry, Mum.'

I turned to my father, who had regained some of his colour but still looked unwell, his skin an odd yellowish-grey.

'Are you all right, Father? Shouldn't you see a doctor?'

'Happen I will,' he replied, surprising me as he leaned towards me, his lips just grazing my cheek in an awkward kiss. 'Have a good time, girl – and don't concern yourself about me.'

'Thank you.' I blinked hard as unexpected tears stung my eyes. 'Take care of yourself, Father.'

Then Richard was by my side, urging me to remember we had a train to catch. I went with him, laughing as an absolute deluge of confetti showered down on us from our relatives and friends. I squealed, feeling suddenly excited as we ran together and jumped into the waiting car, which was driven by one of Richard's friends and had been suitably decorated with a string of empty cans that made a terrible noise as it clattered behind us on the road.

'You're all right now, aren't you?'

I slid my hand into his. I had taken Gran's advice to heart and knew the next few hours might be the most important of my life. I wasn't in love with Richard, but he'd stood by me and saved me from the shame of bearing an illegitimate child. I owed him at least respect and a smiling face.

'I was a bit nervous earlier, that's all.'

'You'll be all right with me. I know you've had a hard time of it at home, but things will be different now we're married. We'll go out, Emma. Pictures and dancing sometimes. I thought you might like to go somewhere this evening?'

'Could we?'

'After we've booked into our hotel.' He grinned at me. 'There's usually a dance on Saturdays in Ely. We could go for a while, if you like?'

'I'd love that, Richard.'

He leaned towards me, his fingers stroking my cheek.

'I reckon you've been only half alive until now. It's different being wed, Emma. I'll be good to you, lass.'

'And I'll be good to you,' I promised.

I had three port and lemons at the dance. Richard kept buying them for me and I didn't refuse. They gave me a lovely warm feeling inside, making me relax. I couldn't help enjoying myself. It was the first real dance I'd ever been to and the live music was wonderful.

'It's so much better than dancing to records,' I said, nestling my head dreamily against Richard's shoulder. 'I've never had this much fun. Not ever.'

'Not ever?' He glanced down at me, frowning slightly. 'Even when you were out with *him*?'

'Paul didn't take me dancing,' I said. My breath caught in my throat as I saw the tight look in his face. 'Please don't, Richard. That's all over. Let's forget him. Please?'

'Sorry.' I saw a flash of jealousy in his eyes. 'I didn't mean to spoil things. Do you want another drink?'

I hesitated, then shook my head. There was no point in putting it off any longer, and another drink might be one too many.

'No, not for me, thanks. Why don't we go back to the hotel?'

'Are you sure?'

'Quite sure.'

We walked back beside the river, stopping now and

then to look at the moon reflected in the dark surface of the water. It was a warm summer night, peaceful and romantic.

How wonderful it would have been if I'd been with Paul! I felt the grinding ache inside me, then pushed it away. I was Richard's wife and must never, never let myself think that again.

We went into the riverside hotel and up the stairs to our room. It was a nice room with its own bathroom and a good view; I knew it must have cost extra. Richard had obviously done everything he could to please me. I picked up my nightdress and went into the bathroom to change, glad now that I'd taken notice of my mother and bought something pretty.

My hair was loose on my shoulders when I returned to the bedroom. Richard had changed into a pair of blue striped cotton pyjamas. He looked so different that I was reminded of Gran's words and had to struggle not to laugh.

Suddenly, I knew what I had to do. I walked over to him, looking up at him, sensing that he was almost as unsure as I was.

'Kiss me,' I whispered huskily. 'Let's start from tonight, Richard. Let's pretend that this is—'

I got no further. He groaned and reached out for me, gathering me into his arms, crushing me against him, his mouth seeking mine greedily, hungrily. I let him kiss me. My hands moved in his thick hair, stroking the back of his neck, and my body was pliable, willing and warm, as he picked me up and then laid me down on the bed.

At first I felt nothing. I was deliberately closing my mind to what was happening to me, trying not to remember. I had expected it to be swift, over in a few minutes, but gradually I became aware that this was different. Richard was taking his time in arousing me, stroking and kissing my breasts, touching me with his big hands in a way that was surprisingly tender. It was having a powerful effect.

My lips parted in a sigh. I moved my head on the pillow restlessly as something came to life deep inside me. It was like the feeling I'd had at the start with Paul, but stronger, more urgent, more compelling. My body arched and trembled as the sensation of pleasure intensified.

'Oh . . .' I murmured. 'That's so nice . . .'

My words seemed to work on him powerfully. He covered my body with his own, thrusting up inside me, but even now he was controlled, sure, deliberate. I clutched at his shoulders, nails scoring his flesh as I shuddered with the waves of delicious sensation coursing through me.

Oh! Oh! I had never believed I could feel like this. It was so gorgeous, so delicious and exciting. I was panting, gasping, legs gripping him as the rhythm of his thrusting became faster, and he plunged deeper and deeper inside me. I felt as if I were falling . . . there was such pleasure I was dissolving into it.

I gave a little scream as the feeling gathered and my body suddenly convulsed with such an intensity of sensation that I could hardly bear it. Then it was over and I felt Richard's whole weight fall on me as he too reached a shuddering climax.

Tears trickled down my cheeks as he gave a grunt and rolled off me. So this was what all the fuss was about! I'd wondered after my first experience of sexual love, but now I understood.

'Richard . . .' I wanted to share my feelings with him. To thank him for giving me such pleasure. 'Richard, I . . .'

'Go to sleep,' he muttered. 'We've got to be up early for the train.'

He turned his back towards me. I didn't know why but I felt as if he'd slapped me. I wanted to talk, to tell him that he'd made me happy, that he'd banished some of the hurt and emptiness I'd been feeling since Paul deserted me – that I was no longer nervous of being his wife.

Richard's gentle snores told me he'd fallen asleep almost at once. I lay awake, staring at the ceiling. Gran was right, it did feel strange sharing a bed with a great lump of a man – and yet there were compensations.

It was strange that Paul's lovemaking had given me so little pleasure. Richard had managed to awaken something locked deep inside me. Yet I had thought I didn't like him! I'd loved Paul – a first, innocent love that had died a cruel death. Perhaps it was my innocence, my guilt that had prevented me from feeling pleasure in Paul's loving – or perhaps he'd been in too much of a hurry? Taking rather than giving. I had expected Richard to take rather than give. His patience – and skill – was surprising.

I thought about the man I'd married and how little I knew of him. I had no idea of what he liked to do with his time, of his thoughts, hopes or plans for the future. What kind of a man was he really?

I had tumbled into this marriage without thinking what I was doing. So far it had brought me more pleasure than I'd expected.

Closing my eyes, I drifted into sleep. As I was floating away, I murmured a name . . .

I did my best to enjoy my honeymoon. Yarmouth was a noisy, busy seaside town and had once been the centre of a thriving herring industry, though the trade was not now as good as it had been before the Great War. Perhaps because of that, the town was now turning itself into a resort visitors liked to come to for their holidays and weekends, boasting piers, theatres and cinemas showing the latest films.

'Isn't this fun?' I asked as we walked arm in arm

along the front after going to the show at the pier. 'I love it here, Richard. Can we come again one day?'

'Maybe for a week next year,' he said. 'Do you fancy a drink before we go back?'

'Yes, why not?'

I knew he wanted a beer. It wasn't meant to be a question, more a statement of intent. He would have sulked all night if I'd said no, or left me at the hotel and gone off on his own.

'Is everything all right, Richard? You're not annoyed with me, are you?' I gave him an anxious look.

'Why should I be?' He turned towards one of the seafront pubs. 'Come on, don't sulk, Emma. It's our last night, let's make the most of it. We shall be back home soon enough.'

I made no reply. His moods puzzled me. Sometimes he seemed to want to please me, taking me wherever I wanted to go, the next minute he was abrupt, scowling at me for no good reason.

The exquisite pleasure of our first night had not been repeated. He hadn't touched me for three nights, then he'd taken me with a careless disregard for my feelings that came close to rape. I'd lain in the darkness for ages with tears on my cheeks, feeling the pain of my hurts and wondering what I'd done to make him angry.

In the morning, he'd apologized and made love to me tenderly. I had responded, but a part of me held back, remembering his brutality the previous night. Oddly, my reserve had seemed to please him. He had been especially nice to me all day, buying a pair of pretty earrings to go with the pearl beads he'd given me as a wedding gift. Since then he had hardly touched me.

The pub he had chosen was noisy and smelled of stale beer. My stomach turned as soon as we went in. I had been feeling queasy the last couple of mornings but hadn't yet been sick. I'd hoped the sickness wouldn't start until we got home. This *was* supposed to be our honeymoon. Richard wouldn't want constant reminders of the child I was carrying.

'What do you want?'

'Oh, just lemonade, please.'

I watched as he went off to the bar. There was a crowd and he had to wait to be served. My stomach heaved. The smell in here was awful. Oh, damn! I was going to be sick. I got up hastily and ran to the ladies' cloakroom.

I was sick twice. I felt terrible as I came out of the toilet and looked at myself in the streaky wall mirror. What a mess! My face was white and my hair was wet at the front. I splashed water on my face and hair, trying to get rid of the horrible stench of vomit that seemed to cling about me.

It was several minutes before I felt well enough to go back to the bar. I was walking towards the table I'd left minutes earlier when a young man deliberately stepped in front of me, blocking my path. He couldn't have been more than nineteen or twenty, and had a cheeky grin.

'Where are you going, darling?'

'Please, let me pass.'

'Supposing I don't want to?' He leered at me, obviously a little drunk. 'You on your own then? Or have you got a friend?'

I tried not to laugh. I wasn't in the least intimidated by him. His manner reminded me of a boisterous puppy, who was a little too bold.

'I'm with my hus—'

'Emma!' Richard's voice was harsh. I swung round, seeing the angry look in his eyes, my heart sinking. 'Where the hell have you been?'

'I had to go to the cloakroom,' I said. 'I'm sorry if you wondered where I'd gone.'

Someone had just taken our table. I looked round as the young man who had accosted me melted into the crowd. It was hot in here, so stuffy. I felt as if I couldn't breathe.

'Do you think we could take our drinks outside?' I asked. 'I'm not feeling well.'

Richard looked at me sullenly. 'We might as well, since you've let someone else take our table. Why you couldn't have waited until I came back, I don't know.'

I didn't feel like explaining. He was in one of his odd moods again, but at the moment all I could think about was escape. My head was swimming. If I didn't get some air I would faint.

We went out and crossed the road, finding a wooden bench at the edge of a green which overlooked the sea. There was a stiff breeze that evening and the waves were quite rough, crested with a yellowish foam. I breathed deeply. The sickness passed and I began to feel better.

I looked at my drink and frowned. 'This is port and lemon. I wanted lemonade.'

'You drank enough of the stuff at the dance in Ely,' Richard muttered. 'I thought it might put you in a good mood for later.'

I turned away. I didn't want the drink and I wasn't in the mood for making love, especially after the way he'd spoken to me in the pub. I put the glass down on the bench beside me, untouched.

'Drink it. I didn't pay good money for you to waste it.'

'You shouldn't have bought it. I didn't ask you to.'

'No, of course not. You didn't ask me to marry you – but I did.' I caught the bitter note in his voice and turned to stare at him. He was so angry! 'Drink it or I'll pour it down your throat.'

'What's the matter with you? I've told you I don't want it. I've already been sick – this would make me sick again.'

'I said drink it!' He picked up the glass and thrust it at me, spilling a few drops on my white blouse. 'Get it down you.'

I hesitated, then drank the contents of the glass straight down, replacing the empty glass on the bench. I got up and started to walk away from him.

'Hey! Where do you think you're going?'

I kept walking, ignoring him, though my heart hammered wildly.

'I asked you where the hell you think you're going?' Richard had run after me and caught my arm. He swung me round to face him. He was livid with rage, eyes glittering in the light of the street lamps. My heart began to race with fear. 'You little whore! Do you think I'm blind? Do you think I didn't see you making eyes at that bloke just now?'

'What man?' I was astonished. 'You mean the one who spoke to me?' I laughed at the ridiculous accusation. 'You can't mean it? He was just being silly.'

'I won't stand for you making a fool of me!'

Richard's arm went back. I recoiled as he hit me across the face, almost sending me flying.

'Here, mate!' someone shouted. 'What's all this about? That ain't the way to treat a lady!'

Two young men had stopped to remonstrate with him. Richard swung round on them, clearly in the mood for a fight.

'What the hell is it to do with you?' he yelled. 'If I want to give her a good hiding, I will!'

'Now then . . . now then,' the first man taunted,

obviously a little the worse for drink himself. 'No call for all this. If you want to hit someone pick on me. I'm more your size.'

I stared in horror as Richard threw a punch at him.

'No, please don't,' I cried. 'Don't fight.'

The man Richard had punched shoved him away, then his mate joined in. They were tall, well-built men, working men with strong backs and large fists. Richard tried throwing punches at each of them in turn, but he was caught between them as they jostled and shoved. Then one of them stuck his foot out and tripped him. Richard went down hard. One of the men kicked him in the ribs, but there was the sound of shouting and a whistle being blown further down the promenade. The two strangers looked at one another and took off, laughing as they ran across the green and disappeared down the steps that led to the beach.

Richard got to his feet a little unsteadily. I went to him at once, looking at him anxiously.

'Are you all right?'

'No thanks to you.'

'Richard, don't!' I said. 'Please don't.'

'Are you all right, sir?' The policeman had reached us. 'I saw two of them attacking you. Did they rob you? Was it your wallet they were after?'

'It's all right,' Richard said. 'They didn't take anything. I think they had been drinking. They insulted my wife and picked a fight with me.'

'We get that sort sometimes,' the policeman said, shaking his head sorrowfully. 'Would you like me to take you to a doctor, sir?'

'No, thanks. I'll be all right. My wife and I were just on our way back to the hotel, weren't we, Emma?'

'Yes.' I bit my lip, unable to look at the officer as I lied. 'I can look after my husband, sir. But it was a good thing you came when you did.'

'I usually walk this way at about this time.' He glanced across the road at the pub. 'Gets a bit rowdy there now and then. My advice is to stay away from it in future. Take care of yourselves, sir – and madam. Enjoy the rest of your holiday.'

'Thanks. We shall,' Richard said, and took my arm. 'Come on, love. We'll get back to the hotel.'

We walked in silence. When we reached the hotel, I went straight to the bathroom. Richard's ring had caught my mouth but it wasn't bleeding, though I thought it might swell by morning. I held a flannel under the cold tap and pressed it against my cheek, then went back to the bedroom. Richard had taken off his shirt and was looking at himself in the mirror.

'I'll be black and blue in the morning,' he muttered. 'Damned lucky they didn't kick my ribs in. I'd have been off work for a couple of weeks at least.'

'You shouldn't have tried to hit him, Richard. Not when there were two of them.'

'What was I supposed to do – let them tell me what I could do with my own wife?' He glared at me. 'If you hadn't behaved like a slut, it wouldn't have happened.'

'I wasn't making eyes at that man. For goodness' sake, Richard! I'd just been sick twice in the toilet. I certainly didn't feel like flirting – and he was only a kid anyway.'

'Prefer a man, do you?'

As he moved towards me, I flinched. Was he going to hit me again? He frowned as he saw my reaction, then took the flannel from me, touching the small abrasion on my mouth.

'Did I do that?'

'You know you did.'

'I'm sorry.' The look in his eyes told me what was on his mind. He wanted me. 'I mean it. You didn't deserve that. I shouldn't have called you a whore either. I'm sorry, Emma.'

'No, you shouldn't. I'm not like that, Richard. I know I made a mistake with him, but . . .'

He touched my hair, letting it run through his fingers. 'You know I love you, Emma. I'm not much with words, and sometimes I lose my temper – but I care about you in my way.'

Did he love me? Really love me? Perhaps in his own fashion, but he had an odd way of showing it sometimes. Maybe he would have been different if I had never been with Paul, never fallen for another man's child. I would never be sure about that, and it was too late to change things. I was his wife now. I had to make our marriage work somehow. If I could just help him to forget that I had been with another man, we might learn to be happy together.

My mother had suffered the consequences of a man's terrible jealousy. I was determined that I would not make her mistakes. Life wasn't always what we hoped it would be, but if I tried I could find a kind of happiness with Richard. It wouldn't be perfect, not the kind of loving relationship I had hoped for – but how many women found that?

'Let's just forget what happened. Be nice, Richard, that's all—'

He stopped me with a kiss. It was the kind of kiss he had given me on our wedding night, warm and tender, teasing a response from me. I was still angry and wanted to push him away, but I couldn't. My body was swaying into his, the desire swirling inside me despite my resentment at the way he had treated me earlier. I wanted him and hated him both at the same time. My betraying body was calling out for his as he swept me up in his arms, carrying me to the bed.

'You want me, Emma,' he whispered close to my ear. 'You always did but you wouldn't admit it. Don't deny it, don't fight me. I'll be good to you, I promise. I'm sorry.

Sorry I've got such a bad temper on me, but it won't happen again. I promise.'

I let myself be swept away by the passion he was so skilful at arousing in me. There were tears on my cheeks even as I heard myself cry out in pleasure.

He was lying. I knew he would hurt me whenever he was in the mood, and afterwards he would make love to me like this. I was beginning to think he actually enjoyed hurting me, humbling me: it aroused him.

Afterwards, when Richard was asleep, I rose from the bed and went to the window. I listened to the sound of the waves beating against the shore and felt the sting of humiliation.

I believed my passionate response to him was part of the reason behind his sullen moods. He blamed me for responding to his lovemaking. It was because of the child I was carrying, of course.

He had married me knowing I was carrying another man's bastard, but he would never forgive me.

Chapter Nine

'A letter came for you,' Mother said, taking it from her apron pocket. It was the morning after my home-coming, and the first time we'd had a chance to be alone. 'I put it to one side for you, Emma. The postmark is London.'

'I expect it's from Paul's cousin.' I glanced at it without real interest. 'I'll read it later.' I hadn't expected Jonathan to keep on writing now that I was married, and I wasn't sure how I felt about it. Richard wouldn't like it if he knew Paul was sending me money through his cousin.

'So how was it?' Mother gave me an anxious look. 'You seemed a bit quiet last night, love.'

'I was probably tired,' I admitted. 'I liked Yarmouth. It was nice being at the sea, but I'm glad to be home.'

Richard had been up early that morning, seemingly eager to help with the shop before he went off to work. He had been in a cheerful mood when Mother served him a cooked breakfast, and I was hoping things might be easier between us now we were home.

'Is your mouth a little swollen?' Mother asked with a frown.

'Oh, that's nothing,' I lied. 'We were acting about on the sea front the other night and Richard's ring caught me, that's all. It doesn't hurt.'

She appeared to accept the excuse. Richard had been so nice to everyone the previous evening, handing out the presents we'd bought and enthusing over the holiday. He had smiled at me a lot, and put his arm around my waist as if he really cared about me – and perhaps he did in his own way. There was no point in telling my mother that my husband had hit me; it would only upset her, and there was nothing either of us could do.

I thought about my marriage as I went down to the shop. I didn't love Richard; I wasn't exactly happy, but I wasn't as miserable as I had been when I'd first realized Paul had deserted me. If I'd never met Paul, would I have come to think of Richard as a husband in time? I'd always told my mother I didn't like him, but maybe underneath there *had* been an attraction. I supposed I had been flattered by his attentions, even though I had denied it. I had been very naive, very innocent, and I'd had to do a lot of growing up very quickly. Now that I knew what being married was all about, I had changed.

I thought about the night he had hit me, then made

love to me. It was probably because Richard had realized why I was feeling sick that he'd lashed out at me the way he had, and I couldn't blame him for being upset over the fact that I was carrying another man's child. He had married me despite it, but I couldn't expect him to welcome the idea.

Father nodded to me as I began to tidy the shop shelves, which looked as if they needed some attention. I thought his eyes held a look of satisfaction, as though he was pleased with the way things had turned out.

'That's right, Emma,' he said. 'We could do with a bit of a tidy-up. I've been too busy to bother while you were away.'

'Are you feeling better now?' I asked casually, as I would about anyone I knew who had been ill.

'Yes, thank you. It was just a bit of a stomach upset. Pity it happened at the wedding, though. I must admit I did feel queer that day.'

'You should have gone to the doctor.'

'No need.' He hesitated, giving me an odd look. 'It's nice of you to bother. No hard feelings, Emma? Richard is good to you, isn't he? I knew he was fond of you. I was right, wasn't I?'

As if he cared! It was on the tip of my tongue to tell him the truth and wipe that satisfied look off his face – but what was the point? It was too late.

'If I'd taken more notice of you in the first place it

wouldn't have happened,' I said, knowing it was the plain truth. 'I made a mistake and now I've got to live with it, haven't I?' I didn't smile at him as I spoke. I wasn't ready to forgive him for the way he'd behaved to Mum and me, but I didn't hate him. I wasn't sure why. Surely I ought to? He had never done much for me, except provide a roof over my head, but I believed he was my father and there was a part of me that wished things had been different between us. Perhaps I understood his feelings better since my marriage, because of the way my being pregnant with another man's child had affected Richard's attitude. 'I daresay I'll survive.'

He nodded, seemed as if he wanted to say more, then changed his mind. 'I'm off to the stockroom,' he said as a customer came in. 'Ben should be along later. He wanted to go to the dentist, so I let him – being as you're back.'

I served the customer with his newspaper and pipe tobacco, then went back to tidying the shelves. It was about five minutes later when the doorbell rang again and Sheila Tomms entered; she was wearing her working clothes and wore a scarf tied around her head turban-style.

'So you're back, then,' she said, giving me a strange look. 'I heard you and Richard were married.'

'Yes.' I glanced over my shoulder. The door to the stockroom was firmly shut. 'You gave us all a shock, Sheila. We thought for a while you'd been murdered.'

'So Eric told me.' Sheila grinned. 'It put the wind up him, I can tell you. He has asked me to marry him. I've told him I'll get engaged, and if he behaves himself I might marry him next spring.'

'Next spring?' I was surprised. It didn't sound as if Sheila was in any hurry.

'If you've been wondering same as the rest—' Sheila patted her stomach and laughed. 'It was a false alarm. I thought I was but I'm not.'

'Oh,' I sighed. 'Lucky you.'

'In more ways than one,' she agreed and laughed. 'Give me a quarter of those toffee pieces, Emma. So what changed your mind about Richard then?'

'My father changed it for me,' I replied, giving her a straight look. 'I'm pregnant, Sheila.'

'Is it Richard's?' Sheila's brows went up as I was silent. 'No, of course it wouldn't be. Sorry, Emma. What rotten luck. It always happens to girls like you. It was probably your first time.'

'You won't say anything? Not to anyone.'

'You know I won't. It *could* have been me. I was going to have an abortion – but then I just came on all of a sudden. You won't tell anyone else that, will you?'

'No, of course not.' I smiled. I felt closer to Sheila than before, as if the exchange of secrets had formed a bond between us. 'Richard was talking about going to the dance on Saturday. We'll perhaps see you there?'

'Well, that's one good thing about getting married,' Sheila remarked. 'Your father can't stop you going out anymore.'

'No, he can't,' I replied. I suddenly realized my life had changed for the better after all. 'I'll see you then, Sheila.'

'Righto. I'm off. I've got a new job. Starting in the canteen at the corset factory this morning. It's more money – sixteen bob a week. You want to ask your old man for a raise, Emma. You'll need money for the baby, won't you?'

'Maybe I shall ask him.'

I smiled to myself and touched the envelope in my pocket. Jonathan Reece had sent me fifty pounds this time. He said Paul was going to pay me that sum every quarter from now on. That was two hundred pounds a year! It seemed a fortune to me.

My cousin has come into a small inheritance, Jonathan had written. *Despite your marriage, it is only right he should make some contribution for the child's benefit. If you don't need the money for yourself save it for the child's future.*

I was determined to put the fifty pounds into my Post Office savings account as soon as I got the chance. My secret hoard was growing bit by bit. I wasn't sure why that gave me pleasure, because it didn't change anything. Except that I felt I had a way of escape if I really needed it.

*

I visited Gran on Wednesday afternoon as usual. I had settled back into my old routine, and apart from the fact that Richard slept in my bed at night, it was almost as if nothing had changed.

I took Gran some pipe tobacco and a tin of fudge we had brought her from Yarmouth.

'You're bearing up then,' she said, giving me a shrewd stare. 'I expected you would. You've got backbone, Emma. No matter what comes, you'll cope – in your own way.'

'I've been sick again this morning,' I answered, deliberately misunderstanding the questioning look. 'Can you recommend anything to help?'

'I've something ready for you.' She nodded towards a small, dark bottle on the sideboard. 'It won't stop the sickness, but it will make you feel better in yourself. When your time comes, I'll give you something to ease the birth, lass – and meantime, I'm always here for you. If you're worried about anything, just come and tell me.'

'Thank you.' I kissed her gratefully. 'I do love you, Gran.'

'Humph!' She nodded, her eyes seeming to see what she hadn't been told. 'Make the best of things, Emma. Once you've had the child, life will seem brighter. Children bring love with them, if you let them.'

'Oh, I want my baby,' I assured her and smiled. 'I can't wait to start making clothes – though I suppose

I'd better not buy anything just yet or the tongues will start wagging.'

'You won't stop that,' Gran said. 'I've cut out a few patterns from old magazines for you. If you buy lemon wool you can say it's for a cardigan for yourself.'

'Yes, I suppose I could.' I felt a warm glow all of a sudden. In a way I was lucky. Richard was being nice at the moment, and I couldn't really complain. 'I'm not sorry about the baby. I just wish Paul had really wanted to marry me, that's all. It made me feel used when he just went off without letting me know . . . as if he had never cared.'

'No use crying over spilt milk, girl.'

'No, of course not. I've got over him now, Gran.' I laughed as her old, knowing eyes narrowed in suspicion. 'Really, I mean it. It doesn't hurt half as much as it did. Perhaps I wasn't in love with him at all. And Richard isn't too bad.'

'If you'd had more freedom, you wouldn't have been so easily taken in,' she said. 'It was Harold's fault for keeping you almost a prisoner. No doubt he thought he was doing right by you, but it made you restless. You just tumbled into the arms of the first man who made the effort to get you alone. And he was a charmer, make no mistake about it, Emma. You won't have been the only one to have been deceived, mark my words.'

'I think you may be right,' I agreed. 'His mother said

something to me the day I went there. I think perhaps there was another girl in the same kind of trouble. That makes him a bit of a rotter, doesn't it?'

I was thoughtful as I walked home later that afternoon. I had certainly let myself be misled by Paul, but perhaps it had been inevitable, just as Gran had said. The idea made me feel better about myself, not quite so much of a fool.

My spirits began to lift again. I'd made a mistake, but it wasn't the end of the world. I'd longed for children, and I was having my own; that couldn't be so bad, could it? Maybe I would buy some lemon and some white wool. Mrs Henty sold knitting wool; I could always pretend I was making a striped jumper for myself.

It would give me something to do in the evenings when Richard went off to the pub, as he had every night since our return from Yarmouth. He only stayed for an hour or so, and I didn't think he drank all that much; most men I knew did much the same, though some took their wives with them.

'A man needs a drink with his mates after a hard day's work,' he'd told me when he left me for the first time.

I hadn't argued. I didn't like being in pubs much, and was relieved he hadn't insisted I go with him. It was far more comfortable staying at home with my mother.

'We'll go out at weekends,' Richard had promised. 'To the dance one Saturday, pictures the next.'

I agreed and kissed him on the cheek. As long as Richard didn't turn nasty the way he had in Yarmouth, it was enough to satisfy me. Especially as my father seemed to have lost any desire to interfere in my life. Apparently, I was no longer his concern.

I accepted the port and lemon Richard bought me at the dance, thanking him without comment. I was feeling very much better now that I was taking Gran's herbal tonic regularly. It didn't stop me being sick, but I wasn't as drained afterwards, and my old energy had returned.

I sipped my drink, content to watch the other dancers. Richard had already danced with me twice, but he was on his third glass of beer. He seemed determined to make quite a night of it.

'Saturday night is the best of the week,' he'd told me. 'I don't have to work tomorrow.'

I watched as he finished his drink and went off to join the queue at the bar. Surely he wasn't going to get drunk, was he? Richard wasn't too bad sober, but I still dreaded the nights when he'd had too much – though to be honest, he hadn't been violent since that night on our honeymoon.

I glanced round as someone sat down on the chair next to me. It was Sheila, wearing a very pretty blue-and-white spotted dress with full skirts, wide shoulder straps

Rosie Clarke

and a squared neckline. She had a thin white wool shawl over her arms and looked smart. Obviously, she'd treated herself to a new dress.

'Enjoying yourself then?' she asked.

'Yes, I suppose so.'

'You don't sound too sure.'

'I don't like the smoke in here much. It makes my throat sore.'

'And you work for a man who sells cigarettes!'

'I know.' I laughed. 'How are you getting on at the factory?'

'It's all right. It'll do until I find something better. I wouldn't mind working in a shop, but it isn't easy to find that sort of work round here. Perhaps I should have stayed in London with my cousin.'

'Is that where you were?'

I wasn't to receive an answer that evening, because we were joined first by Richard and then by Eric, both of them carrying drinks for themselves as well as us.

'Drink up, Emma,' Richard said, winking at the other man. 'Got to get you in a good mood for later.'

I knew better than to argue, finishing my drink in silence.

'Eric and I are engaged,' Sheila said, and flashed her hand at us. Her ring was a gold band set with five garnets and three pearls in a row. 'We haven't set a date for the wedding yet, but it will probably be in the spring.'

189

'Eric was just telling me,' Richard said. 'Congratulations. I hope you'll both be as happy as you deserve.'

I thought there was something odd about the way he looked at Sheila, but I didn't make much of it, because Eric was holding out his hand to me.

'Dance with me?' he asked. 'Richard won't mind, will you?'

'Course not,' Richard replied affably. 'Go on, Emma. You'll be safe with Eric.'

I went without further urging. I was learning not to argue with my husband. If I did what he asked and kept my mouth shut he seemed prepared to let me do much as I liked. He just couldn't stand being answered back.

I danced with Sheila's fiancé. He was a pleasant, easy-going man with a nice smile, and he smelled of scented hair oil. I was sorry when our dance ended. He led me back to our seats; Sheila got up at once and took his hand. Her face was expressionless, but I sensed something. Richard was frowning. He looked at me as I sat down.

'I'm having another drink. What about you?'

'I've still got one,' I said. 'Could we dance again, Richard?'

'In a minute,' he said, and there was a hint of belligerence in his manner, as if he were angry about something. I wondered if Sheila had said something to upset him. 'I'll get another beer first.'

We did dance again before Richard suggested we leave. I wasn't sure how many drinks he'd had, but I sensed he was almost drunk, though he could walk well enough. Not wanting to provoke him, I was quiet as we made our way home.

My parents were already in bed. I locked the back door and bolted it, then followed Richard up to our own bedroom. He seemed to be having difficulty in unbuttoning his shirt.

'Can I help?' I asked.

Richard focused his bleary gaze on me. 'What are you staring at?' he muttered. 'I'm not drunk, so don't look at me like that.'

'I wasn't staring.'

'Liar,' he said. 'You're like all the rest of them. Always nagging. Every time a man has a drink.' I picked up my nightgown and turned to leave. He caught my arm. 'Where the hell do you think you're going?'

'I need a wash.'

He glared at me. I tensed, thinking he was about to hit me, then all at once his hand dropped, as if he felt too tired – or too drunk – to bother. I left quickly, before he could change his mind.

In the bathroom, I took my time. I washed all over and changed into my nightgown, then brushed my hair for several minutes. Reluctantly, I returned to the bedroom, wondering what kind of a mood my husband would be in now. I hated it when he was in one of his sullen moods. He could be almost tender towards me at times, but he could also be a brute.

To my relief, Richard had fallen asleep. I lifted the covers and eased in beside him. He didn't move, his breathing telling me he was deep in slumber. I settled down beside him.

I was learning how to manage him now, I thought. Most of the time he was easy enough to please. Drinking obviously didn't suit him, but I would just have to hope it didn't happen too often.

'Your father is late coming up for his tea,' Mother said, glancing anxiously at the mantle clock in the parlour. 'It's shepherd's pie this evening, so it won't hurt for a while. He likes the top nice and crispy, but all the same, I don't want it to spoil.'

'I'll go down and see what's keeping him,' I offered, laying my knitting on the settee beside me.

Nearly three weeks had passed since our return from the honeymoon. I'd almost completed my second coat for the baby, but I was careful not to let Richard see me knitting. Any reference to the child I was carrying was sufficient to put him in an awkward mood, and Richard's moods were worse than Father's – though of late there had been little to choose between them.

Leaving Mother listening to music on the wireless, I

went out into the hall. I was in time to see my Father standing halfway up the stairs, bent almost double with what was obviously severe pain.

'Father!' I cried. 'You're ill. Let me help you.'

'No, no,' he muttered, lifting his head to glare at me. 'I can manage. Get on down to the shop, Emma – and don't fuss.'

'Will you let me send Ben for the doctor?'

He hesitated, then shook his head. 'Not yet. If I'm no better by the time you close up, I'll think about it.'

I was shocked by the look of his complexion. His skin was an odd colour, sort of yellowish-grey, and I thought he must be feeling very ill. What was wrong with him? I hadn't seen him in this much pain before.

The shop was busy when I got there. Both Ben and I were serving customers almost non-stop until well past seven-thirty. Father had not returned by the time I sent Ben home and locked up for the night.

I made sure all the lights were off, then went upstairs to be met by my mother, who looked worried.

'He's been sick three times,' she said, 'and he didn't touch his supper.'

'I think we should have the doctor, Mum.'

'So do I,' she agreed, 'but he won't hear of it. Every time I speak to him, he shouts at me.'

'I know,' I said, feeling sad that she had had such a rotten life. It wasn't her fault and yet it wasn't all my father's. I suspected that they had both hurt each other, the little slights and grievances building up over the years until they had reached a state where there was only harsh feeling between them. 'Is he in bed?'

'Lying on top of it, I think.'

'I'll talk to him. See if I can persuade him to see sense.'

'Would you? I'm really very worried, Emma.'

I thought she looked frightened.

I knocked on the bedroom door, then entered. Father was lying with his eyes closed, but even as I hesitated, he rolled over and grabbed at a bowl. He made a fearful retching sound and brought up a brownish bile, which smelt awful.

'I'll empty that and bring it back.' I took the bowl from him, went across the hall and rinsed it down the toilet, then returned with it and a damp flannel. 'Wipe your mouth,' I said. 'I'll get you a little cold water to rinse your mouth, but I shouldn't swallow if I were you.'

He accepted the flannel and the water, but in another minute he was vomiting again.

'I'm getting the doctor,' I said decisively, leaving before he could argue.

I stopped only to put on my jacket, before running down the stairs and letting myself out of the back door. It was chilly out, but I ran so fast I didn't feel it.

Fortunately, the doctor's house was only two streets away. Having come from attending a difficult childbirth,

Doctor Barton had just finished his own dinner. He listened attentively to my story, gave it as his opinion that something Father had eaten had disagreed with him, and told me not to worry.

'He has hardly eaten anything for days,' I said. 'Please, you must come. I think he might be dying.'

'Very well.' The doctor was reluctant to leave the comfort of his own parlour, but my very real fear decided him that it was his duty. 'I'm sure you are worrying for nothing, my dear – but I shall come.'

Ten minutes later, he was standing by Father's bedside, shaking his head and looking serious.

'You should have sent for me before this,' he said. He took Father's pulse, then examined his tongue. 'This is either an ulcer or your liver, sir. Tell me, how long have you been having the pain?'

'Months – years,' Father said, grimacing. 'But not like this. I thought it was indigestion.'

'More likely an ulcer then,' Doctor Barton said. 'You should be very careful what you eat from now on, Mr Robinson. No spicy foods for you, I'm afraid. Milk and bread – perhaps a raw egg beaten into some milk at night to settle your stomach. Nothing cooked in the frying pan. I'll give Emma a prescription.' He wrote something on his pad and tore it off. 'This should help ease the pain for now – but I should like you to go into hospital as soon as possible. Tests would help establish the cause of your pain.'

'No hospitals,' Father said and bit back a groan. 'It's my own fault for overeating. I'll take that stuff of yours and stick to a diet in future.'

'Harold has always been a martyr to his stomach,' Mother said from the doorway. She looked at him doubtfully. 'Perhaps you should go to hospital – just for some tests, dear.'

'Damn you, no!' he muttered. 'It's already easing. I shall be better soon. Thank you for coming, doctor – but there was really no need.'

'I believe you have an ulcer,' the doctor said. 'If you are wise, sir, you will rest as much as possible – and stick to a diet for several weeks. Then come and see me.'

'I'll see you out,' I said, following him quickly from the room. I could hear my father's voice complaining loudly as we went downstairs.

'How is he really?' I asked before unlocking the shop door to let Doctor Barton out the front way. 'Is it serious?'

'It might be,' he said. 'There's something about his colour I don't like. I can't place it – but it's not right.'

'Is he going to die?'

'I shouldn't think so – not if he's sensible. Unless there's internal bleeding. Did you notice blood in his vomit?'

'No.' I was decisive. 'I'm sure I would have noticed. It was just foul-smelling brown stuff.'

'Then it may not be too serious. Try not to worry, my dear. Send for me if you need me.'

'Thank you.'

I locked the door after him. I was thoughtful as I went out of the back way, walking through the dimly lit streets to the chemist shop in the next road. I had to pass the Cock Inn to reach it, and a burst of noisy laughter from inside made me scurry by.

What had caused Father's sickness? He certainly hadn't been eating too much recently, despite his claims to have done so. Could it possibly be the tablets he dosed himself with regularly? I was sure he hadn't mentioned them to the doctor. He wouldn't have wanted him to know about those, of course. Nor was he likely to visit the hospital. He would probably be annoyed with me for fetching the doctor at all.

I was relieved to find the chemist still open. I handed over the doctor's prescription, waited while it was prepared, and paid for it. Going back outside, I stood for a moment looking about me.

Across the street, a man had caught hold of a woman's arm and was swinging her round to face him. They appeared to be having an argument. As they moved into the light of an inadequate street lamp, I felt a shock of surprise. The man was my husband – and the woman was Sheila.

Before I'd time to digest this, Sheila struck him a sharp blow on the face and ran off. I thought he was about to follow until some instinct made him glance across the street. He looked thunderstruck as he saw me standing there.

'Emma?' He came towards me, his manner half angry, half wary. 'What are you doing here?'

'Father was taken ill,' I said. 'I had to fetch the doctor – and this.' I showed him the medicine. 'Were you having an argument with Sheila?'

'She's a fool!' Richard said, and now he looked scornful. 'Eric is ready to marry her, yet she still can't leave the men alone. She was with some gypsy in the pub just now. Can you imagine that? I told her she was asking for trouble. If Eric heard he would drop her faster than she can drop her knickers!'

'Richard!' I cried, disliking his coarseness. 'That isn't a very nice thing to say.'

'It's the truth,' he said, falling into step beside me as I began to walk home. 'Oh, I know you like her, Emma – but she's a whore. There's no getting away from it.' He glanced at me sideways, as if to reassure himself that I had believed him. 'What's wrong with Harold then?'

'He was being sick and in a lot of pain. The doctor says he may have an ulcer. He ought to go into hospital for tests, but you know my father.'

'He won't go,' Richard said. 'I don't know as I blame him. Those places kill as many as they cure.'

'Of course they don't!'

'What would you know? Ever been to one?'

'No, but—' I was silenced as I saw the expression on his face. 'But they're supposed to help people, aren't they?'

'My grandfather went in for tests, caught some disease or other and died,' Richard said. 'And he isn't the only one. No, it's best Harold stays home with you and your mother to look after him.'

'I suppose so,' I agreed reluctantly, wondering why he seemed so set on persuading me. 'He wouldn't go anyway.'

'There you are then,' Richard said, and looked at me. 'Fancy a drink before we go home?'

'I'd better take this back,' I replied, 'but you go if you want, Richard.'

'Perhaps I will,' he said. 'Don't wait up for me. I might be late. It's my mate's birthday. I promised I'd help him celebrate.'

'Oh . . . all right.'

I hurried on as Richard turned towards the pub. I didn't mind him going – as long as he wasn't drunk when he came in.

Richard had drunk more than usual, but not enough to fall asleep as soon as he got into bed. I was sleeping, but that didn't prevent him from reaching for me.

'Wake up,' he muttered against my ear. 'I want you. Damn you, Emma! I know you're only pretending.'

I came back from the depths to discover Richard was already on top of me. I protested tiredly, but he ignored me, taking me without bothering to kiss or arouse me. It was painful and made me weep bitter tears after he had finished.

Why did he have to do this? Was he punishing me? Every time I made up my mind to try harder in this marriage, he did something that sent me sliding all the way down to the floor again. I wanted to feel tenderness for him. Sometimes, I persuaded myself that I did love him in a way, but then he did something like this and I wondered if it was worth the effort.

Richard was soon snoring. Or pretending to, I thought angrily. I got up and went into the bathroom, washing myself all over in an attempt to wash away my feelings of having been used.

He had never been this cruel before. I came close to hating my husband in that moment. If he had been kind to me, I might have learned to love him, or at least to be content with my lot – but now I was beginning to think it was impossible.

'What's the matter? You've been crying.'

I met my mother in the hall. My eyes were red from weeping, and there was no point in trying to hide it, though I didn't answer at once.

'Is Father worse?'

'No. That medicine helped,' she said. 'He's sleeping

at the moment, but I couldn't rest. I'm having a cup of tea – want one?'

'Yes, please.'

Anything to delay the moment I had to go back in that room.

We went into the kitchen together. I watched as Mother put the kettle on the gas, leaving off the whistle. How often had she done that in the past? I had known nothing about her restless nights then, but now I had a reason to be restless myself.

We smiled at each other, moving softly so as not to make a noise. We were like two conspirators, I thought, not wanting to wake the men.

'Was Richard drunk?' Mother asked. 'I heard him come in late and I wondered.'

'He'd had more than usual – but not enough. When he's drunk he falls asleep before—' I blushed. 'It isn't always like that. He can be almost tender, if he wants . . .'

'Oh, Emma,' she sighed, reading between the lines. 'Harold was just the same. I was hoping it would be different for you.'

'It's my own fault.'

'No, it isn't,' she denied. 'Your father made you marry him. Gran was right. He isn't the one for you. I'm sorry, love. Sorry I went along with it.'

'You couldn't have known. Besides – what else could I do?'

'You should have run away. Why don't you go now, Emma?'

'And leave you here? Have you forgotten what Father threatened?'

'It's different now. He's too ill to follow you. You could be free to live as you wish.'

Her words made me feel wistful, made me long for something more than I had – than I would ever have. Yet I knew it was a forlorn hope.

'I won't go without you. Besides, I'm married. It's too late, Mum. I have to make the best of things.' *However bad they are sometimes.*

'Maybe Richard would give you a divorce.'

'I doubt it.' I pulled a face. 'He likes living here. It suits him. Sheila warned me he would get his feet under the table if he could. I think he and Father . . . I'm not sure, but I think there's some arrangement between them.'

'Richard doesn't pay any rent,' Mother said. 'I know that much. That's probably why he has more to spend on drink these days.'

'Yes, perhaps.' I thought there might be more to it, but wasn't sure. 'Anyway, we couldn't go – not while Father is ill. Who would see to the shop? We couldn't just desert him, despite what he said that night. You know we couldn't, Mum.'

'No.' She looked thoughtful. 'It might be best to stick it out a bit longer – if you can manage?'

'I shall have to,' I replied, a note of bitterness mixed with anger in my voice. 'I married him. In any case, he'll probably apologise tomorrow and buy me a present.'

'Don't be bitter, love.' Mother gave me a quick hug. 'Things will get better, I promise.'

'Perhaps.' I smiled suddenly. 'Yes, of course they will, Mum. When I've had the baby. Richard is jealous. Sometimes I think . . . he hates the idea of it being Paul's.' I placed a protective hand on my stomach. 'He promised it didn't matter, but it does. I suppose it always will – just the same as you and Dad. You can't really blame either of them. Richard does care about me, in his way.'

If I didn't believe that I wouldn't be able to bear my life!

'Yes. Perhaps that's all it is,' she said. 'Maybe he will get over it. If not . . .'

'There's not much I can do, is there?'

'Let's see what happens.' She touched my cheek. 'Just as long as he doesn't hurt you.'

'He won't,' I said. 'Not while Father is alive. It's the money, you see. I think that's a part of the reason why he married me. He likes the idea of there being money in the family.'

'What money?' She looked disgusted. 'If there is any I haven't been able to find it. Harold has a few pounds in the bank, and the shop, but that's all.'

'There must be more,' I said. 'I don't know what he

does with it, Mum – but I know the shop makes a good profit. He takes the money out, but where he puts it—' I shrugged my shoulders. 'Not that it matters. I don't care about the money. I've sometimes thought about leaving. It might be safer for me and the baby.'

'You can't think he would hurt the baby?' She looked at me in horror. 'He isn't that bad, is he?'

'No, not all the time,' I said and shook my head. 'No, of course he isn't, Mum. I'm just feeling down. Sometimes I feel things aren't too bad – then I get miserable and wish I could run away.'

'I know just how you feel, love. It was that way for me for years. When Harold was nice, I enjoyed being his wife. I was proud of his business sense. Then he would think I was looking at a man and he would be furious. I used to lie in bed at night and wish I could go off somewhere, but I wasn't brave enough. I couldn't go and neither can you.' An odd look was in her eyes. 'Not yet. Don't despair, love. It won't always be this bad, I promise you.'

How could Mother say that? I wondered as I washed the cups and went back to bed. Richard was snoring loudly now. I looked at him with a growing disgust. I had tried hard to come to terms with being his wife. I had almost convinced myself that I was happy – but I was lying. Richard could be nice one day and cruel the next. He seemed as if he was driven by a demon – perhaps his jealousy – when the drink got into him. He said he cared for me, but he hated me too. And he wanted to punish me. What sort of a life was that for any woman?

What sort of a woman was I if I let him get away with treating me like dirt? At first I had responded to his lovemaking, but now I was beginning to dread the moment he reached for me. I longed for freedom – for the right to choose whether or not I wanted to make love.

One day I was going to be independent. One day I would have money of my own: I would be in a position to look after myself. And I would never marry again . . .

What was I thinking? I was married. I was trapped and there was no way out for me as far as I could see, no matter what my mother said to comfort me.

Richard brought flowers home the next evening. He looked awkward as he gave them to me, but didn't apologise. 'I was thinking we might go somewhere for your birthday,' he said. 'Perhaps to London? We could see a show and do some shopping.'

I stared at him, not quite sure how to react to this suggestion. My birthday was two weeks away. I'd never been to London, and the idea itself appealed to me.

'I'd like that,' I said, deciding to take him at face value. 'Thank you for thinking of it – but it depends how Father is by then.'

'He'll be all right,' Richard replied. 'It was just a bad attack of his stomach trouble, that's all.'

'Perhaps,' I agreed, though not convinced he was right. There was no real reason why I should care what my father felt, but somehow I did. Maybe the old folk are right when they say blood is thicker than water – or perhaps it was because Father was very different with me these days.

Had ill health made him look at things in a new light? Gran always said that the approach of death was a great leveller.

'It makes folk think, lass,' she had once told me. 'It's not good to go with too much bad feeling left behind.'

Sometimes I saw a look in my father's eyes that I thought was wistful, as though he wished he could turn back the clock.

After a couple of days' rest, during which Father left me to manage the shop alone, he did seem better. His illness had taken something out of him, though, and his manner had continued to soften towards me, losing its old harshness. He often smiled at me now and didn't grumble about me fetching the doctor, even going so far as to thank me for my concern and insisting I let Richard take me to London for my birthday.

'Well . . . if you're sure you can manage?' I looked at him doubtfully. 'I don't want to leave you in the lurch if you're ill.'

He made no reply, but seemed thoughtful. On the

morning we were due to leave for London, he gave me
an envelope with twenty pounds inside.

'It's for your birthday,' he said sheepishly. 'And you'll
be needing things – for yourself and the baby.'

'Thank you.' I was so surprised I hardly knew what to
say. 'It's a lot of money, Father.'

'You're a good girl, Emma. Always have been.' Unable
to meet my gaze, he lowered his own. 'I don't blame you
for what happened, despite the things I've said. I'd just
like to get my hands on the swine who did it to you. Your
mother should never have harboured him here. That sort
are never to be trusted. If she hadn't invited him to tea—'

'It might still have happened. I would have met him
somehow. I was in love with him, no matter what he was.'

I gave him a straight look. Clearly he had decided
to forgive me, but not my mother. The breach between
them had gone too deep to be mended.

It made me feel sad – and once again I decided to try
and patch things up with Richard. He didn't deserve that
I should, but divorce wasn't easy. If only I could wipe out
the hurt in my husband's mind, things might improve.

I would never love Richard, but there must be lots
of women who endured similar marriages. I would just
have to live with it somehow. What else could I do?

Chapter Ten

London amazed me. I'd never imagined it could be so large and noisy. We travelled up on the early train, disembarked amongst the crowds of people flowing in and out of Liverpool Street station, took a bus to Marble Arch, which gave me an opportunity to stare in wonder at the sights, and then spent two hours walking along Oxford and Regent Street. The pavements thronged with people, all of whom seemed to be in a hurry, and crossing the road was a terrifying experience – but I loved the shops.

'What do you want to do now?' Richard asked after we'd had a proper three-course lunch in a smart restaurant. 'We could go to the waxworks if you like – or the zoo? Or would you prefer more shops?'

'More shops, please,' I said. I'd been too bewildered by the choices offered to buy anything that morning, but now I'd made up my mind. 'I think I would like to buy that red wool dress I looked at this morning.'

'I'll buy it for your birthday,' he offered. He looked almost excited at that moment, and I saw the man he might have been if his mind hadn't been soured by bitterness. 'I wasn't sure what to get.'

Richard's moods swung between wanting to please me, and wanting to punish me for not loving him . . . for having let another man touch me.

'You're already paying for all this . . . the theatre and everything. Besides, Father gave me some money.'

'You keep it,' Richard said. 'I'll get you the dress. I want to, Emma. I know I'm a bit of a brute sometimes, but I do love you.' For a moment he looked as though he really meant it.

It was as close to an apology as I was going to get. I smiled and tucked my arm through his, wanting to be fair to him.

'All right,' I said. 'I can buy some shoes to go with it, can't I?'

He grinned at me. 'Come on,' he said. 'Let's go mad for once. It'll be a long while before we can do this again.'

We plunged into an orgy of spending, buying not only my dress and shoes, but also a shirt for Richard, leather gloves for Mother, a tie for Father and a warm winter scarf for Gran. Emerging into the coolness of late afternoon, our arms full of parcels, we paused on the pavement and looked for a bus to take us to the hotel Richard had booked for the night.

'Damn it, we'll take a taxi,' he said. 'If we don't get a move on, we'll be late for the theatre.'

I wasn't really listening. My eye had been caught by a large and expensive car which had just pulled into the kerb. I thought it looked a bit like the one Paul had sometimes driven, only newer, and as the driver got out I saw he was an older man, perhaps fortyish. He was smiling at a very smartly dressed woman, who had also been on a shopping spree judging by the amount of parcels she was carrying.

As I watched, I saw the woman suddenly stagger and start to fall. Some instinct had already alerted me and I dropped my parcels, darting forward to catch her. Because I had acted so swiftly, I was able to grab hold of the woman's arm and support her, preventing her collapse.

'Margaret!' I heard the man's anxious voice. 'Are you all right? What happened?'

'I think she nearly fainted,' I said. The woman was moaning softly, her own parcels scattered on the pavement. 'She needs to sit down.'

'Thank you. Let me have her now. My wife hasn't been well, but I didn't expect this.'

The man put his arm about his wife, helped her to the car, and settled her in the passenger seat. She seemed to come round, though was obviously still unwell. I bent to gather the parcels she had dropped and took them to the car. After making sure his wife was comfortable, the man turned to me and took the parcels from me.

'You are very kind,' he said. 'My wife could have had a nasty fall if you had not been so quick to help her.'

'I'm glad I noticed her,' I replied, smiling at him. 'I hope she will be all right now.'

'We shall have to see what the doctor says about this.' There was an anxious expression in his eyes, which were a blueish-grey and seemed kind. 'Thank you again for helping her.'

I shook my head and turned away as Richard came up to us, having gathered up the parcels I had dropped.

'Is she all right?' he asked, with a cursory glance at the woman. 'Good thing you saw her. I didn't notice. Come on, I've got a taxi waiting.'

About to follow him, I felt a touch on my arm. I looked back at the man whose wife I'd helped, and saw he was offering me his business card.

'I'm Solomon Gould,' he said, his eyes meeting mine for just one second. 'If I can ever do anything for you, please get in touch.'

Richard was looking for me impatiently. I nodded, took the card and slipped it into my jacket pocket. Richard scowled at me as I climbed into the back of the taxi.

'What did he give you? If it was money, you shouldn't have taken it.'

'It wasn't, and I wouldn't have,' I replied, annoyed that

he could even think it. 'He gave me his business card.'

'Whatever for?'

'In case he could ever do anything for me, that's what he said. I expect he was just grateful, and didn't know what to say.'

'Looked like he had plenty of money,' Richard observed with a twist of his mouth. 'He'll forget you by next week, Emma. Throw the card away. You don't want anything from his sort.'

I made no comment. Why was Richard so touchy over it? I knew it was just an instinctive reaction on the part of Mr Gould. He must have realized I would be insulted by an offer of money, but felt he wanted to show his gratitude. I had no intention of ever using the card, but thought it nice of him just the same.

'Yes, all right,' I said. 'I'm hungry – and I want a cup of tea.'

Richard nodded, relaxing again. I wondered if he had noticed the car was very like Paul's. Perhaps that was what had caused his jealous mood – or was there something more?

'I'm looking forward to the show this evening,' I said and smiled at him. 'This is the best birthday I've ever had, Richard. You were good to think of it.'

His frown lifted. 'Good. I'm glad. I want you to enjoy yourself.'

*

The show was even better than those Richard had taken me to on our honeymoon. I giggled over the comedian's jokes, marvelled at the ventriloquist and jugglers, and was enraptured by the beautiful voice of the young female singer's rendition of Cole Porter's *Anything Goes*.

Afterwards, Richard took me out to supper. He had a couple of beers, but wasn't in the least drunk when he made love to me later at our hotel. I let him do what he liked, but didn't respond. It didn't seem to matter, because he just turned over and went to sleep when he'd finished, seemingly satisfied.

Afterwards, I lay awake, staring into the darkness for a long time. This couldn't be all there was to life. Surely there had to be something more?

I recalled the look of concern in the man's eyes as he'd helped his wife into his car. It had been obvious to me that Mr Gould loved his wife very much. He had been so concerned for her, so considerate and gentle. I felt a pang of envy. It must be nice to be loved like that.

I slipped out of bed and went over to the window, looking out over the roofs of the buildings around the hotel. Then, on impulse, I took the small white business card from my jacket pocket and read the inscription.

Solomon Gould. Clothing Manufacturer.

Just that and a business address in the Portobello Road. I replaced the card. Why should I throw it away? I would never use it, of course, but would keep it as a kind

213

of talisman: to remind me there was another way of life.

Perhaps one day . . .

'Emma, what are you doing?'

Richard's voice startled me, making me jump.

'Just getting my dressing gown,' I said. 'I need to go to the bathroom.'

'Take your key then,' he muttered, a note of irritation in his voice. 'Remember it's down the hall to the right – and don't get lost.'

'No, I won't,' I promised.

Tears stung my eyes as I found my way to the bathroom. There must be another way to live, and one day I would find it.

'He was taken bad again in the night,' Mother said one morning, some weeks after the trip to London. She looked at me anxiously. 'I wanted to send for the doctor, but he won't let me. He says he'll stay in bed today though.'

'I'll get down to the shop then,' I said. 'This is the third time he's been really bad, Mum. We really ought to have the doctor.'

'Wait for a bit,' she advised. 'Last time he was better after a few hours – and you know what he's like about doctors.'

'Yes, I do.'

I left her and went down to open the shop. I didn't mind that Father was leaving things more and more to me these days, even though I was beginning to feel the baby now. I was more than four months gone and had started to show, though the loose overall I wore in the shop disguised it for the time being.

'Hello, Emma,' Sheila Tomms said. She was first in after the door was unlocked and was stamping her feet with the cold. 'I reckon it's nearly cold enough for snow. Can I have some toffee pieces please – and I'll have this.' She picked up a copy of *Woman,* then studied me with interest. 'You look a bit pale. Are you all right?'

'I was thinking about my father,' I replied. 'He's been ill again. He's resting today.'

'So you've got to do everything?' Sheila pulled a sympathetic face. 'If you need any help, I could always come in for half an hour before I go to work.'

I smiled at her. I still liked Sheila, despite what Richard said about her being a whore, but I knew neither my husband or my father would tolerate her working in the shop.

'That's kind of you,' I said. 'But I can manage for the moment. If I need help later—' I patted my stomach. 'I'll ask when the time comes.'

'Yes, that might make things awkward.' Sheila looked round the shop. 'I wouldn't mind working here.'

Father would never allow it, of course, but I wasn't going to insult my friend by saying so.

'I expect my father will be better soon.'

'Let's hope so.' Sheila frowned. 'You wouldn't want anything to happen to him. If Richard got his hands on the money he'd soon drink it away.' She laughed as she saw my face. 'Sorry! I shouldn't have said it – but Eric told me he was drinking too much. Something was said about it at work. You ought to stop him, Emma. He only used to do it at weekends, but he's doing it more now.'

'I know – but I can't stop him.'

I dreaded the nights when Richard came home from a heavy drinking bout, and they had happened more often in the weeks since our visit to London. I stayed up for him now, shutting myself in the bathroom until I thought he might be asleep. Quite often he was, but sometimes he was waiting for me; it was those times that made me regret my marriage.

'No, I don't suppose you can,' Sheila said. 'I ought to have warned you before it was too late. I always knew he could be nasty when he'd had a few.'

'You weren't here,' I reminded her. 'And it wouldn't have made any difference.'

'No—' She hesitated, seemed about to say something, then changed her mind as the shop bell rang. 'See you later,' she said, smiled and went out.

I served the next customer, then got on with my work. It was a busy morning and I was beginning to long for a sit-down when the door opened and a man came in. I stared at him in surprise, my breath catching as he smiled and handed me a bunch of dark crimson chrysanthemums.

'Hello, Miss Robinson,' he said, then laughed at his mistake. 'Sorry. It's Mrs Gillows now, isn't it?'

'Emma,' I replied. 'Are the flowers for me? How lovely. It's very kind of you.'

'I thought you might like them,' Jonathan said, seeming almost bashful. 'You look beautiful. Having a baby obviously suits you. I hope you don't mind my calling? I was in the district and decided I would call to see how you were.'

'I'm very well, thank you.' I held the flowers to my nose, inhaling their strong scent. 'I love these. Especially the big ones.' My eyes met his shyly. 'Did you get my letter? It was good of you to send me that money.'

'It's less than you deserve,' he said, looking at me in a way that made me blush and avoid his eyes. 'I'm sorry I didn't come before, when I said I would.'

'Your letter explained,' I replied. 'You couldn't leave your aunt at a time like that. I understood, of course I did.'

'Are you happy, Emma?'

The door of the shop opened. A customer came in. Jonathan waited while I served him, pretending interest in a row of birthday cards on the shelf, then we were alone again.

'Are you all right?' he asked. 'Do you need anything? Is there anything I can do for you?'

'I'm fine,' I lied, wondering why his concern for me made my eyes sting. He was so kind . . . a little like I'd imagined Mr Gould to be. 'I'm very grateful for all you've done for me.'

'If there is ever anything—' He broke off as Ben came in from the stockroom at the back of the shop. 'Anything at all.'

'Yes, I'll remember.' I gave him a bright smile. 'Thank you for these, and for coming.'

'I've had my dinner,' Ben announced. 'You can get off for yours if you like. I'll serve this gentleman.'

'Oh yes,' Jonathan said. 'I'll have a paper, thank you.' His eyes met mine as he offered the exact change. 'Goodbye.'

I took the money, holding it in my hand until he'd left the shop. Then I slipped the coins into the till, picked up my flowers and went upstairs.

'They're nice,' Mother remarked as she took them into the kitchen and filled a vase with water.

'Yes – a customer brought them for Father.'

I wasn't sure why I'd lied, but I didn't want to tell anyone the truth, even my mother.

'I'll take them in and show him,' Mother said, then changed her mind. 'No – you do it, Emma. I'll put your dinner on the table.'

I showed the flowers to my father, but he wasn't interested enough to ask who had sent them. He nodded and told me to take them away, because he didn't like the smell.

'Is there anything you want?' I asked.

'You could fetch me my tablets,' he said. 'A blue box in the top drawer of the chest in the stockroom.'

'Should you be taking them as well as the doctor's medicine?'

'That stuff is useless,' he grumbled. 'Fetch my pills, there's a good girl.'

I gave up and went to do his bidding immediately. There was no point in upsetting him. I opened the drawer of the chest, discovering that all the old boxes and bottles had gone. Only one box of tablets for indigestion remained right at the back of the drawer. As I reached for it a glimmer of something bright caught my eye. I moved a sheaf of old bills and saw the gold sovereign lying there. Picking it up, I turned it over in wonder. It looked new, pristine.

What on earth was it doing in the drawer? I was unsure whether to leave it there or take it to my father. Surely he couldn't have meant to leave it there?

After a moment's thought, I replaced it at the back of the drawer, but when I returned to the bedroom with the tablets, I mentioned it to my father.

He gave me a long, hard look, then grunted. 'It was given to me by someone,' he said, and somehow I knew he was lying. 'I must have mislaid it. Put it back, did you?'

'Yes, Father. I just thought you should know it was there.'

'Good. I'll see to it another day.'

'I could bring it up if you like?'

'No, leave it. I'll attend to it.'

I nodded assent, turning as my mother called that dinner was ready.

'You're a good girl, Emma. I was wrong to disown you. You're my daughter – whether you're my blood or not.'

The implication was clear. He was telling me I meant something to him, even if my mother didn't. I went out without saying anything, a lump in my throat.

Why couldn't he have been kinder to me before this? We might all have been happy together. It had been such a waste, of his life and ours. I felt the sting of tears I refused to shed. I wasn't going to cry, not for him and not for myself.

The next few weeks were tiring for me and my mother. Father's illness seemed to be gaining on him little by little. Some days he would appear to rally, and he even went down to the shop a couple of times, but didn't stop long. He wasn't always sick now, but his body was getting weaker and his eyes looked dull.

I sensed my father was seriously ill. I went into his room to see him every morning, dinner time and evening, giving him news of the shop, making his pillows more comfortable, fetching his paper. There wasn't much else I could do to help him, but I insisted on having the doctor again, despite his protests.

Doctor Barton gave me a long, pointed stare when I took him downstairs afterwards.

'You're looking tired,' he said, his eyes dwelling on the swell of my stomach. 'Isn't it time you came to see me yourself?'

'Should I?' I asked. 'I – I wasn't sure. And I don't have much time.'

'I'll make you an appointment for one evening, after shop hours,' he said kindly. 'I want you to promise me you will keep it – and that you won't do too much.'

I promised to keep the appointment, but knew there wasn't much hope of cutting down on my work. Ben was putting in extra hours to help me, but I couldn't leave him alone for long.

We would need a more experienced assistant when my time came. Mother wasn't used to being in the shop. Besides, she had her hands full looking after the house and Father. Richard was no use at all. He did occasionally lift a heavy box and bring in the coal, but he always complained if I asked him to help me.

Doctor Barton hadn't said as much, but I believed my father was dying. He ought to go into hospital but wouldn't, and his ill health hadn't improved his tolerance of others. He refused to have any tests whatever, though he did take some of the herbal drink Gran had prepared for him.

She brought it after I told her how ill he was.

'It won't kill you,' she told him sourly when he complained of the taste. 'If I'd wanted you dead, Harold Robinson, I'd have done it long ago. You've nothing to fear from me.'

'Curse me, would you?' He gave her a wry smile. 'Perhaps you have.'

'I'll take this with me then.' She picked up the bottle. 'You're a fool to yourself, man. This will ease the pain, believe me. It ain't a cure, there's nothing will stop what you've got if I know anything about it – but this will make you feel better.'

'Leave it then. Maybe I'll drink some of it later. Don't look like that, woman. I know better than to believe stupid gossip. You've a tongue on you like a rasp, but I've always respected you.'

'Aye,' Gran said. 'You're a mean old skinflint, Harold Robinson – but there's worse.'

Her mixture was left on the dressing table. That evening he told me he thought the first dose had done him good, and asked for more. He took it regularly for three days, then declared he was right as rain and got up, coming down to serve in the shop while I got on with some book work.

'That grandmother of yours knows a thing or two,' he told me that morning. 'I should have gone to her months ago. Doctors are a waste of time – and those pills I've been taking. I haven't felt this well in an age.'

'Good. I'm glad,' I said.

He turned his eyes on me, giving me a searching look. 'Yes, you are,' he said, and smiled oddly. 'You're a caring girl, Emma. I've been wrong to treat you the way I have. Things will change for the better now. You'll see.'

'It doesn't matter,' I said, not wanting him to see his words had got to me. 'I'm just glad you're well again. I'd be the same with anyone who had been ill.'

'Would you?' he asked. 'Maybe you would, Emma – and then again, maybe you wouldn't.'

Richard was drunk when he came in that evening. I heard him stumbling up the stairs and caught my breath. Why must he do it? Why did he have to drink so much? What had I done to make him turn from me again?

And yet perhaps in my heart I knew. Since our return from London, I had not tried so hard to please him as I ought. Something in me could not help rejecting him. Richard had recognized that rejection, and this was his answer.

I tensed as I wondered what kind of a mood he would be in. If he went straight to bed I would sit up for a while, give him time to fall asleep.

He came into the parlour. I laid down my knitting. I saw his eyes go to it, saw the anger flare, and my heart sank. He was such a bully when he was in this mood.

'Did you want something?'

'Yes – you,' he muttered. 'Get in that bedroom. I want you where you belong, instead of sulking in here.'

'No, Richard,' I replied. 'I'm too tired – and I don't feel well. Besides, you might hurt the baby.'

'Bloody good job if I did! Best thing I could do. Get rid of the bastard.'

I felt my face drain of colour. I stood up, placing my hands protectively over my stomach.

'I'm not going to let you,' I said, facing him defiantly. Any regrets I might have had for not being more loving towards him were gone instantly. 'You're drunk. I won't be treated like this, Richard. When you're sober you can do what you want, if you're careful – but I'm not going to lie there and let you rape me night after night. I've had enough of it.'

'You'll do as I tell you,' Richard muttered and made a grab at me. 'Come here, you little slut.'

I screamed as he caught hold of my arm. I struggled, pushing at him as he snatched a handful of my hair and twisted my head round.

'Let me go!'

'You're my wife. I can do what I like with you.'

'She's also my daughter,' a voice said from the doorway.

'Take your hands off her, you fool. You promised me you'd be good to her. It was part of our bargain.'

Richard's hand fell away. He swung round in shock as he heard Father's voice, his face a picture of dismay. He was obviously still in awe of my father, even in this state.

'Thought you were sick,' he said, slurring his words and staring stupidly. 'Just having a little fun with my wife, that's all.'

'Fun?' Father's tone held the sting of a whiplash. 'Is that what you call it? You're drunk, man. I disapprove of too much strong drink. I won't have such behaviour in my house. You've broken your word to me, let me down. I'm disappointed in you, Richard. This isn't what I wanted for Emma. I thought you would take care of her.'

'Just a little fun,' Richard muttered, then vomited on the carpet. He stood swaying for a moment before pushing past Harold and making for the bathroom. 'Just a little . . .'

We could hear him being violently sick again.

'I'll get a cloth and clear this up,' I said, looking at my father anxiously. 'You should be in bed, Father. I'm sorry about—' I caught back a sob.

'How long has this been going on?'

I was silent. Father's mouth tightened, becoming white-edged with anger.

'All the time, I suppose?'

'He hit me on our honeymoon.'

'You should have told me—' He stopped as my eyes swept up to meet his. 'No, of course you wouldn't. I wouldn't have listened. I'm sorry, Emma. Believe me. I was mistaken in his character. If I'd known – if I'd realized he could be like this I would never have made you marry him. I thought he cared for you.'

'Perhaps he's the way he is was *because* he cared for me, Father. At the start, I think he did care . . . but watching another man's child grow inside me has turned that caring into hatred.' My eyes looked directly into his. 'You should be able to understand that.'

My words went home. Father's eyes stared at me bleakly and I knew then that he had suffered in his own way all these years, perhaps as much as my mother.

'You shouldn't have made her marry him,' Mother said from the kitchen doorway. 'She's miserable, Harold – and it's your fault.'

'Yes, I can see that,' he admitted, eyes narrowing. His face was cold with anger, but with my husband this time, not her. We heard a door slam downstairs. Richard had obviously gone out again. 'I'll speak to him when he comes back. Don't worry, Emma. I'll make him behave decently.'

I saw him flinch as he spoke. The colour was leaving his face.

'Are you in pain again?'

'Yes. It's just started to come on again,' he said. 'I

think I'll go and lie down for a while. Give me your arm, Emma.'

'Go with him,' Mother urged. 'I'll clear this mess up. If I were you, I'd lock your bedroom door tonight, Emma. Let Richard sleep on the sofa if he comes back.'

'He'll come back,' Father muttered sourly. 'He knows which side his bread is buttered.'

I helped my father back to the bedroom. He had started to shake now; he was clearly very ill indeed. I settled him against the pillows, then fetched some of Gran's herbal drink in a glass.

He sipped it slowly. As I watched, his colour gradually returned. It was obviously easing the pain. I took the glass from him and was about to leave when he stopped me.

'Wait a moment.' He laid a hand on my arm. 'If anything should happen to me, Emma, before I've had time to put things right—'

'Don't,' I begged. 'You're getting better. You've been a lot more comfortable these past few days.'

'That stuff helps,' he admitted, 'but it won't stop me dying. She told me that straight out.' He grimaced. 'She's an old witch, Emma, but honest. A decent woman, which is more than I can say for her daughter.'

'Please,' I said. 'Don't be bitter about Mum. Not now.'

'Not now I'm dying? Going to forgive me when I'm gone, and pretend I was a saint?'

'No, of course not!' I flushed. 'I don't hate you,

227

Father. I might have done for a while, but only while I was angry with you for hurting Mum. And I don't blame you for anything else either. It's my own fault I'm in this mess.'

'Part of it – but I made you marry him. I was wrong.'

'Yes,' I said quietly. 'You were wrong. But it's done now so there's no point in going on about it.'

'If I should die,' he said again. 'There's money for you, Emma. I always meant you to have it one day. It's hidden somewhere safe. Keep it to yourself. Don't tell Richard or your mother. You'll find it in the—' He broke off as the bedroom door opened and Mother came in. 'Never mind, it will keep for another day.'

I nodded. I bent to kiss his cheek, then stopped to kiss my mother on the way out.

I had always suspected Father had hidden money somewhere. I locked my bedroom door and undressed. He had never deposited his money in the bank, and I knew the shop made a profit, though not quite as much these past weeks. I wasn't sure why. Once or twice I'd thought money might have gone from the till, and I believed Richard might have taken it.

I'd seen him behind the counter in the shop on a couple of mornings, and when I'd looked, the money had been less than I'd left in the float the previous evening. Of course Father could have taken it, but I didn't think so. At first it had only been a couple of shillings, then ten or fifteen. If Father had wanted money he would have taken it all, as he had in the past.

I suspected my husband of taking his beer money. I thought he might have been doing it from the beginning, but recently it had been a couple of pounds rather than shillings. It was as if he didn't care any more – as if it didn't matter.

Because he thought Father was dying?

I knew Richard still respected my father, or at least feared his power. What he had been doing was theft, even if the shop did belong to his wife's father. He knew Harold could have made trouble for him if he'd wished.

Richard would have no such respect for me or my mother. If Father were to die . . . I shook my head. I was worrying for nothing. If my father died, Mother would own the shop. We could sell it and go away somewhere else. I could leave Richard.

He would never give me a divorce. Not while there was any money left. I knew he had married me for the money. I wasn't sure what my father had promised him, but he seemed to think he could help himself to the till whenever he chose.

Was that why Father had been going to tell me about his secret hoard – so that I could put it somewhere safe? Did he guess Richard had been taking money? Perhaps he had tolerated it because of their arrangement?

I felt angry and shamed in turn. Father had bribed

Richard to marry me. I felt the tears on my cheeks and made no attempt to check them. It was my own stupid fault.

Yet my father had been planning it even before I became pregnant. He'd agreed Richard could take me to the church social without asking me. He had thought marriage to Richard would make sure I stayed where he wanted me, a prisoner of the shop, at his beck and call.

I dried my tears. Crying wouldn't help me. For the moment I was trapped, but it wouldn't be for ever. One day I would escape somehow. One day I would be free.

I was woken by the frantic pounding on my door.

'Get up!' Mother called. 'Your father has brought blood up all over the bed. You've got to fetch the doctor, Emma. Emma! Wake up.'

I was out of bed in seconds. I rushed to unlock the door. Mother was in a panic, really frightened. She grabbed at my arm.

'I think he's dying,' she gasped. 'There's blood everywhere. It's awful. Oh, Emma! I didn't want this to happen. You must believe me. Honestly, I didn't.'

'Of course not. It's all right, Mum. You put your coat on and go to Mary's house. Ask Mr Baxter to phone for the doctor. I'll look after Father. There's no need for you to worry.'

'Yes. Yes, all right.' She looked grateful. 'I can't go back in there. I can't.'

I left her in a hurry. I felt apprehensive as I went into Father's room, but when I saw him lying with his eyes closed I was overcome with pity. The blood on the bedcovers didn't seem to matter. Reaching out for his hand, I held it and bent over him.

'It's all right, Father,' I said softly. 'Don't worry. The doctor is coming. He'll get you into hospital and—'

'No.' His eyes flickered open. He looked up at me. 'It's too late,' he said, and for a moment his fingers tightened about mine. 'I'm sorry, Emma. Forgive me. Please?'

'It's all right,' I said and touched his face with my free hand. 'Don't worry. I'll be fine. I promise you.'

'The money,' he croaked. 'It's in the sto—' He got no further. Gasping in pain, his eyes rolled upwards and his body jerked for several seconds, then there was a rattling sound in his throat and his hand slipped from mine.

'Father . . .' My throat tightened with emotion. I hadn't loved him, but neither had I wanted to see him like this. 'Oh no . . .' My eyes stung with tears. I blinked them away. It was a senseless, useless waste of a life, but I wasn't going to cry.

I was never sure afterwards how long I sat there by my father's body, alone, stunned, disbelieving. It might have been ten minutes or half an hour before the doctor came.

He sent me out of the room while he examined Father's body. I sat next to my mother on the settee in the parlour, staring at the empty fire grate and thinking how cold it was. Mother never let the fire go out, but this time she had; she seemed numbed, unable to take it all in.

'I always thought it would be me first,' she said, her hands shaking. 'Harold was such a strong man. I never expected him to die.'

I sensed her fear, though not its cause. I reached for her hand and squeezed it. She clung to me, seeming to need comfort, reassurance – as if she felt guilt now that her husband was dead.

'I hated him sometimes,' she said in a strangled voice, 'but I didn't wish him dead, Emma. Not really – not dead.' She choked back a sob. 'Just before the last . . . he told me he was sorry . . . told me he wished he had treated me better.'

I glanced at her. She was very distressed and nervous. What was she frightened of? Or was she just regretting the lost years, blaming herself for his death?

I tried to comfort her. It wasn't her fault that Father had been so ill. He had neglected his health for too long.

'Of course you didn't,' I said. 'It was his own fault, Mum. He should have seen the doctor ages ago, and he should have gone into hospital for those tests. Perhaps they could have done something for him if he'd gone in time.'

'The doctor's coming out.' Her face went chalky white as the doctor came into the hall. She looked at me as if seeking help, her hand reaching for mine. 'I can't—'

I stood up and went to meet the doctor. He held out his hands to me and I took them gratefully.

'What a terrible ordeal for you and your mother,' he said. 'I was afraid this might happen if he neglected himself. You recall we spoke of it the first time I came?'

'Was it an ulcer?' I asked hesitantly. 'Will – will you have to do a post mortem? That's what they call a special examination after someone dies suddenly, isn't it?'

'That won't be necessary,' he said, and I was conscious of an overwhelming relief, though I wasn't sure why. 'I don't doubt my diagnosis was right. Your father had an ulcer. The internal bleeding led to complications and he died of heart failure. There is no need for a formal investigation, my dear. It was not unexpected. I shall sign the death certificate. You and your mother have enough to cope with without a lot of fuss and trouble for nothing.'

'Thank you. You're very kind,' I said. 'I wish Father had taken notice when you wanted him to go into hospital. If he had, he might still be alive.'

'Probably it wouldn't have helped, not at this late stage. His illness had been coming on for years.' Doctor Barton patted my hand kindly. 'At least he isn't in pain now. You must look after yourself and your—' He broke off as Richard came up the stairs. He was unshaven and looked dishevelled. 'Ah, yes, Mr Gillows.' There was disapproval in his voice as he looked at my husband. 'Well, I'll leave you to break the sad news, Emma.'

'I'll see you out first.' I threw a look that spoke volumes at Richard, going past him without a word. The sight of him like that turned my stomach, and I blamed him for making such a rumpus earlier, bringing my father from his bed. What had happened that night had killed any lingering sympathy I had towards Richard. As far as I was concerned, our marriage was finished. 'It was very good of you to come, sir. I am grateful for everything you've done for my father.'

At the door I hesitated. Ought I to mention the pills Father had been taking? I had always thought they might be harmful, that some of them might actually have contributed to his illness.

Something made me hold back. There was no point now. He was dead. Nothing could change that – and I wasn't sure. Besides, the vague, terrible thoughts in my mind horrified me.

'Goodbye,' Doctor Barton said. 'Come and see me soon, Emma. I want to make sure you're looking after yourself properly.'

I thanked him, then walked slowly back upstairs. Richard was waiting for me in the hall. Mother had obviously told him the news and he looked stunned, almost disbelieving.

'I'm sorry,' he said awkwardly. 'I didn't realize he was that ill . . . not dying.'

'Didn't you?' I looked through him. 'You smell disgusting, Richard. If I were you, I would go and clean yourself up before anyone else sees you. I'm closing the shop for the day – and as soon as I'm ready I shall arrange for Father to be laid out. So, if you'll excuse me, I have a great deal to do.' I left him staring as I walked away.

Chapter Eleven

Father was buried. It had been bitterly cold in the church, but at last it was over. We had asked close friends and relatives back to the house – my mother's relatives, not Father's.

'I don't think he had any family,' Mother told me when I asked if we should get in touch with them. 'At least, he never mentioned anyone to me. Not once the whole time we were married.'

I looked through the rolltop desk downstairs in the stockroom, but there were only piles of old bills and accumulated rubbish, amongst which I saw several cuttings from the newspapers advertising various cures for indigestion.

So there was no way of tracing Father's family, if he had any. And now most of our friends had shown their sympathy and gone. Only Gran, Mother, Richard, Father's lawyer, Mr Smythe, and I remained in the parlour.

I was about to disappear into the kitchen to start the washing-up when the lawyer called me back.

'You should be here, Mrs Gillows. Your father's will concerns you.'

I sat down, glancing at Mother. She was still pale, but no longer nervous.

'Mr Robinson revised his will a few months ago,' Mr Smythe informed us, then cleared his throat. 'As you know, Mrs Robinson, your husband owned this shop and house outright.'

She nodded expectantly as he paused.

'You are to have life tenancy and—'

'What does that mean?' She looked shocked, as though she had expected something very different.

'It means this house will be your home for as long as you wish.'

Her face was chalky white. 'You mean I don't own it – he didn't leave it to me?'

Mr Smythe looked uncomfortable. 'No, Mrs Robinson. Your husband's wish was that you should live here and receive the same allowance as before from the income derived from the business.'

'And that's all?' I could see the shock and anger in her eyes. 'After all these years . . . all I've had to suffer?'

'Mum—' I looked at her in appeal. 'Don't – not now.'

'Who gets the shop then?' I could hear the anger and bitterness in her voice.

He cleared his throat. 'Until recently it was left to his daughter, Emma, but . . . Mr Robinson changed it.'

'He left it to me,' Richard said suddenly. His eyes gleamed with triumph as he looked at me, and I knew that he wanted to humiliate me, to punish me. 'It was his part of the bargain we made.'

'Is that true?' Mother asked, staring oddly at the lawyer. 'Can he do that? Leave everything away from his wife and daughter?'

'It is quite legal,' Mr Smythe said. 'Providing he leaves you sufficient to live on. You could contest it, of course, but that would be costly.'

Mother sat back, hands twisting in her lap, obviously distressed and barely controlling her anger.

'There are, however, certain conditions attached to the legacy,' the lawyer went on. 'Mr Gillows cannot sell the property without the consent of his wife. And if there should be a divorce, the property would revert to you, Emma.'

'No! That's not what we agreed!' Richard said, looking furious. 'Harold promised it would be mine.'

'It is, sir.' Mr Smythe frowned. 'But Mr Robinson wanted his daughter to be secure. It is his wish that she be given a free hand to run the business. And everything else is left to her.'

'Everything else?' Mother sat forward, suddenly alert. 'What else is there?'

'I believe there is some money in the bank . . .'Mr Smythe glanced at his papers. 'Three hundred and seventy pounds to be precise.'

'There must be more,' Mother cried. 'He must have left more.'

'Mr Robinson was a very careful man,' the lawyer said. 'He liked to keep his business to himself. If there is anything more, he did not mention it to me.'

'But there must be more,' Mother repeated, eyes filled with tears. 'What did he do with all his money? It's not right. I was his wife. I should get something.'

The lawyer shook his head. 'I was not in agreement with this will. I asked your husband to reconsider, but he was adamant.'

She nodded, took out her handkerchief and wiped her eyes.

'The money from the shop.' Richard was glaring at Mr Smythe. 'That's mine?'

'Yes, sir. Mrs Gillows is to run the business, because of her previous experience – but you own it. You own the property in theory, but you cannot turn Mrs Robinson out while she wishes to live here, nor can you sell without your wife's written consent.'

'And if I contest that part of it?'

Mr Smythe shrugged. 'It might be that a court would decide the will was invalid, made when Mr Robinson was suffering from ill health. It might be revised in favour of his family. It's difficult to say. Again, I would only point out that it could be very costly.'

'The crafty old devil,' Richard said, but he was smiling now, sure of himself. 'We shall just have to live with it, shan't we? I'll see you out, shall I?'

'No,' I said, standing up. 'I'll do that, Richard.'

He glared at me, but made no move to stop me. I led Mr Smythe from the parlour and down to the shop. He smiled and asked me if there was anything else I wanted to know.

'Yes,' I said, looking at him hesitantly. 'When you said everything else is mine – does that include anything I might find amongst Father's things? Money, property deeds?'

'Yes, Mrs Gillows.' He gave me an apologetic look. 'I'm sorry about this will. I tried very hard to persuade him against making it, but Mr Robinson refused to accept my advice.'

'My father never listened to anyone,' I replied and we shook hands. 'Thank you for coming, sir.'

'If there is anything I can do?'

'No, I don't think so. Not for the moment.'

'The money in the bank?'

'Leave it there for the moment. I shall let you know if I need it.'

'Very wise. Very wise.'

I smiled and opened the door for him.

After he had gone, I stood alone in the shop thinking for a few minutes. Father had left me his money. I was sure there was considerably more than the three hundred in the bank – and I believed I knew what he had done with it. All I had to do was find it . . .

When I returned to the parlour upstairs, it was obvious that a quarrel had been going on between my mother and Richard.

'Harold had no right to leave it all to you,' she was saying furiously. 'It should have been mine – or Emma's.'

'He promised me the lot,' Richard said, glaring at us all. 'House, business – and the money. Said he didn't trust you or Emma to look after it. He thought it would be better in my hands.'

'I'll take you to court.'

'Don't be a fool, Greta!' Gran spoke sharply. 'You'll lose what little bit you've got. The only ones to benefit will be the lawyers. You're no worse off than you were – you'll have to make the best of it.'

'You don't know what I've had to put up with all these years,' Mother said bitterly. 'What I've done—'

'What are you talking about, Mum?' I said quickly. 'You've done your duty, nothing more or less – as we both have. We both knew Father was capable of doing this. There's no point in making a fuss. Gran's right, we're no worse off than we were.'

Mother looked as if she wanted to protest, but, seeing

the warning look in my eyes, shut her mouth. She got up and walked away, going into her bedroom and locking the door.

'Well, I'll be off then,' Gran said. She stood up a little stiffly, as if the action was painful to her, and came to kiss my cheek, her voice no more than a whisper against my ear. 'Chin up, love. You'll maybe find a way of working things out. It might not be as bad as you think just now – Harold was always a bit of a mystery.'

I kissed her back, nodding but saying nothing. I knew that she had her own ideas about my father's money, but wasn't going to say anything in Richard's hearing.

'I'll come and see you as soon as I can,' I promised. 'I'll have to see about getting another assistant – part time, anyway.'

'We'll see about that,' Richard muttered behind me. 'Assistants cost money.'

I went downstairs with Gran. 'Your father had more than that put by,' she said, 'but you know that, don't you?'

'He told me there was something,' I agreed, 'he just didn't say what or where.'

'That's typical of Harold Robinson,' she said and chortled. 'If you find it, you'd best keep it to yourself, love.'

'Yes, I know.'

'I know Richard Gillows' sort,' Gran said. 'He's got a taste for the drink. While he had to look after his money it wasn't too bad, but now . . . you'd best keep a cool head on your shoulders, lass. You can't deny him the profits from the shop – and it would cause trouble if you tried – but don't let him get his hands on yours.'

'No, I shan't,' I promised her. 'And I shall come to visit you. If Richard won't let me take on a new assistant, I'll leave Ben on his own for an hour or so. I don't intend to be a prisoner again. I've had enough of that to last me a lifetime.'

'If he causes you too much trouble, let me know,' Gran said. 'I could talk sense into Harold – and I dare say that husband of yours is much the same.'

I kissed her goodbye, but as I walked upstairs, I thought she was wrong. My father had given her her way for the sake of peace – arguments in the shop were bad for business – but Richard wouldn't care about that. As long as there was money in the till when he wanted it, he would be reasonable, but he wouldn't stand for anyone telling him what to do.

Richard was waiting for me when I got back to the parlour. One look at his face told me he was angry about Father's will.

'You need not imagine I'll be ruled by you,' Richard said, eyes glinting with temper. 'Your father made a bargain with me – my name for your bastard child. He thinks he's cheated me of my rights, but I won't be bested by him or you.'

'Your rights?' I raised my eyebrows at him. 'If anyone has reason to complain of being cheated, it's my mother or me. Had I known the truth – that he made such a bargain with you – I would never have married you. *You* lied to me, Richard – *you* cheated me. If you feel my father welshed on your bargain, I'll give you a divorce.'

His eyes narrowed. 'I'll just bet you would! Well, you won't get rid of me that easily. I'm going to stay here and take what belongs to me. I'll never divorce you. And you had better not try to cheat me, Emma.'

'I wouldn't dream of it. The profits from the shop are yours. Just leave me enough to pay the bills.'

'You've got money in the bank for that.'

'Oh, no, Richard. That's mine. It's going to stay with Mr Smythe until I want it.' I raised my head, looking straight at him. 'I might use it to leave you. You can run the shop as you want then.'

'You think I couldn't?'

He took a step towards me, drew his hand back and hit me so hard I fell against the sofa. My ears were ringing and my eyes stung with the tears I was too proud to shed.

'Leave here, and I'll throw your mother out. She won't get a penny from me once you've gone.'

'You can't do that,' I said. 'Besides, I can take her with me.'

'You'll do as you're told – or I'll beat that bastard out

244

of you. You're my wife and you'll stay here whether you like it or not.' He slapped me again, though not as hard as the first time. 'I'm going out.'

I sat down as he left the room, my throat tight with emotion, my hands over my face as I fought for calm.

'He's worse than Harold ever knew how to be.'

I looked up as I heard Mother's voice. She came and sat next to me, her fingers touching the red marks on my face.

'I'm sorry, Emma. This is my fault. I would never have done it if I'd thought it would turn out this way.'

'Done what, Mum?'

She sighed and shook her head. 'Agreed to the marriage. You should have listened to Gran, Emma. I thought things would be better when Harold was dead, but they're worse.'

'It doesn't have to be worse,' I said. 'We've got the money Father left me. We could go away . . .'

'And leave everything for Richard? Are you going to sign away your inheritance? That's the only way he would leave you in peace – if you signed for him to sell this place. He'll never let you divorce him.'

'It might be worth it, Mum. I've got a few pounds put by as well as Father's money. We could manage until I'm fit to work.'

She sighed. 'I'll get a cold flannel for your face. Perhaps we should stick it out for a while – until the baby is born. See if anything turns up. Harold had more money than that – it must be somewhere.'

'He tried to tell me something before he died,' I said. 'He said there was money for me, but he didn't say where.'

Her eyes gleamed with excitement. 'I knew it. Find it, Emma, and then we'll go. Let Richard have the shop.'

'I've been thinking about it,' I replied. 'Father wouldn't have hidden anything where you might find it. I think it must be downstairs – probably in the stockroom.'

'Shall we start looking now – while Richard's out?'

'We'll have to be careful. If he thinks something is going on he will be suspicious. If he knew we'd found something, he'd take it from us if he could.'

'I'll go through Harold's things again,' she said. 'I've already looked, but I might find something. What do you think he has hidden?'

'Gold sovereigns,' I said, and nodded. 'I'm pretty sure that's what he did with the money. I found one shoved in a drawer in the stockroom and told Father. He said it had been given to him. After he was well enough to come down for a few days, I looked and it had disappeared. He had hidden it somewhere.'

'It's just what he would have done. He might have given it to you for looking after him.'

'I didn't want it, Mum. If Richard didn't drink so

much . . .' I sighed. 'I wouldn't have minded the shop being his if he were different. But drinking changes him, makes him violent.'

Why was I trying to convince myself? My marriage had never stood a chance. And if I were honest, I didn't want it to – not any more.

'He wasn't drunk when he did this,' she said quietly and touched my cheek. 'We'll give it until the spring, Emma – and then we'll go, whether you find those sovereigns or not.'

'Richard's mother was a hard woman,' Gran said as we sat over tea several weeks later. 'She drove her husband to drink, and when he lost his job because of it, she never let him forget what a worthless wretch he was. I reckon Richard saw enough petticoat rule when he was a lad to last him a lifetime. Happen that's why he won't stand for any lip from you.'

'As long as he gets his own way, he's not violent,' I said. 'If I try to tell him he can't keep taking money from the shop without running out of stock, he loses his temper. People have already started to ask for things we need to reorder – but what can I do?'

'Don't put your own money into it,' she warned. 'You'll not gain by it, Emma.'

'I know.' I thought of the argument with Richard the previous evening, when he had taken every penny from the till. 'I make him give me some of the change back – but it will run out one of these days.'

'Don't you go short,' Gran said. 'If you need a few bob to keep you going, I've got my savings.'

'As if I would take your money!' I sighed. 'Oh, Gran, you know I wouldn't. I'm only having a moan.'

'I'll not be needing money for much longer,' she said. 'After I've gone, you'll find my bits in a biscuit tin under my bed. I'll tell you now. It's all for you, Emma. There's not much, but it's yours.'

'Oh, Gran, don't! I would much rather have you.'

She smiled at me. 'Aye, lass, I know it – but I know I haven't got long. I'm hoping to see your little one born afore I go.'

'Of course you will, you daft thing! Only another two months to go,' I said, patting my bulge. 'I sometimes think I shall be glad when it's over.'

'It's always difficult at this stage, but when you've your son in your arms, you'll forget how uncomfortable it was.'

'My son?' I quizzed her with my eyes. 'Am I carrying a boy?'

'I reckon it's a boy,' she said. 'But we'll see.'

She wouldn't let me wash the tea things before I left. It was the beginning of January 1939; the weather was bitterly cold and the sky quite dark by the time I reached the High Street that afternoon. I lingered outside

Mrs Henty's window and she beckoned me inside.

'I got some pretty smocks in this morning, Emma. I thought you might like one?'

I had been managing by wearing dresses my mother had let out at the seams, but one of the smocks was a very pretty green print, and I thought it would be nice to wear in the shop – cover my bulge a bit.

'How much is this one?'

'Sixteen shillings – but I'll let you have it for twelve.'

'I think I will have it,' I said. 'I'll bring the money in tomorrow or the next day. Will you keep it for me until then?'

'You take it with you,' she said. 'I know I can trust you. Besides, I may not be here much longer.'

'Not here?' I was surprised. 'What do you mean?'

'I'm thinking of selling up.'

'You're not! Please don't do that. I should miss coming here. It wouldn't be the same without you, Mrs Henty.'

'I might not have a choice,' she said. 'My landlord wants to sell the premises, and I haven't got the five hundred pounds he's asking. It would probably be more if I didn't have a clause in my lease . . . but it might as well be thousands.'

'Five hundred pounds . . .' I looked round the show-room. It was small and crowded with rails and glass cabinets, but I knew she did a reasonable trade. 'It doesn't sound outrageous. And you live over the top, don't you?'

'Yes.' She sighed and looked worried. 'That's what makes it so awkward. I suppose I shall have to move – but I don't want to borrow from the bank.'

'Supposing I lent you the money?' I spoke impulsively, without considering. 'You could pay me back so much a month, couldn't you?'

'I could pay you five pounds a month – which is what I've been paying in rent.' She looked at me hesitantly. 'Or we could be partners, Emma. I'd carry on the same as always, but instead of paying you back, we'd share the profits.'

The idea appealed to me. My money would be safer in property. Richard had already hinted that I should ask Mr Smythe to release it – and I knew what would happen then.

'How much would that be?'

'It depends – from ten to fifteen pounds a month perhaps,' she said, looking excited. 'It brings in less at the moment, allowing for expenditure – but there would be no rent to pay.'

I could have earned almost as much by renting the shop back to her, but it would be a steady income and I thought I would enjoy helping to choose the new stock.

'You tell your landlord you want to buy,' I said. 'I'll speak to Mr Smythe and make the money available.'

'Are you sure you can manage it, Emma?' She looked excited and anxious all at the same time.

'Father left me nearly four hundred pounds,' I told her. 'And I've saved another hundred and thirty.' She looked so surprised that I laughed. 'Not from my wages!'

'I shan't ask, Emma. Where the money came from is your business.' She was folding the smock, putting it into a bag. 'Take this as a present, with my love. It will seal the bargain between us.'

'Thank you,' I said and kissed her. 'You do realize that this has to be a secret between us?'

'Yes, of course. I understand you wouldn't want everyone to know.'

'Richard would be furious,' I said. 'Keep the property in your name, Mrs Henty. We'll have something put in writing at the lawyers'.'

'It might be best that way,' she agreed. 'And call me Madge, Emma – seeing as we're partners now.'

After leaving her, I went straight to Mr Smythe's office. He was on the point of leaving for the night, but was good enough to see me at once. And, after I'd told him what I wanted, expressed his agreement.

'We'll make it an interest-free loan against the property,' he said. 'That way it would revert to you if Mrs Henty were to die.'

'She isn't going to die,' I said, 'but do whatever you think best.'

'Do you want me to arrange a bank loan for the extra money?'

'No. I have a hundred and thirty pounds in the Post Office. I'll get it out as soon as I can.'

If he was surprised, he didn't show it. I made arrangements for an appointment the following week, then hurried home. Ben would be wanting to get off for his tea, and I had to look after the shop.

I was excited at the idea of being Mrs Henty's partner. The money I received each month would make me independent of Richard and the shop. He could drink away Father's stock if he liked.

As yet, I'd had no luck in my search for Father's secret hoard. Perhaps it didn't exist. I intended to go on looking, but at least the money I already had would be safe out of my husband's reach.

It was the end of February. I was very close to my time now and feeling desperately tired. Richard still wouldn't agree to my employing another assistant, so my mother had started to take my place for two hours in the afternoons. To my surprise, she seemed to enjoy it.

'We need some more of those special cigars,' she told me that afternoon when I went down after my rest. 'Someone asked for them – and Fry's dark chocolate. We're down to our last bar.'

'I'll see what I can do,' I said, sighing wearily, 'but Richard takes the money out every night. He only allows me two pounds in change – and your housekeeping money, Mum.'

'If he keeps on at this rate, the trade will suffer,' she said. 'And what are we going to do then, Emma?'

I had told her about the partnership with Mrs Henty. She had been surprised and a little shocked when I explained that the extra money had come mostly from Jonathan Reece. I knew she thought I ought not to have taken it, but I didn't see why I shouldn't. Paul owed me something. If it hadn't been for him, I would never have married Richard and the shop would now have belonged to Mother and me.

'We'll manage,' I said. I raised my eyes to hers. 'Maybe Richard will come to his senses when he realizes what is happening to the profits. We can't sell what we haven't got. And if he doesn't—' I shrugged.

She frowned but didn't say any more. As she went out, I picked up an evening newspaper, scanning the lead stories. The government had recently announced they were intending to spend several million pounds on defence, and the journalist was talking about people making air raid shelters in their own back gardens.

Surely it wouldn't really be necessary? I knew about the troubles in Germany – the way the Jews were being driven from their homes – but all that seemed so far away. I couldn't believe that there would really be a war.

I replaced the newspaper in the rack as the bell went

and a customer entered. My breath caught in my throat as I saw who it was.

'Jon!' I cried, surprised and pleased that he had come. Then I blushed as I realized I'd used his first name. 'Mr Reece, I mean.'

'Right the first time,' he said, eyes going over me anxiously. 'I'm Jon to you, Emma. Should you still be working?'

'I'm fine, really. Just a bit tired sometimes . . .' I hesitated. 'You got my letter? You know my father died last year?'

'Yes, I know, Emma. I'm sorry I didn't reply. I've been busy at Chambers. And my uncle's estate took some sorting out – there were a lot of debts and documents missing. My aunt has been very upset. I've had to spend time with her. We have just managed to find a buyer for the house, that's why I am in Cambridgeshire.'

'Oh . . . does that mean Mrs Greenslade will be moving away?'

'She is going to live in Devon with her sister. That house was far too large for her – and Paul doesn't seem to think he'll be coming back to this country.'

'I see.' I realized with a shock that I hadn't thought of Paul for ages. 'So you won't be coming this way again?'

'Oh, I might have business down here occasionally.' He glanced round the shop, eyes narrowing as he noticed empty spaces on the shelves. 'Are you managing, Emma?

You've been getting the money I sent you all right?'

'Yes. It has been a great help to me.' I explained about the investment I'd made. 'I really don't need the fifty pounds anymore.'

'It's yours by right,' he said, and took an envelope from his inside pocket. 'I'm going to be away for a while, Emma – so I've brought this today.'

I could tell the envelope contained money, and was embarrassed.

'Really, you shouldn't—'

'I want you to have it.'

I saw the expression in his eyes and blushed. 'Are you quite sure?'

'Perfectly sure.'

'Then thank you.' I slipped the envelope into my pocket. 'You have been so kind all this time, looking after me. I had no right to expect anything from you, Jon.'

'Paul owes it to you,' he said and smiled at me. 'Besides, I care what happens to you. You know I would always help if things get too bad.'

'Yes, I know.' I could feel a lump in my throat, and tears stung my eyes. 'Thank you. I—'

Ben came in from the back room. Jonathan looked at him, asked for a paper, paid and went out. I wanted to call him back. I wished that we could have gone on talking . . . that I wasn't tied to the shop and my husband. But I might as well have wished for the moon.

'Can you manage for a while, Ben? I need to go upstairs.'

'Course I can,' he said, and eyed me strangely. 'Ain't I seen that toff before?'

'Mr Reece has been in the shop before,' I replied. 'He is a lawyer from London, Ben.'

'Not much of a looker, is he?'

'He is quite attractive,' I replied, 'and very kind. I like him so you need not be rude about him.'

'Sorry, Emma. Only asking.'

'I'll be down again in a few minutes, Ben.'

I was anxious to go upstairs and put away the money that had just been given me. Richard was on the early shift and he might be home soon. I didn't want him to see it or he would want to know where it had come from.

I opened the top drawer of my dressing table and reached for the old toffee tin at the back. At the moment it contained two pounds and my Post Office book. I had two shillings and sixpence left in it. I'd thought of closing it, but hadn't got around to it. Now, I would be able to deposit some of the money Jon had given me.

I counted the notes, feeling shocked when I realized he had given me an extra ten pounds this time. How had he persuaded Paul to do that? I sat staring at the money, puzzling over it, and then I suddenly understood. I realized what I should have known from the beginning – it wasn't Paul's money. Any of it. Jon had been paying me fifty pounds a quarter out of his own pocket!

How much did a junior partner earn in a London law firm? It couldn't be that much, surely? I felt guilty. I would have to repay him somehow.

'Where did you get that?' Richard's voice startled me. I jumped and snatched the money up as he made a grab for it.

'It's mine – nothing to do with you.'

His fingers encircled my wrist, gripping it so hard that I was forced to drop the money and my savings book. He picked the book up, giving a snort of disbelief as he saw I had withdrawn a large sum some weeks earlier.

'Where did this come from – and what did you do with it?'

'I – it was some of the money Father left me,' I lied, hoping he wouldn't look at the dates it had been deposited. But he was only interested in the withdrawal and what I had done with the money. 'I needed it to pay some bills after he died.'

'If you're lying to me, Emma—' He swore and made a fist at me. 'You said the profits were down because we're low on certain stock. If I find out that you've been helping yourself . . .'

'You can see the account books any time you like,' I said. 'And we do need more stock. Look at the shelves – they're half empty.' I gasped as he thrust the money into his pocket. 'That's my money. I need it – I need things for the baby.'

I caught at his arm. He thrust me away, hitting me with the back of his hand.

'Please, Richard! I have to feed and clothe myself and the baby.'

'As far as I'm concerned the brat would be better dead.' He glared at me, then put his hand in his pocket and withdrew three pounds. 'That's all you're getting – and if I find out you were lying, I'll make you sorry.'

I picked up the money, furious with myself for letting him catch me unawares.

'I hate you, Richard Gillows!'

I was shocked by my own words. How had it got this bad? At the start I had really felt we stood a chance, but little by little he had killed any feeling there was for him in me, and now I was close to hating him.

'Do you now?' he grabbed hold of me, dragging me from the edge of the bed into a standing position. 'Well, maybe I'll give you something to really hate me for one day.' Then he shoved me away so that I stumbled against the dressing chest.

I cried out as the pain whipped through me, clutching at my belly. 'Don't hit me again,' I begged. 'It's the baby. I think I'm starting it. You've brought it on too soon.'

'Let's hope it dies,' he said and turned away with a snarl on his lips. 'You too for all I care!'

I sat on the edge of the bed, doubling up with pain as he went out. It hurt so much – and it was too soon.

It hurt so much that I didn't turn my head as Mother came in. She was across the room in seconds, sitting on the bed beside me, her arm about my waist.

'That devil!' she muttered. 'He hurt you. We'll go, Emma. It doesn't matter about this place. We'll go now, before he kills you.'

'Not tonight,' I gasped, and turned towards her. 'It's coming, Mum. My baby is coming . . .'

Chapter Twelve

'You should have told me he'd actually hit you before this,' Gran said when she visited me the next day. My beautiful new-born son was lying in the cot beside me, waving his tiny fist at her. 'I'll set Richard straight, Emma. He won't hit you again, I promise you that.'

'You don't know him,' I said. I looked at her anxiously. I could see a difference in her. She looked older, more fragile somehow. 'He might hurt you. Please don't risk it, Gran.'

'I'll not let him make your life a misery. Just let him wait until I see him. I'll make his insides turn to water.'

'Do you want to hold James?' I asked, trying to turn the subject. 'I was afraid he might be harmed but the doctor says he's fine – perfectly healthy. He is beautiful, isn't he?'

'Aye, he's that all right,' Gran said. She turned her head as we heard the sound of Richard's voice in the other room. Her expression was grim, determined. 'I'll be back in a moment, Emma.'

'Gran – please don't—'

It was no use, she wasn't listening. I glanced at my son as he lay peacefully in his cot. His birth had cost me several hours of pain and anguish, and I had feared for his life, because I knew Richard's brutality had made me go into labour two weeks early.

The loud voices from the next room startled me.

'You don't frighten me, you old hag!'

'Don't you dare speak to my mother like that!'

'I'll teach you—'

I froze in horror as I heard the argument going on in the parlour. Why hadn't Gran listened to me? She didn't realize that Richard wasn't like my father. He had no respect for anyone he could knock down with his fists, and would not care about hurting her.

'Touch my daughter or Emma again,' Gran said, 'and I'll make sure you won't live the year out, Richard Gillows.'

'What are you going to do – put a curse on me? They say you're a witch,' Richard sneered mockingly. 'Maybe they should have burned you years ago.'

'Aye, happen they should,' Gran said. 'I've never used my powers for evil yet, Richard Gillows, but there's a first time for everything. The next time you hurt my girl, you'll feel a pain in your belly. The pain will grow and burn your insides, and you'll lose your manhood. If you persist in your bullying, you will die within the year.'

Gran's voice sounded so odd. I had been summoning the strength to get out of bed and stop their argument, but something made me fall back against the pillows, unable to move even a finger. I shivered, feeling cold all over. Gran really did sound as though she was cursing him.

'You're just a senile old woman,' Richard shouted, but his voice too was strange, as though he half believed her. 'Damn you! And damn that little whore in there!'

I heard the sound of heavy feet as he stamped along the hall and down the stairs. For a moment there was silence, then a muffled thud as he slammed the door of the shop behind him.

Gran came back into the bedroom. Her eyes glittered, and I knew she had relished the scene with Richard. She looked younger and was definitely pleased with herself.

'That should make him think twice. And if it doesn't, I'll give Greta something to put in his dinner – not to poison him, mind. Just to make him feel a little sorry for himself.'

'Gran!' I stared at her, half shocked, half amused. 'You wouldn't – would you?'

'If it was the only way to stop him hurting you.' She glanced at my mother. 'It's been done before, I daresay. There's more ways than one of drawing the tiger's tooth. I'll do what needs to be done for your sake, Emma. And your mother will do the same.'

Mother wouldn't look at her, but her manner was guilty. I remembered Father's illness at my wedding and wondered. Surely she wouldn't have . . . not deliberately? Was it possible that my mother had put something in Father's food that day? No, she couldn't have. I dismissed the idea hastily.

I looked at Gran doubtfully. 'You haven't really put a curse on him, have you?'

She chortled with delight, her eyes screwing up with laughter. 'Only if he thinks I have, love. It's all in the mind. You can curse some 'til you're blue in the face. Harold would have laughed his head off. I had other ways of dealing with him. But there's some frighten themselves. If Richard wants to believe I've cursed him, he'll mayhap bring on the symptoms I've put into his mind.'

'Oh, Gran . . .' I wasn't sure what to believe. 'You're a terrible woman.'

'I look after those I care for,' she said. 'Richard knows he only has to leave you alone. Nothing will happen unless he hurts you.'

Her eyes glittered suddenly, and I felt a coldness go through me. Father had died of stomach pains and sickness – could he have been poisoned?

No, surely not! Not Gran. Not my mother! Both had wanted to protect me – but surely neither of them would have gone to such lengths for my sake? I certainly hadn't wanted him dead.

'Well, I'll be off, lass.' Gran bent stiffly to kiss me and then the baby. 'If Richard starts on you again, just you let me know.'

I nodded but said nothing. I would need to be careful not to let her or my mother see any bruises Richard inflicted in future. He was a brute but I had no desire for his death – or the trouble their meddling might bring down on our heads.

'He won't,' I said, smiling at her. 'Things will be better now the baby is born. He was just jealous, that's all.'

'I'll see you out, Ma.'

My mother followed hers from the room. I could hear them whispering together at the top of the stairs, but their words were indistinct. A few minutes later, my mother returned. She was smiling, and I thought she looked relieved, as though a weight had somehow lifted from her mind.

'What have you two been hatching out between you?'

'Nothing. Nothing at all, Emma.' She shook her head at me. 'Your Gran knows a lot about herbs and things, love, but she wouldn't hurt anyone. Not really. Besides, curses don't kill people, that's old wives' talk. Like she said, it's all in the mind. Just harmless nonsense. It might make Richard think before he lashes out next time, but that can't be bad, can it?'

'No, I don't suppose so,' I said, but I was uneasy. 'I

just think it's best not to stir things up. I wouldn't want anything horrible to happen – to any of us.'

'It's not going to happen, Emma.'

'I meant what I said, Mum. If Richard hits me again, I shall leave him. I'll have a bit put by soon, and I shall be able to work again. We could go somewhere together. You could look after James while I work. We could manage.'

I thought regretfully of the money Jon had given me. I had made up my mind not to take any more from him. While I'd believed it was from Paul, I had felt justified in accepting it, but now I couldn't. Jon owed me nothing. He had already done far more than I could ever have expected.

Mother looked at me thoughtfully. I could see something in her eyes, some hesitation. 'Yes, we could go whenever we liked,' she said. 'But we must have one last search for those gold coins, Emma. You've been too tired to bother much lately – but I'm sure they are here somewhere. And they belong to you. Why should we leave them for Richard – or a stranger if he sells? And you would have to sign or he'd never leave you in peace.'

'They belong to us, Mum. You deserve them as much as anyone.' I smiled at her as my son began to whimper. 'Give him to me, will you?'

She reached into the cot, placing the child in my arms. Her expression was a little odd as she looked at me. 'All I want is for you to be secure and happy,' she said. 'It doesn't matter about me. It was always for you – always for you, Emma.'

She watched for a few moments, then turned and went out, leaving me to nurse my son.

What had she done for my sake? She had expected Father to leave me most of his property – but would she have killed for my sake?

I prayed that she had not. Father had been harsh to us both, but I believed in my heart that he had cared for me in his way – and perhaps he had once loved my mother. Jealousy and endless quarrels had turned that love to hatred over the years. And some of the blame for that must lie with my mother.

Had she punished him at the end for his harsh treatment of her by putting something in his food? I recalled the fear in her eyes when she'd realized he might be dying.

'I never wanted him to die, Emma.'

I had wondered at her fear then, but now I thought I understood. It was possible that she had tried to make him ill – so that he wouldn't have such a hold over us. Yet I did not believe she would deliberately kill.

Not my mother. Not Gran. It would be too horrible. A wicked evil crime – committed to protect me . . .

I lay thinking about it for a while, then I slept. When I woke it was to laugh at myself and my foolish imagination. Gran had played a silly joke on Richard, that was all.

The room smelt of flowers. There was a vase of early daffodils on the dressing table, and a small jug of snowdrops by my bed.

As I stared at them, thinking of the message of hope and reborn life such flowers always gave, the door opened and Richard entered. I was surprised to see that he was wearing his best suit and his hair was slicked down with oil. He gave me a sheepish look as he apologized.

'I bought you some flowers,' he said. 'I'm sorry, Emma. I shouldn't have hit you like that – and I shouldn't have said those things.' He took some money from his pocket and laid it on the table beside the bed. 'I've spent a few pounds – but that's your money.'

'Thank you. I'll use some of it to order stock we need,' I said, knowing I had to meet him halfway. I didn't want this marriage, I wanted to be free – but Richard would never give me a divorce. 'Why can't we at least try to get on? I don't mind that Father left the shop to you – but I can't run the business properly if you take all the money. And that means it will eventually run out.'

'I'll do better,' he promised, obviously subdued. 'I never meant it to be this way. I'm a devil with the drink in me, always was. Me ma said I'd end up bad – just like my father.'

'What happened to him?'

'He died drunk in a ditch. Ma had him buried on the parish. She said he was worthless, and that I was like him.'

'Sometimes you are,' I said, meeting his eyes steadily. 'But we might have been all right together if you hadn't started to get drunk all the time.'

'I could try again,' he said, looking shamefaced. 'You look after the money, Emma. Run the shop the way you want. I'll stick to my wages – and I'll try to keep sober.'

'If you do that, Richard, we'll manage.'

His hand moved towards me, then fell back. 'Jealousy is a terrible thing, Emma. It drives a man mad.'

'Yes, I know that, Richard. But you have no need to be jealous of Paul. It was just a young girl's foolishness, that's all. All I want now is a proper life – the way you promised it would be.'

'What about the money his cousin has been sending you?'

'I'm going to tell him not to send it anymore.'

Richard nodded, accepting my word.

'We'll go out, once you're well enough,' he said. 'To the pictures and dances, like we did at the start.'

'And you must promise not to hate James. Promise me you will be all right with him, Richard?'

'Aye, I'll try,' he said and turned away. Then he looked back at me. 'I'm going out to see a friend. I shan't get drunk. I promise you, Emma.'

'I don't expect you to be a saint, Richard – just a man I can respect. Let's try to be good to each other – please?'

He nodded, but didn't speak again before he left. I

was thoughtful as I lay back against the pillows. What had brought about this change of heart – surely not that foolish curse? Richard couldn't really believe Gran had the power to make him ill – could he?

Perhaps I'd been right all the time. He had been jealous of Paul's child growing in my womb. And maybe, if we both tried very hard, we might just manage to salve something from the wreck of our marriage.

The doctor wouldn't let me go back to work for two weeks after the birth. Mother and Ben shared the shop work between them, and Gran came to see me every other day.

I told her Richard had apologized, and that we had agreed to try again.

'That's right, lass.' She grinned at me. 'It's wonderful what a bit of a fright will do sometimes.'

It was obvious Gran thought Richard's transformation was a great joke. In a way it was amusing, because the change was so marked. Although a little awkward and subdued, he was trying very hard to please me. He had brought more flowers and fruit from the market, even a fancy cake from the baker's down the road.

I smiled and thanked him, yet I was conscious of a deep sadness. If he had been like this all the time, we might have had a good marriage by now – instead of pretending.

I would never be able to trust Richard again, not deep down in my heart – nor could I love him. He was trying very hard, but suspicion lay just beneath the surface. I sensed it was just a matter of time until it all started to crumble.

Three weeks after the birth of my son, I was in the shop putting out boxes of cigars and jars of sweets that had just come in. Ben had gone to have a cup of tea upstairs with my mother when the doorbell went and someone came in. I turned to see Sheila Tomms standing at the counter.

'How are you, Emma?'

'I'm fine,' I said. 'You haven't been in since I started back in the shop.'

'No . . .' She glanced up at the shelves. 'Oh, good, you've got my favourite toffee pieces in again. Sorry I haven't been to see you, I've been busy.' She laid a little parcel on the counter. 'I've knitted a bonnet and booties for you.'

'Oh, that's nice of you,' I said, unwrapping them. 'They're lovely, Sheila. Thank you.'

'I'm getting married next week. I've come to invite you and Mrs Robinson – and Richard, of course. If he wants to come.'

'Oh, that's lovely,' I said. 'I'm sure Mum would like to come. I'll ask Richard what shift he's on – but I shall come anyway.'

She looked at me oddly. 'I haven't seen Richard in the pub so much recently. Are things better between you two now?'

'Yes.' I turned away to weigh her sweets as I told the lie. 'We get on all right.'

'I've wanted to tell you, Emma . . .'

'Yes?' I waited as she hesitated, looking uncomfortable. 'What is it – something I ought to know?'

'You'll probably hate me for it.'

'No, I shan't. Is it about Richard?'

'You know . . .' She bit her lip. 'Or are you just guessing?'

'There was something between you and him once – am I right?'

She nodded, her gaze dropping. 'I'm not telling you to be vindictive. It's just that I heard he was rotten to you – hit you before the baby was born. But if you're getting on better—'

'You might as well tell me now you've started. It won't spoil anything. I'm not in love with him. I never have been.'

'The baby – the one I'd thought of aborting?' I nodded and she frowned. 'It was Richard's. I'd been seeing him for a while – until he started talking to your father in the pub and got grand ideas. I knew he wouldn't marry me, but I threatened to tell you if he didn't pay for the abortion. He went mad, hit me several times. That's why I cleared off out of it.'

'Yes. I thought it might be something like that.'

'Did he tell you?'

'No – but he was very angry about you. I knew there had to be a reason. And you'd told me why you went away. I knew you thought you were having a baby, and I sort of thought it might be Richard's.'

Sheila hesitated again. 'Do you remember that girl they found in the river – the one people thought might be me?'

'Yes.' I was puzzled. 'What about her?'

'I saw a picture of her in the paper. She looked a bit like me – or she would in the dark. She could have been mistaken for me. It just made me think . . .'

'I remember everyone thought she was you at first.' I felt a coldness at the nape of my neck. 'You don't think . . .?'

'I don't know.' Sheila looked nervous. 'He threatened me one night – about the time your father was taken bad. Said if I opened my mouth they would find me in the river one day.'

'Oh, Sheila!' I felt sick as I recalled the night I'd seen them arguing outside the pub. I'd been to fetch Father's medicine. Richard had been about to follow her, and then he'd seen me standing on the opposite side of the road. 'You don't think he meant it? He was just angry – afraid you might say something to me.'

'I expect so.' She shrugged. 'Perhaps I shouldn't have

told you. It's just that I thought you should know he can be dangerous.'

'He has a temper, especially when he's drunk, but I don't believe he would murder anyone.'

'The police never found that girl's killer,' Sheila said. 'I've often wondered if—' She laughed and shook her head, clearly embarrassed. 'Don't take any notice of me, Emma. It's my imagination. You won't tell him I said anything?'

'No, I shan't tell him, Sheila – but I think you're mistaken. Richard is a bully, but I can't think he would deliberately kill anyone. Why should he?'

She shrugged, looked as though she wanted to say more, but decided against it. 'No doubt I got it all wrong – but take care of yourself, Emma.'

'You too,' I replied. 'I shall look forward to the wedding. It will be an excuse for a new dress.'

Sheila laughed, paid for her purchases and went out.

I felt cold and shivery as I thought about what she had told me. That night I'd seen her with Richard outside the pub – would he have followed her and killed her if I hadn't been there? It was too horrible to contemplate. Richard was a lot of things – but surely not a murderer. . .

'Have I been too long?'

Ben's voice made me swing round. 'Why do you ask?'

'You were frowning something awful.'

'No, you haven't been too long – but I'm going to

have a clear-up in the stockroom. You can manage here, can't you?'

'Course I can,' Ben said cheerfully. 'You get on, Emma.'

I smiled at him, thanked him and went into the stockroom. I had been meaning to clear out some of the old boxes for ages. Father would never let me, but there was no reason I shouldn't now – and I needed something to keep me busy. Sheila had unsettled me more than I cared to admit.

I attacked the accumulation of rubbish with a good will. I hadn't felt like doing it after Father died, but now I was determined to have a good clear-out. I broke up and stacked several rotten crates, putting them out in the yard. They could go in the woodshed to be used for the fire. There were also piles of newspapers and empty cardboard boxes. These joined the crates in the yard. Behind them, I discovered five sealed boxes. My heart raced with excitement – could I have found Father's secret hoard at last?

The first contained children's colouring books; the second, writing paper; the third, envelopes; the fourth, pencils. The last was smaller and very heavy. My mouth went suddenly dry as I picked it up and broke the seal. Inside were several good quality silver cigarette cases and lighters. I supposed they must be worth a hundred pounds or more.

No sign of the elusive sovereigns, but at least I could fill some of the empty spaces on the shelves – and the cigarette cases would look nice in the locked cabinet behind the counter.

I carried the boxes one by one into the shop, leaving Ben to put out the stationery. Removing all the old boxes from the stockroom had revealed the wall, which was unplastered brick, painted a dull cream and showing signs of crumbling. I knelt down, running my hands over the bricks to see if there were any loose ones. It took me several minutes to check properly, but in the end I gave up.

If Father had hidden some sovereigns, it wasn't here. I'd really thought I might have found them under all the rubbish, but my search had been fruitless.

Perhaps there had ever only been one. So what had Father done with his money?

At least my efforts had settled my thoughts. Sheila had let her imagination run away with her – just as I had when Gran had pretended to put a curse on Richard.

Two months had passed since my son had been born. He was thriving and my relationship with Richard seemed to have improved – except that he hadn't tried to make love to me.

I told myself it didn't matter. We lay apart in our bed every night, neither of us attempting to bridge the gap between us. My memories of his past brutality did not exactly encourage me to welcome a return of his lovemaking, but I had promised myself I would try to rescue something from the ruins of this marriage.

Perhaps if Richard had a child of his own he would feel happier, more secure. I'd seen him looking at my son sometimes, and I had tried not to shudder inside or show my feelings. That odd expression on his face meant nothing. He wouldn't harm James. He had promised to be a good husband. And yet I accepted Mother's offer to have my baby sleep in her room, and when I got up for his nightly feeds, I was always careful not to wake Richard. But as much as I disliked the idea of any further intimacy with my husband, I knew the initiative had to come from me.

'Richard.' I turned towards him, putting a hand on his shoulder. 'Are you asleep?'

'No,' he muttered, obviously on the verge of going off. 'Is something wrong?'

I moved a little closer, so that our bodies were almost touching. I didn't want to do this, but I knew it might be the only way to guarantee a good life for my child and myself. If Richard could be made to think I cared for him even a little, he might be kinder towards my son. It was an effort to make myself, but I forced the words out.

'It's two months, Richard. I'm all right now – if you want to . . . you know.'

He seemed to freeze for a moment, then he reached out for me, drawing me closer. I could smell beer on his breath, but he hadn't drunk too much.

'I thought you wouldn't want me to touch you.'

I stroked his face in the darkness, then stretched up to brush my lips over his. 'It's all right, Richard. I want things to be good between us – the way they were at the start.'

He moaned low in his throat. His mouth fastened on mine, his hands beginning to knead my breasts beneath my flimsy nightdress. I stiffened without meaning to as he moved his body on top of mine, waiting for the inevitable – and then he stopped, rolling on to his back with a grunt.

'Richard?' I said. 'It's all right. I'm just a bit nervous.'

'Go to sleep, Emma,' he muttered. 'I don't want to force you.'

'You weren't,' I whispered, but I turned away from him. I had made the effort but could not deny my feeling of relief. 'Another night, then. Perhaps I'm just tired.'

Tears slipped down my cheeks as I lay sleepless long after Richard was snoring at my side. All I could think of was the empty years ahead.

I turned my thoughts towards other things. I had written to Jon telling him he must not send me any more money. I had thanked him for his kindness, but insisted he must not give me his own wages in future.

I supposed it would mean the end of our friendship.

He had kept in touch out of a sense of duty, of course – but it could not go on.

Eventually, I drifted into sleep. I might have mentioned his name. I might even have cried a little.

The news in the papers was worrying. It seemed that a war was creeping ever nearer. The government had brought in conscription, and a lot of young men were being sent their call up papers.

I wondered if Richard would have to join up, but when I mentioned the possibility he gave me an odd look and said it was unlikely.

'They'll need men to drive the trains,' he said, his eyes narrowed and accusing. 'You'll not get rid of me that easily, Emma.'

'I didn't want to get rid of you, Richard. I was just wondering, that's all.'

I sighed as I saw his scowling look. There were days when his moods were as bad as ever, but at least he hadn't hit me – not since Gran had threatened him.

It was now the middle of May. The sun was shining as I wheeled my son's pram along the High Street. I stopped outside Mrs Henty's shop, looking at a pretty dress in the window. She came to the door to speak to me.

'It's smart, isn't it?' she said. 'I thought of you when I bought it. It's from a new supplier in London.'

'I like it a lot,' I said. 'But I ought not to buy another new dress. I had one for Sheila's wedding.'

'Yes, I know. It was that nice blue one with the gored skirt. But this is special, Emma; better quality than we usually stock.' She felt in the pocket of her suit jacket and took out a business card to show me. 'The salesman told me there was a lot more on sale at their workrooms in the Portobello Road.'

I glanced at the card, feeling a shock of surprise. 'Solomon Gould – I met him once. When Richard took me to London for my birthday. His wife was ill. I helped her and he gave me a card like this one.'

'It wasn't Mr Gould himself who came here.' She looked thoughtful. 'You wouldn't like to go up, would you, Emma? I couldn't leave the shop. Besides, you have such good taste.'

'I should like that.' I looked at her in dawning excitement. 'It would be nice to get away.'

'Why don't you?'

'I'm not sure that Richard would let me.' The excitement faded almost at once. 'He doesn't know about our arrangement. No, I couldn't go, Madge. I'm sorry.'

'It was just a thought. I expect the salesman will call again.' She bent over the pram, cooing at James. 'He is a little love, Emma. Come and see me at the weekend. I'll have some money for you.'

I nodded and began pushing the pram again. People

stopped to look at my son and congratulate me. I was feeling relaxed and happy when I became aware of a car drawing up at the kerb. Turning to look, my heart caught as I saw Jon smiling at me. He was driving his uncle's car – the one Paul had been using the first time we met. Jon opened the window and called to me.

'I was coming to the shop,' Jon said. 'Then I saw you. You look lovely, Emma. You seemed so low the last time we met. I've been worried about you.'

'I'm fine,' I said. It was so good to see him. I hadn't realized how much I'd missed his occasional visits. 'Did you get my letter?'

He frowned and looked serious. 'That's partly why I came. I need to talk to you. Could we go somewhere? Perhaps have tea together?'

'I would need to take James home. His pram wouldn't go in the car.' I hesitated, knowing I was taking a risk. 'Why don't you come to the house? We could have tea upstairs, and you can hold James. If you would like that?'

I read the answer in his eyes before he spoke, and I knew he wanted to make this visit last a little longer as much as I did.

'Are you sure?'

'Yes, of course. My mother will be there – she would enjoy meeting you.'

'Shall I follow you?'

'Park your car, then come through the passage to the back yourself. I'll let you in.'

Jon nodded. My heart was racing as I pushed the pram back to the house. By the time I'd put it in the shed in the yard, Jon was at the back door of the house. He took James from me while I unlocked it, holding the child gently and with great care.

'He's beautiful. You must be very proud of him, Emma.'

'Yes, I am.' We smiled at each other as I led the way up the stairs. I called to my mother as we reached the landing. She came out of the kitchen, wiping her hands. Her expression was almost comic in her surprise.

'Emma?'

'This is Jonathan Reece, Mum. He's Paul's cousin. I've told you how generous he has been to me. He was passing, so I asked him up for tea. That's all right, isn't it?'

'Yes, of course.' I took James from him as he came to shake Mum's hand. 'It is so nice to meet you at last, Mr Reece. You have been very kind to my daughter.'

'Please call me Jon,' he said, clasping her hand with both of his. 'I hope you don't mind my turning up out of the blue?'

'Not at all. I'll put the kettle on.'

I took Jon into the parlour, then went to put James in his cot near the settee. My son looked at me with his big eyes and blew bubbles. He looked so beautiful that my throat caught with love for him.

Jon sat on the settee. I knelt down by the cot. When I glanced up, he was smiling down at me.

'I've imagined this so many times,' he said. 'I think of you often, Emma.'

My heart contracted with pain as I saw the naked longing in his eyes, and realized something that I had known in my heart for months. He cared for me, far more than he ought.

'You mustn't, Jon,' I whispered. 'It isn't right for you.'

'Are you happy?'

'No, not very.' I couldn't lie to him. 'I have been very unhappy since my marriage – but it is a little better at the moment. Richard was jealous about the child. My marriage was a mistake.'

'Then why . . .?'

I stood up and walked over to the window, looking down at the yard and Mother's tiny garden at the bottom. I wasn't sure how to answer him. Why didn't I leave Richard? Because of my father's will. And because I had been trying to save my marriage – but in my heart I knew it would never work out for us. This was just the lull before the storm.

Richard had tried to make love to me twice since the night I had invited him to do so, but both times he had turned away – even though I had tried to welcome his advances. And he was drinking again. Not as much as before, not enough to make him violent, but enough to make him fall asleep every night without touching me.

I felt a gentle touch on my shoulder. I turned and gazed up into Jon's eyes, making no attempt to resist as he took me into his arms. His kiss was so sweet, so tender, that tears sprang to my eyes.

'I love you, Emma,' Jon said huskily. 'I think I've loved you almost from the first moment we spoke.'

'You couldn't have,' I choked, tears blinding my eyes. 'You knew about . . . you had seen me with Paul.'

'That didn't stop me thinking you were the prettiest girl I'd ever seen. Then when I found you crying, I just wanted to look after you.' There was sadness in his eyes, and love. 'I was afraid to speak out that first afternoon. You were in trouble and upset – how could I tell you how I felt? It was too soon. I meant to talk to you the next time we met, to ask you if you would consider marrying me – just to make things easier on yourself. If my uncle hadn't died I would have but I couldn't come to you as I'd promised. And then it was too late. I've wished a thousand times I had told you how I felt at the beginning, but I've never been much with words.'

'You're doing very well at the moment,' I said, blinking back tears. A watery laugh escaped me. 'Oh, Jon . . . If only you had . . . if only you had.'

'Come with me, Emma,' he urged, and the longing was in his eyes. 'I'll take care of you and James. We'll find a way for you to divorce your husband.'

'He would never let me go. You don't know him, Jon. You don't know how violent he can be. Or what's at stake for him.'

'Go with him, Emma. It's your best chance of happiness.'

I turned to stare at my mother as she carried in the tea tray and set it down on the table.

'What about you?'

'It doesn't matter about me. I'll find somewhere to live. This is your chance to escape, Emma.'

'I could help with a house for Mrs Robinson,' Jon said, looking at me intently. 'I meant to tell you, Emma. My uncle left me a collection of valuable books – that's how I was able to send the money. If you're worried about your mother—'

'Oh, Jon.' I stared at him helplessly. It was so tempting to say yes and let him take me away – but we hardly knew one another. I had already made so many mistakes. I was almost sure we could be happy together, but I was afraid to commit myself. 'I'm not sure. I need to think about this.'

'Go with him, Emma,' my mother urged, 'while you have the chance.'

'You don't have to make up your mind this minute,' Jon said gently. 'If you decide to come, just telephone my office.'

'Jon—' I was on the verge of saying I would go with

him when we all heard feet pounding up the stairs and then Ben burst into the room.

'Emma,' he gasped, face white with shock. 'You've got to come. There's someone in the shop . . . he says your gran's hurt bad. You've got to come straight away.'

'Gran hurt?' My gaze flew to Jon in immediate appeal. 'Where is she?'

Ben was clearly in a state of shock and distress. 'At her cottage. The doctor has been sent for – but they say she's bad. She's had an accident, Emma.'

'I'll take you to her,' Jon offered at once. 'Forget everything else for the moment. There will be plenty of time for us. Your gran has to come first.'

'I'll stay here with the baby,' Mother said at once. 'It's you your gran will want to see, Emma.'

'Oh, Mum,' I rushed to hug her as the tears threatened. 'I'll tell her you love her. I'm sorry. I have to go . . .'

Chapter Thirteen

I was tense and anxious as Jon drove me to Gran's cottage, hardly speaking the whole of the journey. When we arrived I saw there was a little crowd of people outside. They looked at me oddly as I jumped out of the car and ran inside. Doctor Barton was waiting for me. He stopped me as I would have gone into the bedroom.

'She's very poorly,' he said in a low voice. 'I doubt she'll last the night – but she *is* conscious and she wants to see you.'

I swallowed hard, holding back the tears. 'What happened? Was it an accident?'

'I don't think so. She has a severe wound to the back of her head. I think she was struck from behind. She was found by one of her friends, a lady who often calls to see how she is.'

'She has many friends,' I said. 'Where was she?'

'In the kitchen, lying on the floor – and this was near her.'

He indicated a biscuit tin. At the moment it contained only a broken string of coral beads and some papers.

'Someone must have robbed her. She told me her bits and pieces were in a tin under her bed.'

'When was this?'

'Just after my father died. She said there wasn't much – but it was meant for me.'

He nodded gravely. 'You didn't tell anyone – anyone at all?'

'No. Why?'

'It may not mean anything, Emma – but when she first regained her senses she mentioned a name. It was your husband's name.'

'No!' I grabbed at the back of a kitchen chair as the room seemed to spin around me. Richard couldn't have done this terrible thing! It was too horrible to contemplate. 'He wouldn't, would he? I know he drinks but this is murder.'

'Perhaps it means nothing,' Doctor Barton said. 'But I thought it best to tell you. You can go in now.'

I was reeling from the double shock as I went into the bedroom. Gran was lying flat with her eyes closed, but she opened them as I approached, her lips forming a smile of welcome.'

'Emma, lass . . . there isn't much time.' Her hand moved restlessly on the bedcovers. I took it in mine. It felt cold and she was trembling. 'It's my fault. I put the fear into him, but it was for your sake. Forgive me, lass. I never thought he would do something like this . . .'

'Oh, Gran.' Sickness rose in my throat as I realized what she was saying. It had been Richard who had attacked her! 'Don't talk. Don't tire yourself.'

'I haven't told anyone else,' she said. 'They don't know it was Richard. It's your choice, Emma. If you want to be free . . . or it could be a hold over him.'

'Please don't talk, dearest. Don't worry about me.' The tears were so close. I loved her and she was dying – because she had tried to protect me. 'I knew it was wrong. He's so violent . . .'

'He accused me of stealing his manhood.' A faint chuckle escaped her. 'At least he hasn't been bothering you, lass.'

I remembered the way Richard had turned away from me in bed. Something had prevented him from being a proper husband – was it only in his mind, or had there been another reason?

The game Gran and my mother had been playing was a dangerous one. It had driven Richard into a corner, and like a wild beast, he was most unpredictable when wounded.

Gran had closed her eyes. I felt an overwhelming grief. She had clung on to life for my sake. Now there was nothing more to hold her. I could see the colour fading from her cheeks. She was slipping away from me – and I couldn't bear it.

'Gran,' I sobbed. 'Don't go. Don't leave me. I love you so much.'

She opened her eyes once more, smiling as if in blessing. But then there was a horrid rattle as her last breath was spent and I knew she had left me.

'Oh, Gran . . .' I wept openly now. It hurt so much. The pain swept over me. It was all Richard's fault! He had lied to me, beaten me – and now he had killed Gran. I felt a surge of anger and of hatred. 'Gran. I love you so. I love you so . . .'

'So she's gone, then?'

I glanced over my shoulder as the doctor came in. I sobbed out my grief, tears streaming down my cheeks.

He laid a sympathetic hand on my shoulder. 'Mr Reece asked me to tell you he would be in touch soon. He left because he thought you might prefer to be alone.'

Did I want that? I wasn't sure. Jon had done what he felt right, but at that moment I needed a shoulder to cry on.

'Gran told me – it was Richard who attacked her. He killed her and stole her things.'

'Are you prepared to make a statement about this?'

'Yes, I am. My husband is a violent man. He has abused me ever since our honeymoon. Because of what he did to me, Gran tried to threaten him, to make him leave me alone – and this was his revenge.'

Doctor Barton looked serious. 'You understand what this will mean? He will be arrested and tried for murder – it will be in the papers. If he is found guilty, he could hang.'

'If he is guilty—' I choked back a sob. 'He will deserve to be punished, won't he?'

'In my opinion he should hang,' Doctor Barton said. 'But I wanted to be sure you were prepared for the consequences, Mrs Gillows. It will be your testimony, and my own, which will convict him. There are no witnesses. You will have to stand up in court and give evidence.'

I stared at him, a sense of horror sweeping over me. Gran had given me the choice, because once again she had wanted to protect me from what would be an unpleasant experience. In a small town like ours there would be bound to be gossip and pointing fingers. But I could not allow Richard's crime to go unpunished.

'Yes, I am prepared,' I said, my head going up. 'My husband is not a good man, sir. It is just possible that he might have killed before: a girl he mistook for someone else.'

'What do you mean?'

I explained, telling him what Sheila had told me that day in the shop – that he might have mistaken another girl for her.

Doctor Barton nodded, looking grave. 'I see. I shall report this to the police. Do you think she would repeat her story to them?'

'I don't know. She might not want to now that she's married.'

'Well, we'll have to see what happens. In the meantime, you may be in danger. Your mother and son also. Richard will be frightened and angry. He may try to harm you – especially if he thinks you might give testimony against him.'

'Perhaps.' I looked at Gran. She was so white, so still – yet she looked peaceful, younger somehow. 'I don't want to leave her like this.'

'There are others who will look after her, Emma. Friends who cared for her. Mother Jacobs was loved by many. There will be many to mourn her – and to call for justice when this gets out.'

'Yes, I know. She was always getting little presents from folk who cared for her. A lot of the young lads who work on the railway called regularly. If some of them find Richard before the police—' I shuddered. 'I think they would make him sorry he ever lived.'

'Go home, my dear.' Doctor Barton touched my arm. 'Leave your grandmother to me. And be careful.'

'Yes,' I said. 'I shall. Thank you, sir. You are very kind.'

*

Emma

'Richard killed her?' Mother stared at me in horror. 'I can't believe it, Emma. No! Oh no . . . It's all my fault. I shouldn't have done it . . . but I thought it would help.'

She looked pale and distressed, suddenly sitting down on the settee with a bump. She was in such a state that I knew my suspicions had been right. My mother and grandmother had been plotting something together.

'Did you put something in his food?'

'It was harmless,' she said, giving me a guilty glance. 'It wouldn't have killed him, Emma. I just wanted to punish him a little for what he'd done to you. Gran gave me a herbal mixture. She said to give him a small dose occasionally. It was supposed to make him less inclined towards – well, you know.'

'So you planned it together.' I looked into her eyes. 'Did you do the same to Father? Put something in his dinner to make him suffer?'

She nodded, biting her bottom lip. 'I never meant Harold to die. You must believe me. It wasn't my fault. I asked Gran the day she cursed Richard. I told her what I'd used. She said it wouldn't have killed him – it just made him sick.'

'What did you give him?'

'I don't even know what it's called. It's a herb that grows wild. Gran used it to make poultices. Once, when I was a child, I ate some – just chewed at the leaf. It made me violently sick, but I got over it within hours.'

'Oh, Mum. Perhaps it didn't kill Father, but it didn't help him.'

'It was only a few times. After you'd fallen pregnant and he'd threatened us both. Never before that, and that's the truth. I promise you, Emma. I wouldn't have poisoned him. I just didn't want him to turn violent. I thought if he didn't feel good he'd have enough on his mind.'

She looked ashamed of herself, and I sighed.

How could I blame her for doing what she had? Father had been so unkind to her. For years he had bullied and carped at her. She had put up with his mental and physical cruelty for my sake, knowing that I had the chance of a better life as his daughter. She wasn't strong enough to stand on her own feet and make a living for us both. So she had endured her husband's taunting and the occasional blow for the sake of what he might leave me.

In a way it was poetic justice, and yet it left an unpleasant taste in my mouth. She ought to have found the courage to leave my father when I was still a child. What she had done was attempt to protect me, but it was wrong. It was wrong, and yet I could not be angry with her, I could not condemn her. I loved her.

'I know you didn't kill him, Mum,' I said, moving to hug her, my eyes misting. 'I know what you did was for me – but that doesn't make it right.'

'I know.' She sniffed hard and I gave her my handkerchief. She accepted it with a watery smile. 'But I couldn't stand to see you hurt, Emma. And when Richard started hitting you . . .' A tiny sob escaped her. 'But now it's all gone wrong. I've killed Gran . . .'

'Of course you haven't,' I said. 'It was her own idea to put the curse on Richard. I begged her not to do anything silly. I was going to leave him when I was ready. I wouldn't have put up with his bullying for ever – not the way you did, Mum.'

She looked at me, a strange expression in her eyes. 'No, you wouldn't have, Emma. I can see that now. You're stronger than I am. You must get that from your father. Harold had his ways . . . but he wasn't a bad man. If I'd been a virgin when we wed, who knows? We might have been very happy.' She sighed. 'But he couldn't forgive me for that, and it ruined everything.'

'Did you ever love him, Mum?'

She shook her head. 'Not really. I put money above love, and look where it got me. You'll never do that, will you, Emma? Promise me you'll marry for love next time.'

'But I'm still married to Richard.'

'Perhaps not for much longer.'

A shudder ran through me. I got up from the sofa and walked over to the window, gazing out at the back yard. It was getting dark now. Richard was out there somewhere.

What was in his mind? He had killed once – was it his intention to kill again?

'The back door is bolted inside,' I said, without turning round. 'And I'll make sure the shop is secure after Ben goes off for the night – but if Richard is desperate he'll get in somehow. I should lock your door from now on, Mum.'

'You've no need to remind me,' she said. 'You do the same, Emma. I shan't feel safe until he's been arrested.'

'No, nor me,' I replied. 'We shall just have to be careful, that's all.'

'I could ask a friend of mine to move in for a while,' she said tentatively. 'Just to sleep – in case Richard tries to break in while we're asleep.'

'A friend?' I was puzzled, then I recalled the man she had danced with at the church social. 'Do you mean Mr Fitch – the man you were dancing with the night we went out with Richard?'

There was a faint flush in her cheeks. 'Yes. I haven't told you before, Emma, because it was too soon. And I couldn't think of leaving you while Richard was around, but Bert has asked me to marry him.'

'Do you want to?' She didn't answer at once, but there was something in her eyes. Suddenly the penny dropped. 'He's the one, isn't he? He asked you to marry him years ago, but you said no and he went away.'

'I regretted it as soon as he'd gone,' she admitted. 'I didn't realize how much I loved him until I'd lost him.'

'Oh, Mum,' I said, feeling pity for her. She had been

tied to a man she didn't love for years. 'Why didn't you write to him – ask him to come back?'

'I didn't know where he'd gone. Besides, Harold was courting me. He seemed such a wonderful catch, Emma. He would never discuss his folk, but I think he came from a good family. There was always some mystery about that; he would never talk about the past – even when he cared about me. And I think he did . . . at the beginning.'

My throat caught as I pictured her life, her regret and disappointment when nothing turned out as she had hoped.

'You should have left Father years ago, Mum.'

'I had you to think of,' she said. 'But you're grown up, Emma. You've a good head on your shoulders. I shan't do anything just yet, but when this is all over . . .'

'Yes, you should marry him, Mum – if it's what you want.'

'It is,' she said. 'Bert still loves me, even after all this time. I think we can make each other happy.'

'Good, I'm glad.'

James started to cry at that moment. I gathered him up and took him into the bedroom to feed him. Stroking his downy head, I crushed the worm of suspicion in my mind. Mother would not lie to me, surely? Yes, she had wanted to be free of her unhappy marriage, and she admitted making my father sick. But somehow, I didn't think that the herbs she'd given him were totally responsible for his death. She would not have poisoned him.

Yet I had a terrible feeling that someone might have done just that.

I woke with a start as I heard the splinter of breaking glass and knew it came from the back yard. Someone was breaking in. And I knew who it was.

Richard had a key to the back door, but it was bolted inside. He would not have let that stop him. I lay listening, and then I heard someone moving about downstairs. I crossed my fingers and hoped Richard had come looking for money, praying he would be satisfied with what I'd left in the till.

I heard it ring as the drawer was opened, then something went flying and I heard a smash as if a glass jar had broken. No, it was probably the cabinet with the silver cigarette cases. I had left that locked, and they were the most valuable items in the shop. Richard might be able to sell them somewhere, and he would need money now that he was on the run from the law. Would he come upstairs?

I lay waiting, hardly able to breathe, for some time. The noises had stopped downstairs. Was Richard still there, waiting for me to go down and investigate? It would be the worst thing I could do in the circumstances. Locked in my room, with a chair lodged under the handle, I was surely safer than I would be downstairs.

The minutes passed slowly. Had he gone by now? I got up, reaching for my dressing gown and slipped it on. Creeping softly to the door I leaned my head against it, straining for the slightest creak. It was ages since I'd heard the last sound.

I unlocked my door and stepped out into the darkness. Immediately, I sensed danger. He was here, waiting. I could smell the strong odour of oil which always clung about him. Reaching for the light, I switched it on, flooding the hall, to see him standing just a few feet away from me. He had bread and cheese in his hand, and a bottle of beer.

He sneered at me. 'I knew you would come if I waited long enough,' he said. 'So you've been telling tales about me. You know what that means.' He moved towards me. I retreated, my heart racing wildly.

'Stay where you are, Richard!' I said, holding out my hand to ward him off. 'If you touch me, I'll scream.'

'So what?' he sneered. 'Who's going to rescue you now? Your mother – or your precious Gran?'

'I know you killed her. Only you made one mistake, Richard. She wasn't quite dead. She told us it was you who attacked her.'

'I thought she was dead,' he muttered. 'I should have hit her again to make sure.'

'Yes, you should,' I said. I could see that the door to the spare bedroom had opened just a crack and my fear of Richard faded. 'That was your mistake. You killed my grandmother and you'll hang for it. The police will arrest you and I shall stand up in court to—'

'I'll shut your mouth once and for all,' Richard took a step towards me, his fist raised. 'I showed that old hag what I thought of her and I'll show you. Harold cheated me of my rights. The mean old bastard! I thought I'd fixed him good and proper. He had the last laugh, after all, but you . . .'

'What do you mean?' I was seized by a sudden suspicion, my blood running cold as everything began to slot into place. 'You gave him something. Something to make him ill . . .'

Richard's lip curled over his teeth. 'I found some tablets in that desk downstairs. I was looking for money but I found the tablets instead – there was arsenic in them. The fool had been taking them, and they were making him ill – so I helped him along a little. He was taking some foul medicine or other. I crushed the tablets up and put them in that stuff your grandmother gave him.' He laughed triumphantly. 'If they had suspected murder it was her they would've blamed.'

'You devil!' I cried, my voice rising angrily. 'You murdered my father to get the money you knew he had left you – and now you've killed Gran. You'll hang for certain, Richard Gillows.'

'No one knows but you,' he said. 'And if you were to

have a little accident, like falling down the stairs, who would know?'

He made a movement towards me, then stopped as the door to the spare room opened wide and a man stepped out, carrying a shotgun.

'I'd know for one,' Bert Fitch said. 'I've heard every word you said, Gillows – and I'll stand up in court and repeat it for a judge. I'll see you hang cheerfully. And if you lay a finger on Emma or her mother, I'll shoot you like the dog you are.'

Richard stared at him, his mouth open. 'What the hell are you doing here?'

'Mrs Robinson sent for me,' Bert said. 'We're friends, see, and I'm staying here to protect her.' He glanced at me. 'Emma, put your coat on and run for the police.'

Richard looked at me. He was between me and the stairs. He could have tried to grab me, but Bert was raising the gun to his shoulder, taking aim. Suddenly, he threw the beer bottle at Bert, then turned and made a dash for the stairs as the gun went off, but misfired, the barrels winging upwards to the ceiling, bringing down a shower of plaster.

'Damn!' Bert said. 'Sorry about that, Emma. I never meant to fire, that bottle jerked my arm.'

'Bert!' Mother had come to the door of her room. She looked terrified. 'What happened? You promised me you wouldn't fire that thing in the house.'

'It wasn't his fault,' I said. 'Richard was here. He was going to hit me. Mr Fitch came out and stopped him.'

'He threw a bottle at me,' Bert said. 'Sorry, Greta. I didn't mean to scare you.'

'It's all right,' she said, although the colour had left her face. 'It's a good thing you were here, Bert.'

'Yes, it was,' I said. 'I didn't really think he would try to harm us, but Mum was right. I'm glad you were here.'

'It was a pleasure,' he said, his eyes narrowing. 'That man is a menace, Emma. Neither you nor your mother will be safe while he's around. I'm going to go next door to ask Mr Baker to alert the police, then I'll come back here and sit up all night.'

'I don't think he will come back,' I said, smiling as I recalled the look on Richard's face as he'd seen the shotgun. 'He doesn't know you didn't mean to fire. He won't risk coming here again.'

'Perhaps not,' he said and grinned. 'But I'd best make sure, just the same. You go with your mother, Emma, and lock yourselves in until I get back.'

'Leave the gun with us,' I said. 'Just in case he does try.'

Bert hesitated, then put the gun into my hands. 'It still has one barrel loaded. Be careful. Look – this is the safety catch, don't touch that unless you have to.'

'I shan't,' I promised and smiled at him.

I took the gun into my mother's bedroom, leaning it in a corner with the catch on as Bert had showed me.

James had started to whimper in his cot. I bent over him, stroking his face with the tips of my fingers.

'You're not hungry,' I whispered, 'no, you're not. It isn't time yet. Go back to sleep, little one.'

Mother was sitting on the edge of the bed. Her face was still very pale. She glanced at me as I left James to settle and went to sit beside her, taking her hand.

'I heard what Richard was saying,' she said, and I felt her tremble. 'I never dreamed what he had done. Harold had asked for more of Gran's mixture. I gave it to him, Emma. It was after that he started bringing up the blood.'

'You didn't know what Richard had done. None of us knew he was capable of murder. You can't blame yourself.'

'No . . .' She raised her head, her expression one of determination. 'No, I shan't any more. I'm going to put it all behind me. I'm going to marry Bert as soon as you're settled.'

'Yes, Mum,' I said and kissed her. 'You do that.'

'You should go with that nice Mr Reece,' she said. 'You'd be safe then, Emma.'

'We'll see,' I replied. 'I'm not sure yet. I can't think properly – not until all this is over.'

The police came round the next day to take my statement about the break-in and advise about new locks on the doors and windows.

'We are looking for him, Mrs Gillows,' the young

officer told me,' but so far we haven't been able to find him. All we can do is keep a watch on this place.'

'I don't think he will come back,' I said. 'Mr Fitch scared him off. He thought we were alone, but now he knows my mother's friend is staying, he won't risk coming back.'

'It depends how desperate he is,' the constable said. 'He'll know he's being hunted, and he'll need money to get away.'

'He took money and some valuable cigarette cases last night – but they were his to take under the terms of my father's will.'

'Well, just you be careful,' the officer said. 'We're doing our best, Mrs Gillows, but it may be a while before he is apprehended.'

I thanked him and he left. Afterwards, I went down to the shop. Ben had cleared away the mess of the smashed cabinet. I looked at the empty space on the wall and shivered, remembering the look on Richard's face the previous evening as he had threatened to kill me.

'It's all right, Emma,' Ben said as he saw my face. 'If he comes in here, I'll protect you.'

'Thank you, Ben,' I replied, not allowing my smile to show. 'But I don't think he will – not during the day.'

'He deserves a birching afore they hang him,' Ben said. 'There are a good many around here would be pleased to do it, given a chance. Your Gran was a nice old lady. She cleared a wart off Ma's hand once, never charged her a penny for it – and Ma ain't the only one neither. I reckon there's some would do for that so-and-so if they could – they'd teach Richard Gillows a lesson he'd never forget.'

'Yes, I expect so,' I said, and shuddered convulsively. 'Could you manage in here if I go into the stockroom, Ben?'

'You know I can,' he said. 'Do anything for you, Emma.'

I smiled at him and went into the stockroom. I was feeling upset by everything that had happened. All the things I'd discovered about my father's illness and his death. If I had never married Richard . . . if I hadn't let Paul make love to me . . . none of this need have happened.

And yet Father had been planning even before that – he had been thinking about marrying me off to a man he trusted. A misplaced trust, as it turned out.

How could he? How could he have made such an scandalous bargain with Richard? By doing so, he had made both Mum and me hostages for life – or that's what he had intended. He had wanted to make sure that neither of us could ever leave this shop. But I would. I would leave as soon as Richard was arrested. I wouldn't stay here a moment longer. I felt angry. So angry that Father had tried to manipulate our lives. It wasn't fair, it wasn't right.

I was standing next to his roll top desk and, in my fury, I suddenly gave it a tremendous thump. Damn Father! Damn him for leaving Mother and me with nothing!

As I thumped the top of the desk, the roll front fell down with a clatter. I thumped it again for good measure, taking my frustration out on the old piece of furniture. Then, as my anger left me, I laughed instead and pushed the roll back again, revealing all the little drawers and pigeon holes. For a moment as I stared at it, I couldn't think what was different. Then I realized that one of the little pillars which separated the pigeon holes had somehow shot forward. I reached out to push it back, then realized it was a secret drawer – open at the top.

I had heard of them, but never imagined there was one in Father's desk. I took hold of it, trying to pull it out, but it fell from my hand because it was so heavy. My heart raced as I tipped the contents out onto the desk. It had been packed with small brown envelopes and each one made a thud as they landed on the wooden surface. I picked one up and looked at the writing on the envelope.

'Golden guinea, 1860'

'Golden half guinea, 1790'

The writing was my father's, and it was on every envelope, listing the coins inside. Every one of the coins was gold, some were sovereigns, some guineas – some Roman coins.

My father had been a collector of coins. So this was where his money had gone.

I stared at his secret hoard. Most of them gave no

indication of the value, but even at face value there were hundreds, perhaps a thousand or more, pounds.

It was quite a find, and it was mine. My eyes stung with sudden tears as I realized Father had left me my independence after all. He might have made his bargain with Richard, but he had left me a way of escape.

Yet why couldn't he have spent some of this money on Mum and me? Why hadn't he let me make up my own mind about marrying Richard? Had he only been kinder, he might still be alive.

I glanced in the drawer again. At the bottom there was a scrap of paper which hadn't come out with the coins. I stuck a pencil down and levered it free, shaking it down into my hands. Opening it, I saw it was a message in Father's writing, and it was to me.

'I knew you would find this if you looked hard enough, Emma. You maybe hate me for what I've done to you – but I thought it was best. You needed someone to protect you, look after you, but perhaps I picked the wrong man. I'm sorry. You've been a good daughter. There's enough here to start you off in a new life. Use your head, Emma. If there's any of me in you, you won't let life get you down.'

I felt my throat close with emotion. He had done what he thought was right. My whole family had tried to protect me, but it had all gone sadly wrong.

'Oh, Father. Why didn't you let me decide for myself?'

'They must be worth a lot of money.' Mother looked at the coins as I spread them on the parlour table for her to see. She clasped my hand, excitement in her eyes. 'I knew there must be something. I'm glad he left them to you.'

'To us,' I said. 'They're as much yours as mine, Mum.'

'No, Emma, I don't need them. I'm going to marry Bert. Besides, I don't want them. I don't want anything of Harold's. I married him for money and that was wrong. When I leave this place, that will be the end of it as far as I'm concerned.'

'Are you sure, Mum? I would much rather share the money with you.'

'You'd best put them in the bank, love – until you decide what to do with them.'

'I thought I might take them to London,' I said. 'Have them valued – perhaps sell them.'

'Well, if that's what you want,' she said, 'but be careful, Emma. If your father said they were worth a bit, they will be. Don't let those dealers cheat you.'

'No, I shan't,' I said and smiled at her. 'I've been wanting to go to London for a while. Madge asked me to pick out some stock for her shop, but I knew Richard wouldn't let me go, but now . . . I can do anything I want now, can't I?'

'Yes, I suppose you can.' She looked at me uncertainly. 'Do you want me to come with you?'

'No, I can go on my own,' I said. 'Will you stay here – or go to live with Mr Fitch?'

'I'll ask him to stay here,' she said. 'I shan't move in with him until you're settled, love.' She hesitated, then, 'What about the shop?'

'Ben can look after it for a couple of days.'

'I meant . . . afterwards?'

'Oh, I don't know. It belongs to Richard, Mum. I'll have to ask Mr Smythe what I should do.'

'It's yours by right,' she said. 'Harold wouldn't have wanted him to have it if he'd known.'

'No,' I shook my head. 'We'll have to see, Mum. But whatever he says, I'm not going to stay here much longer.'

For the first day or so after Richard's nocturnal visit, we lived in apprehension of another unwelcome surprise, but it didn't happen. People came into the shop to sympathise and praise Gran – no one had a good word for Richard.

Feeling was growing in the town. Sheila told me she'd heard several threats made against him.

'Some of the young lads are keeping an eye out for him,' she said. 'If they do what they're promising, there won't be much left for the police to pick up.'

'Oh, don't,' I said. 'I want him to be caught and punished, Sheila, as much, perhaps more than anyone. But this isn't right. It's like a lynch mob out of a cowboy picture.'

'I shouldn't worry,' she said, laughing. 'Most of them are all talk and no do.' I smiled and she went out, but her visit had left me feeling cold all over and I had a premonition that something terrible was going to happen.

The next day was Gran's funeral. The church was packed to capacity and a crowd had gathered outside to show their feelings. I heard several whispers of shame, and some of the women reached out to touch me as I passed, trying to give comfort.

I wept throughout the ceremony, partly because the church was throbbing with love. Gran *had* been loved, even by strangers who hardly knew her and simply looked forward to seeing her as they passed by her cottage each day in their train.

After the service, a feeling of peace came over me. Gran had been near her time. I felt she was beside me, her kindness and love wrapping about me as her arms had done in life. And I knew she was at peace. It was as if she was talking to me, telling me not to grieve for her, telling me to go on with my life. And that was just what I intended to do. I wasn't going to let the thought of Richard hiding, waiting in the shadows, deter me from doing what I wanted. And first of all, I was going to take a little trip to London.

Chapter Fourteen

I came out of the coin dealer's shop feeling disgusted. It was the third I'd visited that morning, and not one of them had treated me decently. Only one had offered a price, and that was hardly more than face value. The other two had asked me what I wanted, refusing to give me a valuation for the coin I'd shown them.

It was obviously going to be harder to sell Father's collection than I'd imagined. But for the moment that would have to wait. Glancing at my watch, I saw that it was time for me to meet Mr Gould at his showrooms in the Portobello Road.

I had telephoned him from my hotel on the evening of my arrival in London, making an appointment for today at noon. It had been my intention to have Father's coins valued before that, perhaps to sell them. Now I would have to take them with me, and they were heavy. The weight of my shopping bag was making my arm ache.

I hailed a cab to take me to Mr Gould's showrooms. My appointment was with him personally, though I hadn't told him we had met before, just that I would like to see what he had in stock that might be suitable for Mrs Henty's shop.

'I'm sure we can find something,' he'd promised. 'I shall look forward to meeting you, Mrs Gillows.'

Getting out of the cab some fifteen minutes later, I stood outside the showroom and stared at the window. It had blinds behind the three dummies, which were all that were being shown, and looked rather dingy from the outside. However, the clothes displayed – two dresses and a smart costume – were good quality and very stylish. I thought of Sheila and the other girls I'd come to know while working in Father's shop. Any one of them would go wild for clothes like these. But I supposed they would be far too expensive for us to sell.

Across the street, a man was pushing a rail of coats along the pavement, another was taking a pile of shirts into a tiny showroom. It was a busy road, with vans, bikes, cars and a red bus adding to the confusion. I paused for a moment, absorbing the atmosphere. It was exciting, like a living, throbbing pulse. So different from the quiet streets at home, which only seemed to come alive like this on market days.

I pushed open the door of Gould's and went in, setting the bell on the jangle. A woman turned to look at me over the top of her glasses, which perched precariously on the end of her nose.

'Yes, can I help you?'

'I've come to see Mr Gould.'

I could see him standing at the back of the large room, in what looked as if it must be his office.

'Have you an appointment? Mr Gould is a busy man.'

'I am Mrs Gillows. I spoke to him yesterday evening.'

She looked disbelieving but went off to inquire. He glanced in my direction; then she returned to tell me I was to go to the office. As I approached, Mr Gould came out to greet me and we shook hands.

'Mrs Gillows. You wanted to see some stock for your shop I believe?'

'It's Mrs Henty's shop – but I am her partner in the business.'

He nodded thoughtfully. 'What were you looking for in particular?'

'I'm not sure. I liked the dresses in the window. How much are they?'

'They would cost you thirty-five shillings – which means they would retail at about three pounds and ten shillings.'

I was surprised. I had thought they would be more expensive. He chuckled as he saw my face. It was a nice sound, pleasant and comforting.

'You've come direct to the manufacturer, Mrs

Gillows. It was a shrewd move on your part. This way you cut out the middle man, which means you can either charge a bigger mark up or sell more cheaply than your competitors.'

'That sounds like good business to me.' I smiled at him. 'Mrs Henty says I can spend fifty pounds with you this time.'

'That's a good start,' he said, wrinkling his brow as his eyes went over me. 'I can't help feeling we've met before – but I can't think where.'

I blushed. 'We have met before, very briefly. Your wife had been shopping and . . .'

'You saved her from a nasty fall,' he said, striking his forehead with the heel of his hand. 'Well, bless my soul! This is a turn up for the books. I've often thought of you, wished I'd asked for your name. I wanted to thank you properly.'

'There was no need. I did very little.'

'You were kind and thoughtful. Not many would have noticed Margaret was ill.'

'Really, it was nothing.'

'It meant a lot to me.' He smiled. 'Let me show you the rails, Mrs Gillows. Forget the prices on the tickets. I'm sure we can do better for you.'

I laughed, caught up in the excitement of my adventure.

'This is my first go at buying for the shop. I shall need some help.'

'Don't buy everything in your own size,' he joked. 'Not everyone is as slim as you are, Mrs Gillows. You need to think about your regular customers.' He pulled a pretty blue dress out to show me. It had a gored skirt and three-quarter length sleeves, but the neck was unusually shaped with a little roll collar. 'This is for an older customer, someone like your mother, perhaps?'

'Yes, it would suit her,' I replied. 'She could wear it with a white hat for a wedding.'

'And this would look nice on someone of your own age . . .'

He went through all the rails with me, patiently pointing out the latest fashions, but advising me to stick with the tried and tested lines.

'Nothing too outrageous for a country town.'

I made my selection, sometimes choosing a dress that was a little more expensive, a little smarter than the average. By the time we had finished there were thirty dresses and five costumes hanging on 'my' rail.

'I should like to have them all,' I said. 'But I may have gone over my budget.'

'Come into the office. We'll see what we can do.' I had left my shopping bag on a chair and he picked it up to hand it to me. 'That's heavy – got the Crown Jewels in there, have you?'

'Almost,' I said and laughed. 'My father left me some

coins. I've been trying to sell them, but no one will give me a valuation – at least, not a sensible one.'

'I'm a bit of a collector myself. Would you like me to take a look at them for you?'

I didn't hesitate. 'Would you mind? I'd like to sell them but I don't know how, or what they're worth.'

I opened my bag and laid the coins on his desk. 'I've been offered just over face value on this one, but I thought it might be worth more?'

He looked at the coin, nodded and drew a pad forward, making a mark on it. Then he began to open the envelopes one by one, looking carefully at each coin before returning it to its envelope. He wrote on his pad each time. The minutes ticked by and I felt awkward; I hadn't expected him to be so thorough. This was taking a lot of his time, which must be valuable.

After he had examined all the coins, he sat frowning over his notes for so long that I couldn't stand the suspense any longer.

'Are they any good?'

He glanced up, still frowning. 'Your father was a very shrewd man, Mrs Gillows. This is a remarkable collection. I should say at a guess that you have two or perhaps three thousand pounds worth of coins here. I'm not sure of the exact value until I check them out properly, but I could do that. I could get a price for you. A genuine price that would reflect their value.'

I felt a thrill of excitement. I hadn't dreamed the coins would be worth so much.

'Would you do that? Is it too much to ask you to trouble yourself for my sake?'

'It isn't a trouble at all, I like coins. I shall enjoy researching these properly.' He smiled, then looked at me inquiringly. 'If you wish me to undertake the sale on your behalf, I shall give you a receipt for them, and I shall advise you of the best price before I sell.'

'I don't need a receipt. I trust you.'

He smiled but shook his head. 'Now I *am* disappointed in you, Mrs Gillows. You've been showing a flair for business, but the first rule of success is never to trust anyone completely. You need a receipt. I might die. You might be knocked down by a bus before you have the chance to tell anyone what you've done. Then what would your husband say?'

I glanced down at my lap, twisting my gloves in my hand. 'My husband has . . . left me.'

'Left a lovely girl like you? The man's a scoundrel or a fool.' His eyes twinkled at me. 'I'll put these away in the safe, then we'll ask my assistant to make out your invoice and, if you're agreeable, we'll have lunch together. To thank you for your kindness to my wife a long time ago and also because I should like to know a little more about you, Mrs Gillows.'

'My first name is Emma,' I said, responding to his

humour and charm. 'Yes, I would like to have lunch with you, but I must see this invoice first. Mrs Henty told me not to spend more than fifty pounds.'

'Spoken like a true professional,' he said and chuckled. 'Business first, then pleasure. Let's get on with it then.'

Solomon Gould took me to the Savoy Hotel for lunch. At first I was a little overawed by my surroundings, but the friendliness of my host and the waiters, whom he seemed to know by name, soon put me at ease. Solomon, or Sol, as he preferred to be called, chose all manner of delicious things from the varied menu: fresh salmon, asparagus, tiny minted new potatoes, then a strawberry mousse with thick cream followed by coffee and handmade chocolates. He also bought me champagne.

Afterwards, I sighed with pleasure. 'I've never eaten anything like this before, and this is my first taste of champagne.'

'I thought we should celebrate the beginning of our business association,' he said, a gleam in his dark eyes. 'It is the start of a new era for you, Emma, and now I want you to tell me everything. All the bits you've left out.'

There was something about this man that made me want to tell him my story. He was like the father I would have loved to have had: solid, dependable, caring and generous. As I recounted my story, I could see the play of emotions across his face, and when I finished speaking, he laid his hand on mine for a moment.

'It sounds to me as if you've had a rough time, my dear.'

'It hasn't been easy,' I admitted.

I had given him only a brief outline, leaving out much of Richard's brutality and glossing over the years I'd spent almost a prisoner of Father's shop and strict discipline, but I knew he understood. He had read deeper into my story, sensing the things I could not bring myself to say.

'Well, you deserve to enjoy yourself now,' he said. 'Don't you worry. I'll get you the very best price for those coins. What are you going to do with the money?'

'I'm not sure. Invest most of it, I expect. I might put some into the shop, but I'll have to think about it.'

'I might be able to come up with some ideas, but we'll see.' He glanced at the gold pocket watch hanging from a fancy chain on his waistcoat. 'I have an appointment shortly so I'll bid you good day, Emma. I hope you will come and see me again? I am sure Margaret would like to meet you next time.'

'I should like that,' I said. 'Thank you for being so kind to me.'

'My pleasure. Enjoy the rest of your day. The dresses you purchased should arrive at the beginning of next week. Let me know how you get on with them, won't you?'

We parted. It was almost three o'clock. I could probably just catch the next train home if I hurried, but I wasn't ready yet. I wanted to stay in town for one more night, to go shopping and perhaps to the pictures. I had never been on my own before, but there was a first time for everything.

I wandered round the shops for almost two hours, buying a toy for James and a pretty hat for my mother, who was looking after him. We had recently managed to wean him on to a bottle and I knew he would be well cared for, but I couldn't help worrying about him a little. Was he taking his food? Was he missing me?

In my heart I knew he was safe enough. It was good for me to have this break away from the trauma of the past few weeks. I needed to think about what I was going to do with the rest of my life.

My situation was very strange. I wasn't divorced or widowed, but I was no longer married either. I could never live with Richard again, no matter what happened. He was guilty of murder, whether he was ever convicted of the crime or not. I had to make a new life for myself and my son, and I had begun that today by coming to London alone.

I didn't want to stay on at the shop for much longer. I had spoken to Mr Smythe about it before I came up to London. He had told me that my present situation was awkward.

'Very awkward, Mrs Gillows. In law, the shop and

its profits still belong to your husband. If you continue to manage it in his absence, you are entitled to a wage, and your mother will of course continue to receive her allowance. But until Mr Gillows is tried and convicted . . .' He shrugged his shoulders. 'You could divorce him or you could contest your father's will. It will need sorting out. But it will take time, and I think it best you wait for a while . . . to see how things go.'

'Supposing I let the business to someone else?'

'The rent and anything the stock realized would belong to Mr Gillows. It is a difficult position for you.'

'But I could leave it empty?'

'There is nothing in law that says you are forced to look after the shop, but what would you do? What would you live on?'

Mr Smythe knew nothing of my father's secret hoard. I hadn't told him. I supposed I ought to declare it, but why should I? It was security for my future and that of my son. What if I left March? What if I went to London? I could find work of some kind – or I could divorce my husband and marry Jon.

I had thought of telephoning Jon at his office, to let him know I would be in London for a couple of days – but something held me back. I was attracted to him, and when he'd kissed me I had felt something stir inside me. I knew I would miss Jon if I never saw him again, but was I in love with him? Did I want to be his wife?

Two men had betrayed me. I believed Jon was different, more caring and gentle. Yet I was reluctant to make my decision. Besides, I wasn't free. In law I was still Richard's wife, and until that was settled, I could only wait and see what happened.

Once back at home, my life settled into its usual routine. At times, I could almost believe that things were as they had been, that my father was still alive – that I had never been married. But of course I had, and nothing could ever be the same again.

'Richard has gone,' Mother said about a week later. 'I'm sure he's gone somewhere else. Perhaps abroad. He wouldn't stay here.'

'It does seem unlikely that he would wait around to be caught,' I agreed, although a part of me wasn't convinced. Richard had a stubborn streak in him and he felt he had been cheated. He might hang around in the hope of getting even. 'But the papers have been saying the police are watching the ports for him. I still keep thinking he will come back – try to get at us in some way.'

'No, he's gone for good,' she said. 'We've got to think about the future now, Emma. Bert wants to have the banns read in church. He wants to get married now. After all, there's no sense in waiting. We've wasted too much of our lives already.'

'Yes, you should make the arrangements,' I said and squeezed her hand. 'You don't want to wait forever. Richard might never be caught. He might just disappear.'

'And where does that leave you?'

'I think I shall have to close the shop, either sell off the stock or . . . I don't know.' I sighed and wrinkled my brow. 'It's awkward. Father's will was so complicated.'

'But surely if you divorced Richard,' she said thoughtfully, 'doesn't it all revert to you? After all, you have sufficient grounds for divorce now.'

'It would be difficult. I think it might be easier in the long run to close the shop. Besides, I don't want to stay here. I want to make a change, Mum. If I close the shop, I can see what happens . . .'

'Well, that's up to you, Emma – but it's yours by right.'

'Yes, I know.' I stood up, kissing her on the cheek. 'I'm going down to the shop now, Mum. Ben needs a break. But don't worry about me. Let Bert do what he thinks best. I shall make up my own mind when I'm ready.'

I was thoughtful as I went downstairs. I still wasn't sure what I really wanted to do with my life. Jon had written me two lovely letters, telling me how sorry he was about what had happened, assuring me of his love, asking me to marry him.

'We'll find a way for you to divorce Richard,' he had said in his last letter. 'Even if the police never find him.'

Jon would look after me. I knew he would never be

cruel, not in the way Richard had been – but did I want to marry again? I thought I might one day, though perhaps not yet.

All my life I had been told what to do. Other people, even those I loved and who loved me, had ruled my life, telling me what I ought or ought not to do . . . and in some cases doing irrevocable things for my sake.

I was beginning to think there might be another way to live. I was just experiencing my first taste of freedom, and I was starting to like it.

Ben and I were in the shop that afternoon, almost three weeks after Gran's funeral. It was now the beginning of June and the threat of war loomed ever closer. Ben had been talking endlessly about the possibility of his being called up.

'You're only seventeen,' I told him. 'Surely you don't want to fight?'

'Just give me the chance!'

He was too young to be called up in the first wave of conscripts but, I realized now, if there was a war Ben would leave the shop anyway. The papers were full of reports about the country needing workers for the munitions factories. Everyone would be looking to help the war effort. I could not expect to keep Ben in the shop for much longer.

It seemed a decision was being forced on me. I would

soon have to make up my mind, one way or the other, and it might as well be now.

'Ben,' I began. 'If you want to . . .'

The door bell jangled and a customer came in. The words died on my lips. I stared at the man who had entered in disbelief. It couldn't be! He was in America. Jon had told me Paul had no intention of returning to this country.

'Emma . . .' Paul was hesitant, oddly unsure of himself as he stood looking at me. 'I suppose I should have written or something, but I hoped we could talk. Jon told me . . . about the boy. About everything.'

'Paul?' I felt my mouth go dry and my knees had turned to jelly. It was such a shock. I'd believed I had managed to forget him, but seeing him again was disturbing. 'Perhaps we should go upstairs? Ben – you can manage for half an hour or so?'

'I've got to go early,' Ben said, giving Paul a hostile look. 'You haven't forgotten that, Emma?'

'No, I haven't forgotten. I shan't be long.'

I lifted the counter flap so that Paul could pass. He followed me through the back and up the stairs without saying a word.

'Is that you, Emma?' Mother came out of the kitchen as she heard us. Realizing who was with me, her eyes narrowed in anger. 'Oh, it's you.'

'Yes, it's me,' Paul said, looking awkward. 'I know

what your opinion of me must be, Mrs Robinson. I let you down, and Emma.'

'Your behaviour was despicable!'

'I know that. I never dreamed . . .' He halted as he saw the expression on her face. 'I shouldn't have gone off the way I did. It was thoughtless and careless. I don't really have an excuse. I was offered an exciting contract in America. I took it and once it was signed I couldn't walk out on the company – there were severe penalties attached. But I did write, Emma. Once before I left England, and again from America.'

'I didn't get either of them.'

'That doesn't mean I didn't send them.'

'No, it doesn't,' I agreed. Father could easily have taken the letters in an attempt to stop me contacting Paul, to make certain I did as he intended. 'Come into the parlour, Paul. We do need to talk – and you might like to see your son?'

'Yes, thank you. I should appreciate that – if you don't mind?'

My mother made an angry sound in her throat, and I knew she believed I should have sent him packing straight away.

'I'll put the kettle on. Don't do anything silly, Emma. Don't trust him. He's let you down once, he'll do it again.' Mother gave me a sharp look, then disappeared into the kitchen. I led Paul into the parlour, sitting on a hard, upright chair next to the table. Paul stood by the fireplace, obviously ill at ease.

'Sit down,' I said, 'and don't look so nervous. I shan't attack you with the carving knife and nor will Mum. If my father or Richard were here they might well have had a go at you, but they aren't.'

Paul seemed embarrassed. 'I read about your husband, and Jon told me about Mr Robinson. I'm very sorry.'

'Yes. I am too. That may surprise you?'

Paul shook his head. 'Your father was fond of you in his way. He was only trying to protect you from men like me.'

'From rotters, you mean? Men who seduce naive country girls and leave them to sort out the mess alone?'

'I know I behaved badly,' he said and smiled oddly. 'Don't be bitter, Emma. It doesn't suit you.'

I laughed harshly. 'How should I be? Grateful that you've bothered to remember me?'

'I know I let you down. I'm sorry. It was a terrible thing to do, and I can't blame you for being angry. I did care for you, but things were difficult.'

He wasn't going to get away so easily. I *was* very angry. He had caused so much pain and suffering.

'I wasn't the only one you seduced, was I?'

'Did Jon tell you about Marion?' Paul had the grace to look embarrassed.

'No. I was there at the house when he brought your

money back – remember? I heard enough to guess what might have been going on. And another girl wrote to your mother. She thought I was trying to blackmail her when I went to see you. Did she tell you that?' He shook his head. 'I thought you would marry me if you knew I was having your child. I didn't know there was a prior claimant.'

'Marion's child wasn't mine,' he said defensively. 'We've known each other for years. Our parents were friends years ago, but they fell out and Mother hadn't seen Marion since she was a child. I suppose she thought you were her.'

'Yes, I'm sure of it.' I gave him a long, hard look. 'Why should I believe any of this, Paul? I don't have much reason to trust you, do I?'

'No, but it is true. Marion has tried every way in the book to get me to marry her. She swore the child was mine, of course, but it only happened once, at a party. I was drunk and so was she. But I wasn't her only lover. I knew there had been others. It wasn't the same as you and me, Emma. I give you my word. And I *would* have married you if I'd been here. If I'd known about the baby.'

'Would you?' I gave him a hard look and his gaze dropped, a red flush creeping up his neck. Perhaps he had convinced himself that he would have done the decent thing, but I didn't believe him. 'I'm sorry, Paul. I don't think you know when you're lying yourself. You make excuses because you just don't have the courage to face the truth.'

Paul looked surprised, as though he didn't think me capable of such thoughts.

He took a step towards me. 'I've come to try and put things right. We'll get a good lawyer to look after the divorce . . .' He paused as he saw my expression. 'We could be married . . . My son needs his father.'

'Your son?' I asked scornfully.

'James is my son. You aren't denying that?'

'No, but I have no intention of marrying you, Paul. If that's why you came, you've wasted your time.'

'Don't dismiss my offer out of hand. I think we could be good together.' He smiled, clearly thinking his charm would bring me round, as it would have once.

'Why are you bothering with this, Paul? Why now? I'm sorry to be suspicious, but I keep thinking there must be a reason.'

'Why should you think I need a reason, Emma? You were always an attractive girl, you're even more so now, and I'm fond of you. Surely you believe that?'

'I believe you think you are, Paul,' I replied, staring at him intently, a faint suspicion creeping into my mind. I couldn't believe he'd travelled all this way just to do the right thing. 'There's something else, isn't there? A reason why getting married is important to you.'

He looked annoyed, as if he resented my self

confidence. I realized he'd expected me to accept his offer at once, to be grateful that he was giving me the chance to be his wife. But my father's pact with Richard had made me suspicious.

'Does it have something to do with money?' I saw a tiny pulse in his throat and knew I had guessed correctly. 'I know I'm right Paul, so you might as well tell me.'

His eyes flashed with sudden temper as I pushed him too far. 'I wouldn't have put it quite so bluntly, Emma. And I do care for you, but my father changed his will just before he died. He left my inheritance in trust. I can't touch a penny until I marry, and I would rather marry you than anyone else I know.'

Because when he had last seen me I had been an innocent, adoring and biddable girl!

A coldness crept down my spine. Any feeling I might have retained towards him vanished in that moment. I saw him for the selfish man he was and had always been.

'Jon is worth ten of you,' I said. 'You can see James this once if you want to, but that's it. I don't ever want to see you again.'

He stared at me in silence for a moment. I had shocked him. He did not know quite how to react or how to treat the new Emma, so he resorted to resentment, putting the blame on me.

'You've changed. You've become hard. It isn't very becoming.'

'If I have changed, you had a part in it.'

He nodded. 'I suppose I did,' he said. 'In that case, I'm sorry. I preferred you as you were, Emma.' He turned to leave.

'Don't you even want to see James once?'

Paul glanced at me, the expression in his eyes a mixture of regret and annoyance. 'There doesn't seem to be much point, does there? Anyway, he probably isn't mine anyway.' His parting shot was meant to hurt, because I had wounded his pride.

The old Emma might have wept or screamed at him, but his hurtful remarks meant nothing to me. I smiled serenely as he paused for a moment, unsure, then went out without another word.

Mother came in with the tea. 'I'm glad you sent him packing, Emma. It's what he deserved.'

'Yes, it was,' I replied. 'Paul wanted to use me, Mum, and I don't intend to let anyone do that again.'

'Not all men are like that,' she said, frowning. 'I've been hurt too, Emma, but I've discovered that it is possible to love again.'

'I know.' I smiled and kissed her cheek. 'Are you telling me I ought to marry Jon?'

'That's up to you. He's a decent man, but do you love him? Enough to marry him?'

'I'm . . .'

I was interrupted by the sound of Ben's voice calling

to me from the bottom of the stairs. I went out to the hallway, looking down at him.

'What is it, Ben?'

'Emma, there's some people here to see you and I've got customers. Shall I send these gentlemen up?'

'Who are they?'

'It's the police, Inspector Martin and a constable.'

My heart took a flying leap. 'Yes, of course. Ask them to come up now, Ben.'

I smoothed a wisp of hair behind my ear. I was beginning to tremble and I felt breathless.

A man wearing a dark suit came up the stairs. He was accompanied by a young constable in uniform.

'Mrs Gillows?' he asked.

'Yes.' I took a deep breath to steady myself. 'Will you come into the parlour, Inspector?'

'Are you alone here, madam?'

He had reached the hall. I could see what he had to say was serious.

'My mother is here. Please come through. We were just going to have a cup of tea.'

He followed me into the parlour. Mother was sitting in her armchair by the fire. She looked at me and I could see she was nervous.

'Will you join us in a cup of tea?' I asked.

'I think you should sit down, Mrs Gillows. I have something to tell you. Something unpleasant, I'm afraid.'

I perched on the edge of the sofa. Inspector Martin stood by the fireplace. I held my breath, waiting for him to go on.

'This may be a shock for you, madam.'

I expelled my breath on a sigh, sensing what was coming. 'Is it about Richard? Have you caught him?'

'Your husband was seen down by the railway this morning.' He paused and frowned. 'Apparently some lads spotted him.'

Mother gasped. 'He's come back? You were right, Emma. He's not going to give up that easily.'

'He won't be causing you more trouble, Mrs Robinson,' the young constable said, then went red as Inspector Martin looked at him.

'Unfortunately, the lads didn't come to us,' the Inspector went on. 'They ran home and told their parents. It seems some of the men got together. There has been bad feeling towards Mr Gillows because of what happened to Mrs Jacobs. Several local men decided to go after him . . .'

'Did they find him?' I asked, a cold shiver trickling down my spine. 'I was afraid something like this might happen. Gran was well liked. Is Richard hurt? I know some of the men have threatened to teach him a lesson.'

The Inspector cleared his throat. 'I'm afraid your husband is dead, madam. As you said, Mrs Jacobs was well liked locally. The men went after Mr Gillows.

I understand there was a bit of a fight. Mr Gillows managed to break away from them. He ran across the track, in front of a non-stop train. He must have been killed almost instantly.'

Mother's hand went to her mouth, but she didn't say anything. She was obviously shocked.

'Will any of the men involved be arrested?' I asked, feeling numb. At that moment I neither hated nor pitied Richard. I had no feelings at all. It was as if I was listening to a story about a stranger. 'I know what they did was wrong, but it was for the right reasons. I know Richard killed Gran. If he had been taken he would surely have been hanged. My husband was a train driver, sir. He knew the times of the trains better than anyone. If he ran across that track . . .'

'Are you suggesting that he might have done it deliberately?'

'Perhaps. I don't know.'

'None of us will ever know,' he agreed. 'As far as I have been told, none of the men concerned have actually been named.'

I felt relief wash over me. 'I'm glad. There has been enough grief already, Inspector. It might be better if Richard's death was the end of the matter.'

He was silent for a moment; then he nodded. 'I think I agree with you, Mrs Gillows. In the circumstances, this may be easier for you and Mrs Robinson. A trial could only have caused you both further pain, prolonged the gossip and unpleasantness.'

'Yes.' I looked at my mother. 'We want to put all this behind us now, don't we, Mum?'

She smiled as the tension left her. 'Yes. I am to be married soon, Inspector Martin. A trial would have been most unpleasant.'

He nodded and expressed his good wishes, then turned to face me. 'I'm sorry, Mrs Gillows,' He was looking at me with sympathy. 'I have to ask you if you would mind identifying the body.'

'I'll do that,' Mother said. 'Emma has been through enough. I've known Richard Gillows all my life. Surely my word will be enough?'

'It's all right, Mum,' I said. 'I can do this. You go down and relieve Ben. He has to go to a dentist this afternoon.' I looked at the Inspector. 'Do you want me to come with you now?'

Chapter Fifteen

I gave a little cry of admiration as Mother came out of her bedroom that morning. 'You look lovely, Mum,' I said. 'That dress I bought from London suits you, and the hat.'

'Thank you, Emma. I feel grand. I've never had anything as smart as this before.' She moved towards me and we embraced, laughing but also close to tears. 'Mr Baker said he would be here at eleven, and the cars are booked for a quarter past.'

'We've been through all this, Mum,' I said teasing her. Everything is going to be all right. There's no need to worry.'

She nodded but still looked anxious. 'Are you sure you don't mind staying here alone?'

'I'm not in the least nervous. Besides, it won't be for long. Ben is leaving next week. Mr Smythe is going to sort everything out for me, and then he'll let the shop to a tenant, who will buy the stock at valuation. I'm going to give that to you and Bert, Mum. It's my wedding present to you.'

'You've already given me this dress and . . .' She smiled as I shook my head at her. 'All right, if it's what you want, love. You're quite sure about leaving here?'

'I'm sure.'

She nodded, then looked thoughtful.

'You did invite Mr Reece to the wedding?'

'Yes, Mum. I invited Jon.'

'But you haven't heard anything?'

'No. He hasn't replied to my letter.'

'That seems a bit odd.'

It was so easy to read her mind. She wanted me to marry Jon, because she thought I would be safe with him.

'There may be lots of reasons. Jon isn't like Paul. He'll be in touch as soon as he can. Stop worrying about me, I'm a big girl now. I can look after myself.'

'Of course you can.' She laughed at herself. 'I don't know what's wrong with me. It's wedding nerves, I expect.'

'Yes, I expect so.' We both heard the shop doorbell. 'I should think that's Mary and Mr Baker now at the door. I'll run down and let them in. Sit down and relax, Mum. I promise you, nothing is going to go wrong.'

I was singing to myself as I went downstairs and through the shop. It was closed for the day because Ben was coming to the wedding with his parents. I stared at the silhouette of the man outside the shop window. That wasn't Mary's father . . .

Opening the door, I hesitated as I saw the distinctive uniform of the RAF. Then its wearer turned and I realized it was Jon. My heart took a flying leap as I stared at him in surprise.

'You've been called up!'

'Actually, I didn't wait for the summons,' he said. 'I volunteered for service as a navigator. I've been away for a couple of weeks, Emma, being assessed and going through the medical checks. That's why I didn't get your letter until now.'

'Come in,' I said, standing back to admit him. 'I knew there had to be a reason, but I didn't expect this. You look very splendid, Jon.' I moved towards him impulsively. 'I'm proud of you. I think it was a wonderful thing to do.'

'You look lovely,' he said, 'but then, you always do. I've missed you, Emma.'

'I've missed you. Very much.' We moved closer, then Jon bent his head, kissing me very gently on the mouth.

'I love you.' His eyes sought mine. 'Paul came to see you?'

'Yes. He came, and I sent him away.'

'When he told me he was going to ask you to marry him, I thought perhaps you might accept?'

'I could never marry him, Jon. Surely you know that?'

'He told me you had refused him. Are you sure about that?'

'Quite sure.'

'Does that mean . . .'

We were interrupted by the arrival of Mary, her father and her husband. The frustration in Jon's eyes made me want to giggle, but I controlled the impulse.

'If you'd like to go upstairs,' I invited, 'Mum is waiting for you.'

I caught Jon's arm as they went past us, holding him back.

'We can't talk properly now,' I said. 'Can you come back here this evening, after everyone has gone?'

'I have two weeks leave before training begins,' Jon said. 'I thought we might possibly spend them together?'

'We'll talk about it later,' I promised. 'Come on, Mum will be wondering where I've got to and she's already in a fret.'

Despite Mother's fears, the wedding went smoothly. I shed a few tears as she took her vows and I thought about my father and all the wasted years. Then Jon took my hand in his and I smiled up at him as the regrets slipped away. There was no point in looking back. The past was over and done. I was free now, free to choose my own way.

The ceremony was soon over. We followed Mum and

her new husband from the church to the sound of pealing bells. People were outside waiting to throw confetti and taking photographs.

Jon took several with his own camera, including some of me holding James, who had slept throughout the service. Everyone was laughing and talking excitedly. It was a happy occasion and I could see the love in my mother's eyes as she looked at her new husband. I felt so glad that at last she had found something to make her life worthwhile.

The reception was being held at a nearby hotel. Mum and Bert went in a car with flowers and ribbons all over it, but it was a nice day, warm and sunny, so most of the guests walked across the road and round the corner.

'We've only invited a few friends,' I told Jon. 'And there isn't going to be an evening party. Just a sit-down meal for twenty of us.'

'Which means we'll be soon be alone.'

The smile he gave me made my heart jerk. Jon was obviously intending to ask me to marry him again and I didn't know what answer to give him.

I watched as he moved amongst the other guests at the reception, meeting our friends, all of whom were strangers to him. He had an easy, friendly manner. People laughed when he made a joke. It was obvious that he lived in another world from most of them, yet they weren't uncomfortable with him.

Jon was truly a gentleman, much more so than Paul. He was kind and generous, and I couldn't imagine him ever raising his hand to anyone in anger, especially a woman. He had an air of authority about him, and I thought he would scarcely need even to raise his voice to make himself heard. He was the kind of man others looked to with respect.

He turned at me as the toasts were drunk, and smiled. 'To Greta and Bert,' he whispered. 'And to us, Emma.'

I nodded and sipped my drink. 'To happiness,' I said, 'for all of us.'

It was past six o'clock when we returned to the shop together. Jon had driven my mother and Bert to the station, then returned to the hotel to fetch me after I'd seen all our guests on their way. Mary had taken James home with her earlier and had promised to give him his bottle.

'I'll bring him round later,' she'd told me. 'After you and Jon have had a little time together.' She cuddled James to her, kissing the top of his head. 'Perhaps I'll keep him. He's such a little love, Emma.'

I smiled, thinking that Mary was getting broody. It wouldn't be long before she wanted a baby of her own.

'Yes, he is. I'm very lucky.'

It was odd, but after all the pain and grief of the past months I was beginning to feel very different. I loved my son and life seemed sweet, full of promise for the future.

Jon was no longer using his uncle's old car, but a smart Rover.

'I thought I'd treat myself,' he told me when I mentioned it that evening. 'I've got some money put by, Emma. And things may be difficult soon. I doubt if there will be many new cars available soon, or the petrol to run them. We all ought to make the most of the next few months.'

A shiver went through me. Caught up in my own problems, I hadn't given much thought to the threat of war, which had been looming for a while now.

'Is it really coming then? You don't think it will all go away if we cross our fingers and wish very hard?'

Jon laughed, then his expression became serious. 'No, Emma. I don't think we can wish it away, however hard we try.'

I nodded, swallowing hard as I led the way upstairs. I was frightened, by the thought of war and also by what Jon was about to say to me.

'I'll just put the kettle on. I don't know why, but hotels never make a really good cup of tea.'

Jon nodded but followed me, watching as I filled the kettle and put it on the stove.

'I know it's too soon,' he said. 'You've been through so much. I can't expect you to give me an answer yet. But do you think you might feel like marrying me one day?'

I took a deep breath, then turned to face him. 'It is too soon, Jon. I wasn't in love with Richard. There were times when I came close to hating him, but I did marry him. And I believed I was in love with Paul when we were together. I'm not quite ready to marry again just yet.'

'You do care for me?'

I smiled and moved towards him. 'You are the nicest man I've ever met, Jon. I care for you very much. Forgive me if I can't give you my promise now. I need time to catch my breath and think about things, what I want to do with my life. I've been hurt . . .'

'I know that,' he said swiftly. 'Of course I do, Emma. I'm willing to wait, for as long as it takes.'

'Oh, Jon,' I sighed. 'Please kiss me.'

'Emma . . .'

He drew me into his arms, his kiss gentle at first, then more demanding. I felt the pleasure intensify into desire and I smiled as I gazed up at him.

'I want to spend the next two weeks with you,' I said. 'I want us to be together, to get to know each other. We don't have to rush things, do we? It would be easy to throw myself into your arms, Jon. But this time I want to do it right.'

'I wouldn't have it any other way,' he said. 'I love you, Emma. I want to be with you for the rest of my life, if it's what you want, too. But most of all, I want to make you happy.'

'Thank you. You really are the dearest man.'

'Where would you like to go for our holiday?'

'To the sea, but not to Yarmouth. Somewhere I've never been.' I laughed, pushing back my hair from my face. 'Which gives you plenty of scope. I've never been anywhere much.'

'I've always loved Cornwall.'

'That sounds wonderful. Yes, let's go there, Jon.'

He kissed me again, then the kettle began to whistle behind us and he let me go, laughing ruefully.

'I think I should leave now, for the sake of your reputation, and my sanity. Sleep well, my darling. I'll pick you up at seven in the morning. It will give us a good start.'

'I'll see you out then.'

Downstairs in the shop, we kissed again, parting reluctantly. It would have been so easy to let Jon take me to bed, but we both wanted to do this properly.

I locked the door after he had gone. Mary would ring the bell when she brought James back. I was going to ask her if she would look after him for me while I went away with Jon, and I knew what her answer would be.

As I turned to go upstairs, I saw a letter lying on the counter. Someone must have picked it up earlier, probably Ben when he came in to do the morning papers. I bent down to retrieve it. The postmark was London, and I tore open the flap as I went back upstairs. I read the contents as I made tea.

'Dear Mrs Gillows,' Solomon Gould had written. 'I read of your husband's death in the papers. It must have been very distressing for you. However, I have some news that may be a comfort to you . . .'

His next words took my breath away. He had been offered three thousand and two hundred pounds for the coins.

'If you wish, I shall sell on your behalf,' he went on. 'Again, if you wish, I can invest all or part of the money for you. I am myself about to open a new factory, making uniforms for the Armed Forces. In view of the uncertain times that face us, I feel these will be in ever greater demand. I have secured various contracts, which I should be happy to show you, should you be interested in becoming my partner in this venture.

I folded his letter, returning it to its envelope. It was a surprising offer and one that did interest me. I should have no immediate need of my legacy, for I was beginning to accumulate money from my share of Mrs Henty's business. And I would soon have rent from Father's shop, which was, of course, now mine.

And I intended to find myself work in London, but not just yet. For the moment I had other things on my mind.

We drove down to Cornwall in easy stages, stopping to eat lunch, then tea, planning to spend the night at a little bed and breakfast place in Exeter. I telephoned Mary and was told James was well. She held the phone to his ear to let me talk to him, and I could hear his gurgle of pleasure.

'You should have brought him with you,' Jon said that evening as we went out to dinner. 'I wouldn't have minded.'

'I thought we should have a few days alone,' I said. 'We might collect him and go up to London towards the end of your leave, Jon, if that suits you?'

'Anything you want, Emma.' He smiled at me. 'I shall enjoy getting to know your son.'

'And I'm enjoying being with you, having a holiday,' I said, smiling at him. 'This is an adventure for me, Jon. I want to go everywhere and see everything.'

'We will,' he said, laughing at my pleasure. 'I'll show you all the places I know and love, Emma.'

We continued the next morning, reaching the hotel Jon had booked after stopping for lunch on the way. I had never dreamed life could be so easy, so relaxed. Nor had I ever enjoyed myself this much.

Jon had booked two rooms, just as he had the previous night. It was a modest hotel, right on the sea front at Torquay. My room was comfortable, and the view out over the bay was magnificent. I could see the sea boiling and crashing around a spur of rock below, hear the cry of the gulls as they circled overhead. Wonderful! I felt as free as those birds circling over the sea. I unpacked, then went to meet Jon in the lounge for a cup of tea.

'Is your room all right?'

'Very nice. Comfortable, and the view is lovely.'

'I've been here once or twice as a child with my parents. I thought it would suit us.'

'Are your parents still alive, Jon?'

'My mother is. She lives with Grandfather in Hampstead. My father died years ago. He wanted me to be a lawyer and he managed to set me up as a junior partner in a respected firm. It wasn't really what I wanted, but I've always felt obliged to carry out his wishes.'

'Yes, I think *you* would,' I said and smiled at him. 'What would you have liked to do, given the choice?'

'I think I should like to farm. Does that surprise you?'

'No.' I laughed, then admitted, 'Yes, actually it does. I can't see you working on the land. But perhaps you're going to be a gentleman farmer? Now, that might suit you. You could ride around your land and smile at the labourers, charm them into working for you.'

'Is that how you see me?' He frowned, then saw the mischief in my eyes. 'You're pulling my leg!'

'Yes. Do you mind?'

'No.' He looked amused. 'I think I rather like it that you want to tease me. You have hidden depths, Emma. There's more to you than meets the eye, my girl!'

'Yes, I think perhaps there is,' I agreed, becoming

serious for a moment. 'You see, I don't think I really know myself, Jon. All my life people have taken care of me, whether I wanted them to or not. I've been told what to do, what to think . . . watched over, protected, ordered to do what other people felt was the right thing for me. My father, Gran, even my mother always did what they thought best for me. Everything was for my sake. I suppose that's why I was such a fool over Paul. If I'd been allowed a little freedom, things might have been different.'

'Yes, I do understand.' Jon looked thoughtful. 'It wouldn't be that way for us, Emma. I love you. I want to share things with you. I don't want to make you my prisoner.'

'I'm beginning to feel that,' I said. 'But I need a little time, Jon.'

'Yes, of course you do. We've plenty of time, Emma.'

The next few days were as near perfect as life can ever be. The weather was kind to us as we walked on the beach, our bare feet sinking into the warm sand. Jon encouraged me into the water, but he couldn't persuade me to swim. I splashed around and had fun, but kept both feet on the bottom.

'Cowardy custard!' Jon teased. 'Just let yourself go, Emma, and you'll float.'

I tried once and sank, coming up spluttering with indignation. 'I thought you said I would float!'

'Oh, my poor Emma!'

Jon rescued me, sweeping me up in his arms and carrying me up the beach to our rug. He set me down, then knelt above me, gazing into my eyes before drawing me close. His kiss was tender and sweet, making me want to swoon with love for him. I felt my resolve weakening. Why was I holding out? Jon loved me. I was happier now than I had ever been. Why didn't I just give in to this feeling between us? All I had to do was say yes and I could be Jon's wife. I would be secure, adored, taken care of for the rest of our lives.

And yet a little voice in my head warned me to wait. If I married Jon now, I might never come to know the real Emma.

'Why so serious?' Jon asked as we lay side by side on the blanket, the sun warming us after our swim. He bent over me, touching my mouth with the tips of his fingers before lowering his lips to mine. 'Are you worried about something?'

'I was wondering . . .'

'What?' He kissed the tip of my nose. 'Are you missing James? Do you want to collect him and go up to London? I ought to see my mother. I could telephone her. We could stay with her for a couple of days, if you would like that?'

'Does she know about me?'

'She knows there is someone special, but nothing more.'

'Don't you think it would be best if I took James to a hotel? I'd like to meet your mother, Jon, but it might be a shock for her when she discovers who I am. I've been married. I have a child, and my husband's name has been in the papers.'

Jon silenced me with a kiss. 'She will love you, because I love you. I promise you, Emma.'

I reached up and kissed him on the lips. 'I've loved being here with you, Jon, but I think I've left James for long enough. I need to fetch him and to take care of a few things at home. Why don't you drop me off, go to visit your mother, and I'll come up to London for the last few days of your leave?'

'If it's what you want,' he said. 'We'll go tomorrow.'

I sensed his disappointment. The peace and tranquility of our time by the sea would be broken as soon as we returned to our own lives, but I knew it was too dangerous to go on as we were. Jon had behaved impeccably, but it wasn't fair to expect such restraint. If we stayed here much longer we would become lovers. In town there would be more distractions. Besides, I was beginning to feel guilty about leaving my son, and I was missing him.

'We'll have the last few days together, Jon,' I said. 'And there will be other leaves, other times when we can be together.'

'Yes, of course.'

I sensed I had hurt him. He couldn't really understand

my reasons for holding back, even though he accepted them. But why should he, when I hardly understood myself? I felt guilty because I knew how much he loved me, and also angry that I was being so foolish. I touched his cheek.

'Don't be angry, Jon. I do love you. You know that.'

'Yes, I know, and I'm not angry.'

He kissed me again, but I knew that he was holding back. He was hurt because I wasn't prepared to throw my hat over the windmill and marry him.

'I told you I would wait, Emma, and I will.'

'You needn't have come back for another week,' Mary said. She handed James over reluctantly. 'He was no trouble, I promise you. I loved having him.'

'I'm very grateful,' I said and kissed my son as he gazed innocently up at me. 'It was lovely having a few days on our own, but I missed James. And I've got to pack some bits and pieces Mum wants from the house and my own things, too. Most of the furniture will stay for the benefit of whoever takes the shop over, but Mum will store my things.'

'Are you really going to London for good?' Mary looked upset. 'I'll miss you, and little James.'

'I'll come back to visit,' I said. 'I'll still be buying stock for Madge Henty. I dare say we'll see each other almost as much as we ever did.'

'Well, that's all right then.' She looked at me curiously.

'Are you going to marry that nice Mr Reece?'

'He has asked me,' I admitted. 'I'm not sure yet, Mary.'

'I would if I were you. You'd be mad to throw away a chance like that, Emma.'

I laughed and shook my head at her, but Sheila said much the same when she called at the shop the next day.

'I saw you in here,' she said. 'Ben told me the shop would be closed after he left last Saturday.'

'It is, really,' I replied, 'but I'm listing the stock for Mr Smythe and I thought I might as well leave the door unlocked. I'm going to London the day after tomorrow. The shop will be closed then until we find a tenant. I've decided to let it, but I don't know what kind of a shop it will be.'

'I wanted to ask you . . .' She looked uncertain. 'Eric has a bit of money put by, and you know I've always fancied working here. Do you think we stand a chance of taking it over?'

I was too surprised to answer for a moment, then I nodded. The idea of Sheila running my father's shop would make him turn in his grave, but I thought it was marvellous.

'I think the stock is going to be valued at between three and four hundred pounds, Sheila. And the rent is two pounds ten shillings a week, that's for the upstairs as well. If Eric thinks he can manage that, I'd like you to have the place.'

Her cheeks went pink with excitement. 'I'm sure he will,' she said. 'I'll talk to him this evening and let you know. And while I'm here, I'd like some of those toffee pieces, please.'

'You'll have to watch you don't eat all the profits,' I said and laughed. 'Don't pay, Sheila. I was going to put the jar out anyway. I'm only listing the full ones.'

I went back to my task as she left, pedalling off on her bike at a terrific pace. I wondered what people would say if Sheila took over the shop. Father would have been horrified, of course, but he couldn't stop me now. I could do whatever I liked.

'I've decided I would like to sell the coins,' I told Solomon Gould when we met for lunch three days later. I had invited him to lunch at a modest restaurant, nothing as grand as the Savoy but well recommended. 'And I would like to invest all but two hundred pounds of the money with you – if that's all right?'

'I shall be delighted to have you as my partner. I'll get my lawyer to draw up an agreement for us both to sign.'

'Good. That's settled then.' I smiled as we raised our wine glasses. 'I wanted to ask your advice about finding work in London.'

'What kind of work?'

'In the clothes trade if possible. I'm not sure what I could do. Work in a shop, or perhaps as a machinist in a factory. Mum taught me to sew, but I'm not as good as she is.'

Sol looked at me thoughtfully. 'Would you be interested in learning the trade? You would have to start at the bottom, but I could find a place for you.'

'Would you?' I stared at him in surprise and pleasure. 'That's what I would really like. I'm going to be buying for Mrs Henty from now on. She says trade has gone up since I picked out those dresses, but I should like to know more about the business at this end.'

'What about your son?'

'James will be weaned on to soft foods soon. He doesn't need so many feeds now. I'm going to find somewhere decent to live, then I shall employ a nurse to look after him while I'm at work. Mum was always at home, but she's married now. Besides, I want to live in London. I want a chance to make something of myself, learn about life.'

'Well, London is probably the right place to do that.' He nodded, seeming amused but approving. 'I can see you've got it all worked out. Would you consider living with us? We could never have children. Margaret loves them. She would enjoy having James around, and you could still employ your nurse. You would have your own rooms, and be independent.'

'I should like to think about that,' I said. 'Perhaps I could talk to Margaret this afternoon when we have tea together?'

'Why don't you do that?' He signalled to the waiter. 'The bill please.'

'I'm going to pay,' I said after the waiter had gone. 'This is my treat, Sol. If we are going to be partners, I have to pay my way.'

'You are a very determined young woman, Emma,' he said, his eyes glinting with amusement as he put away his wallet. 'I have a feeling I am going to gain a great deal from knowing you.'

'Don't look so nervous,' Jon said, glancing at me as we stopped outside the large, red brick house at the edge of the heath in Hampstead. 'No one's going to eat you.'

'You didn't tell me your grandfather lived in a house like this!'

'Don't be fooled by appearances,' Jon said. 'It's a nice house, but Pops doesn't have a lot of money. He has an income, as Mama does, but there's no huge fortune tucked away.'

'Who is Pops?'

'My grandfather. Everyone calls him Pops. You'll see why when you meet him.'

An elderly, white-haired man wearing a pair of worn corduroys and a loose brown cardigan was working in the garden as we went in through the wrought iron gates. He glanced up and smiled as we approached, wiping his muddy hands on his breeches.

'Ah, there you are, Jon,' he said. 'Your mother is

waiting. Go in, my boy. I'll be along later, when I've cleaned up a bit.'

'This is Emma, Pops. Emma, my grandfather.'

I was too surprised to answer immediately. I had taken him for the gardener.

'Welcome, my dear,' he said, a twinkle in his eyes. 'I'm actually known as Sir Roy Armstrong, but you can call me Pops or Roy, if you would prefer.' He glanced at James. 'And who is this little charmer?'

'This is my son, James,' I said, finding my tongue all at once. It would have been impossible to be shy with this man. 'He's being good at the moment, but he can be less than charming at times.'

'No doubt, no doubt. They all can, when they like. Go along in, my dear. Anne has been fretting all day. She thinks you're some kind of a miracle. This young feller here has dragged his feet in the courting game. We had begun to despair of ever getting ourselves a grandchild to spoil. Now here you both are to order, so to speak.'

I blushed, then laughed.

'You're scaring the life out of her,' Jon said and took my arm, steering me towards the front door. It opened as if by magic. A woman dressed smartly in grey stood in the doorway.

'There you are, Mr Jonathan,' she said. 'Mrs Reece is in the parlour. She's in such a state. You'd best go in to her straight away.'

'Yes, Mrs Chalmers.' He winked at me as she stepped aside to allow us to enter. 'Mrs Chalmers keeps us all in order,' he said to me but loud enough for her to hear.

She turned, giving him a quelling look. 'You will have your little joke. I'm Sir Roy's housekeeper, madam. I've been with him for some years.'

'I'm very pleased to meet you.'

I almost giggled as Jon gave me another wink.

Then we were entering the parlour. It was a large room with high ceilings, furnished in soft shades of green and blue, but slightly shabby in a comfortable, lived-in way. A woman was sitting in a chair by the window. She was small and looked fragile, dressed in a flowing gown of some silky material. I thought how sad and wistful she seemed. Then she smiled and stood up, coming towards us with her hands outstretched.

'Jon, my dearest,' she said and kissed him before turning to me. 'And Emma. I am so pleased to meet you, my dear. Jon has told me all about you. I know he loves you, and I'm sure we shall get along. Is this your son? May I hold him?'

'Yes, of course.' I passed James to her. 'He's rather heavy, I'm afraid.'

'I'm quite strong,' she said, looking down at James as she cradled him. 'Oh, how lovely he is. He reminds me of someone. I'm not sure who, but it doesn't matter. Sit down, Emma, and you, Jon.'

James let out a wail. She laughed and gave him back to me as I sat on the sofa. I rocked him and his cries ceased.

'He knows what he wants,' she said, and sat down herself. 'I'll ring for tea when Pops gets here.' She smiled as if well satisfied with what she saw. 'So tell me, Emma, when you are going to put my son out of his misery and marry him?'

'Mama!' Jon said and frowned at her. 'I told you – Emma hasn't said yes yet.'

'And why not? It makes sense to have the wedding soon, before this wretched war starts.'

'Mama . . .'

'We're still getting to know each other,' I said. 'I'm sure that's best for both of us.'

Mrs Reece hesitated, then smiled as her father came in. I sensed that despite her fragile looks, she was used to having her own way.

'There you are, Pops,' she said. 'Now I can ring for tea.'

'I'm so sorry, Emma,' Jon said as we left later that afternoon. 'I can't think what Mama was about. I told her you needed time before you made up your mind, that you hadn't said you were going to marry me yet.'

'It doesn't matter,' I replied. 'I liked your mother, Jon. And Pops is absolutely lovely.'

'They liked you, Emma.' He looked at me expectantly. I knew he was hoping the warm reception from his family would help me to make up my mind.

'Shall we go out this evening?' I asked. 'Margaret Gould said I could leave James with her. She is very nice, Jon, and both Sol and Margaret are looking forward to meeting you. We could have a drink with them and then go on to the theatre. Make it special as this is your last night in London for a while.'

'It's the last time I shall see you for some weeks,' Jon said. 'We're not likely to get another pass until training is over.'

'But I'll come to the station tomorrow to see you off?'

'No, Emma,' he said. He reached out to touch my cheek. 'I don't like tearful farewells. We'll enjoy this evening together, and leave it at that for the moment.'

'You will write?'

'You know I shall. As you said, there will be other leaves. We can see each other the next time I'm in London.'

'Yes, of course. And I'll write often and tell you how we are.' I smiled at him, but I could see that he was disappointed.

He had hoped that I would make up my mind to marry him before this, that we would be planning our wedding by now.

I woke the next morning feeling uneasy and a little weepy. Jon had kissed me tenderly as we parted the previous evening. I had clung to him, reluctant to let him go.

'Take care of yourself, Jon.'

'Of course. You too, Emma.'

I glanced at the clock as I fed James. He was slow taking his feed that morning. It was half past nine, and Jon's train was due out of Liverpool Street at a quarter past ten. It would probably be months before I saw him again. My thoughts began to wander. Supposing the war started and he was sent on a mission? Supposing his plane was shot down? Already the papers had begun to talk about how awful this new war would be. I had read of the tragedy of the *Thetis*, a submarine which had sunk during trials in Liverpool Bay. Aeroplanes were no safer.

Jon could be killed in an accident even before the war started.

I was shocked at the pain that thought caused me. All at once I realized how much he meant to me, what it would be like if he never came back to me.

What a stupid fool I had been, wasting these last precious days! Yes, I wanted a little freedom, but Jon wasn't like my father or Richard. He knew and approved of my wanting to learn about the clothing business. He would never try to dictate to me as the others had.

The time was creeping by. Jon hadn't wanted me at the station to say goodbye, but I had to be there. I had to tell him how much I loved and needed him.

Grabbing my son and my purse, I ran down the hotel stairs and out into the sunshine. A taxi was passing. I waved frantically at him from the side of the road and he pulled into the kerb.

'Where to, love?'

'Liverpool Street Station. I've got to get there before quarter past ten.'

'Bit tight,' he said. 'You've left it late.'

'My . . . my fiancé is catching a train. He's in the RAF. I shan't see him for ages, and I need to tell him something.'

'Had a bit of a tiff?' He grinned as I nodded. 'Jump in. I'll do my best but I can't promise.'

I got into the back seat, clutching James. My heart was pounding wildly and I was terrified I was going to be too late.

I mustn't be! I had to see Jon. I had to tell him I loved him. Why hadn't I agreed to marry him after Mum's wedding? Everyone had told me I was a fool. I was stupid. Stupid!

I thrust a pound note at the cab driver when he stopped and jumped out of the car, not stopping for change. Where would I find Jon? Which platform? There were three minutes left . . . where should I look?

I was close to despair, breathless, my heart pounding madly. I didn't even know exactly where he was going. Every platform was busy as I looked frantically from side to side. It was impossible. I would never find him. And then I saw him. He was standing next to a train, which looked almost ready to depart, obviously about to board.

'Jon!' I screamed at the top of my voice, uncaring of people turning to stare. 'Jon! Wait!'

He turned as I rushed up to him, surprise mixing with pleasure in his eyes as he saw me. Then he moved to catch me in his arms.

'Emma,' he said. 'I was just wishing I'd let you come. You must have known how much I wanted to see you, my darling.'

'I had to come,' I cried, tears beginning to trickle down my cheeks as he kissed me. 'I couldn't let you go without telling you I love you. I will marry you, Jon, on your next leave.'

'My darling,' he said, hugging me so tightly that James protested with a wail of outrage. 'I love you so much. You don't know what this means to me.'

The guard was slamming doors. Jon kissed me again, then released me and jumped on to the train as the whistle was blown. He let the window down, leaning out to me. I began to walk beside the train as it lurched forwards. I was crying and laughing at the same time.

'Take care of yourself, Jon. Write to me soon.'

'I will.' He blew several kisses. 'I love you, Emma. I love you. And James, too.'

'I love you . . .'

The platform was running out. I couldn't go any further. The train was taking him away from me. I stopped walking and stood waving to Jon until the train was finally out of sight. For a moment I was desolate, filled with regrets for what might have been. We might have been lovers. We might have been married. I had been such a fool to waste those beautiful, sunlit days by the sea.

'Please come back safely,' I whispered. 'Come back to me, Jon. I do love you. I do . . .'

I thought wistfully of what might have been had the war not been imminent. Jon loved me and I loved him, there was nothing to stop us being happy together. I hated the train that had taken him away from me, and the war that meant we could not be together for weeks or even months.

Then, as I left the station, emerging into the sunlight, I began to smile. It was settled now. All the doubting and hesitation were over. I was going to marry Jon on his next leave. In the meantime, I would move in with Margaret and Solomon Gould, and tomorrow Sol was going to start teaching me all there was to know about cloth and the 'rag' trade.

The future looked bright, full of interest and new relationships. I held my life in my own hands, to shape as I wished. From now on, I could do it my way . . .

Read on for a sneak peek at the
next book in the *Emma* series

Emma's War

Also by Rosie Clarke

Coming soon from Ebury Press

EBURY
PRESS

Chapter One

'Daring raid liberates British prisoners . . .' The news-
boy's strident tones caught my attention and I went to buy
a paper. 'That's right, love, read all about it . . . rescued
from the *Altmark* . . . British prisoners in daring escape.'

I smiled and walked on, scanning the headlines in the
paper. It was February 1940 and at last there was some
good news. Something to cheer us up after weeks of
gloom in the papers. Though London itself was still far
from gloomy despite the official black-out, and I had just
come from a lunch-time chamber concert. They were
drawing crowds. People were determined to make the
best of things, to enjoy themselves where they could, and
most of the theatres were opening up again after closing
down when the lights first went out all over the city.

'Watch out, sweetheart!'

'Oh, I'm so sorry!'

Absorbed in my paper, I had walked straight into a

man. He caught my arm, steadying me, a huge grin on his face. I noticed that he had very dark, almost black hair, and that his eyes were a dark, bitter chocolate brown. He was also very good looking!

'If you're not careful, you'll hurt yourself,' he said, seeming concerned for my welfare.

'I'm fine – but did I hurt you?'

'Not so as you'd notice. I guess I'm pretty tough.'

His smile was infectious, making me respond with one of my own. 'Perhaps that's as well, seeing as I must have trodden on your foot. It was clumsy of me. I wasn't looking where I was going, because I was just so pleased to read about those prisoners being rescued . . . it's marvellous news, isn't it?'

He seemed to know what I meant, nodding agreement. 'Yes. It's always good when something like that happens.'

'Especially at the moment.'

'Yes.' He looked serious now. 'It can't be easy for you British at the moment, and I'm afraid it's going to get a hell of a lot rougher before this is all over.'

'Yes, I'm sure you're right . . .' I smiled at him again. 'Forgive me, but I must go. I have to get back to work.'

'I guess so . . .'

'Bye then.'

He caught my arm as I tried to pass him. 'I'm Jack Harvey. American, single, free, here on business, and feeling lonely. You wouldn't have time for a drink one night? Maybe tonight even? I promise I don't bite . . .'

'I'm sorry,' I said, shaking my head at him but smiling because he was looking so eager. 'I'm engaged to someone, a man I love. It was nice meeting you, Mr Harvey – but I must go.'

'OK. It was worth a try.'

He let me go with a rueful grin. I walked on, smiling to myself. It wasn't the first time I'd been asked out by a stranger. There were a lot of young men at a loose end in London at the moment. Young servicemen on leave from their units. Many of them were alone in a strange city and feeling a bit lost . . . or frightened. Mr Harvey wasn't one of them, of course. His country wasn't officially at war, though Sol believed the Americans were helping us more behind the scenes than anyone yet knew.

Thinking of Sol made me remember I was going to be late for work, and I began to run. That afternoon was an important one for me and I didn't want to start out on the wrong foot.

I was in the workshop when the telephone rang that afternoon, but didn't take much notice. This was the first time Sol had trusted me with the good cloth, and I wanted to get it exactly right.

I was concentrating very hard as I cut carefully round the edge of the dress pattern. We couldn't afford to waste cloth, even though clothes rationing had not yet begun.

Sol said the Government was only waiting for the right moment before they imposed it Besides, it was a matter of pride that I should be able to cut well. The cutting was the most important part of tailoring. Sol had impressed that on me from the very beginning.

'A good cutter is worth his weight in gold,' Sol had told me that first morning. 'Never forget it, Emma. In this trade you can cut corners in a score of ways, but never economise on your skilled labour. They *are* your business.'

Sol should know. He had started out as a cutter himself, the son of impoverished immigrants, and now he was an extremely wealthy man – also a very wise and a very kind man.

I glanced behind me. Mr Jackson, Sol's top cutter, was watching me from his corner of the workshop, though trying not to let me see it. He gave me an encouraging smile, but let me get on with it. Sol had given strict instructions that I was to be given no help, and I wasn't going to ask.

'Emma!' One of the girls from the showroom came to fetch me. 'Telephone – for you!'

My heart stopped then raced on wildly. It wasn't very often that anyone telephoned me at work, and my mind was starting to invent worrying images. Had something happened to my son, to my mother . . . or Jon?

'Who is it?' I asked when I reached the office and

saw the receiver lying by the side of the phone. The girl shrugged, and my heart jerked with fright as I put the receiver to my ear. 'Yes . . . Emma Robinson here. Who is it please?'

'It's me, Emma . . .' Relief flooded through me as I heard Jonathan's voice. 'Didn't that girl tell you?'

'No . . . just that I was wanted on the phone.'

'No wonder you sounded breathless. It's good news, Emma. I'm getting a two week leave. I'll be home on Sunday. We can arrange the wedding at last . . .'

'Oh, Jon,' I said, a catch in my throat. 'That's wonderful . . . really good news. I'm so pleased.'

'I can't wait to see you, to be with you, my darling.'

'Me too . . .' I laughed with relief. 'Have you told your mother yet? She will want to get started with all the arrangements.'

'I'll ring her now, but I wanted to tell you first, Emma.'

'I'm so glad you did.'

'Look, there's someone waiting to use the phone. I'd better go. I'll see you on Sunday.'

'Yes. I'll be watching for you. Take care, Jon.'

'I love you . . .'

'I love you, too . . .'

I was smiling as I left the office. Sol had been showing a regular customer the new stock when I answered the telephone call, but he came to me now, brows raised.

'Good news, Emma?'

'The best. Jon is coming home for a two week leave on Sunday. It means we can arrange the wedding at last.'

'That is good news,' Sol said, his thoughtful, grey eyes narrowing as he looked at me. 'Got that dress cut yet?'

'No, not quite,' I replied. 'You can come through and look in another five minutes.'

I went back to my task, determined that I was going to make this dress myself without anyone's advice or help: it had to be good enough to go out on the rails with the others, or I would have failed the test. Only when Sol declared himself satisfied that I understood the basics of the trade, could I move on to the showroom, which was out front of the cramped workshop.

I had been surprised when I saw the workshop the morning I started to work for Solomon Gould. Somehow I had expected it to be larger because of all the racks of dresses in the showroom, but I now knew that as soon as something was finished a girl took it out to the front. Nothing was allowed to linger in this place!

The working conditions for the two cutters and three tailors had seemed cramped and airless in the beginning, but I had soon become used to it, and now, when I visited the main factory with Sol, I found it noisy and somehow impersonal.

Sol's new factory – which he had set up just before the start of the war to manufacture uniforms for the Armed Forces – was outside of London.

'Safe from the bombs,' Sol had told me when we were discussing our joint venture. 'The East End will catch it once they start. And the dock area. We don't want all our money to go up in smoke. Some of the women grumbled about the move. They don't like living in the country, and I can't blame them, but once the Government started to evacuate the children . . . well, they saw the advantages.'

'You mean like eggs?' I'd asked with a smile. Fresh produce was becoming harder to find in London.

For the first few weeks after war was declared, I had wondered if it would be better to send my own son out of town for his own sake. My mother had offered to have James with her, but I was reluctant to be parted from him, and he was so happy at home with Margaret. When the expected bombs had failed to arrive, I was glad I hadn't lost my nerve and sent James away.

It was some months now since I'd moved in with the Goulds. They had a Georgian terraced house in a pleasant garden square. Although narrow, the house was built on four separate floors. Sol had had the attics converted into a nursery and playroom for James.

'Plenty of room for you and the boy, Emma,' Sol had said to me over and over again. 'There's no need for you to move out when you and Jon marry. You know we love having you with us. And Margaret is so fond of James . . .'

It was a convenient arrangement. I could take the underground or a tram to the Portobello Road on the days when Sol didn't drive me to the workshop. Despite being Sol's partner in the new factory, I preferred to make my own way to work, and I had made it clear to Sol from the start that I wanted to be treated like any other worker during business hours.

Sol had been scrupulous about keeping to our agreement. He was teaching me the trade, and if I made a mistake I was put right very firmly – which was exactly the way I wanted it. However, on the days when Sol drove down to the new factory, he treated me and James as if we were his daughter and grandson.

He and Margaret would have loved children of their own, but unfortunately Margaret hadn't been able to have a child. She was very close to being an invalid, though she refused to give into her illness and tried very hard to hide her suffering from us all. I had noticed it was getting more difficult for her to walk up and down stairs, but when I'd suggested she see her doctor, she had sworn me to secrecy. Sol must not know she was feeling worse. He had enough problems with the war restrictions and red tape.

Because of Margaret and Sol's kindness, I wanted to be an asset to the business. I was in the fortunate position of not having to work unless I chose, because I had some money of my own. However, I wanted to work. I had asked Sol to teach me the trade, and I wanted to learn and understand it all properly.

My pattern was cut. I glanced towards the showroom door just as it opened and Sol came in. He was frowning as he approached the table where I was working, and I felt a shiver of apprehension trickle down my spine. If I hadn't done my work properly, it would be as big a disappointment to Sol as it would to me.

He took his time looking at what I'd done, checking the run of the cloth and whether I'd made the best use I could of the length I'd chosen to cut, then he looked at me. He was trying very hard not to grin, and I knew he was pleased.

'Not bad,' he murmured. 'Not bad for an apprentice . . .'

'Oh, Sol!' I cried impatiently. 'Is it good enough? Will you put it on the rails with the others?'

'We'll see when you've finished it,' he said, nodding at me. 'I was thinking of taking a run up to the factory tomorrow, Emma. If you want to come with me, you'd best get on. I haven't got time to stand about all day if you have.'

If he hadn't been satisfied with the cut he would have said as much. He was just teasing me as he so often did these days. Sol was only in his early forties, twenty years or so older than me, but I loved him as dearly as if he were my father. He had shown me more love than my own father ever had, and I was so grateful.

'Of course I want to come,' I said. 'Go and serve some customers, Sol, and let me get on with my work.'

Our factory was in Chatteris, a small market town in Cambridgeshire. Sol had chosen to set up there, because I'd mentioned the availability of suitable premises – or that was his excuse. I suspected a part of it was because it was close to my home.

I had lived in March for most of my life. March itself was a railway town with one of the largest marshalling yards in Europe, and Sol thought it might be vulnerable to attack from the air because of all the trains. Chatteris was tucked away in the heart of the fenland, and he had hoped to avoid some of the risk when the bombing finally started . . . but the Air Ministry had opened an airfield at a village just down the road, so the factory was now between two likely targets.

Not that we had seen any sign of the air raids starting yet. After all the talk and preparation it almost seemed as if it was a phoney war, but Sol told me not to become too complacent.

'Hitler has been busy elsewhere,' he warned, 'but he hasn't forgotten us, Emma. It's going to be bad when it starts. When it does, you ought to think of going somewhere safer.'

I hadn't argued with Sol, but I had no intention of leaving London. Coming here in the first place had been a big step for me, but I had never regretted it despite sometimes missing my mother. She still worried about me and wrote often, giving me all the local news and asking me when Jon and I were going to get married.

We had planned to marry sooner than this, but Jon's training as an Airforce navigator had been intensive, and though he'd had one or two short spells of leave, he hadn't been able to fit in the wedding. At least, not the kind of wedding Mrs Reece wanted.

It was of course the second time for me. My first unhappy marriage was behind me now, and the grief of losing my beloved *Gran* was becoming easier to bear – except when I remembered how she had died, and then sometimes I woke from a bad dream with tears on my cheeks.

My husband – Richard Gillows – had murdered Gran. Of that there was not the slightest shadow of a doubt, though his other wicked deeds could not be proved. He had met a violent and sudden death by running in front of a fast train, and I believed that act had been quite deliberate. Richard had known it was only a matter of time before he was caught and tried for Mother Jacob's murder.

After his death and my decision to live in London, I had decided to use my maiden name. I preferred to be called Emma Robinson rather than Mrs Gillows, and not just because my husband's name had been in all the papers at the time when the police were hunting for him.

James was not my husband's child. He was the son of a man called Paul Greenslade. Paul was Jon's cousin, and we had first met through him. Jon had helped me after I became pregnant and had no one else to turn to. Although my son had been registered as my husband's child at birth, I had since had his name changed to Reece by a legal deed. Jon had arranged that for me so that James would not grow up to believe himself the son of a murderer.

Neither Jon or I saw anything of Paul these days, and I believed he might have gone back to America where he had been working for some years. I never thought of him. Paul and all that his brief presence in my life had meant belonged to the past – as did my first marriage.

The events leading up to the murder of Gran and Richard's death were something I did not wish to remember. I had a new life ahead of me now, and I was determined not to let the shadows of the past spoil my new found happiness.

Sometimes it surprised me when I found myself singing and realized that I was truly happy for perhaps the first time in my life. As a young girl, I had suffered from my father's strictness and this was my first taste of freedom. And I was looking forward to becoming Jon's wife . . . once the wedding reception was over.

Mrs Reece wanted to invite so many people. I had tried to tell her all we needed was a quiet ceremony and a small reception for family and friends afterwards, but she had been so upset that I had somehow found myself agreeing to her hiring a hall and giving us the kind of wedding she thought we deserved.

'Jonathan is my only son, Emma,' she'd said, looking at me anxiously. 'You won't deny me the pleasure of giving you a special day – a day you will always remember?'

It would have been ungracious of me to refuse her, especially as *Pops* was nodding at me from behind her back. Jonathan's grandfather was a dear man, and it would have been beyond me to have refused his request when he asked so little.

I decided to telephone Mrs Reece that evening. We could discuss anything she wanted to know over the phone, and I would see her with Jonathan at the weekend.

'You look very nice this morning, my dear,' Margaret said to me when I came downstairs carrying James the next day. She kissed the child, then me. 'Have a lovely time – and give my love to your mother, Emma. Tell her that she and her husband must come and stay with us for your wedding. I wouldn't dream of them going to a hotel.'

'It's very kind of you,' I said, gazing at her anxiously. She was still an attractive woman despite her illness, but she looked very tired and I was worried about her. 'Are you sure you wouldn't like to come with us? You could stop with my mother while we visit the factory?'

'The drive would be too much for me,' Margaret admitted with a sigh. 'I am going to have a nice lazy day here alone. Perhaps sit in the garden if the sun comes out later . . . or read a book . . .'

'As long as you rest,' I replied, kissing her again. 'We shall be back by supper.'

I glanced at myself in the mirror. I was wearing a smart grey dress and a coat with a black fur collar, black shoes and a matching leather bag. My long brown hair was swept up and back from my face in a rolled style that I'd copied from one of Bette Davis's films, and I was wearing a hat with a cheeky feather at the front. I had never thought of myself as being pretty, but I did have a certain style these days – very different from the Emma who had worked in her father's shop!

'Are you ready, Emma?'

Sol was getting impatient. He was always slightly on edge when we visited the factory. It wasn't easy complying with all the new rules and regulations the Government kept throwing at us, though being an official supplier to the Armed Forces did have its compensations.

I went out to the car. Sol had the door open for me. He held James while I settled myself in the front seat, then placed the child in my arms.

'I swear he gets heavier every day,' he said. 'What do you feed him on, Emma, lead puddings?'

I laughed and shook my head at him. My son was

thriving, and Sol was as proud of him as if he had been his own flesh and blood.

'I telephoned Mum,' I said. 'She says she has some eggs for us, and a few extra goodies she managed to buy somewhere or other.'

'Your mother will get herself locked up for trading on the black market one of these days.'

'Sol! It isn't the black market. It's just that in the country people grow their own food, and Mum happens to know someone who makes farm butter and has just slaughtered a pig they kept in the back yard.'

'Yes, of course,' Sol agreed, amused by my mother's excuses. 'I'll drop you off with your mother, Emma, and go to the factory alone. It's all rather boring stuff these days, nothing for you to worry about. You'll be much happier enjoying a chat with Greta.'

'If you're sure there's nothing I can do to help?'

'I'm going to check on quality, and look at the stock control,' Sol said. 'It would be a waste of your time to come with me. No, you treat it as a little holiday, and visit all your friends.'

'You spoil me, Sol,' I said, and smiled at him. 'But I would like a little time to visit my friends.'

'That's what I thought,' he said. 'You'll want to talk, with the wedding coming up.'

'Oh, you do look lovely, Emma!' Sheila exclaimed as I went into the shop. 'Really smart. And your son is just gorgeous!'

'Thank you.' I glanced round the shelves. So far the rationing of sugar hadn't affected Sheila's sweet stock, though I supposed she had bought in as much as she could before the shortages started to bite. 'How are you managing?'

'Not too bad so far,' she replied and pulled a face. 'Some things are slow coming in, but others don't seem to have suffered yet. Our suppliers say we shall get our share same as everyone else – but once the Government makes us have coupons for sweets I shall go potty.'

'Is it getting too much for you, working here?' Sheila was in the middle stages of her pregnancy. 'If you wanted to give the shop up, I would understand.'

'You don't want it back, do you?'

She looked so anxious that I laughed and shook my head. 'No, of course not. I was just concerned for you, and Eric, of course. I wouldn't want you to feel tied just because you've signed a lease.'

'What would you do if we packed up?'

'I'm not sure. Things are going to be difficult for a while. I might just leave it empty and try to sell after the war is over . . . whenever that is.'

Sheila looked thoughtful. 'Would you sell to us, Emma? If we could raise enough money to buy?'

'Are you sure you want it?'

'Eric was talking about selling other things – maybe groceries or alcohol, if we could get a licence. Make it an off licence . . . He thought about packing in his job and running the shop himself.'

'Won't he be called up?'

'He's got a weak chest.' Sheila frowned. 'Eric failed his medical last month. It threw him a bit I can tell you. That's why he's thinking of expanding the shop . . .'

'I'm sorry he isn't well. I didn't know, Sheila.'

'Nor did we. He gets a bit chesty in the winter, but . . .' She shrugged but I could see she was concerned. 'He would be better off working indoors.'

'You can do what you want with the shop,' I said. 'You don't have to buy it. Apply for the licence. If I can help in any way, just telephone me.'

Sheila's face lit up. 'You're a real friend, Emma.'

'Let me know how things go,' I said. 'I'm going to see Madge Henty now.'

Sheila nodded. 'I buy all my things there now. No one else in town has such pretty dresses. I hope the Government isn't going to stop us buying clothes next?'

'Sol is sure it will come. He has a lot of contacts, Sheila, and he knows things – so if you want something new buy it now while you can.'

I left the shop as a customer entered. At first it had seemed a little strange to see Sheila standing behind the counter of Father's old shop. He would have hated it, of course: he had never approved of her, but the property belonged to me now, and I had always liked Sheila. She paid her rent regularly, and that was all that counted as far as I was concerned. Besides, she was married and perfectly respectable. Whatever people had said of her once, they had to admire her these days. She worked hard, and it was quite something for her and her husband to own and run their own business.

A few doors further along the High Street was the dress shop run by Mrs Henty. She was another close friend, and my partner in the dress shop. Trade had been brisk these past few months. I chose most of the stock myself in London and had it sent down to her by rail.

Sol didn't make costumes or knitwear, but he had been able to advise me on the best places to buy at the keenest prices, and my own instinct for what would sell in a country town had proved reliable.

Mrs Henty was serving a customer with a pretty blouse when I went in. I amused myself by rocking James in his pushchair and glancing through the rails. Judging by how thin the stock was, my friend had been rushed off her feet.

'I could do with a cup of tea,' she exclaimed as the door shut behind her last customer. 'I was going to telephone you, Emma. Everyone has been going crazy these past two weeks. I am sure they are all terrified the Government is going to ration clothes!'

'They will before long. I'll sort some more stock out for you, Madge.'

'Yes, please do,' she said. 'We could probably double or treble our usual orders at the moment . . . for as long as the panic lasts anyway.'

I liked to keep the stock fresh, sending Madge a few of the most attractive new dresses from Sol's rails at a time, but now I saw that it might be wise to build up our stock a little.'

'I'll send whatever I think you can sell,' I promised as I followed her through to the back room and watched her put the kettle on. 'Sol won't mind if we owe him for a few weeks. So, how are you? Other than being busy?'

Madge laughed. 'Very well, Emma. I'm comfortable here in my own little way – but tell me what you've been up to, my dear.'

'I'm getting married next week.'

'To that nice Mr Reece?' I nodded and she looked pleased. 'Well, I think that's lovely. I like Mr Reece – he's a real gentleman. So kind and gentle, and polite too. You will be settled at last, Emma.'

'Yes, I'm sure I shall,' I said. Jon was kind and gentle, and I loved him. 'Do you think you could come up for the wedding? Or is it too difficult?'

'I can get a girl to look after things here.' Madge beamed at me. 'Lily is a nice little thing, helps out sometimes on a Saturday when I'm busy. I can leave her in charge for once. I wouldn't miss your wedding for the world!'

I stayed for nearly half an hour talking to Madge, then made my way back to my mother's house. Sol would return in a little while, and I wanted a few minutes alone with Mum.

She had been baking when I went into the kitchen, her face flushed and smeared with flour.

'I had some sugar put by,' she told me as she brought a sponge cake from the oven. 'You take this back with you, love.'

I went to kiss her cheek. 'You needn't worry about us, Mum. Honestly, we're fine.'

'London food isn't worth the eating,' she said. 'I've got a box of fresh stuff for you to take back, so you won't starve for a while.'

'No, we shan't starve.' I smiled. She was convinced I had lost weight since I'd been living in London, which might have been true, but was due more to the fact that I was always busy than any shortage of decent food. We were still managing despite the recent rationing of butter, sugar, ham and bacon. 'Thank you, Mum. We shall enjoy that sponge.'

'I do worry about you, Emma, but you'll be all right when you're married to Jon. I trust him – he will look after you.'

'I'm fine now. I don't need looking after. Besides, Margaret and Sol are so good to me.'

'Yes, I know.' She sighed and reached out to touch my

cheek. 'It's just that . . . well, I can't forget how it was for you. I want you to be happy, love.'

'I am happy, Mum. Very happy.'

She nodded, then reached into her apron pocket and brought out a letter. 'This came for you last week,' she said. 'I opened it, Emma. I thought it might be important. It's from a solicitor down in the west country . . . I wasn't sure whether to give it to you. If I were you, I should just tear it up.'

'Mum?' I stared at her, seeing the unease in her eyes. 'Why? What does this solicitor want? Why are you frightened?'

'I'm not exactly frightened, Emma. I just feel it might be best to let things stay as they are.'

I took the letter out, made curious by her attitude. It was from a firm of solicitors that I had never heard of before. They had been contacted by a relative of the late Harold Robinson . . . someone wished to know if he had an heir. Apparently, they had seen a notice of his death and now wished to trace any family.'

'They've heard he left money,' my mother said. 'Depend on it, Emma. They're scroungers, out for what they can get.'

'You don't know that,' I said, laughing at her expression. 'Aren't you curious about them?' I turned the page, looking for more information. 'The solicitor says he believes I may be the person he is looking for, and will I reply at my earliest convenience.'

'Tell him you don't want to see them, whoever they are,' my mother said. 'Your father didn't want to know his family. In all the years we were married, they never tried to contact us. Why should you bother with them now?'

'I don't know. Perhaps I shan't.' I slipped the letter into my pocket. 'I'll send this to our lawyers, Mum, let them find out what it's all about. Don't worry, I shan't get taken in by someone who wants money.'

'Well, just be careful, Emma.'

'How is Bert?' I asked, changing the subject. 'You said he had a nasty cold when you last wrote.'

'He's better now. We're both fine, Emma. Happy . . .' She bent down and took James from his pushchair as he held out his arms to her, kissing his cheeks. 'I miss you and this little fellow – but I wouldn't change my life. Bert is the man I should have married years ago. If I had how different our lives might have been ...'

'Don't look back, Mum,' I said, squeezing her waist with gentle affection. 'I've made up my mind I won't, not ever. I'm not going to waste time in regrets. Life is what you make it, and I intend to make the most of mine.'

'Yes, you must,' she said. 'But you will, I know that. We all underestimated you when you were a girl, all tried to take care of you – but you're in charge now, aren't you? You look so different, Emma – such a smart woman, a townie . . . not a country mouse any more. Sometimes I hardly recognize you in your posh frock!'

'But I'm still me underneath,' I said, and reached out to take James from her as he started to grizzle. 'I think that's Sol coming back now. We shall have to go in a few minutes, Mum. We don't want to be too late back. Sol never says anything, but I know he worries about Margaret.'

'It was good of him to bring you down,' she said. 'A man like that . . . I can't help wondering why he's taken to you the way he has . . .' She frowned. 'I mean, what does he get out of it?'

'Mum! Why should he want anything?' I said. 'I've told you. I trust Sol. He and Margaret are good people. Now, please, stop worrying about me and let him in . . .'

Chapter Two

I had been eagerly anticipating Jon's arrival, but it was a bitterly cold day, the mist freezing so that it was impossible to see more than a short distance. Jon had telephoned to say he was on his way, but that had been ages ago and I was beginning to fret.

'Don't worry, my dear,' Margaret said as I went to the front windows yet again. 'Jon will . . .'

The front door bell pealed at that moment, and then we heard Jon's voice answering the housekeeper's anxious inquiry.

'I'm fine, thank you, Mrs Rowan. The mist is pretty bad, but I managed to . . .'

I flew into the hall. Jon opened his arms, catching me and crushing me to him. We kissed passionately in front of a slightly startled Mrs Rowan and an approving Margaret, who had followed me into the hall and was smiling benevolently as she watched us.

'I've missed you so much,' Jon said. 'You smell gorgeous, Emma, like a wood after a shower of rain.'

I laughed with pleasure. Jon always said nice things to me. Sometimes, I thought he ought to have been a poet. He had been a solicitor before the war, though it was not a job he particularly enjoyed. Once, he had confessed to me that he would have liked to be a farmer. I had teased him then, but the slow, gentle life, caring for the land would have suited this man who had come to mean so much to me. Perhaps after the war was over we would think about making a new life together in the country.

Jon always said of himself that he was a plain, ordinary chap, the kind of man you might pass in the street without giving him a second glance. Perhaps his sandy coloured hair and rather square features were not remarkable, but inside he was beautiful. There was something fine, almost noble about Jon at times. Of course I would never dream of telling him that – he would cringe with embarrassment.

'I'm so glad you're home,' I said now, clinging to his arm as I drew him into the warm, comfortable room where we had been sitting round the fire. 'I can't believe we've got two whole weeks together!'

'It's good, isn't it?' Jon smiled at Margaret. 'How are you, Mrs Gould?'

'Quite well, thank you,' she replied. 'Your uniform looks rather smart. I believe congratulations are in order, lieutenant?'

I realized Jon had various new stripes and badges sewn to his uniform jacket. 'Does this mean you've passed everything?' A tiny shiver went down my spine as he nodded. 'So the training is finally over . . . that means . . .'

'Yes.' Jon touched a finger to my lips. 'We don't need to talk about any of this, Emma. We have a wedding to plan, and two glorious weeks to spend together.'

'Lovely,' I said and smiled up at him. 'Your mother has the wedding planned for next Wednesday . . .'

'She wanted to wait until Saturday, but I said no.' A gleam of determination showed in Jon's eyes. 'Anyone who can't make it by then can send their apologies. I want to spend my leave with my wife. I'm not prepared to waste time . . .'

'Well said, Jon!' Sol came in at that moment carrying a tray of fine crystal glasses. Behind him, was Mrs Rowan with an ice bucket and a magnum of champagne. 'This is vintage,' Sol announced triumphantly. 'I've been saving it for the right moment . . . and I think this must be it, don't you?'

'That's rather splendid of you, sir,' Jon said and grinned. 'Much appreciated.'

Sol opened the champagne. It popped beautifully and we all toasted one another, Mrs Rowan staying to wish us health before taking her glass away with her.

'To a long and happy life for you both,' Sol said. 'May all your troubles be little ones.'

We all laughed, sipped our champagne and talked about the wedding. No one mentioned the war, or the fact that Jon would be flying combat missions once his leave was over. I knew he didn't want to discuss or even think about war when he was with me. He said our time together was special, and must not be wasted.

'It's always there,' he'd told me on one of his flying visits home. 'I live, breathe and sleep war when I'm in camp, Emma. I don't want to think about it when we're together.'

I wondered if Jon was afraid. Surely any man would be? But somehow I sensed Jon's feelings went deeper. In his heart he probably felt that war itself was wrong: killing and death were something so foreign to his nature that he must hate the very idea. Perhaps that was why he had chosen the Airforce instead of the Army? To keep the death and killing at a distance . . .

'What are you thinking about?' he asked suddenly. 'Why the frown?'

'I was wondering if we ought to leave. We don't want to keep your mother waiting, Jon.'

'No, of course not.' He laughed. 'I was told not to be late for lunch.'

'We mustn't keep you,' Margaret said, and waved us away with a smile. 'Now don't worry about James, Emma. Nanny will see he eats his lunch, and I shall sit with him while he has his nap afterwards, as I always do.'

Emma's War

'Don't let him tire you then.' I kissed her cheek. 'I expect we shall be back by teatime.'

'You look very well, Emma.' Dorothy Reece smiled at me in her sad, wistful way. 'It seems ages since I saw you, my dear.'

Immediately, I felt guilty. It was almost a month since I had last brought James to see her and *Pops* – known to the rest of the world as Sir Roy Armstrong.

'Yes, I know,' I apologized. 'I've been so busy. Sol wanted me to produce a dress from start to finish, just to prove that I really understand what goes into the production of a finished garment. It was just a classic cut with a gored skirt and fitted waist, but I had to practise and study Mr Jackson's work for several weeks . . .'

It was a weak excuse and we both knew it. The workshop was closed on both Saturdays and Sundays. I could visit every week if I chose, but the truth was I found Mrs Reece difficult to please. It wasn't that she criticized me openly, but I was always aware of something . . . a look of disapproval or a lift of those fine brows.

She was a small, fragile woman who dressed in pretty, flowing gowns that made her look rather like a doll. However, I had soon discovered that beneath that wistful air was a very determined woman, a woman who usually knew how to get her own way.

'Well, you are here now,' she said with another of

392

those smiles. 'I've drawn up a list of guests I've invited. Most of them by telephone, Jonathan, since you insisted on such short notice . . .' She frowned as she handed me the list. 'You haven't invited many friends, Emma. Are you sure you remembered everyone?'

'I don't have much family,' I replied. 'Just three uncles on my mother's side, but they are scattered all over the place and Mum says not to bother inviting them. Sheila couldn't leave the shop – but Mrs Henty is coming. I invited Mary and her husband, but she says it's too far to come for a day and she can't leave her father because he isn't well. Mum and Bert are coming, of course, and Sol and Margaret. They are the only ones who really matter. I can send a piece of cake to the girls at work and a few other friends . . .'

'Oh yes, the cake.' Mrs Reece looked pleased with herself. 'As you may imagine, wedding cakes are going to be in short supply, but I had made arrangements weeks ago. Your cake was already made and stored, Emma, and the icing sugar was bought and saved.'

'She's a clever girl,' Pops said, beaming at us. 'You should see the tinned food Dorothy has in the cellar. Fruit, salmon, ham . . . enough to feed an army, let alone a few wedding guests.'

'I thought about it in advance,' she said. 'I didn't need to rush out and spend all my sugar rations in one go. Not like that silly woman in the newspaper!'

'You mean the one who was fined for being greedy and unpatriotic?'

'Yes. So foolish. One only had to think, Emma. It was obvious months ago what was coming. I bought a little more than I needed every time I went shopping, and it has mounted up, that's all.'

'Don't you believe her,' Pops said, chuckling. 'She has been like a general in the field preparing for a siege.'

I smiled and thanked Mrs Reece. She had been so determined to give us a splendid wedding. All I wanted was to marry Jon. If I were honest, I would have preferred a quiet ceremony and a small reception, but I didn't want to spoil her pleasure.

'You've been so kind,' I said now. 'I really will try to visit more often in future.'

'But surely . . .' She looked shocked. 'You will be living here once you and Jonathan are married.'

'No.' I glanced at Jon. 'Didn't Jon tell you? We've decided to stay with Sol and Margaret for the time being. It's easy for me to get to work from there, and James is settled. I don't want to move him until Jon and I can find a home of our own.'

'I did tell you, Mama,' Jon said. 'You might not have been listening, but I did tell you Emma wants to stay where she is for the moment.'

'But surely Emma doesn't need to work,' she said. 'Not when you are married. I had expected her to come here, to live with us. I was looking forward to it so much.'

'Jon understands that I want to work,' I said. 'It is important to me. I've always been honest about this, Mrs Reece. I'm learning a trade. One day I hope to be in business for myself. I'm not sure whether I want to make clothes or sell them to the public, but working with Sol is teaching me so much . . .'

'In business . . .' She looked horrified. 'But is that quite nice, Emma? In my day ladies didn't . . . well, it wasn't done. Respectable women just didn't dabble in trade.'

Pops laughed. 'Nor would you have wanted to work, Dorothy. But that doesn't mean Emma shouldn't. She is a very intelligent young woman. I think it's a splendid idea. Why shouldn't women run their own businesses if they choose?'

Mrs Reece frowned but made no further comments. She was forced to accept defeat this time, but I had a feeling that she was not going to give up the battle. She was used to having her own way.

'Luncheon is ready, madam.'

The housekeeper's announcement put an end to the discussion. After lunch we talked of other things. Pops gave us a beautiful silver tea and coffee service complete with its own tray, and Mrs Reece presented me with two sets of wonderful embroidered linen sheets and pillowcases, much nicer than anything I had been able to buy recently.

I thanked them both. Jon said we had to leave because of the fog, which was as bad as ever and didn't look as if it would clear all day. He gave me a meaningful look as we went out to the car.

'Thank goodness you didn't cave in over living there, darling. I couldn't put up with it. We'll have to look for somewhere of our own when things calm down, but for the moment I think it best if you stay where you are. After all, I shan't be around that often . . .'

'No . . .' I smiled at him. 'Only two days and nights, then we'll be together. Where are we going for our honeymoon?'

'It ought to be Paris. That's where I would like to take you, darling. One day I shall, I promise.' He gave me a regretful look. 'But it can't be . . . but we'll go somewhere.'

'You're not going to tell me?'

His eyes were bright with mischief. 'It's a surprise, darling.'

I nodded, my lips parting in anticipation as he leaned towards me. We kissed, a slow, lingering kiss that made me tingle with pleasure.

'I can't wait. Oh, Jon . . .'

'We've waited this long,' he said. 'We'll wait a bit longer . . .'

*

Rosie Clarke

I found it difficult to sleep the night before my wedding. My dress was hanging in the wardrobe. Not white this time, but a simple plain ivory satin with long sleeves and a high neck.

Once before I had lain wakeful, thinking about marriage. I had been desperately unhappy then, carrying the child of the lover who had deserted me and forced by my father to marry a man I did not love.

What terrible results had come from that marriage! A man's love – if Richard had ever truly loved me! – had turned to hatred. Greed and jealousy had played their part, and I had been caught between them.

How different were my feelings now. I wanted this marriage with all my heart. I was looking forward to being Jon's wife. I loved him, but I also trusted him: he was my friend.

It was all going to be so wonderful! I could hardly wait for the moment we were alone at last.

The wedding itself was beautiful. I carried a small bouquet of snowdrops and lily of the valley, which Pops had grown specially in pots under glass for me. The perfume of their delicate flowers was sweet, and the thought that had gone into Sir Roy's loving gift to me was even sweeter.

Tears gathered in my eyes as I took my vows that morning. I was so lucky to have such good friends . . . people who loved and cared for me. I could hardly believe it was all happening. Life had been so hard, so bitter for a time, and now I had so much.

We were showered with confetti as bells rang out joyously, and then the wedding car was speeding through the damp streets to the reception.

So many of the guests were strangers to me. The thought occurred to me that this wedding was more for Mrs Reece than either Jon or I – that the people I met for the first time were her friends, not ours.

It did not matter. They were pleasant, kindly people and the gifts they had given us were generous: linen, silver, good china and expensive glass, quite different to the gifts I'd received on my first marriage. None of it was important. All that mattered was the look in Jon's eyes when he smiled at me, and the certainty that I was loved.

At last, at long last, the taxi arrived to take us to the station. Jon had decided to travel by train rather than drive all the way up to Scotland. He had told me our destination the night before, warning me to pack plenty of warm clothes.

'It's going to be cold, darling,' he'd whispered, 'but not for us. I promise I shall keep you warm . . .'

We said goodbye to all our friends, kissing and hugging, thanking them for coming and for their good wishes and gifts.

'Be happy, Emma,' my mother said as she held me close. 'You deserve happiness, my darling.'

'I am happy, Mum. Jon loves me and I love him. I couldn't ask for more.'

'Be happy, Emma,' Margaret said, 'and don't worry about James. He will be safe with us, and as loved as if he were our own.'

'He loves you,' I said. 'Kiss him for me every night.'

'Of course I will,' she promised.

'Be happy, Emma,' Sol said, his eyes twinkling. 'Take care of that man of yours. He is about as good as they come.'

Sol and Margaret had refurbished our bedroom for us, giving us the choice of whatever we wanted: a truly magnificent gift we would be able to treasure throughout our married life. But more than that, they had both given me so much support and love.

'I know that, Sol,' I said. 'I'm so lucky in my friends . . .'

At the station, Jon bought magazines and chocolates for the journey. It would take several hours and he had booked a sleeper cabin for us. Now we were truly alone. The cabin door was closed and locked. We were man and wife, and as Jon reached for me I knew true happiness – and it was as if the past had never been.

The narrow beds in a sleeper cabin are perhaps not the most comfortable place to make love, but for me it was all we needed: with a few bumps of arms and legs and elbows, and some laughter, we managed. Jon was so sweet, and tender, so careful to give me pleasure.

I had never known a man to be so unselfish in his loving, but Jon was always the same in everything he did: he would not have known how to be any different.

'You are so lovely, Emma,' he whispered as he caressed my breasts, kissing me, teasing me with his tongue, setting me on fire. 'I've dreamed of you like this, wanted you so much . . .'

'And I want you, Jon,' I said, kissing him back. I was no shy virgin to be afraid of love, but a woman who wanted to give her man the love he needed. 'I do love you, Jon. So much . . . so very much.'

We came together, gently at first, a soft blending of hearts, minds and bodies, passionate but not desperate, not frantic. This was a new experience for me. It was as if we were somehow comfortable together, almost as though we had been married for some years, had always known each other's thoughts and needs.

Afterwards, I felt warm, safe, loved. There had been no crashing of drums, no wild, tempestuous crescendo of feeling, just contentment.

I knew that it was possible to feel more excitement, but I was not disappointed as I nestled in my husband's arms. Sexual desire was only a small part of what I felt for Jon. He had been so good to me, was so loving, so generous in all he gave of himself. I loved him and I wanted to make him happy. I wanted to be happy. I wanted quiet and contentment, the ordinary things of life . . . the respect decent people gave to each other every day.

I was ready to settle for what I had. It was so much more than I had ever had before.

Our days in the Scottish highlands were very precious: days of mists and bright clear mornings when the sun broke through, of dark nights and wood fires, and beauty that touched the soul.

Jon had rented a wonderful cottage where we could be alone. It was part of a large estate and set in huge grounds, with a lake, a mountain in the distance, purple and grand, smudged against the skyline, and gentle hills where deer roamed amongst the heather.

A gigantic hamper of food was waiting for us when we arrived. It was packed with all kinds of luxuries, from venison to pots of pates and peaches in jars of brandy syrup. Each day we were there, a man came down from the house with baskets of fresh provisions. Some of it was ready prepared, needing only to be reheated in the wood-burning oven, but there was also bacon, which I cooked for our breakfast, and fresh

trout or salmon. Jon showed me how to poach these in a special fish kettle, and I discovered he was good at preparing these kinds of dishes. Yet another surprising aspect of this man who was so dear to me.

'Where do you think all this food comes from?' I asked Jon once. 'Do they know there's a war on?'

'What war?' Jon laughed. 'Look around you, Emma. How can there be a war in such a perfect place?'

'It is perfect,' I said, leaning my head back against him as his arms surrounded me. 'You were so clever to find it for us, Jon.'

'I've been here before,' he said, his breath warm against my ear. 'For the fishing. It's wonderful here in September, Emma. We'll come again one day.'

'Yes, please. I should love that.'

'It would be wonderful to live in a place like this,' Jon went on dreamily. 'Don't you think so, Emma? You said you wondered where the food comes from, but this estate must be almost self-sufficient, wouldn't you think? They have so much game in their woods . . . deer, grouse at the right time of year, fish in the lake. I'm sure they live as people used to in the old days, make their own bread, milk their own cows . . .'

I turned to look up at him, gazing into his eyes as I heard the wistful note in his voice. 'Is that how you would like to live, Jon? Away from all the noise and turmoil of the city?'

'Sometimes I think it would be paradise,' he replied and then laughed. 'I'm a dreamer, Emma. Life isn't that simple, is it? Even here they must have their serpent.'

I sensed something in him then . . . a kind of fear. What was Jon afraid of? I knew he hated the idea of war, of the wanton waste of life and destruction of all that made living good. Was he afraid of death – or that life would become too ugly?

'Now what are you thinking?' He lifted my chin with his finger. 'Are you bored here, Emma? Would you rather I had chosen a city? Do you miss the noise of your beloved London?'

'I think I might if I lived here all the time,' I admitted. 'I was born in a country town, Jon. I love the bustle of London. I love being able to go to a theatre when I want, and I love shopping – but this time here with you has been wonderful. Being together, walking, talking, listening to music on the radio when the fire is warm . . . I wouldn't have changed it for anything.'

'But we'll spend the last two nights of my leave in London,' Jon said. 'I mustn't be selfish. I want to please you, my darling. We'll go to the theatre, and we'll go shopping . . .'

'Oh, Jon,' I whispered as I turned in his arms to kiss him. 'You could never be selfish . . .'

'Don't be too sure of that,' he murmured as he bent his head to mine. 'I want you so much, Emma. When a man loves a woman as much as I love you . . . pleasing her *is* selfish. I want to see your eyes light up, to see you smile and hear your laughter.'

I laughed then as he kissed me. Jon's idea of being selfish seemed funny to me. I was beginning to realize there was so much more to this man I had married than I had yet guessed. He went so deep, his thoughts so complex, way beyond my understanding. I could not hope to follow all the secret, twisting trails of his mind. I knew only that he was a sensitive, loving, gentle man, and that I loved him.

When I thought about it, I realized we had met only a few times before our wedding. Jon had been there at a difficult period of my life. He had helped me when I needed a friend, but our meetings had been brief – apart from one holiday by the sea.

It took more than that to know a man like Jon. But we had a lifetime before us, and I was sure deep inside of me that he would be worth the knowing.

And so our lovely, special time drifted away, the days passing with a dreamlike quality as we walked the hills, the wind blowing fine, powdery snow into our faces when the weather turned colder, then racing back to the warmth of our cottage – to our bed. Was any woman ever as loved as I? Had lovers ever been so content as we were then?

All too soon, we were back in London. James wept as he saw me for the first time, and held out his arms to Margaret. I felt guilty as I saw the accusation in my son's eyes. For several days I had almost forgotten him.

However, when he saw the teddy bear I had bought for him, he decided to forgive me. His arms closed about my neck, his tears drying as I held him to me and kissed his soft, baby curls and his face. He smelled so good, and I felt a wave of love for him.

'Mummy is sorry,' I whispered. 'She won't go away again, darling.'

'We should have taken him with us,' Jon said, a note of regret in his voice. 'It was selfish of me, Emma. He loves you, too.'

We both knew it had not been possible. James could not have shared our idyll. It would not have been the same. Besides, we had needed that special time alone together. Jon had needed it, and for this once at least his needs had necessarily come before my son's.

Now that we were back in London, Jon was more like the man I had known before we were married. Whatever part of him I had glimpsed during our time in the highlands was now safely hidden. He was his usual polite, smiling self.

True to his word, Jon took me to the theatre two nights running. He also took me and my son to the park. We watched the horses parading past the palace, and Jon helped my son to sail a boat on the lake, then bought us all cream cakes and tea, most of which James managed to get all over his clean sailor suit. We were just like any other family on a day out.

This was how I had always thought family life should be. It was what I had longed for, and it made me so happy.

The night before Jon was due to return to camp, I clung to him after we had made love. I was crying, but trying not to let him see it.

'Don't, Emma,' he whispered against my hair. 'Please don't cry. I can't bear it. I can't bear it that I may never see you again . . .'

I leaned over him, my hair brushing his naked shoulder. For one terrible moment his soul was as naked as his flesh. I could see his fear, almost touch it. He was afraid of losing all that we had, all that we meant to each other.

'It isn't that I might die,' he said, his throat caught with emotion. 'We all have to die one day . . .'

'What then, my darling?'

'If something should happen . . . if you have reason to believe I am dead . . . don't waste the rest of your life, Emma. I want you to be happy. More than anything else, that is what matters to me. I think I could face death if I knew that you would go on . . . that you would live for me.'

'Oh, Jon . . .' I could not hold back my tears now. 'I can't bear the thought that . . .'

He kissed me. 'Forgive me, darling. I just want you to be happy.'

'I am happy, here with you.' I bent to kiss his face. I touched my lips to his eyelids, his forehead, his cheeks, the tip of his nose, and then his mouth. 'I never want to be with anyone else,' I vowed. 'I love you, Jon. You've given me so much – and I don't mean material things.'

Jon smiled, reaching up to stroke my cheek. 'I'm a fool, Emma. Take no notice. I have dark thoughts sometimes, but they are just bad dreams. I love you. I can't die. I have too much to live for, my darling.'

'Of course you do,' I said. Then I began to kiss his body, tiny, teasing kisses that made him moan and throb with desire. I laughed as I moved lower, knowing what I was doing to him. 'Just so as you remember exactly why you have to come home to me . . .'

I didn't go to see Jon off at the station the next morning. He wouldn't let me.

'Stay with James,' he told me, kissing me goodbye. 'He needs you, Emma. He needs you as much as I do. You mustn't forget that, my darling. I know you enjoy your work, but make time for James. Think about me, my darling, and about the way it will be for us when all this is over. We shall be a family then. You, me and James ...'

'Yes, of course. I always do think of both of you.'

I was a little hurt that Jon should think I would neglect my son. I spent as much time as I could with him, but perhaps it wasn't enough.

Watching him with Margaret later that day, I realized he went as easily to her as to me. For a moment I felt a pang of regret. James was very precious to me. I had never intended to neglect him, but perhaps I had without realizing it.

Jon was so observant, so thoughtful. Damn this wretched war! I wished so much that we could be together as a family, that we could have our own home, live as we pleased . . . but I was not alone. All over the country women were wishing for the same thing, hiding their tears as their men went off to war, perhaps never to return.

I held James on my lap after I had bathed him that evening, rocking him in my arms before putting him in his cot, my cheeks wet with tears.

For a little while, a precious fragment of time, I had forgotten reality. I had believed in Jon's paradise, but now the shadow of war loomed large. Until this moment, I had not really seen it as more than a nuisance, as an excuse for the Government's petty restrictions – but quite suddenly I realized how terrifying it was.

The dangers of training seemed puny against those Jon would face once he began flying missions for real.

'Come back to me, Jon,' I prayed. 'Please come back – for both of us. We both need you.'

I smiled as I touched my son's head, stroking the soft downy hair. He had fallen asleep almost as soon as I laid him down.

I would spend more time with my son, even if it meant cutting down my hours a little at the workshop. And I would go to visit Mrs Reece when I could. I owed Jon that much.

As I went downstairs, the telephone rang. I answered it.

'Emma . . .' Jon's voice came to me sure and strong. 'I just wanted to tell you . . . I'm all right. Last night, it was silly . . . all the chaps feel the same when they've been home. But I'm back now and it's all right. Do you know what I mean?'

'Yes, of course, darling. I felt the same. It's just the thought of saying goodbye.'

'I'll be home when I can,' Jon said. 'Just a few hours next time, but this damned war can't go on forever, can it?'

'No, of course it can't,' I replied, knowing that this was what he wanted me to say. 'Don't worry about us, we're all fine. I've just put James to bed. I read him a story, and he's fast asleep. He looked so sweet, Jon, all warm and pink and soft . . .'

'Good – that's how I shall think of you,' Jon promised. 'Sitting by his bed, your hair glinting with gold in the lamplight . . .'

'My hair is a mousy brown,' I said, laughing. 'You ought to write poetry, Jon. You see everything with a rosy glow.'

'You don't see yourself the way I do,' he replied. 'Sometimes your hair looks like silk . . . and you *are* beautiful, whatever you say.'

'Flatterer!'

'Take care, Emma. I'll telephone you again soon, my love.'

'Yes, please do. I love you, Jon.'

'Bye . . .'

I replaced the receiver. My hand was shaking. Jon had not told me, but I knew he was going on his first mission that night . . .

Also available from Ebury Press:

The Downstairs Maid

By Rosie Clarke

She is a servant girl...

When her father becomes ill, Emily Carter finds herself sent into service at Priorsfield Manor in order to provide the family with an income.

He will be the Lord of the Manor...

Emily strikes up an unlikely friendship with the daughters of the house, as well as Nicolas, son of the Earl. But as the threat of war comes ever closer, she becomes even more aware of the vast differences between upstairs and downstairs, servant and master...

If you like Downton Abbey you'll love this!

EBURY
PRESS

Also available from Ebury Press:

Wartime Sweethearts

By Lizzie Lane

The Sweet family have run the local bakery for as long as anyone can remember.

Twins Ruby and Mary Sweet help their widowed father out when they can. Ruby loves baking and has no intention of leaving their small Bristol village, while Mary dreams of life in London.

But as war threatens there will be changes for all of the Sweet family, with the youngest sister Frances facing evacuation. But there will be opportunities too, as the twins' baking talent catches the attention of the Ministry of Food...

EBURY
PRESS